About the A

Shoma Narayanan started reading Mills & Boon romances at the age of eleven, borrowing them from neighbours so that her parents didn't find out. At that time, the thought of writing one herself never entered her head. But a couple of years ago, Shoma took up writing and was amazed at how much she enjoyed it. Now she works at her banking job through the week and tries to balance writing with household chores during weekends. Her family has been unfailingly supportive of her latest hobby.

Tessa Radley loves travelling, reading, and watching the world around her. As a teen, Tessa wanted to be a foreign correspondent. But after completing a Bachelor of Arts degree and marrying her sweetheart, she ended up practising as an attorney in a city firm. A break spent travelling through Australia re-awoke the yen to write. When she's not reading, travelling, or writing, she's spending time with her husband, her two sons or her friends.

Karen Booth is a Midwestern girl transplanted into the South, raised on '80s music and way too many readings of *Forever* by Judy Blume. Married to her real-life Jake Ryan, she has two amazing kids with epic hair, a very bratty cat, and loves getting up before dawn to write romance. With plenty of sparks.

Workplace Romance

Workplace Romance:
Office Fling

SHOMA NARAYANAN

TESSA RADLEY

KAREN BOOTH

MILLS & BOON

First Published in Great Britain 2024
by Mills & Boon, an imprint of HarperCollins*Publishers* Ltd,
1 London Bridge Street, London, SE1 9GF

www.harpercollins.co.uk

HarperCollins*Publishers*
Macken House, 39/40 Mayor Street Upper,
Dublin 1, D01 C9W8, Ireland

ISBN: 978-0-263-32327-6

AN OFFER SHE
CAN'T REFUSE

SHOMA NARAYANAN

To my family

CHAPTER ONE

DARIUS MISTRY WAS NOT used to taking orders from anyone. And especially not orders that came from a woman he was supposed to be interviewing. The fact that the woman had turned out to be surprisingly attractive was neither here nor there—this was strictly work, and her behaviour right now seemed more than a little strange.

'Hold my hand,' she was saying. 'Come on, she's almost here.'

Her current boss had just walked into the coffee shop, and Mallika was reacting as if it was a massive disaster. Granted, being caught by your boss while you were being interviewed for another job wasn't the best start to an interview, but it wasn't the end of the world. Mallika's expression suggested a catastrophe on a life-threatening scale—like the *Titanic* hitting the iceberg or Godzilla stomping into town.

'Please, Darius?' she said, and when he didn't react immediately she reached across the table and took his hand. 'Look into my eyes,' she pleaded.

He complied, trying not to notice how soft her skin was, and how her slim and capable-looking hand fitted perfectly into his.

'At least try to *pretend* you're my date,' she begged despairingly.

He laughed. 'You're not doing a great job either,' he pointed out. 'The whole "deer caught in headlights" look doesn't suggest you're crazy about me.'

She managed to chuckle at that, and her expression was so appealing that he sighed and put on what he hoped was a suitably infatuated look. Actually, after a second he found he was quite enjoying himself. He had a keen sense of humour, and despite his attempts to remain professional when faced with such an attractive interviewee, the situation was so completely ridiculous it was funny.

He was supposed to be evaluating Mallika for an important role in his company, and instead here he was, holding her hand and gazing deeply into her eyes. Rather beautiful eyes, actually—the momentarily helpless Bambi look was gone now, replaced with an apprehensive but intriguingly mischievous little sparkle.

'My goodness, Mallika, what a surprise!'

The woman who'd stopped by their table was middle-aged and plump and terribly overdressed. Purple silk, loads of fussy jewellery, and make-up that would have put a Bollywood item girl to shame.

'Hi, Vaishali,' Mallika looked up with a suitably friendly smile, but she didn't let go of Darius's hand.

'So this was your "urgent personal meeting", was it?' Vaishali leaned closer to Darius. 'Mallika's kept *you* a pretty closely guarded secret, I must say.'

'We…um…met recently,' Darius said, trying not to gag at the cloud of cloying perfume. It was like being smothered to death by lilies—the woman must have poured an entire bottle of perfume over herself.

'Ah, well, you deserve to have some fun,' the woman

was saying to Mallika, patting her hand in a surprisingly motherly way. 'I'll leave you with your young man, shall I? See you at work tomorrow!'

Her husband had been waiting patiently by her side, and Vaishali tucked her hand in his arm and trotted off with a final wave.

Mallika sighed in relief. 'Close shave,' she said as she released Darius's hand.

Clearly it was no longer of any use to her, but Darius felt absurdly bereft. When he'd first seen her he'd thought Mallika strikingly good-looking, in a natural, outdoorsy kind of way—not his type at all. Now, however, he found himself wishing that she'd held on to his hand just a little bit longer, and the feeling surprised him.

He wasn't entirely sure how he had lost control of the situation, and why he had not asserted himself in his usual role. He usually went for graceful, ultra-feminine women—the kind who'd learnt ballet when they were young and who dabbled in poetry in their spare time. While she was conservatively dressed, in a business suit, Mallika looked as if she'd spent her youth playing cricket with boys and beating them in every game.

Writing off his reaction to her as a momentary aberration, Darius tried to make sense of what had just happened.

'Is she that scary?' Darius asked, and when Mallika didn't answer, he prompted, 'Your boss?'

She bit her lip. 'No, she isn't,' she said after a brief pause. 'She's actually rather nice.'

He was about to ask her why she'd been so nervous, then, but he held the words back. This was a business meeting, and the fewer personal questions he asked the better. Only he didn't feel very businesslike right now.

When she'd bitten down on her lower lip his eyes had been automatically attracted to her mouth, and now he couldn't look away. Her lips were full and soft-looking and utterly feminine, and completely in contrast to her direct gaze and the firm lines of her chiselled face...

Okay, this was crazy—sitting and staring at a woman he'd met fifteen minutes ago. One whom he was supposed to be interviewing for a directorship.

'We didn't get very far with our discussion,' he said, trying to sound as if his interest in her was limited to her suitability for the role he'd been telling her about. 'There's a decent restaurant on the twenty-first floor. Would you prefer going there? Less chance your boss might pop up again.'

Mallika hesitated. It had seemed so glamorous when someone from the Nidas Group had headhunted her to discuss a director level role. Nidas was big—it had been set up by a bunch of young dotcom entrepreneurs a decade ago, and they'd struck gold in almost every business they'd tried their hand at.

They'd started off with online share trading and investments, but later branched off into venture capital and real estate and done much better than players who'd been in the market for thrice the time. Being considered for a directorship in the firm at the age of twenty-nine was a huge ego-boost—it wouldn't have been possible in any other firm, but at Nidas the directors were quite young, and they didn't hold her age against her.

Her first few meetings with Nidas had been preliminary ones, screening her for this final interview with Darius Mistry. For a few days she'd actually thought she could do it—be like any of the other women she'd gone to business school with, take charge of her career, interview with other employers, pretend that she had a *normal* life like everyone else. Reality was sinking in only now.

She glanced across at Darius. When she'd heard the name she'd imagined a paunchy, cheerful, white-haired man—she'd had a Parsi drama teacher at school who'd also been called Darius, and he'd looked just like Santa Claus minus the beard. Darius Mistry had come as a bit of a surprise.

True, his Persian ancestry showed in his pale colouring and hawklike features, but he was in his early thirties, tall and broad-shouldered, and as unlike her former drama teacher as an eagle from a turkey. Not good-looking in the traditional sense, more disturbingly attractive, and he emanated a quiet power and control that had Mallika caught in its glow.

He was still waiting for her to answer, she realised. 'No, I'm fine here,' she said. 'Actually, I just made up my mind. I don't think I want to take the interview any further. I'm sorry—I should have thought this through properly.'

Darius frowned. This afternoon really was *not* going to plan. Mallika had been interviewed by his HR team, as well as by one of his colleagues, and everyone who'd met her had been very impressed. Apparently she'd come across as being sharply intelligent and very, very good at what she did. He'd also looked at the performance of the real estate fund she managed. It had done extremely well, even in a volatile and completely unpredictable market, and before he'd met Mallika he'd built up an image of a hard-nosed, practical businesswoman.

The reality was different enough to be intriguing.

For a few seconds he wondered if she was playing hard to get. People used all kinds of techniques to drive up the benefits package they were offered, but very few started so early in the process. And Mallika looked troubled, a little upset—whatever the reason for her sudden decision to stop the interview process, it definitely wasn't a hard-nosed or practical one.

'You've spent almost five years with your current firm,' he said. 'I know the thought of switching jobs can be a bit overwhelming, but there's no harm going through with the interview process, is there? Once you hear what we're offering you can always say no.'

'I guess...' she said slowly. 'I just don't want to waste your time.'

'My whole night is dedicated to you,' he said.

Promptly Mallika thought of all the things they could get up to together. Her cheeks flushed a little and she took a hasty sip of water, hoping he hadn't noticed her confusion.

'So, how much has Venkat told you about the job?' Darius asked.

'He told me about how you and he set up the share trading division,' she said. 'And how you got a real estate fund going, and that you now want to concentrate on the venture capital side and hire someone to manage the fund for you.'

'That's right,' Darius said. 'The fund was an offshoot of our investments business and it's been doing well— we've consistently outperformed the market.'

She seemed interested, Darius noted as he began telling her more about the role. She was frowning in concentration, and the few questions she asked were focussed and showed that she'd done a good deal of research on the firm and on the job. He asked a few questions in turn, and it was clear that Venkat hadn't been wrong. Mallika knew pretty much everything there was to know about running a real estate fund.

'Does it sound like something you'd like to do?' he asked finally.

It was as if he'd shaken her out of a daydream—her vibrantly alive expression dulled, and her shoulders slumped just a little.

'I love the sound of the job,' she said, almost unwillingly. 'But the timing's not right for me. I have a lot going on right now, and I think maybe it's best I stay where I am.'

'Do you want to take a day to think it over?'

Mallika shook her head. 'No, I…I think I'm pretty clear that it won't work out. I'm so sorry—I know you have a busy schedule, and I should have thought this through properly before agreeing to meet you.'

She looked so genuinely contrite that he impulsively leaned across the table to cover her hand with his, making her look up in surprise.

'Don't worry about it,' he said, masking his disappointment. 'I'm meeting other people as well, but if you do change your mind let me know.'

Mallika blinked at him, uncharacteristically at a loss for words. It was like being hit by a train, she thought, confused. She'd been so focussed on what he was saying, on trying to stay professional, that she'd forgotten quite how attractive he was. Then he'd smiled and taken her hand, and the feel of his warm skin against hers had sent her long-dormant hormones into overdrive.

We like this man, they were saying excitedly. *Where did you find him? Can we keep him? Please?*

So much for a dispassionate admiration of his looks, she thought, trying to quell the seriously crazy thoughts racing through her brain. There was good-looking, and there was scorching hot—and Darius definitely fell into the second category. The first time she'd grabbed his hand she'd been too worked up to notice—this time a simple touch had sent her hormones into overdrive.

Gingerly, she slid her hand out from under his and gave him what she hoped was a sufficiently cool and professional smile.

'I'll tell you if I change my mind,' she managed as she pulled together her scattered thoughts.

'The salary is negotiable,' he added.

She shook her head. 'It's not about the money,' she assured him. 'But thanks for letting me know.'

Darius knew when not to push—and he also knew he wasn't going to give up so easily.

Mallika looked as if she was all set to leave, and he glanced at his watch. 'It's almost eight-thirty,' he said. 'I'm starving, and I'm sure you are too. D'you have time for a quick bite?'

Perhaps he could get to the bottom of her sudden withdrawal and convince her otherwise.

He was almost sure she was going to say yes, but then her phone pinged and she gave the display a harassed look.

'I need to go,' she said, her attention clearly torn between him and whoever had just messaged her. Her expression was distracted as she stood up hurriedly, her short curls swinging around her cheeks. 'Thanks for being so nice about everything.'

She put her hand out, and Darius got to his feet as he took it. 'Nice' wasn't the impression he wanted to leave her with. 'Nice' suggested she'd forget him the minute she stepped out of the hotel. And he wasn't going to let *that* happen.

'I'll be in touch,' he said, keeping her hand in his a fraction longer than strictly necessary.

She didn't reply, but she blinked once, and he realised that she wasn't quite as unaffected by him as she was pretending to be. It was a cheering thought, and he smiled as she walked away.

He'd found her intriguing—an unusual mix of the ultra-competent and the overcautious. And the attraction between them had been hot and instantaneous—if it hadn't been a work meeting he would definitely have taken things further. As it was, he was forced to let her walk away with only a tepid assurance of being in touch later.

The smell of freshly baked bread wafted past, reminding Darius of how hungry he was. He glanced around. Eating alone had never appealed to him, and if he stayed Mallika's boss might see him and come across to ask where Mallika was. He felt strangely protective of the intriguing woman he had only known for a couple of hours.

Mentally he ran through his options. Going home and ordering in. Calling up a friend and heading to a restaurant. Turning up at the excruciatingly boring corporate event he'd earlier declined.

The corporate event was the least appealing, but it would give him an opportunity to network with a bunch of people who could be useful to Nidas in the future. It wasn't too far away, either, and if he left now he'd be able to get there, hang around for an hour or so and still get home in time to catch the last bulletin on his favourite news channel.

He was handing the attendant his valet parking ticket when he spotted Mallika getting into an expensive-looking chauffeur-driven car. She was talking on the phone, and he caught a few words before the doorman closed the door for her and the car zoomed off.

'I'll be home in twenty minutes,' she was saying. 'I *told* you I had a meeting, Aryan. No, I haven't decided. I'll talk to you later...'

Whoever Aryan was, he sounded like a possessive control freak. Darius frowned. He hadn't asked Mallika, but he could have sworn she wasn't married. No *mangalsutra* necklace or rings—but lots of married women didn't wear those. And the way she'd looked at him for that one instant...

Darius shook himself. He was rarely wrong about these things, but meeting Mallika seemed to have seriously addled his brains. He was missing the obvious. She'd hardly have asked him to pretend to be her date if her boss knew that she had a husband.

Restored to his normal confidence once he'd figured that out, he tipped the valet parking attendant lavishly as he got into his car. Not married, and probably not in a serious relationship either. Hopefully this Aryan was her interior decorator, or her tax advisor, or someone equally inconsequential.

'What d'you mean, she wasn't interested?'

'She doesn't want to change jobs,' Darius explained patiently.

He and Venkat had joined the Nidas Group on the same day, and had spent the last decade setting up the businesses they now headed. Darius was the stable, intelligent one—the brains behind most of what they'd achieved together. Venkat was a typical sales guy—competitive, pushy, and notoriously impatient. Outside of work he and Darius were close personal friends, but right now Venkat's expression was that of a bulldog being asked to let go of a particularly juicy bone.

'*Why* does she not want to change jobs? Did you tell her how much we're willing to pay?'

'I did,' Darius said. 'She said she doesn't need the money.'

'You need to meet her again,' Venkat said flatly. 'I have absolutely no clue about this fund management stuff, and if you're leaving we'll go under before you know it. This girl's really good, and she seemed keen until she met you. I'd have thought it would be the exact opposite—girls usually fall for you on first sight. What in heaven's name did you do to put her off?'

'Told her that she'd be working with a bunch of total scumbags,' Darius said, deadpan. 'Look, I'm not prepared to let her go, either, but it will be better to give her some time to think things over and change her mind. I'll make it happen. But in the meantime I've got a bunch of other CVs from HR. Some of them with equally impressive track records.'

Venkat grunted. 'I'll go through the CVs, but you need to work your magic with this girl. Otherwise you can jolly well put your exciting plans on hold and stay here until you can find someone to replace you. I'm terrible at all this HR sort of stuff—you're the one who gets everyone eating out of your hand. Make this Mallika an offer she can't refuse.'

Darius bit back a sigh. Once Venkat decided he

wanted something he was like an unstoppable force of nature.

'I'm a businessman, not a Mafia don,' he said drily. 'Let me do it my way. I have an idea on how to win her…'

CHAPTER TWO

THE FLAT WAS DARK when Mallika let herself in, and she felt a familiar pang of loss as she put the lights on and surveyed the empty living room. Nothing was the same without her parents, and having a brother who'd completely retreated into his shell emphasised her loneliness rather than reduced it.

It had been a gruelling week. Her job involved meeting builders and visiting construction sites and then spending hours hunched over her computer, calculating the possible return she'd get from each investment she made for her fund.

The Mumbai property market had been at its volatile best these last few months, and investors were wary. Which meant that there was a risk of projects stalling—which in turn meant that buyers who'd already invested found themselves with large amounts of capital locked up and no hope of returns in the short term. And the fund that Mallika worked for was seriously considering stopping investment in properties that were under construction.

The kitchen was dark as well. The cook would have gone home some hours ago, leaving dinner out in microwaveable dishes for Mallika and Aryan. She wasn't particularly hungry, but dinner was the only meal she could make sure her brother actually ate.

The lights in his room were on, and she knocked before entering.

'Aryan? Dinner?' she asked, her heart twisting as she watched him hunch over his laptop. It was as if he didn't see the world around him any more, finding reality in the flickering screen of his computer instead.

'In a minute,' he said, not even looking up.

'Did you have lunch?' she asked, and he shrugged.

'Lalita gave me something,' he said. 'You go ahead and eat—you must be tired.'

It was a measure of how little she expected from him that she actually felt pleased he'd realised how exhausted she was. Leaving him to his computer, she went back to the kitchen—she'd make sure he had something to eat later.

For the last couple of days she'd not been able to get Darius out of her head. The way he'd looked at her, his smile, his voice—it felt as if she'd spent hours with him rather than just a few minutes.

He'd said he'd be in touch, but two days had gone by and he hadn't called. Maybe he'd found someone else more suitable for the role. Someone who *didn't* spot their boss and freak out halfway through a discussion, or run out on him without warning.

Idly she opened the contact list in her phone and stated scrolling down it. Darius Mistry. She had his mobile number and his email ID, and the temptation to drop him a text or a short email was huge. She could apologise once again for running out on him. Or tell him that she'd changed her mind about the job.

When it came to professional communications she

was confident and practical, but somehow with Darius she found herself prevaricating. Her shyness prevented her from getting in touch for anything other than strictly business reasons.

She was still mulling things over when her phone rang, and she almost dropped it in surprise.

'I was just thinking about you,' she blurted out, and then blushed furiously. Darius was probably already convinced of her weirdness—she didn't need to make it worse. 'I mean…I was just thinking over what you said about this being the right stage in my career to change jobs…'

'Reconsidering, I hope?' he said smoothly, and went on without waiting for her to answer. 'Look, I know you've said you're not interested, but I've interviewed around a dozen completely unsuitable people and I'd really like a chance to pitch the job to you again. Preferably in a place where your boss isn't likely to land up and ruin my sales pitch.'

One part of her felt disappointed that he hadn't called just to speak to her, but she shook herself crossly. *Of course* his interest in her was purely professional. What had got into her?

'I'm really not interested in changing jobs, Darius,' she said, firmly suppressing the little voice in her head that told her to go and meet him anyway. 'And I've wasted your time once already—I wouldn't want to do it again.'

Darius briefly considered telling Mallika that time spent with her would definitely not be wasted, but he bit the words back. This wasn't a seduction, and he'd already made it clear that when it came to business he was as determined as she to get what he wanted.

'It's part of my job,' he said lightly. 'Even if you don't want to join us now, at least I'll get to tell you about the company—and who knows? Maybe you'll want to join at some later time.'

'All right, then,' Mallika conceded. 'When shall I meet you?'

'Tomorrow,' he said decisively. 'Lunch at one of the restaurants in Lower Parel? That's nearer my office than yours, and hopefully we won't run into anyone you know.'

Darius was beginning to wonder if he'd been stood up when Mallika finally walked into the restaurant. The first thing that struck him was that there was a strained expression in her lovely eyes. The second was that she looked anything but tomboyish now.

Granted, her hair was still styled for convenience rather than glamour, and her make-up was kept to the bare minimum. But she was wearing a sari today—a dark blue silk affair, with a muted print—and her figure was spectacular in it. And her spontaneous smile when she saw him was the best welcome he could ever have hoped for.

He stood as she walked up to him, and Mallika began to feel ridiculously nervous. It was a Friday and he was dressed casually, in a white open-necked cotton shirt over jeans. His thick hair looked slightly damp from the shower, and she had a second's insane urge to reach up and run her fingers through it.

To cover her confusion she held out her hand, and he took it, briefly clasping it between both his hands before he let go.

'Hi,' she said. 'I'm not too late, am I?'

He shook his head. That smile had lit up her face, but now the worried expression was back in her eyes.

'Is everything okay?' he asked quietly once they were both seated and the waiter had put their menu cards in front of them and retired to a safe distance.

Her eyes flew up to his. 'Yes, of course,' she said, sounding just a little defensive.

Aryan was going through a particularly problematic phase, and in the normal course of things she wouldn't have left him alone at home. But she'd promised Darius, and there were meetings in the office that she couldn't avoid. Just this once Aryan would have to manage on his own, with just Lalita the cook to check on him.

'You look tense,' he said. 'Like you're trying to remember whether you locked your front door when you left. Don't worry about it—burglars are usually deeply suspicious of open doors. If it's unlocked, there's absolutely no chance of a break-in.'

She laughed at that. 'What if I did lock it?'

'Ah, then I hope you have a good security system.'

'A simple lock, and a brother who won't notice if someone puts every single thing in the house into packing cases and carries them away under his nose. As long as they don't touch his computer.'

He smiled, his eyes crinkling up at the corners in a maddeningly attractive way. 'Sounds like my kind of guy. Younger brother?'

Mallika nodded. She hardly ever mentioned Aryan in casual conversation, and the ease with which the reference had slipped out surprised her. Darius was beguilingly easy to talk to—she'd need to be on her guard a little.

The waiter was hovering behind her, and she turned her attention to the menu.

'The fish is good,' Darius said.

'It looks delicious,' Mallika said, glancing at the next table, where another waiter had just deposited two plates of grilled fish. 'I'm vegetarian, though.'

'Then the gnocchi?' he said. 'Or the spaghetti in pesto sauce?'

Mallika finally chose the spaghetti, and a glass of wine to go with it—Darius, who'd never paid good money for a vegetarian meal before in his life, found himself ordering grilled vegetables and pasta. A lot of strict vegetarians were put off by someone eating meat at the same table, and he definitely didn't want to risk that. He was on a charm offensive today, and determined to win her over.

'How's your boss?' he asked.

'She's miffed I didn't tell her I was dating someone,' Mallika said with a sigh. Vaishali was a lovely person, but the concept of personal space was completely alien to her. 'She wanted to invite both of us to her house for dinner—I had a devil of a time wriggling out of that one.'

'What did you say to her?' Darius asked, unable to keep a glint out of his eye.

'That I'd been wrong about you and you were actually really self-centred,' Mallika said, delighted she'd managed to keep a poker face. 'And possessive—and controlling.'

She sounded remarkably cheerful about it, and Darius's lips twitched.

'So we aren't dating any longer?'

'We are,' Mallika said. 'You have a few redeeming qualities, but I'm not as sure about you as I was. We're dating, but I'm not introducing you to friends and family just yet.'

'Wouldn't it have been easier to remove me from the scene altogether?'

'If I'd written you off she'd have tried setting me up with a perfectly horrible second cousin of hers. She's spent the last two years trying to palm him off on every unmarried woman she knows.'

'Maybe he's not so bad?' Darius suggested carefully. 'You should meet him—keep your options open.'

Mallika shuddered. 'No, thanks. I've met him once, and that was once too often. He spent forty-five minutes telling me how rich he is, and how he made his money. And he breathes really heavily.'

'Hmm…'

Darius's eyes were dancing wickedly, and Mallika felt a little jolt of awareness go through her. It had been so long since she'd spent any time with an attractive man that she was ridiculously susceptible.

'Can I ask you something?'

She gave him a wary look. 'Yes.'

'Are you atoning for the sins of a past life by working for Vaishali?'

'She's been very good to me,' Mallika said stiltedly, and when he raised an eyebrow she went on in a rush. 'No, really. She can be a bit overpowering at times, but I owe her a lot. I didn't mean to make her sound like a nightmare boss.'

She sounded as if it really mattered, and Darius nodded.

'If you say so.' He was silent for a few seconds as the waiter put their drinks in front of them. 'So, should I tell you a bit more about the job and the company? You can make up your mind then.'

She nodded, and listened carefully as he explained again about the company structure and the role that he was offering. Unlike her current company, which invested solely in real estate, the Nidas Group had evolved into a conglomerate of companies that included a brokering house, a consumer lending company and the fund where Darius was offering her a job. Darius himself was moving on—he didn't give her any details, but she assumed it was to head up a new division—and he didn't have enough capacity to manage the fund as well.

'I have a question,' she said, once he'd finished telling her about the job. 'Why do you think I'm right for the position?'

'You have a superb track record,' Darius said. 'And Venkat was very impressed after he interviewed you.'

'But *you* haven't interviewed me,' she pointed out. 'Or do you trust Venkat that much?'

'I have every intention of interviewing you,' Darius said, his brows quirking. 'The second you tell me that you're actually interested in the job I'll start firing questions at you.'

Mallika stared at him for a few seconds, and then burst out laughing.

'You have a point,' she said. 'So—the job sounds perfect. It's the logical next step in my career and like you said, I've been in my current job for five years and I'm beginning to stagnate.'

'I can see a "but" coming,' he murmured.

'Yes… I mean…'

'It's not convenient from a personal point of view?' Darius supplied when she hesitated.

Mallika nodded. 'That's it. I can't tell you the details, but...'

'I don't need to know the details,' Darius said. 'But if you tell me what exactly it is that your current company is doing to help you maybe I can see if we can work something out.'

Darius could smell victory, and he wasn't about to let this one go.

'I don't have fixed hours,' she said in a rush. 'Some days I reach work at eight, and some days I go in only in the afternoon. And I do site visits on my own when it's convenient to me. Sometimes I work from home, and there are days when I'm not able to work at all.'

She ground to a halt, her eyes wide and a little apprehensive. Clearly whatever was happening on the personal front was very important to her. He wondered what it was. The kind of flexibility she needed was normally required only if an employee had to care for a sick child or an elderly parent. Mallika wasn't married, and from what she'd said her younger brother sounded responsible. A parent, then, he decided.

The unwelcome thought that she might be going through a messy divorce came to mind, but he pushed it away. A divorce might need her to take time off work, but it wouldn't need her to work from home. It was far more likely that one of her parents needed to be cared for.

He thought for a while. 'We might be able to let you do the same,' he said slowly. 'Can I work this out and get back to you?'

'But when I asked Venkat he said you don't have a flexible working policy!' she said.

'It hasn't been formally approved yet,' Darius said. 'We're still working on it. Yours could be a test case.'

Their food had arrived, and Mallika took a bite of her spaghetti before answering. 'You know,' she said conversationally, 'the job market's really bad nowadays.'

'It is,' Darius agreed, frowning a little.

'And bonuses are dropping and people are getting fired every day.'

'Yes.'

'So you could probably hire anyone you wanted, right? With just as much experience and no complicated conditions. Why are you still trying to convince *me* to take the job?'

When it came to work, Mallika was sharp and to the point. She was intelligent—obviously she was, or Venkat wouldn't have considered hiring her. But Darius found himself wondering why exactly he *was* trying so hard to convince her. He'd never tried to recruit an unwilling candidate before—he'd never had to. And while she was definitely his first choice for the job, there were at least two others who could do the job equally well.

Had this just become about winning? Or perhaps he hadn't been thinking clearly since taking her hand in that coffee shop several days ago. What was going on?

'Venkat's interviewed pretty much everyone in the industry,' he said. 'You're the best fit for the role.'

'But the second best might end up doing a better job,' she said. 'He or she'd be more inclined to take the offer to begin with.'

'It's not just about technical skills,' Darius said. 'We think you'd adjust well to the organisation's culture. And we also need to improve the firm's diversity ratio, now that we're likely to get some foreign investment into the company. That's one of the things investors are likely to look at. There are a lot of women at junior levels, but very few at middle or senior management. There weren't too many CVs that fitted the bill *and* belonged to women—and other than you none of them made a decent showing at interview.'

'But I'm sure you have male candidates who're suitable,' she said, her brow wrinkling. 'Surely this diversity thing isn't so important that you've not interviewed men at all?'

'Venkat's interviewed quite a few,' Darius said. 'Apparently you did better than them as well. Diversity's not more important than talent—it's just that now we've found you we don't want to let you go.'

His gaze was direct and unwavering, and Mallika felt herself melting under it. The attraction she'd felt the first time she'd met him was back in full force—if he told her that he wanted her to join a cult that ate nuts and lived in trees she'd probably consider it seriously. Shifting jobs was a no-brainer in comparison—especially when he was guaranteeing a higher salary and no change to her timings.

She was about to tell him that she'd join when a shadow fell across their table.

'Darius!' a delighted male voice said. 'It's been years, my boy—how are you?'

The speaker was a stalwart-looking man in his early forties, who beamed all over his face as he clapped Darius on his shoulder. The blow would have pitched a weaker man face-down into his grilled vegetables, but Darius hardly winced.

'Gautam,' he said, standing up and taking the man's hand in a firm grip. 'Long while... I didn't know you were back in Mumbai.'

'Just here for a visit. And…? You're married and everything now? Is this the new Mrs Mistry?'

He looked as if he was about to clap Mallika on the shoulder as well, and Darius intervened hastily.

'No, Mallika is…a friend.'

'Aha! A Miss Mystery, then, not a Mrs Mistry—is that right?' Clearly delighted at his own wit, Gautam smiled even more broadly. 'I'll leave you to it, then. Catch you online later—I'm in Mumbai for a week more…we should try and meet.'

'Yes, I'll look forward to that.'

Darius waited till the man had moved away before sitting down, shaking his head.

'It's fate,' he said solemnly. 'Last time it was your boss—this time it was Gautam. We can't meet without running into someone we know.'

Mallika chuckled. 'He seemed a cheerful guy. He reminds me of a story I read as a kid—there was a man who smiled so wide that the smile met at the back of his face and the top of his head fell off.'

'That's such an awful story,' Darius said. 'Were you a bloodthirsty kind of kid?'

'I was a bit of a tomboy,' she said, confirming Darius's first opinion of her. 'Not bloodthirsty, though.'

She frowned at her plate as she chased the last strand of spaghetti around it. Finally managing to nab it, she raised her fork to her mouth. The spaghetti promptly slithered off and landed on her lap.

'And *that's* why my good clothes never last,' she said, giving the mark on her sari a resigned look as she picked up the pasta and deposited it back on her plate. 'I'm as clumsy as a hippopotamus.'

Anything less hippopotamus-like would be hard to

find, Darius thought as he watched her dab ineffectually at the stain with a starched table napkin. Her curly hair fell forward to obscure her face, and her *pallu* slipped off her slim shoulder to reveal a low-cut blouse and more than a hint of cleavage.

Darius averted his eyes hastily—looking down a girl's blouse was something he should have outgrown in high school. The one glimpse he'd got, however, was enough to make him shift uncomfortably in his chair. Really, Darius was so off-kilter he could hardly understand the effect she was having on him.

'Here, let me help with that,' he said, after Mallika had dropped the napkin twice and narrowly missed tipping her plate over. He got up and, taking a handkerchief out of his pocket, wet the corner in a glass of water and came to her side of the table to attend to the sari.

Mallika went very still. He wasn't touching her—he was holding the stained section of sari away from her body and efficiently getting rid of the stain with the damp handkerchief. But he was close enough for her to inhale the scent of clean male skin and she had to fold her hands tightly in her lap to stop herself from involuntarily reaching out and touching him.

'Thanks,' she said stiltedly once he was done.

'You're welcome.' Darius inclined his head slightly as he went back to his side of the table. 'Dessert?'

'I should choose something that matches the sari,' she said ruefully as she recovered her poise. 'I love chocolate, but I'm not sure I dare!'

'Blueberry cheesecake?' he asked, his eyes dancing with amusement again. 'Or should we live life dangerously and order the sizzling brownie with ice cream?'

'The brownie, I think…' she started to say, but just

then her phone rang, and her face went tense as she looked at the display. 'I'm sorry—I'll need to take this call,' she said.

'Haan mausiji,' he heard her say, and then, *'Ji. Ji. Nahin,* I had some work so I had to go out. Calm down… don't panic. I can get home in ten minutes—fifteen at the most, depending on the traffic.'

Her face was a picture of guilt and worry as she closed the call, and his heart went out to her.

'I'm sorry,' she said. 'I need to go. It was a lovely lunch, and thank you so much for putting up with me. I'm really sorry about rushing off again…'

'Don't worry about it,' he said gently. 'Do you need a lift anywhere?'

She shook her head. 'I have a car. Is it okay if I go now? I hate leaving you like this, but I really do need to get home as soon as possible.'

'It's not a problem at all,' he said. 'Take care, and we'll talk soon.'

He put enough money on the table to cover the bill plus a hefty tip, and walked her to the door of the restaurant. Her driver took a couple of minutes to bring the car round, and Mallika was clearly on tenterhooks until he arrived.

'Bye,' she said as the car pulled up and she slid into the back seat. 'I'm really, really sorry about this.'

She clasped his hand impulsively before she closed the car door, and Darius was left with the feel of soft, smooth skin on his. The subtle fragrance of her perfume hung in the air for a few seconds after she left.

He gave himself a shake before turning away to walk back to his office. This was not the way he'd planned to end their meal. He'd sensed she was on the point of accepting the role when they'd been interrupted and he could not be more frustrated with his lack of success so far. But it wasn't over—not when he was this close to getting what he wanted.

CHAPTER THREE

'WELCOME TO NIDAS,' Venkat said, giving Mallika a broad smile. 'I'm so happy you finally decided to join.'

'Same here,' Mallika said cautiously as she shook his outstretched hand.

All the old doubts about changing jobs had come flooding back now that she'd actually done the deed. She'd told Vaishali about the job the day after she'd met Darius, feeling like a complete traitor. But Vaishali had been surprisingly nice about the whole thing. Apparently she had been toying with the idea of taking a sabbatical herself, and she wasn't sure if Mallika's flexible working hours would be acceptable to her replacement.

Feeling a bit like a fledgling, shoved out of its nest before it could fly, Mallika had emailed Darius, confirming that she'd be able to join Nidas in a month. He'd been travelling, and someone from his HR team had got in touch to figure out her salary structure and joining date. Darius hadn't even called her, and Mallika couldn't help feeling a little upset about it. And now that she was actually part of Nidas and about to start work, she was very nervous.

The sight of Venkat wasn't exactly inspiring either.

Short and squat and rather belligerent-looking, Venkat was as different from her previous boss as possible.

'We've set up an orientation for you with the team,' he was saying now as he ushered her into his room.

'Darius told me—' Mallika began, but Venkat interrupted before she could complete her sentence.

'Oh, Darius is a busy chap—he won't be able to take you through everything himself.' He peered at her owlishly. 'You do know he's moving out of the firm, right?'

Mallika drew in a sharp breath. A lot of things were suddenly falling into place. Darius's insistence that she join as soon as she possibly could. His asking Venkat to set up her induction plan instead of doing it himself. The lengthy meetings with the other directors, ostensibly to help her get to know them before she joined.

A black curl of disappointment started up in the pit of her stomach. He'd had multiple opportunities to tell her and he'd consciously decided not to. It felt like a betrayal, unreasonable though that was. Unconsciously, a large part of her decision to take the job had been based on the assumption that Darius would be around and that she'd be working closely with him.

Serve her right—trusting a man she hardly knew, she thought, squaring her shoulders and doing her best to keep Venkat from noticing how upset she was.

'He didn't tell me that he was moving out altogether,' she said crisply. 'Though I did get the impression that he'd be cutting off from this part of the business in a month or so.' She was determined to cover her disappointment with cool professionalism.

'Even less, if he has his way,' Venkat said, and an expression of bewildered loss crossed his face for an instant. 'It was a shock when he told me. We've worked

together for years—we set up this business together—
and out of the blue he tells me he's quitting. I still don't
understand why he's doing it.'

Strongly tempted to find out more, Mallika bit down
on her questions. It shouldn't matter to her where Darius
was going or why.

'When you interviewed me *you* didn't mention that
Darius was leaving the firm,' she reminded Venkat.
'Why did you assume I'd know now?'

He had the grace to look embarrassed. 'I couldn't
tell you before you joined,' he said. 'Darius is a pretty
big shareholder, and the news of his leaving isn't public
yet. I thought he might have told you since—I got the
impression you guys are pretty friendly.'

He took in Mallika's suddenly stormy expression and
changed the subject in a hurry. 'Now, I thought I'd first
introduce you to some of the key people in your team,
and then you can start going through our current investment strategies. The team's brilliant—I've been working with them pretty closely for the last few months. I've
put them on to a few good things as well. Of course now
you're here you'll be in full control, but you can reach
out to me whenever you want.'

As the day went by Mallika found herself feeling more
and more confident. Venkat evidently valued her input,
and his style of working wasn't as different from hers
as she had feared.

She was packing up for the day when there was a
knock on the door of her room. Assuming that it was
the overzealous tea boy, who'd been popping up every
half an hour, she said, 'Come in!' and continued stuff-
ing files into her laptop bag.

It was a few seconds before she realised that the man in the room was about twice as large as the tea boy.

'Darius!' she said, her brows coming together in an involuntary frown as she saw him. 'I was wondering if I'd see you today.'

'I meant to come over in the morning, but I had one meeting after another. How was your day?'

'Good,' she said. 'I think I'm going to like working here.'

'Did Venkat manage to spend any time with you?'

'A lot,' she said drily.

Darius laughed. 'He believes in throwing people in at the deep end,' he said. 'But he's a great guy to work with. If you're done for the day d'you want to catch up over coffee? There's a decent café nearby.'

Mallika hesitated. She really wanted to confront Darius about him leaving, but her upbringing made her shy away from any kind of direct conflict.

Some of her indecision must have shown in her face, because he was beginning to look puzzled.

'Or some other day if you need to leave,' he said easily.

Mallika made up her mind.

'I need to get home, but I have time for a coffee from the machine down the hall,' she said.

Compromise—that was one thing she'd learnt early in life. And also that attacking issues head-on sometimes made them worse. She got to her feet and Darius followed her down the hall.

'On second thoughts, I'll have a soft drink,' she said, taking a can from the fridge next to the coffee dispenser. 'You can have that coffee if you want,' she said, gesturing at the mug Darius had just filled for her.

She picked up a second mug and half filled it with warm water from the machine before putting her un-opened can into it.

'It's too cold,' she explained as Darius raised his eye-brows. 'I'll leave it in the mug for a bit and then it'll be just right and I'll drink it.'

Darius's lips curved into a smile as he followed Mal-lika back to her room. She was wearing black trousers, a no-nonsense blue shirt, and extremely sensible shoes. The whole outfit looked as if it had been chosen to down-play her looks, but the most boring clothes in the world couldn't conceal the narrowness of her waist and the ath-letic grace of her walk. Quite contrary to the intended effect, the clothes made her *more* appealing—at least to him.

'Is Venkat involved in the day-to-day running of the fund?' she asked, perching herself on the edge of her desk and swinging her legs idly.

'Not really...' he said cautiously, and she gave him a quizzical look, 'Okay, he's *very* involved in it—but his area of expertise is sales. You won't be reporting to him, if that's your worry—all the directors report straight to the board.'

'Hmm...no, that isn't what was bothering me.'

She smiled at him, and Darius felt his heartbeat quicken in response.

'But tell me—is it true that he's interfered in some of the investment decisions the team have made in the past?'

It was very likely to be true. Darius had heard rum-blings from his team, but he hadn't paid much attention up till now. Mallika's pointing it out after being exactly one day in the job, however, hit him on the raw.

'He's talked to them about a few deals,' he said. 'I wouldn't go so far as to call it interference.'

'Maybe it wasn't brought to your attention, then,' she said, clearly unfazed by the sudden chilliness in his tone. 'But he's made some bad calls, and the fund's asset value has dropped. It'll take me a while to undo the damage.'

It was her air of knowing exactly what to do that got to him.

'I'd suggest you take a few days to understand the business properly first,' he said firmly, though he was feeling uncharacteristically defensive. 'Before you jump in with both feet and start undoing things.'

Mallika frowned. 'I thought the whole point of my being here was that I already know the business,' she said. 'I researched the fund before I even started interviewing with you guys, and it's obvious that you have problems. Logically, it makes no sense to wait to fix them.'

'There's a lot of stuff you wouldn't know from the outside,' Darius insisted. 'Venkat might have his...quirks, but not all the decisions he's made have been bad.'

She shrugged. 'Statistically speaking, even if you made decisions by rolling dice you would end up making some decent ones. But from what I can make out Venkat is superstitious, and his judgement is coloured.'

It had taken Darius months to realise that Venkat's superstitious side sometimes overruled his normally sharp business brain. Mallika had taken exactly one day to figure it out. She was extraordinarily perceptive and he felt slightly wrong-footed. *Again.*

What was this woman doing to him?

Mallika was leaning forward a little. 'Look, you hired me to run this fund,' she said. 'Not because you liked my face. So let me get on with my work. If I mess up you can play the hero and come in and rescue me.'

For a second Darius was tempted to tell her exactly how much he liked her face, but hard as it was he bit back the words. Being her colleague meant that he had to keep a certain professional distance. Speaking of which... Darius realised just how close he was to Mallika, and rolled his chair a few paces back. Unfortunately as soon as he started to speak again Mallika scooted her shapely butt closer to him once more, robbing him of his train of thought.

'You're right about Venkat,' he said, trying to sound as detached as possible. 'The whole superstition thing....' He hesitated a little while trying to find the right words. 'It's a little...'

'Kooky?' she supplied, putting her head to one side. 'Eccentric? Odd?'

'Unconventional,' he said. 'But it's not uncommon.'

'And it's unimportant too, I assume?' she said before she could stop herself. 'As far as you're concerned anyway. Because you're not planning to be around when the problems kick in.'

If she'd expected him to look guilty she was disappointed, because he threw his head back and laughed. 'I mightn't be around, but the fund's performance is still pretty damn important to me. I have a fair bit of my own money invested in it, and I don't fancy seeing it go down the tube.'

'I suppose I should be flattered,' she said drily. 'Here I was, thinking you'd given me the fund to run because you didn't care what happened to it.'

'And now you know I've put my life's savings in your hands,' he said. 'Who told you I was moving out? Venkat?'

'Yes,' she said.

'It's not supposed to be public knowledge yet,' he said. 'The board has asked me to stay on for a few months, and they felt it best that the rest of the firm be told I'm leaving only when it's a lot closer to my last day here.'

'Funny...Venkat assumed you'd already told me,' she said. 'Perhaps he thought it was only fair—given that you recruited me and everything.'

Darius leaned a little closer, his brow creasing. 'Are you annoyed that I didn't tell you?' he demanded, putting a hand under her chin to tip her face upwards. 'Even after what I just said?'

Mallika jerked her head away, trying to ignore the little thrill that went through her at his touch.

'Not annoyed...just a little...concerned,' she said, hoping her words would hide how much she longed to work alongside this charismatic man. 'There might be other things you omitted to mention. I pretty much took everything you said at face value.'

'Now, wait a minute,' he said incredulously. 'Are you suggesting I *lied* to you about the job? What makes you think that?'

'You weren't open at all,' she said. 'All this while you've let me think that you'd be around—that you were simply taking on something within the firm. If I'd known you were leaving...'

'You wouldn't have joined?' He looked quite genuinely puzzled. 'Why not? You seem like you have a handle on things already. My being here or not doesn't make a difference, surely?'

Darius was struggling to keep a smug smile off his face—he wasn't the only one who felt what was between them then.

Oh, but it does, Mallika almost said. The thought of working at Nidas without Darius was unsettling in a not very nice way, and she had to scramble to think of a logical explanation for her anxiety.

'I'm just wondering why you're leaving,' she said. 'I something's going wrong with the company... And I did discuss my working hours with you...'

His brow cleared immediately. 'Oh, the flexi-time thing?' he said. 'Don't worry about that at all—I've cleared it with the board. And give Venkat some time—he's a great guy to work with once you get past his superstitious streak.'

He was probably right—he'd worked with Venkat for years, after all, and she'd only met the man today. And she hadn't known Darius for very long either—there was absolutely no reason for the sinking feeling in the pit of her stomach when she thought about him leaving Nidas.

'Hmm....' she said. 'I think I'll get along well with Venkat—I'll have to. I'll need a lot of help from him for the first few months.'

'Will you?' he asked, feeling oddly jealous.

If Mallika needed help *he'd* have liked to be the one to provide it. For a few seconds before his rational side had kicked in he'd actually thought that she was upset because she'd miss him. Now he was left with an absurd feeling of being sidelined—just another stepping stone in Mallika's life.

Their timing was completely off, he thought ruefully. If he'd met her either a couple of years earlier or later he'd have tried to get to know her better—perhaps even acted on the growing attraction between the two of them. Right now it was completely out of the question. By the time they were no longer colleagues he'd be long gone.

'You still haven't told me why you're leaving,' Mallika said, and he blinked.

'Personal reasons,' he said, standing up to leave. 'Don't worry—the company's not about to go under.'

Mallika laughed at that. She had a particularly appealing laugh, Darius thought. It was as happy and uncomplicated as a child's, but it had a woman's maturity as well, and a sexy little undertone that was irresistible.

'That's reassuring,' she said, slipping off the desk to land on her feet right next to him.

Darius looked into her eyes and there was an instant of absolute connection that made his earlier thoughts irrelevant. A small part of his brain recognised how clichéd the moment was, and he was even amused. The rest of him was completely overwhelmed, and he kept on looking at her stupidly until she blinked and looked away.

'Goodness, look at the time!' she said, her voice slightly more high-pitched than normal. 'I really need to get going.'

'You haven't touched your drink,' he said, and she blinked at the can as if it had just materialised on her desk. 'I'll…um…carry it with me,' she said. 'What about your coffee?'

'I hate that stuff from the machine,' he said. 'Next time we'll go to a proper café.'

The way he said it made it sound like a promise he couldn't wait to keep.

'See you around, Darius,' she managed to squeak, before making a hasty exit.

The next time he saw her was a few days later, with over fifty other people in the same room. Venkat had called for an investor conference, and Mallika was the main presenter.

Darius came in late, slipping into the back of the room. He very rarely attended investor events, but Venkat had been unusually insistent, and he hadn't been able to resist the thought of seeing Mallika in top professional mode.

She was an impressive speaker—economical with words, but leaving her listeners with no doubt of her grasp over the subject. Slim and graceful in a raw silk printed sari, she exuded an aura of confidence and authority that was strangely attractive. Some people would probably think that it detracted from her femininity but, standing at the back of the room, Darius had to work hard to maintain a professional veneer.

She was quite something.

'She's brilliant, isn't she?' Venkat said, materialising next to Darius.

Mallika was answering a question raised by a grizzled investor old enough to be her father—and by the way the rest of the audience was nodding they were as impressed as Venkat was.

'It's been a while since we've held an event of this sort—it's bloody expensive, paying for the dinner and the booze, but it's worth it if we get the monies to come in. And people *are* interested—the market's looking up. We'll get a couple of hundred crores of investment after this event.'

'So does that mean you guys are doing perfectly well without me?' Darius asked, giving Venkat an amused look.

'We are,' Venkat said. 'Mallika's probably the best person you could have hired to replace you—in spite of all that flexible working rubbish. But, man, this place isn't going to be the same without you.'

The event wound to a close, and Mallika stepped off the dais to mingle with the guests. Venkat had been called back for the vote of thanks, and Darius stood alone at the back of the room, watching Mallika as she moved from one group of middle-aged men to the next, her smile firmly in place.

There were only a handful of women in the audience, and Darius noted that she spent longer with them, explaining something at length to one group and patiently allowing a much older woman to peer at the necklace of semi-precious stones she was wearing.

It was a while before the audience dispersed, most of them heading towards the buffet dinner.

Mallika's shoulders sagged a tiny bit, and the smile left her face as she walked towards the exit. It was as if she'd turnedt off a switch, changing from a confident, sparkling professional to a young woman who was just a little tired with life.

Darius waved to her, and she came across to him.

'I didn't see you come in,' she said. 'Did you just get here?'

'A while ago,' he said. 'I'm impressed, Mallika. You had everyone eating out of your hands.'

She shrugged. 'I've done this kind of event many times before,' she said. 'They're exhausting, but it's part of my job.'

'What do you find exhausting?' Darius asked.

'Talking to people,' she said. 'It's a strain. Everyone asks the same questions, and by the end of it I get so sick I could scream. Don't tell Venkat,' she added, looking up with a quick smile that lit up her face. 'He's planning a whole series of these events.'

'I was about to tell you that,' Darius said, a smile tugging at his lips. 'He's thrilled with the way you handled this one.' She made a little grimace, and a spurt of chivalry made Darius ask, 'Should I talk to him? He can handle the events himself—or one of the other fund managers could speak in your place.'

'The other fund managers aren't lucky for Venkat,' she said drily. 'I doubt he'll agree. Anyway, it's part of why you hired me, right?'

Darius nodded. It had been unprofessional of him to suggest he intervene, and he couldn't help admire Mallika's determination to do every part of her job well. Even when she obviously hated what she was doing.

It was intriguing, the way her ultra-professional mask slipped at times to betray her vulnerability. He had a feeling she didn't let it happen often, and all his protective instincts surged to the forefront whenever it did.

'Aren't you having dinner?' Venkat asked, popping up next to them. 'Or a drink? Mallika?'

She shook her head. 'I need to leave,' she said. 'My driver's taken the day off, so I've called a cab. The cabbie's been waiting for half an hour already.'

'Wouldn't it have been simpler to drive yourself?'

'I don't drive,' she said. 'I've tried learning a few times, but it's been an unmitigated disaster.'

'And you don't drink either! What a waste,' Venkat said sorrowfully. In his opinion, the best part of an event of this sort was the company-sponsored alcohol. 'Darius?'

Darius shook his head. 'I need to leave as well,' he

said. 'Got some people coming over. And I'm driving, so I can't have a drink either.'

Venkat looked ridiculously disappointed, and Darius laughed, clapping him on the shoulder.

'I'll take you out for a drink this Friday,' he promised. 'Come on, Mallika—I'll walk you to the lobby.'

Their event had been held in a rather exclusive mid-town hotel, and there were several other corporate events in full swing there. The banquet hall next to theirs was hosting an annual party, and the waiting area outside the banquet hall was dotted with entertainers. Jugglers in clown costumes, living statues, and even a magician or two.

Mallika paused next to a gigantic plastic sphere with a girl playing the violin inside it, and stared at it critically.

'What's the idea?' she asked. 'Why's the girl in the bubble?'

Darius shrugged. 'It's supposed to add a touch of the exotic,' he said. 'In the last party I went to of this sort they'd flown in a belly dancer from Turkey to dance for about ten minutes.'

'Ugh, what an awful job,' Mallika said, wondering which was worse—the few men who were openly leering at the blonde violinist in her low-cut green Tinker Bell dress, or the people who were walking past without even acknowledging her as a human being. 'I'm suddenly feeling a lot better about my own work.'

'No plastic bubbles?' Darius said solemnly as they went down the stairs that led to the hotel lobby. 'That *is* a significant upside, I agree. And wonderful colleagues to work with, perhaps?'

She giggled. 'Like Venkat?'

'Like *me*, I was going to say.' Darius held the door

open for her as they went out into the night air. 'But clearly I've not done enough to impress you yet.'

Mallika looked up at him. In the warm light pouring out from the lobby he looked incredible. His hair was slightly mussed, and a few strands fell over his forehead in sexy disarray. He'd come from work, but he'd taken off his tie and undone the top button of his shirt, and it was difficult to take her eyes off the triangle of exposed skin. And when she did it was only to lose herself in *his* eyes—dark and amused, with a hint of something that was disturbingly exciting.

'Consider me impressed,' she said lightly, and turned away to dig for her phone in her bag, ignoring the sudden movement he made towards her.

'What d'you mean, you've *left*?' she demanded a few minutes later, having finally got through to the cabbie.

She listened to what sounded like an incredibly complicated explanation, and sighed.

'He got another fare and went off,' she said. 'I'll have to ask the hotel to get me a cab.'

'Or I could drop you home?' Darius suggested.

'Isn't it out of your way?'

'Not terribly,' Darius lied. 'We'll take the sea link.' Dropping Mallika home would add forty-five minutes to his drive, but it was worth it.

'If you're sure, then,' Mallika said, heaving a sigh of relief.

It wouldn't be difficult getting another cab back, but the thought of the lonely drive home was singularly depressing. And, whether she admitted it to herself or not, the prospect of spending more time with Darius held a lot of appeal.

Darius handed his valet parking token to an attendant

and put a hand under Mallika's elbow as he steered her to one side. By Mumbai standards it was unusually chilly, and there was a strong breeze blowing. He felt Mallika shiver a little, and gave her a concerned look.

'Do you have a wrap or something?' he asked, and she shook her head, drawing the *pallu* of her sari around her shoulders.

'No, I didn't think it would be cold,' she said.

'And I've left my jacket in my car,' Darius said. 'All my life I've wanted to be chivalrous like in movies—put my jacket around a shivering girl's shoulders—and when I get the perfect opportunity...'

'You find you've forgotten the jacket?' she said, laughing up at him. 'Don't worry about it—I'm not likely to die of frostbite.'

'You could catch a cold, though,' he said, sounding quite serious. 'I'll take you back inside till the car comes up.'

Or you could put your arm around me, Mallika almost said. That would be another favourite Hollywood moment, copied faithfully by Bollywood in multiple movies. Even suggesting it was out of the question, of course, but oh, how she wished she could!

Before she could turn around, a slim woman with waist-length hair came up to them and tapped Darius lightly on the shoulder. A man followed her, a long-suffering look on his face.

'It's Tubby Mistry, isn't it?' she asked, after hesitating a little.

Darius looked around, his face breaking into a smile. 'Nivi! How are you doing?'

'It *is* you!' the woman said, giving a little squeal of delight before throwing herself into his arms.

The man, presumably her husband, gave Mallika a resigned look. Mallika smiled at him, though inwardly she was feeling absurdly jealous of the woman. It was particularly ironic, her turning up and flinging herself into Darius's arms just when Mallika had been wishing she could do exactly that.

'My goodness, I almost didn't recognise you,' Nivi said, stepping back after giving Darius several exuberant hugs and leaving a lipstick mark on his cheek. 'I spotted you when you were walking out of the hotel. You looked so familiar, but I just couldn't place you.'

'She thought you were a TV celeb,' her husband interjected, earning himself a reproachful look.

'You can't blame me for that—he's turned out so utterly gorgeous!' she said. 'You should have seen him in school! He was overweight and gawky and he wore a perfectly hideous pair of glasses. No girl would have turned to look at him twice.'

Her husband cleared his throat, jerking his head towards Mallika.

'Oh, I'm so sorry,' Nivi said, looking genuinely contrite. 'You don't mind, do you? I'm Nivedita. I knew Darius in school, and we've not met in years. I moved back to Kolkata, and I've lived there ever since. We only got here today, and he's the first person I've met from my old life.'

'You must send me some of his school pictures,' Mallika said promptly, and Darius groaned.

'Nivi, if you do anything of that sort I'll have to break that solemn blood oath you made me swear in school.'

'Blackmailer!' she said, giving him another affectionate hug. 'Don't you dare, Darius. Remember all the help I gave you for your Hindi exams?'

'Yes, well, I passed the exams, but I still can't speak a sentence without making mistakes,' he said, and Nivedita laughed.

'You'll learn the language some day,' she said. 'Okay, I'm off now—I can see the two of you are dying to be alone. I'll get in touch with you soon, Tubby.'

'It's our *karma,*' Darius said sadly once Nivedita and her long-suffering husband were out of earshot. 'Faces from the past popping up wherever we go.'

'It's happened exactly once for me—and that time it was a face from the present,' Mallika retorted. 'And Vaishali didn't start drawing up a list of my most embarrassing moments for the whole world to hear.'

'What can I say? Your past isn't as chequered as mine,' Darius said as he took his car keys from the valet parking attendant. 'Come on, let's go.'

'You said Nivedita swore you to a blood oath when you were in school,' Mallika said curiously after she got into the car. 'What was that about?'

'I caught her kissing our house captain,' Darius said as he manoeuvred the car out of a particularly complicated set of barricades at the hotel exit.

'Would that matter now? I'm sure her husband wouldn't be particularly shocked.'

'The house captain was a girl,' Darius said, grinning as Mallika's jaw dropped. 'Nivi was going through an experimental phase.'

'I suppose she finally decided that she preferred men,' Mallika said. 'Bit of a loudmouth isn't she? Were you really that hideous, or was she exaggerating?'

Darius sighed. 'I was a blimp,' he said. 'I weighed almost a hundred kilos and I wore glasses. My mother loved baking, and I loved eating. Luckily I managed to get into my school football team, and the coach made me run twenty rounds of the field every day before the others even turned up for practice. I was down to skin and bone in three months.'

'That explains a lot,' she said, and as he gave her a quizzical look went on, 'You're not vain about your looks. Most good-looking men act like they're doing you a favour by allowing you to breathe the same air as them.'

Darius, who hardly ever thought about his looks at all, felt absurdly flattered. He knew he was a lot more attractive now than he'd been in his schooldays, but he hadn't realised that Mallika liked the way he looked.

'So what happened to the spectacles?' Mallika asked. 'Contact lenses?'

'Laser correction,' Darius said. 'D'you realise you sound like you're interviewing me for a reality show?'

'Serves you right for having become so good-looking,' Mallika said.

They were heading onto the highway that connected North Mumbai to South, and she groaned as she caught sight of a sea of cars.

'We'll be here for ever!' she said. 'There's a new fly-over being built, and three of the six lanes are blocked off.'

'If you'd told me just a little earlier I'd have taken a different route,' Darius murmured, edging the car into the least sluggish lane.

'They're all as bad,' she said, sighing. 'Anyway, at least we have each other for company.' There was a short pause after which Mallika said, 'Darius, can I ask you something?'

'Yes,' he said, though his eyes were still on the road. 'Ask away.'

'Where are you going to be working after you leave Nidas?'

She'd expected him to say that he'd got a better offer from a competitor, or perhaps that he was working on a new start-up. What he actually said came as a complete surprise.

'Nowhere,' he said, as casually as if it was the most obvious answer.

Mallika waited a bit, but when he didn't qualify his answer she said tentatively, 'What are you planning to do, then?'

He turned to give her a quick smile.

'Travel,' he said. 'And some volunteer work—but only after a year or so. For the first year I'm planning on Europe and Africa, perhaps a few months in China and Russia. I've made enough money to last me for several years—if it runs out I'm sure I'll find some way of making some more.'

'You're serious?' Mallika asked. 'I mean, I know people do that kind of thing in the West, but I've never heard of anyone in India quitting their job just to...*travel*.'

The way she said 'travel' was impossibly cute, as if it was a strange, slightly dangerous word that she was trying out for the first time—Darius found his lips curving automatically into a smile.

'I'm serious,' he said. 'Not planning to work for the next five years at least. After that... Well, I'll figure it out when I need to.'

Mallika sat silent for a few minutes, trying to digest what she'd just heard. Darius had struck her as a responsible, steady sort of a man—the last kind of man she'd have expected to leave his job and go wandering around the world on a whim. Showed how bad she was at reading people, she thought. Her own father had been careless to the point of being irresponsible, but this was the first time she'd met someone who was consciously and collectedly plunging into uncertainty.

'You don't approve?' Darius asked wryly as the silence stretched on.

She shook her head in confusion, 'It's not that,' she said. 'It's not my place to approve or disapprove—it just seems like such a drastic thing to do. I guess I don't understand why. I mean, you can travel on holidays, can't you? And what about your family?'

'My family understands,' he said. 'They're as crazy as I am, and they won't let a small thing like my being on a different continent affect the way they feel about me. And travelling on holiday isn't the same thing as being completely free, exploring and having adventures. Setting up Nidas was great, and I've loved that part of my life. But now that it's a success it's slowly becoming like any other large company. I don't find it as fulfilling as I did in the days when we were struggling to make a mark. I wasn't born to be a corporate suit.'

'Unlike me,' Mallika said with a little smile. 'I love the structure and safety of working for a large company.'

Her mother had set up a successful business of her own, but she'd hated the uncertainty and the ups and downs, and she'd taught Mallika to hate them as well.

Before he could reply her phone rang, and she frowned as she took the call.

'Hi, Aryan… Yes, I'm on my way back… No, I'm not coming that way. I'm taking the sea link… No, I can't, Aryan. I've taken a lift from someone, it's completely out of our way, and I'm exhausted.' There was a brief pause, and then she said wearily, 'Aryan, can't this wait till Saturday?'

Evidently it couldn't.

'Look, I'll do my best, but I'm not promising anything. Message me the specs.'

She stared out of the window unseeingly, and Darius hesitated a little before asking quietly, 'Everything okay?'

Mallika turned towards him. 'Yes,' she said with a sigh. 'My brother wants a new memory card for his camera. Actually for my camera—he's sort of taken it over, because I don't have time for photography any longer. I just got a little upset with him because he wants me to stop and buy it for him right now.'

'We can stop if you like,' Darius said, wondering why Aryan didn't go and buy the memory card himself. Maybe he was a little spoilt, and used to his sister running errands for him.

'No, it's fine,' Mallika said. 'I'll try calling a few stores and if they have it I'll get off at the nearest point and take a cab.'

'Assuming they're still open by the time we get to South Mumbai,' Darius said, indicating the traffic outside. 'It's already past nine.'

'So it is,' Mallika said.

Her phone pinged and she glanced down, laughing in spite of herself.

'He's figured out there's a shop that sells memory cards and is open till ten-thirty,' she said. 'And he's told the guy who owns it to wait until I get there.'

'Is it on the way?' Darius asked.

Mallika shook her head. 'No, it's in Worli. You can

drop me where the sea link ends and then you can go home. It'll save you some time. I can grab a cab.'

'I'll come with you,' Darius said, feeling unreasonably irritated with Mallika as well as with Aryan. 'I'm not sure how safe it is, you traipsing around on your own in the middle of the night.'

'It's perfectly safe,' Mallika said crisply. 'But if you're sure it's not inconvenient...' Here, her lips curved into a disarmingly lovely smile. 'I'd love it if you came along.'

'It's not inconvenient,' Darius said, and it took all his self-control not to lean across and kiss her.

Clearly Mallika didn't believe in the fine art of dissembling—if she wanted him around she came right out and said so, instead of pretending that she'd just feel safer if he came with her. It was an unusual and refreshing trait in a woman, and Darius felt himself fall just a little bit in love with her as he smiled back.

'Aryan isn't as spoilt as he seems,' Mallika said suddenly. 'He's got a bit of an issue with stepping out of the house.'

'His health?' Darius asked.

She shook her head. 'No, it's more of a mental thing. He was pretty badly affected when our parents died, but he didn't show it for a while. And then he started going out less and less, and now he doesn't step out at all. And he doesn't like people coming over, though he's usually okay talking on the phone. That time we went out for lunch and I had to leave—my aunt had come over to look after him and he refused to answer the doorbell. She thought something had happened to him, and she was so upset when she found out that he was perfectly okay—just not in the mood to open the door.'

She ground to a halt, wondering why she'd said so

much. Aryan and his peculiarities weren't a good subject for casual conversation.

'So that's why you need a flexible working arrangement,' Darius said slowly, a lot of things he'd found odd about Mallika clicking into place. 'I'm so sorry. I didn't realise that your parents....'

'They died in an accident,' she said hurriedly. 'It was more than two years ago. I don't talk about it much, but it gets more awkward the later I leave it.'

'I get that,' he said, and he looked as if he truly did.

Most people she told either looked awkward or felt terribly sorry for her and gushed over her—both reactions made holding on to her temper tough. Darius looked sympathetic, but not pitying.

'Car accident?' he asked, and she shook her head.

'Gas cylinder explosion,' she said, and he winced.

'That sucks,' he said. 'I'm sorry. Come on, the traffic's finally moving—let's go and get that memory card.'

He kept the conversation light until they'd picked up the memory card—the shop was in an unsavoury little lane, and his lips tightened a little as he thought of Mallika going there alone. He didn't say anything, however, answering her questions on his travel plans instead, and listening to her stories of a holiday in Switzerland that she'd taken with her mother.

It was the first time that Mallika had really opened up and talked, and Darius found his respect for her growing as he listened. She had obviously been very close to her mother, but she was handling her loss with dignity and restraint. Darius had been through his share of family problems, and he could catch the undertone of strain in her voice when she mentioned Aryan. But she didn't complain, and Aryan's name only came up in the context of a hilarious scrap she'd got into with an online clothing store when they'd delivered a set of women's underwear instead of the shirt Aryan had ordered.

Darius still got the impression that ever since their parents died she'd made Aryan the sole focus of her life, and that she felt deeply responsible for him.

They were almost at her flat when he asked, 'Have you tried taking Aryan to a doctor?'

'Several times,' Mallika said. 'Nothing's worked. You see, he needs to be interested in getting better. Right now, he doesn't want that. He seems happy as he is.'

Darius wished he could ask her if *she* was happy, but it was too personal a question, so he contented himself with giving her a light hug before she got out of the car. Her hair smelt of orange blossom and bergamot, and her slim arms were warm and strong around his neck as she hugged him back.

'Thanks,' she said as she straightened up. 'For dropping me home, and for listening to me chatter about things.'

She turned and went into her apartment block quickly, and she heard him start the car and drive away as she got into the lift. The lift man was off duty and the lift was empty—Mallika got in and pulled the old-fashioned door shut behind her before sagging onto the lift man's chair.

It had been a long while since she'd last talked about her family, and the conversation with Darius had brought the memories flooding back. For perhaps the hundredth time she wished she'd gone with her family to Alibagh that weekend.

It had been one of those totally pointless accidents—the kind that could have been avoided easily if only someone had been around at the right time. The cylinder of cooking gas had probably been leaking slowly for a while, but her mother hadn't smelt it because she'd had a cold. She'd picked up the lighter and clicked it on to light the gas stove, the way she did every evening—only this time there'd been a swooshing sound as the petroleum gas pervading the air had caught fire.

Her mother had screamed once, and the scream had brought her father rushing to the kitchen.

They hadn't stood a chance.

The wall of flame had hit the leaking cylinder, and the spare one next to it, and in the next second both cylinders had exploded, turning the kitchen into a blazing inferno. Aryan had been outside in the garden, but he hadn't been able to get anywhere near his parents. And Alibagh was a small, sleepy seaside town—it had been almost twenty minutes before a fire engine reached the house.

It had been in time to save the rest of the house, but far too late to save Mallika's parents. The firemen had told her later that both of them must have died within a few minutes of the explosion, and her only consolation was that at least it must have been quick.

She'd been in shock, but she'd managed to hold herself together long enough to let her relatives know, organise the funeral, and get her brother back to Mumbai. Then, when everything was done, and she'd been about ready to fall apart in private, she'd realised that something was seriously wrong with her brother.

CHAPTER FOUR

MALLIKA KNEW SHE was going to be at work late the next day. A neighbour had complained about Aryan's habit of taking photographs from the windows using a telescopic lens—apparently she thought he was spying on her. It had taken some time to soothe her ruffled feathers, and now Mallika had spent almost an hour trying to explain to Aryan that he couldn't go around peering into other people's houses.

'I was trying to take a picture of a crow on her windowsill,' he said. 'I mean, look at her—d'you think it's likely I'd want a picture of *her* taking up disk space?'

'She doesn't know that,' Mallika said, as patiently as she could. 'And that was *my* camera you were using without asking me. Aryan, look…things are tough enough without you trying to make them tougher. Be a little more considerate, will you? Please?'

He didn't reply, and she almost gave up. Another woman in her place might have lost her temper, or created a scene, but Mallika had had years of training from her mother. However upset she'd been, she'd always concealed her true feelings from the men of the family and soldiered on. For years she'd watched her mother deal with her grandfather and father, and with Aryan as he grew up—the other two men were gone now, and so was her mother, but Mallika found it difficult to shake old habits.

'I'll see you this evening, then,' she said. 'Make sure you eat your lunch, okay?'

He mumbled something that she couldn't catch.

'I didn't get that,' she said.

'I'm sorry,' he whispered, without looking up. 'I didn't mean to upset you.'

Mallika felt her heart twist painfully within her. Aryan was demanding, and sometimes troublesome, but he was very different from her father—and he was the only part of her family left to her.

She went across to him and patted his shoulder awkwardly. 'It's all right,' she said. 'Just be a little careful, *baba*. We can't afford to antagonise the neighbours.'

'I'll be careful,' he said, and looked up, his eyes pleading. 'Do you *have* to go to work?' he asked. 'Can't you work from home today?'

Mallika hesitated. She *could* work from home, but the last time she'd spoken to Aryan's doctor he'd told her that she should try and gently wean him from his excessive dependence on her. She hated leaving him when he'd asked her to stay—it filled her with guilt and worry. But she knew she had to do what was best for Aryan, to try and help him. He was her responsibility.

'I'll come back early,' she promised. 'Why don't you go downstairs and sit in the garden for a bit? Then when I come back we can try going for a drive. Wouldn't that be fun?'

Aryan's face clouded over and he shook his head. 'No,' he said.

Mallika sighed. She'd been trying for months to get Aryan to step out of the flat with absolutely zero success. 'Why, Aryan?' she asked. 'I know you're finding it tough without Mum and Dad, but you need to try and get back to normal. I'll be with you—we don't even need to go anywhere far...'

His grip on her hand tightened painfully. 'I just... can't.' he said, and she had to be content with that.

She couldn't push him any further. If he didn't want to get better she couldn't make him. Something had broken in Aryan when their parents died, and all her love didn't seem enough to set it right.

Her phone was ringing as she let herself into her room at work an hour later.

'Nidas Investments, Mallika speaking,' she said automatically as she picked up the phone without looking at the caller ID.

'Very businesslike,' a familiar voice said approvingly, and her mood was immediately lifted by several notches.

The scene with Aryan had left her feeling drained and helpless, but just the sound of Darius's voice made the world seem like a better place.

'I've called to ask you for some help,' he said. 'I'm looking for a flat to rent, and I'm kind of desperate now. Since you know the real estate business inside out...'

'Don't you have a flat of your own already?'

'It's a long story,' he said. 'I have a flat in the same building as my parents. My sister's moving back to India, and I offered it to her when I thought I'd be leaving Nidas this month. But now that the board's asked me to stay on for another three months I need a place to stay. Only it's difficult to get somewhere for three months—I'm okay with paying rent for six, but not too many people offer leases that short. I really liked a condo in Parel, but it got snapped up by the time I got around to making an offer.'

'That's a pity,' Mallika said, wondering what kind of flat Darius would like. You could tell a lot about a person from the type of home they chose, and she thought she could picture the kind he'd go for. Big, airy and luxurious, but in an understated way. 'Which building?'

He told her, and added, 'It was a great flat—really large living room, with a massive balcony and two bedrooms. But there are only a few flats in the building with that plan. The rest have normal-sized living rooms.'

'Yes, it's only the flats next to the fire refuge areas that have that layout,' Mallika said, chewing her lip thoughtfully. 'I know the building pretty well.'

She was silent for a few seconds, and Darius could hear her slow, careful breathing over the phone line.

'If you're really keen on a flat like that I might be able to get you one for three months,' she said. 'Reasonable rent, and you won't have to pay brokerage. But you'd need to keep the flat in good condition, be careful not to upset the neighbours and all that.'

'I'm keen,' he said, smiling slightly at her tone. 'And I'm housetrained.'

'Hmm...' she said, as if she was only partially convinced. 'Meet me in the parking lot at lunchtime—say at around one—and I can take you to see the flat. It won't take more than half an hour.'

'You mean today?'

'You were the one who said you were keen!'

'So I did.' Darius got to his feet. 'We'll take my car. See you downstairs at one.'

The building was only a couple of kilometres away, and Darius crossed his fingers as they drove through the gate.

He'd been trying to make the best of it, but living with his parents again after a gap of fourteen years was far more stressful than he'd anticipated. So far he'd found only that one place to rent that he'd liked, and he'd been seriously considering choosing one at random from the row of sub-par flats and service apartments his agent had lined up for him.

Mallika's suggestion was a godsend—even if the flat wasn't precisely the same layout as the one he'd initially chosen he was inclined to take it.

He glanced across at her. She was more casually dressed than usual—perhaps because she had no meetings to attend. A black top in some silky material clung lovingly to her curves, and he could see a tantalising hint of cleavage. Her trousers were well cut, and her shoes as sensible as always—the only dash of colour in her outfit was provided by a turquoise blue stole that matched her leather tote.

'You always carry a funky handbag,' he said suddenly as a security guard waved the car to a stop just inside the gate. 'But you wear sensible-looking shoes. Not seen too many girls do that—it's usually neither or both.'

She gave him a quick smile. 'I can't wear heels,' she said. 'Always trip and fall over. But I love bags, and I buy a new one almost every month. I'm surprised you noticed.'

She wasn't just surprised, she was also flattered he'd paid that much attention. Most men didn't notice anything about women's fashions beyond necklines and hemlines.

'I've grown up with a shopaholic sister,' he said, laughing. 'And every girlfriend I've ever had has been crazy about shoes and bags.'

Mallika wrinkled her nose a little at the thought of his girlfriends—she was sure he'd had several, and she found herself thinking negative thoughts about all of them.

The security guard came up to the car and Mallika had to get out and talk to him. Darius tapped the wheel idly as he looked out across the sprawling private garden that was one of the most attractive features of the building.

A tall man came out of the main entrance, and Mallika smiled at him, driving all thoughts of property prices out of Darius's head. The man put an arm around Mallika and gave her a hug that was halfway between friendly and proprietorial, and Darius felt an unfamiliar surge of jealousy as Mallika hugged him back. He knew that Mallika wasn't in a relationship, and it hadn't occurred to him that she might have close male friends. The thought was surprisingly unsettling.

'I have the keys,' Mallika said, sliding back into the passenger seat. 'There's parking for visitors at the back of the building. Take a left after the ramp... Left, Darius—*this* is your left.'

She tugged at his arm as he narrowly missed driving into a flowerbed and Darius grinned as he swung the wheel to the left. 'Sorry, I'm a bit directionally challenged,' he said. 'Especially when bossy women bark into my ear.'

'I'm not bossy!' Mallika protested. She'd let her hand linger on his arm a bit longer than strictly necessary, and now she squeezed it hard. 'Park by the wall. No, not behind the truck—there's more space behind that little red car.'

'Not bossy in the least,' Darius murmured, and she made a face as she got out of the car.

'I'm bossy only when the situation demands it,' she said, linking her arm through his. 'Come on, let's go see the flat.'

'Who was the man you were talking to outside?' he asked as they walked towards the building. 'The guy who gave you the keys? You seemed to know him pretty well.'

He sounded faintly jealous, and Mallika felt her mood improve even further.

'He's an old friend,' she said. 'We were at college together, and he worked with my mother for a while. He and his wife bought a place here last year, and they've been keeping an eye on the flat I'm taking you to.'

Darius nodded. It was ridiculous—it shouldn't matter to him in the least—but he felt a lot better now that he knew the man was married.

The lift man saluted when they got into the lift, and Mallika gave him a quick smile.

'Twentieth floor,' she said, and the man nodded.

'*Sahib* is going to stay here?' he asked.

'*Sahib* is going to figure out first if he likes it or not,' Mallika said. 'What do you think, Shinde? Will he like it?'

'*Sahib* will like it definitely,' Shinde said.

His expression suggested that *sahib* would have to be a blithering idiot not to like it, and Darius suppressed a smile. Mallika had an automatic air of command that Shinde was clearly not immune to—if she'd said that she was taking Darius up to the twentieth floor to persuade him to jump off it she would probably still have had Shinde's wholehearted support.

'It's a beautiful flat, madam,' Shinde added, giving

Darius a disapproving look as the lift doors opened at the twentieth floor.

Shinde was right—the flat *was* beautiful. The layout, of course, was excellent, with a living room that was huge by Mumbai standards, two respectable-sized bedrooms and a compact but very well-designed kitchen. Unlike the stark, unfurnished flat Darius had seen the last time he'd come to the building, this one was fully furnished—right down to elegant white leather sofas and sheer silver curtains with a blue thread running through them.

The colour scheme was predominantly blue and white, but lampshades and rugs made little splashes of vibrant colour. There were a couple of framed vintage Bollywood posters on one wall, while another had a collection of masks from across the country. The overall effect was one of laid-back luxury, and Darius could imagine a high-end interior designer working very hard to produce it.

'You can get rid of the posters and the masks, if you like,' Mallika said as she walked across the room to open the large French windows leading onto the balcony. 'And if you have furniture of your own we can get this put in storage.'

Darius followed her out onto the balcony. The flat overlooked a racecourse and the view was amazing. It was an unusually clear day, and the sea shimmered in the distance, the steel girders of the Bandra-Worli sea link providing a counterpoint to the expanse of blue water. The cars crossing the sea link were so far away that they looked like toys, but Mallika seemed unusually fascinated by them.

'Think of all those people driving from one place to

another, feeling ever so busy and important,' she said as Darius came to stand next to her. 'From here they look just like ants—completely insignificant. And if they look at us we'll look like ants to them too.'

Darius turned to face her, leaning his back against the balcony railing. There was a slight breeze ruffling her curls, and her eyes sparkled beguilingly as she smiled up at him.

'It seems to please you,' he said, laughing as he lifted a hand to tuck a stray curl neatly behind her ear. 'The insignificance of humanity in general and the two of us in particular.'

Mallika laughed, and her dimples deepened. Darius's fingers trailed to her cheek and he traced the line of her jaw, his thumb rubbing very close to her mouth. She went very still, but her large eyes held not even a hint of alarm as he bent down to brush his lips lightly against hers.

Her lips were soft and tempting, and they parted very slightly against his. He deepened the kiss, his arms going around her to pull her closer to him. She came willingly, her arms twining eagerly around his neck and her slim body fitting perfectly against his. Kissing her felt completely natural and wildly erotic at the same time, and it took a huge effort of will to finally stop.

He hadn't wanted to—it had been a last remnant of sanity that had prevailed before he could get completely carried away. It was too soon, he hardly knew her, and he was going away in three months. There were all kinds of things wrong with the situation. But the feel of her in his arms had been so right that stopping the kiss had been almost physically wrenching.

Mallika swayed slightly as he raised his head, and he put his hands on her arms to steady her.

'Wow,' she said softly, her eyes still slightly unfo-cussed. Then a sudden realisation of her surround-ings seemed to hit her and she stepped back, running a slightly shaky hand through her hair. 'So, anyway,' she said, rushing into speech before he could say anything. 'You should probably look at the flat and...um...make up your mind. Whether you want to rent it or not. I'll wait here for you.'

'Or you could come and look at it with me?' he sug-gested, reaching out and taking her hand. She looked un-characteristically flustered, and he could feel her pulse beating wildly in her wrist.

'Yes, of course,' she said, but she disengaged her hand from his before following him into the flat.

For a few seconds Darius wondered if he should ask her what was going on. The kiss had definitely not been unwelcome—he'd felt the desire surging through her body, and the urgency with which she'd returned it. Even afterwards, the way she'd looked at him had made him think that she wanted to take things further.

The change in her had been sudden—maybe she was just more conservative than she'd initially seemed and was trying to cover up her embarrassment. The tempta-tion to repeat the kiss was huge, but Darius didn't want to crowd her.

It didn't take long for him to look the flat over, and he'd come to a decision by the time they were back in the living room.

'I'll take it,' he said. 'Any idea what rent the land-lord's asking?'

She quoted a number that was around fifteen per cent lower than what his broker had quoted for the unfur-nished flat he'd seen the week before.

'Are you sure?' he asked. 'Not that I'm complaining, but I was told that rents have gone up in the last few months.'

'There's been a market correction,' Mallika acknowledged. 'Not very major, though, and this building was overpriced to begin with. The landlord will be okay with the rent—she's…um…a little particular about the kind of person she gives the flat to.'

Darius looked around the flat. 'Whose is it?'

'Mine,' she said, and as he turned to look at her in surprise, she said, 'My mum bought up some flats in this building when it was still under construction.'

'When you say "bought up some flats"…?'

'Two,' Mallika said hastily. 'She bought two flats—one each for Aryan and me. The rates were lower when the project was first floated.'

Darius's eyebrows flew up. *His* family was reasonably wealthy, but buying a single flat in this building would use up at least half their life's savings. Buying two at a time was as inconceivable as sauntering off and buying a sack full of diamonds because you were getting them at a discount.

'Did she…um…do this kind of thing often?' he asked.

'Not really,' Mallika said, her voice guarded. 'Real estate is expensive.'

But between Aryan and her, they owned six flats in Mumbai, three in Bangalore and a farmhouse in Alibagh. It was a fact she usually tried to keep hidden—this was the first time she had voluntarily told anyone even about the flat they were standing in.

'Did the previous tenants leave just recently?' Darius asked, instinctively changing the topic. 'The flat looks as if someone was living in it until yesterday.'

Mallika shook her head. 'I got it furnished a year ago,' she said. 'Sometimes I just need a place to...to think in.'

'Most people do their thinking in the bathroom,' Darius said drily.

She flushed, wishing she'd kept her mouth shut. It was too much, expecting him to understand when he didn't know the first thing about her.

'I meant to rent it out eventually,' she muttered. 'I guess I got a little carried away, doing up the place.'

'Clearly you have more money than you know what to do with,' he said, sounding amused. 'Why d'you need a job?'

'To keep myself from going crazy,' she said.

And her voice was so serious that Darius felt she actually meant it.

CHAPTER FIVE

'This is so typical of a government office,' Darius said, glancing at his watch in annoyance. They were waiting in the property office to register his rent agreement—the appointment had been for seven in the morning, but it was already seven-thirty and the clerks hadn't yet turned up.

'It's always like this,' Mallika said, shrugging. 'Do you have morning meetings?'

He shook his head. 'No, but there's a ton of work I need to get done. And I thought I'd get started on the paperwork for my Schengen visa.'

'Stop thinking about it,' Mallika said, sliding down in her uncomfortable-looking moulded plastic chair and leaning her head against the back to look at the ceiling. 'We're here now. Let's talk about stuff until the clerks turn up.'

'What kind of stuff?' Darius asked, giving her an amused look.

Since the kiss in the flat they hadn't seen each other alone—Darius had been travelling, and after he'd come back Mallika had worked from home for a week. They'd agreed on the rental terms over email and, sensing that she needed some space, Darius hadn't suggested that they meet.

He glanced around the rather seedy office, with its broken furniture and *paan* stains on the walls where it had been chewed and spat out. It wasn't exactly romantic, but at least he was with Mallika, and she looked relaxed and pleased to be spending time with him.

"'Of shoes and ships and sealing wax,'" she said dreamily. "'Of cabbages and kings.'"

'*Alice in Wonderland*,' Darius said. 'It's from The Walrus and The Carpenter poem, isn't it?'

'Is it?' she asked. 'My dad used to keep saying it whenever I asked him what he was thinking about. I didn't realise it was a quotation.'

It was the first time she'd spoken about her father, though her mother figured prominently in her conversation, and Darius took it as a good sign. She was still looking up at the ceiling, as if she found something particularly fascinating in the stains and cracks.

"'*Paisa toh haath ka mail hai,*"' she said after a pause. 'My dad used to keep saying that too. "Money is like dirt on one's palms. Here one moment, washed away the next."'

'He piled up one huge mound of it all the same, though, didn't he?' Darius said without thinking.

Luckily Mallika didn't seem offended. 'Actually, he lost money as fast as he made it,' she said, her mouth curving up into a wry grin. 'It was my mum who was the careful one.'

From her tone, it sounded as if she wished she could admire her mum for it, but couldn't quite bring herself to do so.

Sensing his enquiry, even though Darius hadn't said anything, she went on.

'She was into real estate,' she said. 'My mum. She started off as a real estate agent, but when the markets improved and my dad got back some of his capital she started investing in property herself.'

'Impressive,' he said.

She shrugged. 'I don't think she had much of a choice. My dad couldn't think of any way of making money other than the stock market. If she hadn't taken charge we'd have been out on the streets. Aryan and I were little kids when the stock market crash happened.'

'The Harshad Mehta one?' Darius remembered the crash, but it hadn't affected his life at all. His parents' money was all in fixed deposits and blue chip stocks, so the crash had made good dinnertime conversation—nothing else.

'Yes. My dad lost pretty much all the money we had. Not just his own money but his parents' as well. We used to live in my grandmother's flat in Malabar Hill, but she had to sell it and we moved to a tiny place in Kandivali. Even there, he could barely afford to pay the rent.'

'Must have been tough.'

She shook her head. 'It wasn't. When you're kids it doesn't matter, not living at a good address or having a car and a driver. My dad had more time to spend with us, and he made the whole thing seem like an adventure. He'd take us on bus rides to the zoo and to parks, and he'd invent games for the three of us to play... When I look back, it feels like the best time of my life. It was hell for my mum, though.'

It had been years later when she'd realised that her father had had a mild case of bipolar disorder. The whacky, fun Dad she remembered was the persona he'd taken on during his manic phases. When he'd been going through a depressive episode her mother had concealed it from Aryan and her, telling them that their father was busy at work when he'd locked himself up in a room for hours on end.

'Was that when your mum started up with the real estate thing?'

Mallika nodded. 'She'd been brought up in a rich family, but the dowry she brought with her went with everything else during the crash. And she was too proud to ask her parents for anything more.'

'Why real estate?'

'I guess because that was the only business she understood. Her father was a builder in Gujarat, and she knew how the industry worked. In those days there were very few women property brokers, and she was one of the first to figure out that wives play a huge role in deciding on a house. Most brokers ignored them, but whenever my mom met a couple who was trying to buy a house she went out of her way to understand what kind of layouts the woman liked, how big she wanted the kitchen to be. And kids—no one had heard of pester power, but she made sure she told them about the great play area downstairs and the guy who sold cotton candy across the street...'

'She sounds smart,' Darius said, thinking of his own mother. She was smart too, but she'd been a schoolteacher—selling anything at all was completely alien to her character.

'Yes...' Mallika sounded a little sad. 'But along the line she forgot to have fun or spend time with her family or relax. All she did was work hard and make money.

And every rupee she made had to either go into the bank or into property or gold. I probably have more gold jewellery than the Queen of Oman, even though I hate every piece of it.'

Darius gave her a quick smile. 'It sounds like a problem lots of women would love to have,' he said.

Mallika immediately wondered if she'd sounded too self-obsessed, too demanding and needy. It was difficult to explain the various things that had gone wrong in her family without mentioning stuff that she'd rather not talk about. Which begged the question—why the heck had she started moaning about her parents in the first place?

Giving herself a rapid mental slap, she straightened up.

'You're right,' she said. 'Perhaps some day I'll melt all the stuff down and make a dinner set out of it. I've always wanted to eat off a gold plate.'

'Or give it away to charity?' he suggested.

Mallika shook her head with a laugh. 'There's too much of my mum in me to actually give it *all* away. I do the usual annual donations to charities, and to a couple of religious trusts, but not much more.'

Used to people who claimed to do a lot more for society than they actually did, Darius found Mallika refreshingly upfront. He did a fair amount of volunteering, and he supported a small NGO financially as well, but it wasn't something he talked about much. He was beginning to understand the differences between them. Mallika craved stability, structure and security, whereas he longed for adventure, risk and new experiences that pushed boundaries and frontiers.

'What about *your* family?' Mallika was asking. 'What are *they* like?'

Darius grinned. 'They're a bunch of lunatics,' he said. 'Each one's nuttier than the next. Look—I think someone's actually arrived to open up the office.'

He was right—a surly clerk in a bright magenta sari was making a big show of opening a counter and ignoring the people who'd been queuing up for over forty-five minutes waiting for her.

Registering the agreement took around forty minutes—the last step involved putting their thumbprints onto the documents before signing them, and Darius grimaced as the clerk held out a stamp pad with purple ink to him.

'I thought you just took an electronic thumbprint?' he asked.

The clerk gave him a steely look. 'It's part of the procedure, sir,' she said severely.

Mallika suppressed a little giggle. Darius's thumb was now covered with bright purple ink, and he was looking at it with the kind of horror people usually reserved for maggots and slugs.

'Here, let me help,' she said, taking a pack of cleansing tissues out of her bag.

Darius eyed the packet. 'What're those?' he asked, clearly deeply suspicious of anything in pink packaging.

'Make-up-removing tissues,' Mallika said, taking his hand and beginning to rub the ink off his thumb.

They were out of the office and halfway down the dingy stairs, and there was a curious intimacy in the situation. Mallika took her time, her mouth puckering as she concentrated on getting the ink off. Darius stood still and watched her. The temptation to pull her close and kiss her was immense, but they were in a very public place—and already they'd attracted curious looks from a couple of people.

'Thanks,' he said, once she was done with scrubbing his hand. 'Mallika, the other day in the flat...'

Mallika cringed inwardly. She'd behaved stupidly at the flat, and she knew it. She was very thankful Darius had left the topic alone so far—the reason for her behaviour was solid enough, only it was so incredibly embarrassing that she didn't want to talk about it.

'Yes?' she said.

'Did I upset you? Because you've been a little...different ever since.'

'I wasn't expecting it,' she said. 'And I've been feeling a little awkward—I'm sorry.'

She looked up at him, and for a second Darius forgot what he'd been going to say as he looked into her lovely brown eyes.

'I'm sorry if you think I crossed a professional line,' he said after a bit. 'I kissed you on impulse—I wasn't thinking straight.'

'I'm told that the best kisses happen on impulse,' she said, so solemnly that he burst out laughing.

'Really? Who told you that?'

Mallika shrugged. 'I've forgotten,' she said. 'Anyway, whoever it was, they definitely would know more about it than me.'

Darius gave her a curious look. She didn't come across as being prudish or inexperienced—maybe she meant that her previous lovers hadn't been impulsive.

There was a little pause as they walked out of the building. Mallika was looking straight ahead, her lips pressed tightly together. Embarrassing or not, she'd have to tell him if she didn't want a repeat of what had happened in the flat.

They'd agreed to go back to the office together in Darius's car, and Mallika waited till they were safely inside before she said, 'It was the first time.'

He looked puzzled, as well he might—there had been enough of a pause for him to start thinking of something totally different—like national debt, or the future of the economy. Still, Mallika couldn't help feeling peeved at his not understanding immediately. She'd had to muster up a fair bit of courage to say it the first time, and having to repeat it was just piling on the embarrassment.

'It was the first time anyone had kissed me,' she announced, adding firmly, 'I'm warning you—if you laugh I'm going to have to kill you.'

It didn't look as if there was any danger of his laughing—his eyes widened slightly, and he switched the car engine off.

'You mean—ever?'

'Ever,' she said, wishing he wouldn't stare at her as if she was an alien with three heads and a beak. India was still pretty conservative—surely even in Mumbai it wasn't that unusual to have reached the age of twenty-nine without having been kissed?

Except clearly it was, because Darius looked completely gobsmacked. It took him a few seconds to find his voice, and when he did all he said was, 'Does that mean that you're...a...?'

'A virgin?' Feeling really cross now, Mallika said, 'Yes, it does. And I'm surprised you're asking. What kind of person would have sex and not kiss the person that they're...um...'

'Having sex with?' Darius supplied helpfully.

She glared at him, though that was exactly what she'd wanted to say. 'Anyway, so that was why I was feeling awkward,' she said. 'Can we go now?'

'In a minute,' Darius said, and then he leaned across and kissed her again.

Given that this was the second time it had happened, she should have been better prepared. But the kiss was so different from the first that she was left completely stunned. His lips barely grazed hers, and there was something tender, almost reverential in his touch. Unfortunately her long-dormant hormones weren't in the mood to be treated reverentially, and before she knew it her hands had come up to bunch in his shirt and pull him closer.

The kiss suddenly became a lot less tender and a lot more exciting. *Yessss!* her hormones said happily. *Got it right this time. Don't stop!*

She'd have probably gone with the flow, but catching sight of a large and interested audience of street children outside the car had a sudden dampening effect on Mallika. She pulled away abruptly, straightening her hair with unsteady fingers.

'Sorry,' she muttered. 'I got a bit carried away.'

'So did I,' Darius said, his voice amused. 'You have that effect on me.' Then her suddenly horrified expression registered, and he said, 'Are you okay?'

'Your shirt!' Mallika squeaked, and he looked down to survey his once spotless white shirtfront. Not only was it creased where Mallika had grabbed at it, the top button had popped off and her thumb had left purple ink stains all over it.

'I forgot to use the make-up remover on my own hands,' she said ruefully.

He laughed. 'I have a wardrobe full of white shirts,' he said. 'I won't miss this one.'

'I'll get you a new one,' she said. 'I'm so sorry—I'm a complete klutz when I get carried away.'

'Your getting carried away is worth ruining a shirt for,' he said, his smile warm and sexy as he put out a hand to lightly brush her curls back from her face.

She smiled back, though her heart was thumping at twice its normal rate.

'You're pretty amazing—you know that, right?' he said as he leaned across to kiss her again.

The second kiss was less explosive, but it made her feel cherished and incredibly desirable, and it was like stepping out into the sunlight after months of being locked in a cellar. The sensible part of her mind knew perfectly well that Darius was leaving in a few months, and that they had no future together. But somehow it didn't matter—what mattered was the feel of his strong arms around her and his firm lips moving against hers.

When he finally drew away she gave a little moan of protest.

'I know. I feel that way too,' he said regretfully, though his eyes were dancing with amusement. 'But we need to go—we're providing free entertainment to half the street population of Mumbai.'

He was right—the children had gathered closer to the car and were peering in curiously, and Mallika gave a little sigh.

'All right,' she said, though it felt as if she'd been pulled back to earth with a thump.

'There's a bike parked right in front of the car—I'll have to move it,' Darius said, opening the car door and getting out before Mallika could stop him.

The children followed to watch him, offering their help in shrill voices as he wrestled the locked motorcycle a couple of metres down the road. Mallika got out as well. This was the first time she'd seen Darius do anything...well...*physical*, and he was a treat to watch. He must work out often, she thought, admiring the muscles in his back and shoulders as he lifted the bike. And he was strong—the bike weighed a lot more than he did, and he made moving it seem absolutely effortless.

'Today's not my day,' he remarked as he handed the children a handful of loose change and walked back towards the car. 'First ink and then grease.'

Sure enough, his shirt now had a black grease stain on it.

'Give an old woman something...I haven't had a proper meal since yesterday,' a beggar woman whined from the kerb, and Darius gave her the rest of his change before sliding behind the wheel.

'Blessings on you and your pretty one,' the woman called out after them in Hindi. 'May you have a hundred handsome sons!'

'I like the sound of my "pretty one",' Darius said, sounding amused as Mallika spluttered in annoyance. 'Though having a hundred sons sounds a little impractical.'

'I thought you didn't understand Hindi,' she said crossly.

'Oh, I can get by,' he replied. 'Where to now? I need to get out of this shirt before I show up at work, but I can drop you there before going home to change.'

'You could come to my place,' Mallika suggested impulsively. 'It's nearby, and one of Aryan's shirts would fit you.'

Her body was still tingling in the aftermath of the kiss, and she wanted to keep Darius by her side for as long as she could. It was completely out of character for her to suggest such a thing, and it was reckless and spontaneous, but Darius's kiss had opened a door inside her that could not now be closed. She felt free, and she didn't want that feeling to end.

'Are you sure?' Darius asked.

Going to her place implied taking their kiss further, and he wasn't sure at all if that was a good idea. Kissing her had been on his mind for weeks now, and he hadn't been able to resist any longer. But he should have stopped once she'd told him she was a virgin. He had no intention of getting into any kind of long-term relationship—not at this stage in his life—and he couldn't imagine that Mallika was up for a casual fling.

'Sure that the shirt will fit?' Mallika asked, purposely misunderstanding him. 'It will—Aryan's skinnier than you, but he wears his shirts loose.'

She wasn't sure how Aryan would react to her bringing a man home—either he wouldn't even notice or he'd withdraw even further into his shell—but she found she didn't care. Her home had begun to seem like a prison to her. She loved Aryan to bits, and she felt responsible for him, but he seemed to be getting worse, becoming increasingly difficult to manage, and demanding more and more of her time.

The thought of taking Darius home was strangely liberating. She'd spent the last two years of her life mourning her parents and helplessly watching Aryan get worse. Her friends had gone through the usual ups and downs of relationships and heartbreak before settling down, but she'd listened to her ultraconservative mother and steered clear of men. And after the accident she had been so wrapped up in Aryan that she'd had no time for anyone else.

If she hadn't met Darius she probably wouldn't even have realised that she was living a half-life, and every instinct told her to make the most of the time she had with him. With her mother gone, her links with her conservative extended family had weakened, and she didn't really care what they thought of what she did. And right now she wanted to be with Darius more than anything else.

It took them less than ten minutes to reach her apartment complex, and Darius parked in a free spot outside the compound wall.

'Should I wait here?' he asked in a last-ditch attempt to keep his distance.

She shook her head. 'Better come with me,' she said. 'You'll need to try on the shirt. And I'll give you the keys to your flat too. Now that the paperwork's done, and everything, you'll probably want to move in this weekend.'

A neighbour coming out of the building looked a little surprised to see Darius, but Mallika gave her a sweet smile and swept him into the lift without stopping to talk. The neighbour had known her for years and was a notorious gossip. Mallika would bet her last rupee that she'd make an excuse to call or come over in the evening, with the sole purpose of finding out who Darius was.

The lift stopped on the third floor and Darius followed her to the door of her flat. She dug around in her bright blue tote for the keys—while Aryan was at home, there was only around a ten per cent chance of him opening the door if she rang the bell. Mostly, unless he'd ordered something for himself on the internet and was expecting it to be delivered, he didn't bother answering the door.

Mallika used her own keys to let herself in and out, and she'd got duplicates made for the cook and the cleaner.

Darius's clear, warm gaze on her made her fumble a little, but she finally got the door open, flushing a little as she ushered him in. He stopped as he stepped in, looking around the flat in surprise. He'd expected it to be done up in the same way as the flat he was renting—clean lines, lots of light and space. This flat, however, was crammed full of heavy furniture in some kind of dark wood. The upholstery was in shades of brown and maroon, and the oil paintings on the walls were depressing landscapes in dingy colours. Mallika herself seemed to have shrunk a little after stepping into the flat.

'We…um…usually take our shoes off before going into the house,' she said as she pushed the door open, slipping her own flat-soled pumps off and putting them on a rack just inside the door.

It was a common enough rule in conservative households, and Darius gave her an impish wink as he sat down on a bench next to the shoe rack and pulled off his shoes and socks.

'Sorry,' she said. 'My mum used to be very fussy about shoes in the house, and we've stuck to the rule even without her being around to yell at us.'

'It's a sensible rule,' he said, suddenly understanding why the house looked the way it did. She'd probably changed nothing after her parents had died.

He knew how much she hated any kind of pitying overture, so he didn't say anything, but his heart went out to her.

'I'll get the shirt—give me a minute,' she said, and went into a little corridor and knocked on Aryan's door.

There was no response, and after a minute she gave an exasperated little huff and went into the kitchen.

There was a little service area beyond the kitchen, and a pile of ironed clothes was lying on top of the washing machine. She took two shirts out of the heap and went back to the living room. Darius was still standing, and she held the shirts out to him.

'Here—one of these should fit,' she said. 'You can change in my room.'

Her room turned out to be at the end of the corridor, and unlike the intensely depressing living room it was painted a bright, clean white, with blue curtains and a turquoise bedspread. It was a cheerful room, and Darius felt a lot better as soon as he stepped into it.

'I'll find you a bag to carry your messed-up shirt in,' Mallika said as she shut the door behind her, and she went across to the small dressing table that occupied one corner of the room. 'Here you go.'

She handed him a medium-sized plastic bag and then went to sit on the bed, her eyes on him. The kiss earlier in the car had left her in a confused, half-aroused state so that she could hardly think straight. All she knew was that she wanted to kiss him again, and his suddenly formal attitude was making her feel so frustrated she could scream.

Darius caught her eye and started undoing the top button of his shirt.

Mallika was mesmerised. She couldn't move. 'Uh… maybe I should leave?' she eventually managed to say, but he laughed mischievously.

Darius continued to unbutton his shirt, a gently teasing smile on his lips, and Mallika knew she couldn't leave now. With a boldness that surprised her she slipped off the bed in one fluid movement and came up to him.

'I can help if you want,' she said softly, her hands going to the buttons of his stained shirt.

In the back of her mind Mallika was aware of a lifetime of duty, responsibility and conservative values. But faced with Darius, this beautiful man with his quiet strength, who challenged her but never tried to control her, she found herself responding with an uncharacteristically coy smile. This wasn't her, but it was the person she wanted to be—even if only for a little while. And it felt good...really good.

Darius stood very still as she undid the first two buttons, her hand slipping under the cloth to slide over his bare chest. Inexperienced she might be, but Mallika was very aware of what she was doing and the effect she was having on him. The height difference between them was only a few inches, and she leaned up to press her lips against his, her hands still busy with the buttons. Her tongue lightly teased his mouth, and finally that proved too much for Darius's self-control.

With a muttered oath, he pulled her into his arms, his mouth hard and demanding against hers. His shirt had fallen open, all buttons finally undone, and Mallika could feel his heart pounding under velvety hair-roughened skin.

Without quite knowing how she'd got there Mallika found herself lying on the bed, pinned under his heavy body as he began to kiss his way down her throat. Her hands knotted in his hair and she arched her body to get as close to his as she could without actually breaking skin. Her own clothes were in disarray, her top having ridden up to expose most of her torso, and the feel of his bare skin against hers was indescribably good.

They were probably a nanosecond away from having hot, messy sex on the bed when the sound of a door closing in another part of the flat made Darius jerk away from her.

'Damn, I'm so sorry,' he said.

His eyes were still hooded and a little unfocused as he groaned under his breath and wrapped his arms around Mallika to hold her tightly against his body.

'Bad timing,' he said softly as he dropped a kiss onto her forehead. 'I wish I'd met you a couple of years earlier, Mallika, before I decided to leave India.'

'You could delay going a little,' Mallika said, but she stopped trying to get the rest of his clothes off. She could feel the moment slipping away and she couldn't bear it. 'Or we could just be together until you leave.'

'It's not fair to you,' he said gently. 'Not that I wouldn't love to take this to…to a logical conclusion. I shouldn't have kissed you to begin with, and what happened right now was pretty inexcusable.'

Feeling frustrated, and a little hurt, Mallika sighed. He was right about their timing being completely off, and Mallika wished desperately that she *had* met him a few years earlier. Not that she was in the market for a serious relationship either, but at least they'd have had time to work something out. At least she could have explored all the new sensations and desires that were currently flooding her system. But it looked as if she was going to have to imagine where they might take her instead.

'Go latch the door and put on one of the shirts,' she said, pushing him lightly away.

He groaned reluctantly but got up, giving her an

opportunity to admire his perfectly toned torso as he shrugged off the shirt and put on a clean one. She'd been right—Darius was broader built and more muscular than Aryan, but the shirt fitted perfectly. And the colour suited him. So far, she'd seen Darius only in white or cream formal shirts. This one was a dark blue, and set off his golden skin and jet-black hair perfectly.

'Looking good, Mr Mistry,' she said as he bundled up his old shirt and shoved it into the plastic bag. 'Time for a cup of coffee before you go?'

Darius nodded and Mallika slid off the bed and headed for the kitchen, hastily rearranging her clothes into some semblance of normal.

'Black or with milk?' she asked.

'Black, but with plenty of sugar,' he said.

He took a minute before following her out—his body had reacted with indecent haste to her kisses and he wanted to be sure he was fit to be seen before he left the room. Once he was sure he had everything under control, he tucked the shirt in, gave himself a cursory look in the mirror and strode out.

Mallika was tapping a foot nervously on the floor as she spooned instant coffee powder into two mugs. Her frustration at having to stop was turning into an irritation with everything around her—especially Aryan, who'd disturbed them by slamming his door shut.

'D'you want to grab something to eat before we leave?' she asked Darius when he walked into the kitchen.

It wasn't food he was thinking about just then, but he shrugged. 'A sandwich or something,' he said. 'I'm not particularly hungry.'

She handed him his coffee and went to the fridge.

'I'm sure I can figure something out. The cook will have made lunch for Aryan...I'll just need to see if there's enough for all of us.'

'Mally, do you know where my camera is?'

Darius had built up a mental picture of Aryan, and the reality was so different from the weedy, sallow-looking youth he'd imagined that he blinked in surprise. The resemblance between brother and sister was so close that they could have been twins if not for the obvious differences of gender and age. If anything, Aryan was better-looking than Mallika, and other than his skin being a little pale there was nothing to indicate that he hadn't been out of doors in months.

Mallika had turned at the sound of his voice, and she said curtly, 'It's in my room. And you're not getting it back until you promise to stop taking photos from your window.'

'I promise,' he said. 'Can I have it back now?'

'I'll tell you in the evening,' she said. 'Say hello to Darius, Aryan.'

Aryan's brow furrowed a little as he turned.

'Hello, Darius,' he said slowly, and it was difficult to tell if he was being sarcastic or not. His brown eyes, disconcertingly like Mallika's, flicked over Darius, stopping a little to take in the shirt.

'I lent him one of your shirts,' Mallika said. 'His got ruined by ink and grease—long story. Have you had lunch?'

'Fruit and some milk,' Aryan said. 'There were only oily *parathas* for lunch.'

'Those'll do for us,' Mallika said, locating the *parathas*

and sliding them onto two plates with a little heap of pickle on each. 'Here you go, Darius.'

Darius took the plate. Their hands touched briefly, and a slight blush suffused Mallika's face. Aryan gave her a thoughtful look, but he didn't say anything.

Mallika looked up at him. 'Did you get any work done today, Aryan?' she asked.

'Lots,' he said, stretching like a cat, his mouth curving into a boyish smile that was surprisingly charming. 'The market's very active today.'

'Hmm, I saw the alerts,' Mallika said as she finished her last *paratha*. 'Be careful, though, it'll be very volatile until the elections. Shall we go, Darius? Venkat's probably tearing his hair out—I was supposed to submit a report to him before lunch.'

Aryan watched them leave, an indefinable expression in his eyes. There was clearly a lot going on beneath the surface with Mallika's brother that Darius could only guess at.

'See you around,' Darius said as he brushed past him to get to the door. 'I'll get the shirt cleaned and sent back to you in a couple of days.'

'See you,' he echoed.

His voice was perfectly cordial, though Darius got the impression that Aryan was happy to see him go. It was an odd set-up, and he felt desperately sorry for Mallika, living in that depressing flat with only her reclusive brother for company.

'Aryan works?' Darius asked as they got into the car. He didn't want to talk about what had just happened between them, and felt that Mallika was thinking the same.

'Stock-trading,' Mallika said. 'He inherited the knack from my father and he's doing quite well. Unlike my dad, he knows how to take calculated risks, so he makes money.'

'And your dad?' Darius said eventually.

She shrugged. 'Made a fortune one day—lost it the next. He let his gambling instincts take over too often.'

There hadn't been any photos in the house, Darius realised suddenly. That was what had seemed out of place. The flat was like a museum—all that expensive heavy furniture and dark draperies—with no personal touches at all. No photographs, no tacky souvenirs from foreign trips, no sign that anyone actually *lived* there.

'What did you think of him?' Mallika was asking. 'Aryan, I mean. It's been a while since he met anyone. He doesn't go out, and the only people who visit us have known him for years. I was wondering how he comes across to someone who's met him for the first time.'

'He didn't talk much,' Darius said cautiously. 'It's not that uncommon to be a bit of a hermit at that age, is it?'

'"A bit of a hermit"?' she repeated, and laughed shortly. 'That's a good description.'

He got the sense that she wanted to say more, but she seemed to think better of it and began talking about work instead. Darius felt a strange sense of frustration—not all of it physical. There was something elusive about Mallika…a quicksilver quality that made him feel he was never quite sure of where he was with her.

The admission that he was the first man she'd ever kissed had shaken him up—it was the first indication he'd got that she felt more for him than she'd shown. As for his own feelings—he knew he was already in way too deep to walk away at this point. In addition to wanting her so badly that it hurt, he needed to talk to her, find out what made her tick.

CHAPTER SIX

'NOT THIS WEEKEND. Aryan needs me around,' Mallika said.

She'd tried talking to Aryan again about getting help—it was eight months now since he'd last stepped out of the flat—but she hadn't got anywhere. And he'd been even more distant since he'd met Darius, talking even less than usual and not coming out of his room except for meals. She was really worried about him—afraid he would become so reclusive that she would lose him completely.

'I really want to see you,' Darius said, his voice dropping an octave.

She felt a pleasurable heat curling through her body. And this was in reaction to just his *voice*. A mental image of him shirtless and super-hot intruded, and she squirmed.

'I want to see you too,' she whispered back. 'It's just that this weekend is a bit…tough. I need to figure a few things out.'

As she put the phone down she noticed Aryan at the door, looking at her. It was impossible to gauge how much he'd overheard, and he didn't say anything—just walked off to the dining table.

A surge of annoyance left her cheeks warm and her pulse racing—she badly wanted to meet Darius, and Aryan was one of the main reasons she'd said no. But it seemed a rather pointless sacrifice when it didn't seem to be helping him.

She obsessed over it for a while, before she came to a decision. Her aunt wouldn't mind coming down and being with Aryan for a bit—heaven knew she deserved to have a life of her own. For a minute she wondered what her mother would have thought of her decision and her nerve almost failed her. Her mother had been courageous and independent, but she'd also been rigidly conventional—which was partly why she'd ended up being deeply unhappy all her life. She'd have hated the thought of what Mallika was about to do. But she was gone anyway, and Mallika had her own life to live and her own choices to make.

Picking up her phone, she typed out a quick text.

Are you still free this weekend? Might be able to meet you on Saturday.

Her text arrived in the nick of time—Darius was just about to promise an elderly aunt that he'd drive her to visit a friend who lived around thirty kilometres away.

'Next Saturday instead,' he told his aunt firmly.

The last time he'd driven Auntie Freny to meet a friend she'd insisted on leaving home at nine in the morning, and had subsequently proceeded to party till three the *next* morning.

'*Dikra*, this time you can have a drink too,' Auntie Freny said cajolingly.

Darius promptly felt as if he was six again, being promised a chocolate if he was good.

'Last time, *ni*, you had to drive, no? This time we can stay overnight—just pack some clothes.'

'Next Saturday,' Darius said, and gave his aunt an affectionate hug.

'Some girl you're going to meet—don't think I don't know.'

His aunt made a surprisingly nimble grab for his phone, and Darius managed to whisk it away only just in time.

Balked of her fun, Freny shook her head at him sorrowfully. 'Never do I get to meet these girls. Get married and settle down, *dikra*, this is no time for flirting and having fun. Our race is dying out! I went to the Parsi *panchayat* last week and...'

'And they told you that unless I got married and fathered fifteen children I'd be responsible for the end of the Parsis?'

Aunt Freny gave him an exasperated look. 'No, I met an old friend with a really nice daughter who'd be perfect for you. If you just met her once you'd give up this crazy idea of travelling around in all kinds of strange places, away from your family. Should I call my friend?'

'Thanks, but no thanks,' Darius said firmly. 'I'm perfectly capable of finding a girlfriend of my own if I want one.'

'Freny, he doesn't *want* to marry and settle down,' his mother said tartly as she walked into the room. 'If he did, he wouldn't want to go traipsing across the world like this.' She caught Darius's suddenly stricken look and added in a gentler tone, 'Relax, I'm not trying to make you feel guilty. You've done everything you can for this family, and you deserve a few adventures for yourself.'

Finding something to wear for a date when you possessed a sum total of zero remotely suitable outfits shouldn't have been difficult, but it was.

Mallika grimaced as she surveyed her clothes. She had several shelves of cotton tunics that she teamed with jeans when she went out to indulge her photography hobby, two formal business suits, a couple of silk *churidaar kameez*, and half a dozen saris. Dozens of loose cotton T-shirts...

Even the 'remotely suitable' outfits were beginning to look unusable—one of the tops had a mark on it, and the other two hung loose on her slim frame. Evidently she'd lost weight and not realised it.

Beginning to feel a little desperate, she took everything out of the wardrobe, in the hope that something suitable would surface. Buying new clothes to go out with Darius would be taking the concept of trying too hard to a completely different level...

Perhaps she could wear a silk *kameez* over jeans and pretend that she was going for an arty look.

At the back of the wardrobe, a little patch of flame-coloured matt silk caught her eye. *Ah, right.* That was the dress that an old college friend had given her, evidently not realising that Mallika never wore dresses or skirts.

Tugging the dress from its cellophane wrapping, she shook it out and held it against herself. There was a reason why she avoided anything that showed her legs— there was a narrow, but very visible scar from a bicycle accident that ran up her left leg from mid-calf to knee.

'If it scares him off it's probably a good thing,'

she muttered to herself as she pulled the dress on and smoothed it over her hips.

It should have looked hideous. The colour was anything but subtle, and it was a while since she'd last worn a dress. But the fabric clung softly to her curves, outlining the soft swell of her breasts and emphasising her perfect waist. The hem was asymmetrical, and it hid part of the scar—but she found the scar itself was nowhere as scary as she remembered it being. Her legs were long and shapely, and the scar was barely noticeable.

The dress was probably not suitable for a simple date, but once she'd seen how she looked she didn't feel like taking it off.

'You're looking nice,' Aryan informed her as she stepped out of her room.

Her eyes flew up to his in surprise. She hadn't expected him to come out of his room to see her off. Still less had she expected him to notice what she was wearing.

Feeling the excitement drain out of her, she said tentatively, 'Thanks. Um…are you sure you'll be okay with *mausiji*?'

He nodded, and when she didn't look convinced gave her a crooked smile. 'I'm alone at home when you go to work,' he reminded her. 'Go ahead—I'll be fine today.'

Aryan probably hadn't intended it, but she felt inordinately guilty as she stepped out of the flat. She did her best to work from home whenever she could, but she did end up having to go to the office at least two, sometimes three days a week. Aryan never liked being left alone in the flat, and ever since she'd changed jobs he'd been more on edge—staying in his room and skipping meals if she wasn't around to force him to eat.

Darius was waiting in his car at the end of the lane, and she half ran the rest of the way to reach him.

He leaned across and unlocked the door, giving her a quizzical smile as she slid in, half out of breath. 'Are the Feds after you?' he asked.

She laughed. 'No—worse, I have the snoopiest neighbours in the universe. So, what are we doing today?'

He'd planned lunch and a movie, but one look at Mallika in her flame-coloured dress had driven everything out of his head—all he could think of was taking her home and making slow, delicious love to her.

'Whatever you want,' he said slowly. 'I've booked tickets for a movie, and a table at a restaurant. But most of all I want to talk to you. We left a lot of things unfinished the last time we met.'

His eyes met hers, and it was as if she could read what he'd been thinking a second ago.

'You've moved into the Parel flat, haven't you?' she asked, and he nodded. 'And have you managed to set up your home theatre system yet?'

He nodded again, and she broke into a smile so bright and alluring that he could hardly tear his eyes away from her face.

'Let's go there then,' she said. 'Watch an old movie, order takeaway…talk.'

'Right,' he said, his throat suddenly dry. 'Sounds like a plan.'

Predictably, watching a movie was the last thing on their minds as they tumbled into the flat fifteen minutes later. Darius had pretty much broken every speed limit in town, getting them there, and they were barely inside the flat before Mallika was in his arms, kissing him so eagerly that it took his breath away.

'Slow down,' he said softly, smoothing her hair away from her face. 'We have all the time in the world. And I really do think we should talk.'

It took everything he had not to whisk her straight into the bedroom, but it was important that they laid some ground rules before taking things further.

She sighed and pulled away from him. 'What's there to talk about?' she asked. 'You're leaving in a few months and I'm stuck here.'

'I know,' he said. 'Logically, we should stay away from each other—but that's not happening, is it?' It looked as if she wanted to interrupt, but he went on, 'It's mostly my fault—I've been trying to convince you to meet me. If you want me to, I'll stop.'

'I don't want you to stop,' Mallika said, her voice low. 'Look, I can't commit to a long-term thing either, but I haven't felt like this about anyone ever before. I haven't wanted to do this with anyone before. Maybe it's just physical attraction, but I…I dream about you. And when I'm with you I can't seem to stop myself from…from…'

Touching you, she wanted to say. *Kissing you and wanting to make love to you all night long.* The words didn't come, though—and already she'd said more than she'd meant to.

Darius's expression had changed. Maybe he thought she was throwing herself at him. She quickly tried to dispel the thought.

'I can't marry while I still have Aryan to look after,' she said. 'Until I met you I used to stay away from men and concentrate on work. It was much easier that way.

Only with you I've not been able to stick to the rules I made for myself.'

Mallika took a deep breath. She'd never had such a conversation with a man before, and she had to screw up her courage to get the next words out.

'So I was thinking—maybe I should just forget about the rules for a bit. Do what *I* want for once—with someone who wants it just as much as I do.'

Darius leaned closer to her, capturing both her hands in his. 'Mallika, I don't want to take advantage,' he said. 'I'm crazy for you, but the last thing I want to do is hurt you in any way.'

'You won't,' she said, her eyes meeting his steadily. 'I know you'll leave, and I'm okay with it. I just...' Her voice quivered a bit, but she steadied it with a visible effort. 'I haven't really been able to let go and do what I want. *Ever.* When I was in school and college I was studying hard all the time, because that was the way my mother wanted it. Even when I started working I stayed away from parties and men. She was trying to protect me because she'd had such a tough life herself. By the time I figured out that the world wasn't that bad after all, she was dead. And I had Aryan to look after.'

Darius's eyes were sympathetic now, and she felt she couldn't bear it.

'While you're here, let's be together,' she said, making her voice as upbeat and cheerful as possible. 'And once you need to go we'll separate—with no regrets. How does that sound?'

'Like the last bit's going to be damn tough,' Darius said honestly. 'I'm finding it difficult enough to be objective right now. I don't know what it'll be like three months from now.'

'If we're lucky it'll wear off by then,' she said.

He had to laugh. 'If we're lucky,' he repeated, tracing a line down the side of her face with one hand and watching her quiver in response. 'But—just so that you know—even if we're perfect together I'm not going to stay. I need a clean break from my current life, and that's important for me. More important than anything else.'

'Relax, I get that,' she murmured. 'If you like we'll get the legal team to draft a set of disclaimers for you! I'm not looking for a happy ending, here—just a few weeks of fun.'

'Right,' he said.

There was an awkward moment while they stared at each other, both unsure of what to do next, then Darius muttered something and swept her into his arms, his lips hot and insistent against hers. Mallika melted against him, but a few minutes later, as his hands went to the zip on her dress, she made a little sound of protest and Darius pulled back.

'Are you okay?' he asked, his mouth against her throat.

She nodded her head. 'Yes,' she said decisively. 'Just go a little slower. I'm…nervous.'

The admission shook him more than he would have cared to admit and he changed his touch, skimming his hands over her skin as gently as if she was made of spun glass.

It was only when she made a little sound in her throat and pressed her hips hard against his that he let his lips become a little more urgent, his hands more demanding…

Much later, Mallika raised her head lazily from Darius's shoulder and surveyed the room. Her dress lay in a tangled heap near the foot of the bed, next to his jeans, and the rest of their clothing was strewn around the room. It was a miracle that they'd made it to the bed and not ended up making love on the living room sofa or on the floor.

'That was good,' she said.

'Just *good*? I must be losing my touch,' he murmured, running a finger lightly down her arm. She shivered in reaction and he grinned, twisting her around to kiss her. 'Did I hurt you?' he asked, more seriously.

She shook her head. 'I'm a little sore, but I guess that's to be expected. And I hate to spoil the mood, but I'm starving after all that exercise. Any chance of getting something to eat?'

'We'll have to order in,' Darius said. 'The sum total of food available in this house is one apple and a box of biscuits.'

'I'll take the apple,' she said, turning and burrowing closer to him.

'I have some takeaway menus in the kitchen,' Darius said. What do you feel like eating?'

'I'm not sure,' Mallika said with a sigh. Lying in Darius's arms felt so good she wouldn't move at all if her stomach weren't rumbling.

'Did you live here ever, Mallika?' he asked. 'Before you decided to rent the flat out?'

The place had a sense of having been lived in, despite its pristine state.

'I wanted to move here when my parents died,' she said. 'Our old place reminds me of them every minute I'm in the flat. But Aryan wasn't keen, and now I can't leave him there by himself.'

'That's understandable,' he said.

There was a brief pause as Mallika cuddled up closer

to him and nibbled playfully at his shoulder. She responded enthusiastically when he pulled her in for a hard kiss, but after a bit twisted away from him.

'I'm really, really hungry,' she said. 'Can we order food first?'

Darius groaned and picked up the first of the menus. 'Here you go,' he said. 'I can see I'm much lower in your priority list than lunch.'

Mallika took the menu and gave him a conciliatory little kiss. 'You're *much* more important than lunch,' she assured him. 'I just want to get lunch out of the way so that I can concentrate on you.'

The thought of her concentrating only on him made it difficult for Darius to think straight, but he leaned back and watched Mallika as she went through the menu.

'*Tandoori roti, daal tadka* and *aloo jeera,*' she said. 'What about you?'

'I think I'll have the chicken *sagawala,*' he said, mentioning the first thing he'd noticed on the menu. 'Or, no—you're vegetarian. I'll have the same stuff you're having.'

'I'm okay with you ordering chicken as long as I don't have to eat it,' Mallika said. 'But it's *saagwala*—not *sagawala.*'

Darius frowned. 'What's the difference?'

'*Saagwala* means that it's made in a spinach sauce,' she explained patiently. '*Sagawala* means that the chicken is a blood relative.'

'Seriously?'

'Seriously.'

He looked impressed. 'There's more to this speaking Hindi thing than meets the eye,' he said. 'Maybe you should give me Hindi lessons.'

'Maybe I should,' she said, dimpling as she tossed the menu back to him and went to get a glass of water.

Darius used his cell phone to order lunch, and once he was done wandered back to the bedroom. He lay down and stared at the ceiling. In spite of it being Mallika's first time, the sex had been mind-blowing, and he could hardly stop a goofy grin from spreading across his face at the thought of how good it had been.

Mallika came back into the room a few minutes later, still swathed in the bed sheet. She perched on his side of the bed and looked at him thoughtfully. Darius was sitting up now, his bare chest on display as he gave her a slow smile—and he looked so heartbreakingly perfect that for an instant she forgot the lines she'd been rehearsing in the kitchen.

Impulsively, she leaned across and kissed him, but pulled away when he tried to take her into her arms. Losing her head once a day was enough—it had been amazing, unforgettable, but now she needed to be sensible.

'This is going to be complicated,' she said. 'We should talk.'

CHAPTER SEVEN

'I AGREE,' DARIUS SAID. 'I think ground rules are a very good idea.'

'So that we don't end up making a mess of things,' Mallika continued. 'I mean, you'll be going away, so it doesn't matter so much for you, but I don't want to have to deal with unnecessary gossip.' She thought for a moment, and went on, 'Plus it'll be difficult for me if Aryan finds out. He's very fragile right now—even more so than usual.'

'We don't need to tell him,' Darius said, reacting to the last sentence first. Her expression changed and he added hastily, 'Or anyone else. What's next?'

He looked so tempting, standing there with his shirt still partly unbuttoned and his hair rumpled after making love, that Mallika felt like abandoning the list of rules and going back to bed with him.

Sighing, she turned away and walked to the window. 'Gossip is only part of it,' she said. 'We should probably be careful not to…um…get too close—like talk about our lives too much and all that. Keep it limited to the physical stuff.'

Darius nodded again, a little more slowly this time. What she said made sense, but it made him think that she was perhaps more emotionally affected than she said she was. It sounded as if she was trying to build up walls so that she didn't get hurt when he left.

'What else?' he asked, beginning to wonder if this had all been a huge mistake.

He was a lot more experienced than her, and he should have foreseen the complications that would occur if they slept together. He couldn't get tangled up in something that would make him question his travels. He needed this…he *deserved* this—it had been his goal for so many years and now it was within touching distance. He wouldn't give it up—not again.

'We should…um…be together only in the evenings,' she said. 'I'll come to you.'

That would set some boundaries, she thought. Ensure that she didn't throw herself at him at all hours. And she'd make sure she went to him only on the days that she'd been working from home, so Aryan wasn't alone for more than a few hours.

He nodded again, and she said. 'Just one more thing. I have a lot of stuff going on right now, so while I'd love to meet you as often as you want to it probably won't be possible.'

This was beginning to sound a bit clinical, thought Darius. He understood that Mallika was only trying to protect herself, and goodness knew the rules certainly worked in his favour, but it made him feel concerned that she had already got in over her head.

'Problems with Aryan?' Darius asked, and his voice was so gentle that Mallika felt suddenly very close to tears.

'Yes,' she said. 'He doesn't like me leaving him at home and going out.'

Darius moved to stand behind her, his arms coming around her to pull her gently against him. He would agree to the rules, of course, but he would have to stay on his guard. After all, rules could always be broken.

'Maybe I could help?' he suggested. 'If nothing else, I could take your mind off everything that's bothering you.'

Mallika turned abruptly and buried her face in his chest. 'It isn't so simple,' she said, her voice muffled against his shirt.

'It could be,' he said, his breath stirring her hair. 'Think about it.'

'I should go now,' she said, without looking up. It's getting late and Aryan's alone. My aunt will have left by now.'

For a few seconds Darius felt like telling her that Aryan was a grown man and capable of taking care of himself for a few hours. But he bit the words back. Mallika clearly felt responsible for her brother, and making snide remarks about him wouldn't help matters. Also, he trusted her judgement—if she said her brother wasn't fit to be left alone for long periods she was probably right.

But he was feeling incredibly frustrated—Mallika had got to him in a way no woman had before, and her determination to stay emotionally unattached bothered him more than he would have expected.

'I'll drop you home,' he said, but she shook her head again.

'I'll take a cab.'

'Stop being stubborn about it,' he said. 'Even if someone sees us, we can tell them you're my landlady.'

She nodded obediently, and Darius tipped her face

up so that she was forced to look right into his laughing eyes.

'Come on, landlady,' he said teasingly. 'Let's get you home.'

Perhaps it would have been easier if Darius had taken her rules at face value, Mallika thought a few weeks later. She slipped into Darius's flat almost every alternate evening, and the sex was as hot and passionate as it had been the first time. But Darius didn't seem content with that—she'd expected that he would stay away from her when they weren't actually sleeping together, but he was doing quite the opposite.

'People know that we're friends,' he said. 'It'll seem far more suspicious if I stop talking to you at work than if we continue to hang out together.'

And so, in public, he'd assumed the role of a friend—one who wanted to spend as much time with her as possible. Every couple of days he'd call to suggest meeting up for coffee or a movie—if she said no he'd laugh and suggest an alternative date. Or he'd bully her into admitting she needed a break and take her out anyway.

Once he'd bought tickets for a stand-up comedy show and told Venkat that she needed to leave work early to participate in a personality development exercise.

Venkat had asked suspiciously, 'What's wrong with her personality?'

He'd said, 'Her sense of humour could do with some work—she takes life way too seriously.'

And Venkat, who wouldn't have recognised a joke if it had walked up and hit him on the nose, had agreed with him and forced her to go.

Another time he'd booked both of them onto a heritage walk across the old parts of South Mumbai, which had ended at an open-air music festival at the Gateway of India. The music had been a crazy jumble of jazz, blues, fusion and rock, and Mallika had had the time of her life.

Afterwards, they'd wandered through Colaba and had dinner at a little tucked-away Lebanese café. They'd talked for hours and hours about music and travel and books, and hadn't realised how late it was until they'd been the last people in the café, with the owner waiting patiently for them to pay their bill and leave.

When she'd got home Aryan had been waiting for her, his eyes large and accusing in his pale face, and she'd resolved never to stay out so late again.

The next few times Darius had asked her out she'd made excuses and stayed at home, playing Scrabble with Aryan, or just sitting in his room with a book while he pored over his laptop screen.

Today, Darius was on the phone insisting she get up at this unearthly hour in the morning to go with him to Sewri. A flock of migratory flamingos stopped at the Sewri mudflats for a few weeks every year on their way from Siberia, and Darius was appalled to hear that she'd lived in Mumbai for her entire life and never seen them.

'Darius, I can't,' she protested. 'I've just woken up, and I need to get breakfast for Aryan. And I need to go to my Alibagh house for a few hours in the afternoon. I can't come.'

And I can't be with you and pretend to be friends without wanting much more, she said silently to herself. It was time she put her foot down and made sure they stuck to the rules. She was new at this, and she could feel herself starting to fall for him, to rely on him being a part of her life. She didn't want to get hurt, and of course there was Aryan to consider.

'I'll stop at a café and fetch something for Aryan's breakfast,' Darius said easily. 'And we'll be done with the flamingos by ten—I'll drop you to the ferry after that.'

'I don't want to leave Aryan alone for that long,' she said. 'My aunt can't come over today—she's got a *puja* prayer ritual to go to. And I'm a little tired.'

She'd woken up with a bad headache, and the thought of the Alibagh trip was depressing. The little beach villa was where her parents had died—she'd not been able to bring herself either to sell it or rent it out, and it had been lying vacant for the last two years. It had been repainted after the accident, and there was a caretaker who kept the house clean and tended the lawn, but she'd visited it only four times in the last two years. Now there was a leakage problem and she had to go.

'We can go tomorrow, then,' Darius said. 'Or next week, if you like.'

Mallika sighed, and then said abruptly, 'Darius, why are you doing this?'

'Doing what?' he asked innocently.

'You know what I mean,' Mallika said.

She got up and closed the door to her room, to make sure that Aryan couldn't overhear her.

'Look, we're doing what we said we would—having a fling before you go to Alaska or Mongolia or wherever. But you're also doing this "just good friends" routine. I'm not sure if it's fooling anyone, and it's definitely confusing the hell out of *me*. It just…doesn't make sense.'

'It does to me,' he said. 'I really like you. I like being with you—in bed and out of it. And, maybe I'm wrong, but it feels like you don't have any close friends—not people you can be yourself with.'

'So you feel *sorry* for me?'

She probably hadn't meant to sound bitter, but it came out that way and Darius winced. He hadn't wanted to have this conversation so soon—and definitely not over the phone. What she'd said about never having had a chance to have fun and do what she wanted had struck a chord with him. He'd never had the kind of problems she had, but he understood the need to break loose and he'd been doing his best to help.

Quite apart from that was the fact that he actually loved every minute he spent with her—but he tried not to think about that too much. He knew that their spending time together like this was dancing on the edge of what their rules allowed, but somehow he couldn't stop himself.

'Not sorry, exactly,' he said. 'I just think that you're young and you have your whole life ahead of you—it's a little early to be cooping yourself up at home and only coming out when you need to go to work. You said it yourself—you want to go out and have fun, do all the things you missed doing when you were younger.'

'I might have said it, but it's not practical to think only about myself,' she said. 'I have a brother with problems, remember?'

'I know,' Darius said.

She didn't mention Aryan often, but he had now got a fair idea of what she was dealing with there. He gritted his teeth before plunging ahead.

'But I don't think you can solve his problems by locking yourself away as well. He needs professional help, and the sooner you get it for him the better it'll be for both of you.'

'Perhaps *I* need professional help as well, then,' Mallika said. 'Because I can't see my way to dragging him to a doctor when he refuses to go. And I can't stop caring about him or looking after him.'

'There's always a way out,' Darius said. 'It's just not obvious because you're so closely involved.'

'Maybe I don't want a way out,' she said softly, the hopelessness of the entire situation striking her anew. 'I'm not like you, Darius—I can't just walk away from my family without a backward glance.'

There was a long pause, and then Darius asked, 'Is that what you think I'm doing?'

'Well, isn't it?' she countered hotly. He had pressed her buttons and now her blood was up. She was spoiling for a fight. 'Your parents are old, and there's your grandmother, and your aunt—you're just leaving them to fend for themselves, aren't you?'

'My sister's here,' he said, wondering why he was even bothering to justify himself.

He hadn't talked to Mallika about his family much—their rules forbade it, after all—so it wasn't surprising that she was jumping to all the wrong conclusions. Still, her words stung, and he couldn't help thinking they'd been right about keeping their relationship superficial. Their approach to life was so different that they didn't have a hope of ever fully understanding each other.

'That's not the same thing,' Mallika was saying. 'She's got kids and a husband, hasn't she?'

Shirin was in the process of divorcing her husband. That was another thing Darius had never told Mallika, and this was definitely not the right time. Suddenly his plans for a glorious morning with Mallika had turned into an ugly argument and he coulnd't wait for it to be over.

'Mallika—' he said, but she interrupted him.

'I'm sorry,' she said. 'This isn't any of my business, and I'm getting a bit too emotional about it. I miss my own parents and I can't understand you leaving yours behind while you go off to discover yourself, or whatever. So I'm not being rational, and I've probably said a bunch of things I shouldn't have.'

Her voice was shaking a little, and Darius felt his anger dissipate as quickly as it had flared up.

'It's all right,' he said. 'You're right, in a way. But my family and my decisions don't have anything to do with the situation you and Aryan are in. I really do want to help, Mallika. Don't keep pushing me away.'

'I'm not,' she said. 'It's just…very tough talking about him with anyone. Even you. It feels like I'm betraying him. And I love spending time with you, but I feel guilty every minute because I know he needs me more than you do.'

There was a longish pause, after which Darius spoke. 'I can understand that,' he said slowly. 'But what about what *you* need?'

'I don't know, Darius, but I do know that I have to put him first. That's what you do when it comes to family— you don't just go off and leave them to it.'

Family would always be her priority, but as she began to calm down she realised how harsh that must have sounded to Darius. It had been a long and tiring week, and Aryan's moods and ingratitude had pushed her over the edge. A weak, but insistent part of her kept saying that she should apologise and do whatever he wanted, but she squashed it firmly.

Luckily, before she could say anything, he said, 'All right, then. I guess I'll see you around the office next week.'

His voice was remote and expressionless, and Mallika just got to say a brief goodbye before he cut the call.

She put the phone on her bedside table and flopped back into bed to stare at the ceiling. It was all very well to tell herself that she'd get over Darius in a bit—right now she felt as if she'd succeeded in cutting her heart out with a rusty knife. He had been genuinely trying to help her, to connect with her better, and she'd said some unforgivable things to him. No wonder he'd sounded as if he never wanted to see her again.

She tried to focus on Aryan instead. Darius wasn't the first person to say that he needed professional help, though he'd said it far more bluntly than most. Mallika had done her best to shield her younger brother from the aftermath of their parents' death, but he'd actually been there when the accident had happened. He'd escaped completely unharmed, but since then he'd been a shell of his former self.

Mallika and he had been close when they were growing up, but despite her best efforts she hadn't been able to get him to talk to her about what was wrong. And the more she tried to draw him out, the more silent he became.

The only time Aryan seemed really happy was when he was in front of his laptop, staring at the flickering screen as he traded stocks and moved money around from one set of investments to another. He had inherited just the right mix of talents from his father and mother to be a formidable trader, and he had almost doubled the money they had inherited from their parents over the last year.

Aryan lived most of his life online—he worked online and bought everything he needed on various websites and had it delivered to the flat. They had a cook and a cleaner, and of course he had Mallika for anything else. He no longer needed to go out at all.

After a while, she had stopped pushing him to talk, and that had had the result of making him more and more dependent on her. He tried to stick as close to her as he could whenever she was at home, and messaged her constantly when she was at work. Mallika sometimes found herself wishing he'd leave her alone—he was as demanding as he'd been when he was three and had toddled behind her everywhere like a pudgy little shadow.

Mallika sighed as she got out of bed. There were little sounds coming from the kitchen that indicated that Aryan was awake and foraging for breakfast. She'd forgotten to order groceries the day before, and there wasn't any ready stuff that he could eat. She'd need to make him some *upma* or something before she got ready and left to catch the eleven o'clock ferry to Alibagh.

There was a long queue for the ferry at the Gateway of India and Mallika joined it, cradling her bright green tote in her arms. The sun was beating down uncomfortably on her head and she wished she'd thought to wear a hat in addition to the sunglasses that she'd perched on her nose.

The glasses served the dual purpose of saving her eyes from the sun as well as concealing quite how puffy they were. Post-breakfast, with a morose and monosyllabic brother, she'd gone to her room and had a good cry.

It hadn't done much for her looks, but at least she felt a lot calmer than she had in the morning.

'Excuse me, would you mind keeping my place for me in the queue for a few minutes?' the woman in front of her said. 'My son wants an ice cream, and if I don't get it for him right now he'll whine for the entire hour that we're on the ferry.'

'No, I won't,' the pudgy youngster standing next to her said indignantly.

He had a pronounced accent which Mallika couldn't quite place—it wasn't American, but it was close.

'You promised me an ice cream last week and I didn't whine when you didn't buy it, did I?'

'Of course you did,' his slightly older sister chimed in.

Their mother groaned. 'Can it, both of you,' she said. 'Do you want ice cream or not?'

'Want ice cream,' both of them said firmly.

The woman turned back to Mallika. 'Sorry,' she said. 'They're at a terribly argumentative stage. So—is it okay if I leave the queue for a minute?'

'Yes, of course,' Mallika said.

'Of course it's okay if you *leave*,' the girl said scornfully. 'The point is, will she let you back in the line when you come back?'

'I will,' Mallika promised, her lips twitching slightly. The girl was around nine, dignified, knobbly-kneed and totally adorable.

'Thank you so much,' the mother said with evident relief, grabbing her children's hands. 'Come on, people.'

Mallika gazed after her as she walked towards the ice cream vendor, holding a child's hand in each of her own. She had a slight twang to her accent as well, and there was something about her that was vaguely familiar.

The queue had moved quite a bit before the woman came back, breathless and clutching ice cream bars in each hand.

'Oh, thanks,' she said in relief as Mallika waved to her. 'Here—I forgot to ask you which flavour you'd like. So I got chocolate and vanilla both—you take the one you like and I'll have the other.'

'You shouldn't have,' Mallika said, taking the chocolate bar gratefully. 'But thank you so much—it's so hot I feel like I'm about to melt.'

'It'll be more pleasant on the boat,' the woman said. 'Come on, now, kids—be careful on the stairs or you'll slip and fall in the water.'

'Papa would have carried us if he was here,' the boy grumbled.

His sister glared at him. 'Well, he isn't, so *manage*,' she said fiercely. 'Whine-pot.'

'Cry-baby,' the boy retorted. 'Mud-face.'

'*Muuuummm...*' the girl said.

'Be *nice*, people!' the woman snapped.

'I can carry you, if you like,' Mallika offered. 'Your mum's got too many bags to handle.'

The boy looked as if he wasn't sure which was worse—being carried in public by a *girl*, or having to walk down the stairs on his own. His evident fear of heights won over, and he held his chubby arms up to Mallika.

'I wish Papa was here,' the boy said defiantly once she'd picked him up, and Mallika wondered where their father was.

'He divorced us,' the girl said in a fierce whisper to her brother. 'Stop whining or I'll punch you in the face.'

Their mother sighed. 'So much for being dignified

and discreet,' she said, and gave Mallika an artificially bright smile. 'I'm so sorry you're being subjected to this.' In a whisper, she continued, 'My husband ran away with his secretary a few months ago and we're still trying to deal with it.'

Under the smile she looked tired and defeated, and Mallika's heart went out to her. 'Men can be pigs,' she said quietly once they were all on the ferry. 'I'm sorry—it must be tough for you.'

'I'm thrilled to be rid of the cheating bastard, actually,' the woman replied in an undertone as they climbed to the upper deck behind the kids. 'But it's tough on the kids. If he'd given me a choice I might have actually stayed with him to keep them happy. As it turned out he didn't, so here we are—back in India.'

'Where were you before this?'

'Canada,' she said. 'But I'm happy to be back with my family.' They had reached the upper deck, and the woman looked around. 'Are you in the A/C section as well?' she asked.

Mallika shook her head. 'I prefer the sea breeze,' she said. 'See you in a bit.'

She took a seat towards the front of the ferry, where she didn't have to look at other people, and leaned her head gratefully against the cold guard rail. She'd loved these ferry rides to Alibagh when she was a teenager. Aryan had still been a kid then, and he'd used to run around madly while Mallika stood near the railing, soaking in the sun and the sea breeze.

Even in those days she'd been more of an outdoor person than Aryan was—he'd preferred the lower deck, and after a few arguments their mother had started buying two tickets for the upper deck and two for the lower, so that they didn't fight.

Mallika cast a glance towards the air-conditioned cabin where the woman and her kids had gone. *'I might have actually stayed with him to keep them happy...'* It sounded so terribly sad, when the woman was clearly happier without her husband.

Mallika wondered whether her own mother would have been happier without her father. She'd definitely been more than capable of taking care of herself, but their extended family was extremely conservative. Maybe she'd stayed so that she didn't have to be cut off from them. Or maybe she'd not wanted to separate Aryan and Mallika from their father.

She still felt guilty when she thought of how much trouble they'd given their mother during their growing up years. It had only been when she was in her late teens that Mallika had begun to understand why her mother worked so hard and was so grim and serious most of the time. And even then she'd not known the full story.

As she'd told Darius, her father had lost most of his money in the stock market crash of the eighties—what she hadn't realised for many years was that her mother had been supporting the family ever since. When she'd found out she'd been more sympathetic, but she still hadn't been able to understand why her mother couldn't loosen up a little...be a little more fun.

Her attention was attracted by the girl and her mother coming out of the air-conditioned cabin. The girl's face was distinctly green.

'I'll be all right on my own,' she was telling her harassed mother. 'You go inside and be with Rehaan.'

'I'm not leaving you here on your own,' the mother said. 'Are you still feeling pukey?'

'Not that much,' the girl said, pushing her way through the crowded deck to come and stand next to Mallika by the railing. 'It's better in the breeze.'

'Seasick?' Mallika asked, and the woman nodded.

'The sea's really choppy, and it's a bit disorientating inside the cabin. Rehaan's refusing to come out. I should have just stayed home instead of trying to take these two out for a weekend break.'

'I'll be okay on my own,' the girl insisted.

'I can keep an eye on her, if you like,' Mallika offered.

The woman laughed. 'You know, this is the part I love about being back in India,' she said. 'It feels like being part of one big family. I'm Shirin, by the way, and this is Ava.'

'Pleased to meet you,' Mallika said, grinning back at her. 'So, if you like, you can leave Ava with me and go be with Rehaan.'

'He'll be all right on his own for a bit,' Shirin said, and lowered her voice a little. 'It's Ava I worry about—it's not as safe for a girl as it is for a boy, and I don't know how to explain that to her. And I'd die before I admit it to her, but I'm feeling a bit seasick as well.'

They were both silent for a while, watching Ava as she waved to a flock of seagulls following the ferry.

Ava was too engrossed in the seagulls to hear them, and Mallika said impulsively, 'I don't mean to be intrusive, but you said that you'd have stayed with your husband for the sake of the kids—it's not worth it. You'll be much happier on your own.'

Shirin turned to look at her, raising her brows a little. 'Sounds like you're speaking from personal experience.'

'Sort of,' Mallika admitted.

She'd never spoken about this before, and confiding in a stranger wasn't the kind of thing she normally went in for. Still, there was something about Shirin that made Mallika want to talk to her.

'My dad had affairs,' she said. 'Many of them. My mum put up with them—I guess she didn't have much of a choice—but me and my brother didn't understand why she was unhappy most of the time and we tended to blame her a little. My dad was fun, only he wasn't around much—it was only when I was in my teens that I figured out that he was a pathetic excuse for a husband.'

'No wonder you don't have a high opinion of men,' Shirin said. 'Is your dad still like that?'

'He died in an accident,' Mallika said. 'Along with my mum.'

'Oh, my...' Shirin said sympathetically. 'That sucks.'

Mallika nodded. There was something oddly familiar about Shirin's reaction, but she couldn't put her finger on who she reminded her of.

'Anyway, what I was trying to say is that your kids might be a bit upset now, but it's better for them to be growing up with you.'

'That's good to hear,' Shirin said. 'Most of the time I'm sure I'm doing the right thing, but sometimes I wonder. The kids miss their dad, and they miss Canada, and I'm not really sure how I'm going to manage.'

'Where do you work?' Mallika asked.

'I don't,' Shirin said with a sigh. 'I sponge off my brother. But I'm planning to start once I get the kids settled in school.'

Mallika wondered for an instant what it would be like to have a brother she didn't have to worry about, then shook herself. Aryan might be a bit of a liability, but she wouldn't swap her own life for Shirin's for anything.

'Older brother?' she asked, for the sake of something to say.

'No—younger,' Shirin said. 'I used to make his life hell when he was a kid, but he's—without exaggeration—the best brother a girl could have.'

There was a little pause, and then she went on.

'My parents offered me a place in their flat, but it was impossible to manage. They're old, and set in their ways, and the kids drove them crazy. My brother had a flat in the same building and he's turning it over to me.'

'Has he moved out already?' Mallika asked, though she already knew the answer.

It had taken a while for the penny to drop, but she'd finally realised why Shirin seemed so familiar. She didn't look much like Darius—she was petite and sharp-featured—but some of her mannerisms were just like his, and their smiles were identical.

'Yes, he's rented a hideously expensive place in Parel,' she was saying now. 'He says he's enjoying being on his own, but I still feel terribly guilty. Anyway, he's going overseas in a few months—some complicated "finding himself" kind of journey. I'm happy for him, but I'll miss him like crazy.'

And so will I, Mallika thought to herself, feeling suddenly very shallow and stupid.

It hadn't even occurred to her to ask Darius *why* he'd given his flat to his sister. All this while she'd thought Darius was being callous about Aryan, not realising that he took his responsibilities as a sibling quite as seriously as she did.

'Are your parents okay with your brother going away?'

she asked, the words slipping out before she could help herself.

Shirin nodded. 'He's wanted to do it for as long as I can remember, and he planned his trip a couple of years ago,' she said. 'He's had to cancel it twice already—once because Dad had a heart attack, and a second time because I'd come back to India to have my second baby. Our grandmother fell down and broke pretty much every bone in her hip around the same time, and poor Darius was saddled with looking after all of us *and* paying the medical bills. Luckily he was minting money by then, so the bills weren't a problem, but he went crazy trying to look after everyone at the same time. It doesn't help that we're a bit of an eccentric family too... Anyway, this time hopefully he'll get away before one of us does something stupid.'

Rehaan stuck his head out of the cabin, and Shirin hurried towards him while Mallika tried to get her disordered thoughts back on track. This didn't really change things. If anything, it underlined the fact that she wasn't suited to be with a man like Darius even if he had been ready for a relationship.

Any other woman would have tried to find out about his family—*she* was so hung up about her own that she'd avoided the subject of his completely. From what Shirin had said, Darius was as unlike her father as he could be—he was responsible and trustworthy. And she'd made all kinds of assumptions about him that were totally untrue. Worse, she'd accused him of not caring for his family—and he hadn't even defended himself.

Shirin waved to her as they got off at the jetty, and Mallika saw them get into a car that had the logo of an expensive resort printed on the side. Alibagh had been a sleepy little seaside town during her growing up years, but in the last decade high end hotels and villas had gone up all around the place. Property prices had rocketed as well, and her mother's decision to buy a bungalow there had been more than vindicated.

It took her most of the day to get a contractor to commit on the money and the time it would take him to get the leakage in the Alibagh house fixed. It didn't turn out to be as expensive as she'd feared, but she'd need to make a few more trips to the house over the next few weeks.

She grimaced at the thought. Even now she couldn't bring herself to go into the kitchen and cook a meal for herself, and she ended up sitting in the living room and eating the packed lunch she'd brought with her.

It was ironic, she thought—after all the grief and heartache he'd caused her mother, her father had finally died trying to save her from the fire. If there was an afterlife, perhaps her mother had forgiven him. Mallika still couldn't bring herself to do so.

The weeks after her parents' death would have been horrific enough without having to deal with her father's mistress. She was a virago of a woman, out for all that she could get, and finally Mallika's father's impecuniousness made sense—all this while he'd been supporting her on the side.

Mallika's mother had known, and she'd been careful to make sure that all her investments and the property she'd bought were either in her own name or in her children's. Even so, there had been a bitter battle to hold on to Mallika's grandparents' flat, which her father had inherited, and his mistress had done all she could to claim a share of it. Finally, when she hadn't been able to take any more, Mallika had paid her off—she didn't regret the money, but the experience had left her very bitter.

Once she'd sorted everything out with the contractor and the caretaker, and made advance payments to the workers, Mallika headed back to the jetty. There was just about time for her to catch the last ferry out, and she settled herself into a corner seat with a sigh. She hadn't been able to stop thinking about Darius all day, and impulsively she pulled out her phone and dialled his number.

The phone rang a few times, but Darius didn't pick up and she dropped it back into her bag. Calling him had been a stupid idea anyway—he was probably out partying with his friends.

Feeling suddenly very lost and alone, she shut her eyes and tried not to think about him. The images kept coming, though, and she had to blink very hard to stop tears from welling into her eyes. Damn Darius—he was proving far more difficult to forget about than she'd thought.

CHAPTER EIGHT

IT WAS PAST eleven when Darius finally got back home. He'd gone to the tennis court in his building to see if he could catch a game, and he'd run into an ex-colleague who was now a neighbour. They'd played a couple of gruelling sets, after which they'd walked down to a nearby bar to watch a football match over beer and chicken wings. His ex-colleague was a cheerful, sporty sort of man who didn't go in for deep thinking—he was the perfect companion to take Darius's mind off Mallika.

Once he was back in the flat, though, the morning's conversation replayed itself in his head. He was able to be a little more objective now, and he could see things from Mallika's point of view. She was going through a tough time with Aryan, and she wasn't yet over her parents' death—she couldn't be blamed for not wanting to complicate her life by getting into a relationship with a man who was about to go away for who knew how long.

He'd left his phone in the flat, and picked it up now to see three messages from his sister. Shirin had taken the kids out for a weekend on the beach, and while she said it had got off to a rocky start they seemed to be fine now.

He smiled as he read through her quirky messages

about the kids' reactions to the hotel and the pool—and the last message read: Hired a babysitter and am now off to the spa!!!

He was still smiling as he scrolled through the list of calls he'd missed, and his expression stilled as he saw the call from Mallika. Damn, she'd called over four hours ago—she must have thought he was purposely avoiding talking to her.

He glanced at the time—too late to call her back, but he could text her. They both used the same mobile chat app, and he checked her status. It said she was last on at ten twenty-five p.m., which wasn't that long ago.

Hey—sorry I missed your call, he typed. Had forgotten my phone was at home.

Mallika reached out for her phone as it pinged. She still kept in touch with a few school friends through mobile chat—most of them lived overseas now, and she was used to getting texts at odd hours from them. But this time it wasn't Naina or Kirti messaging about their latest boyfriends…

No worries, she typed. I just wanted to apologise for being so rude when we spoke in the morning.

The reply was almost instantaneous.

I'm sorry too. I shot my mouth off a bit.

Cool, so we're quits.

Mallika thought a bit and added a smiley.

How was Alibagh?

Not bad. I got most of my work done. Guess what—I met your sister on the ferry on the way out.

She took the ferry? I thought she was taking the speed-boat!

Must have changed her mind. She's really nice, by the way. And so are the kids.

She didn't mention meeting you! I saw her messages a minute ago.

We just had a random conversation. I figured out she was your sister from something she said.

You didn't introduce yourself?

No L wasn't sure if she'd know who I was.

I've talked about you. No details, though.

Thank heaven no details.

Mallika typed the words, even though she felt flattered that he'd spoken about her at home.

She's my older sister—what d'you expect?

The text was quickly followed by another.

Can you talk? Texting feels a bit teenagerish…

Teenagers don't type full words. Can't talk L A's a light sleeper and his room's right next to mine.

There was a pause of a couple of minutes, as if Darius was deciding how to respond.

OK, got it.

Will the flamingos still be there tomorrow?

Guess so.

Can we go?

Guess so.

Mallika stared at the phone in frustration. The problem with texting was that she couldn't figure out whether he wanted to see her or not—*Guess so* was as vague as it got. She was about to type a message when his chat window popped up again.

Should I pick you up?

Can meet you there. But no pressure, seriously, if you don't want to go.

Isn't that my line?

It was—this time I'm the one who's asking you to come!

I want to see you. The flamingos are incidental.

They agreed on a time, and Mallika put her phone back on her bedside table, feeling strangely euphoric.

Mallika took a cab to Sewri the next morning. She'd arranged to meet Darius at the path that led to the mudflats, and her body was thrumming with nervous energy—she had to take several deep breaths to calm herself before she got out of the cab.

The cabbie gave her a jaundiced look as she fumbled in her wallet for change. 'Should I wait?' he asked. 'You won't get a cab back from here.'

Mallika shook her head and handed him the fare. 'No, I have a ride back.'

'I can wait anyway,' the man said. 'In case whoever you're meeting doesn't turn up.'

Goodness, she hadn't even thought of that! What if Darius didn't come?

She spotted him as soon as she'd dismissed the thought as ridiculous, and her breath caught in her throat. He looked achingly familiar and wildly desirable at the same time.

'He's here—you don't need to wait,' she muttered to the cabbie, and got out of the cab, standing stock-still as Darius came up to meet her.

He was wearing a dark blue open-necked T-shirt over jeans, and he looked good enough to eat. It took a significant effort of will not to throw her arms around him.

'Hello,' she said shyly—but she didn't get any further. Darius put an arm around her and pulled her against his side in a surprisingly fierce hug.

'Good morning,' he said. 'Come on, let's go.'

There was an ancient shipwreck at the beginning of the mudflats that gave the best view of the flamingos.

There were people milling around, and Darius took his arm away from her shoulders to help her up the rickety ladder.

'I can manage,' Mallika said, but just at that instant her foot slipped a little and she had to cling onto him for support.

'I'm sure you can,' he said soothingly. 'I just feel like holding your hand for a bit.'

Put like that, she could hardly say no, and the ladder *was* rickety...with a thirty-foot drop to the mud below.

The flamingos were amazing—flocks and flocks of them, perched among the mangroves that grew out of the sludgy mud. They were a bright salmon-pink, and they were showing off a little—taking off and swooping back onto their perches in little groups. Some of them were busy looking for food, and a guide nearby was explaining their migratory habits to a bunch of serious-looking kids.

'Did you ever bring Ava and Rehaan here?' Mallika asked, cuddling in a little closer to Darius. Public displays of affection weren't normally her thing, but she could hardly bear to keep her hands off him.

He nodded. 'Last week,' he said. 'I hear Shirin confided in you quite a bit on the ferry yesterday?'

Mallika looked up in surprise. 'Is she back?' she asked. 'I thought they were away for the weekend?'

'She called this morning,' Darius said. 'Thanks for pepping her up. She's going through a bit of a guilt trip, keeping the kids away from their dad.'

'I figured that,' Mallika said slowly.

If Shirin had relayed their conversation to him, she'd probably told him what Mallika had said about her own family.

Feeling suddenly a little vulnerable, she leaned her

head against his arm and said, 'When you told me she'd moved back to India I didn't realise she was going through a divorce.'

'I guess we didn't talk about her much,' he said, even though he'd consciously *not* told her. She had enough problems of her own without him moaning about his family to her as well, and they had agreed not to talk too much about personal family matters.

'I'm sorry about all I said yesterday,' Mallika said. 'I made a lot of assumptions about you that were completely wrong.'

'It doesn't matter,' he said quietly. 'It was as much my fault as yours—it was natural that you jumped to a few wrong conclusions.'

'*Very* wrong conclusions,' she said, her mouth twisting into a wry smile. 'From what Shirin said, you've done far more for your family than I've ever done for mine.'

'And I'm now escaping from them,' he said, holding up a hand when she began to protest. 'It's true,' he said. 'Not exactly the way you thought it was, but it's true all the same. They've come to depend on me a lot over the last few years. My mother says she's fine with me leaving, but I know what she'd really like is for me to marry a nice Parsi girl and settle down in Mumbai for the rest of my life. Shirin would like me to hang around and be a father figure for my niece and nephew. And my father would like me to join his golf club and start taking an interest in fine wines.'

It was the most Mallika had ever heard him say about his family, and it took her a few seconds to absorb it fully. 'It all sounds rather overwhelming,' she admitted.

'It is,' he said. 'I love my family a lot, and if they really needed me I'd cancel my travels for a third time without a single regret. But with Shirin around I think they'll be fine.'

'I'm sure they will,' Mallika said, wanting more than anything to remove the slight uncertainty lurking in his eyes. 'You should go—especially since it's something you've wanted to do for so long.'

'It's bigger than me, in a way,' he said, and laughed slightly. 'This whole need to go out and see the world. Shirin says it's inherited—some ancient Persian wanderlust gene that's skipped a few generations.'

'Maybe she's right,' Mallika said, reaching out to take his hand.

There was a tinge of sadness in her voice as she thought of how different the two of them were. His family sounded like the kind she'd always longed for and, while she understood his motivations a lot better now, she knew that she wouldn't have taken the same decisions in his place. She craved stability and was comfortable with the conservative values of a traditional family, whereas Darius wanted to break out, challenge himself and push boundaries.

He helped her down the ladder, and once they were on dry land again turned her to face him.

'Want to come over?' he asked, and she nodded, her throat suddenly dry.

There was no mistaking his meaning—and there was also no point bringing up the rules again. Their attraction was too strong to fight, and the most she could hope for was that it would die away after a while without doing too much damage.

Neither of them spoke during the short drive to his flat, their heightened anticipation too intense to allow for casual conversation. Mallika found that her knees were trembling just a bit as Darius unlocked the flat and let her in.

She had barely stepped inside when he bolted the door and turned to take her into his arms.

'Welcome back,' he murmured against her mouth, and then there was no room to talk any more as a tide of pure unadulterated desire overtook both of them.

'What next?' Darius asked many hours later. 'I guess a few of the rules just went out of the window.'

'I guess,' she said, trailing her hand slowly down his chest.

She didn't want to think about practical stuff right now, and Darius's question had brought her back to reality with a bump.

'We can take each day as it comes, can't we?' she asked. 'I mean, some of those rules I made were downright silly.'

'I agree,' Darius said, and it sounded so heartfelt that both of them burst out laughing.

Mallika pressed herself closer to him. With her slim, pliant body and sparkling, naughty eyes, Mallika was almost impossible to resist, and Darius bent his head to capture her lips under his.

'You know, Shirin really liked you,' he said.

'I liked her too,' Mallika said, feeling absurdly flattered.

Darius reached out and tucked a stray strand of hair behind her ear.

'I think it's time for you to meet the family,' he said musingly.

Mallika looked up in alarm. 'Whose family?' she asked.

'The Prime Minister's,' Darius said. 'Whose do you think? Mine.'

'I thought we'd agreed not to tell them!' Mallika said.

'We did. You're going to be my scary colleague-cum-landlady. Shirin's guessed, but to my parents you'll be just one more among my many admirers. Come on, I'd like you to meet them—they're a little crazy, but they're fun.'

Mallika couldn't bring herself to say no—she still didn't know *why* Darius would want to take her home, though.

'Aunt Freny's going to be there as well,' he told her. 'You'll like her.'

'What should I wear?' she asked.

'I've no idea,' Darius said. 'We'll be going from work, so regular office gear should be fine. My parents aren't particular.'

Particular or not, Mallika felt devoutly grateful that she'd dressed up a little when she met Darius's perfectly groomed mother the next day. All of five feet tall, she was like a Dresden figurine with her pink cheeks and carefully styled snow-white hair. She gave Mallika a polite kiss on the cheek, her flowery perfume enveloping them as she ushered Mallika and Darius into the room.

'Papa Mistry, this is Darius's landlady,' she announced, and Darius's father peered short-sightedly at her.

'She looks too young and too pretty to be a landlady,' he said firmly. '*Now* I know why Darius didn't want to live here any more.'

'He didn't want to live here because this place is like

a mausoleum,' Aunt Freny grumbled. 'Or a madhouse when those kids of Shirin's turn up. Little devils.'

'Don't you dare call my grandchildren names,' Mrs Mistry said, her eyes narrowing dangerously. 'They're perfectly angelic if you know how to handle them.'

'With a pair of long-handled tongs,' Aunt Freny muttered.

Mrs Mistry pretended not to hear her. 'Do sit down, child,' she said to Mallika. 'How do you take your tea? One cube of sugar? And milk?'

The tea tray had a tea cosy on it with a fat little tea-pot inside, and a tiny jug of milk with a bowl full of sugar cubes next to it. Mallika looked curiously at Mrs Mistry as she poured the tea. She'd seen tea served so elaborately only in British period movies on TV—real, live people drinking it this way was a novelty. Her own mother had always just boiled everything together and then strained it into cups.

'So you met Darius at work?' Mr Mistry asked, leaning forward curiously. 'This is the first time he's brought a girl home.'

'The first time this month,' Aunt Freny said promptly, and Mallika dissolved into laughter.

Aunt Freny was adorable—Mallika's own relatives tended towards the stiff and formal, and she wished she'd had someone like Aunt Freny around when she was going up.

'Freny is our *enfant terrible*,' Mr Mistry said indulgently. 'Tell us about what you do, Mallika. Darius said you work in real estate investments? How did you end up there?'

He seemed genuinely interested, and he knew far more about real estate than most people did.

Shirin trooped in with her children when they were halfway through the conversation, and Rehaan promptly clambered onto his grandfather's lap.

'Where's Great-Granny?' he demanded.

Mr Mistry turned to his wife. 'Is Mummy still asleep?' he enquired.

'No, I'll go and call her,' Mrs Mistry said, and a few minutes later a tiny, very frail-looking old lady emerged from somewhere inside the house.

Darius got up to help her to a chair. 'Meet my grandmother,' he said to Mallika. 'She was an army nurse during the Second World War.'

The elder Mrs Mistry was alert and very garrulous. But with the children running around, and Shirin keeping up a parallel conversation on school admissions, poor Mallika could hardly understand what she was saying, and after a while she gave Darius an appealing look.

'Darius, you should take Mallika out dancing instead of making her sit with us old folks,' Aunt Freny said.

'I used to love dancing when I was a girl,' Darius's grandmother said wistfully. 'My Rustom used to waltz so well.'

'He used to step on everyone's toes,' the irrepressible Aunt Freny said. 'And sometimes he got the steps wrong. But he looked good—I'll give you that.'

'Darius, I'm coming to your building on Saturday,' Ava announced. 'To swim in the pool.'

'You're very welcome,' Darius said. 'I won't be there, but don't let that stop you.'

'Why can't you swim in the club, *dikra*?' Mrs Mistry asked, shooting a quelling look at Darius.

'Because the club pool is full of old hairy men,' Ava said. 'Can I just say—*ewwwww*?'

'Men *should* be hairy,' Mrs Mistry said. 'Not too much, but all these models and actors nowadays with waxed chests—they look terrible. What do you think, Mallika?'

Completely thrown by the sudden appeal for her opinion, Mallika floundered. 'I...uh...I guess it's fashionable nowadays.'

'Darius doesn't wax his chest,' Rehaan volunteered. 'I saw him in the pool last week and he's got hair. Not the orang-utan kind—just normal.'

'Thank you, Rehaan,' Darius said, getting to his feet. 'And on that note I think we should leave. People who aren't used to our family can handle us only in small doses.'

'If you mean Mallika, I think she's made of sterner stuff,' Shirin said, giving Mallika a friendly smile.

'Do you like orchids?' Aunt Freny asked abruptly.

Mallika nodded, and Freny reached behind her chair and produced a flowering orchid in a small ceramic pot.

'This is for you,' she said, handing it to Mallika with a firm little nod. 'Don't overwater it, and make sure it's not in the sun.'

Mallika took the orchid, and as Darius looked all set to leave she stood up as well, and followed him to the door.

'It was really nice meeting all of you,' she said, giving the four generations in the room a comprehensive sort of smile.

'It was lovely meeting you too, *dikra*,' Mrs Mistry said warmly. 'Darius, you must bring her again.'

'Yes, sure,' he said drily, but he was smiling as he bent down to kiss his mother.

He waited till they were in the car before turning to her and raising his eyebrows.

'Well? Did they scare you?'

She laughed and shook her head. 'They were fun,' she said.

And so they were—but she wasn't sure why Darius had decided that it was the right time to introduce her to his family. After all, he was going away, so what they had couldn't go anywhere.

Back at Darius's flat, she shut the front door behind her and leaned against it, her eyes dancing as she looked at him.

'I need to refresh my memory,' she said. 'Exactly *how* hairy is that chest of yours?'

CHAPTER NINE

'ONE OF MY schoolfriends is coming from the US this Friday,' Darius said a few days later. 'We haven't met in years, so I've invited him to stay with me over the weekend. Shirin and a few other people are coming over for dinner on Saturday. Would you like to come?'

Mallika hesitated. She'd insisted that Darius still did not tell his parents the truth about them, the way she'd not told Aryan or any of *her* relatives, but Shirin had guessed anyway—and meeting a few people for dinner trumped not seeing Darius at all for the entire weekend.

'Okay,' she said. 'D'you need help planning the dinner?'

'No, I'll outsource everything,' he said. 'There's a friend of mine who does catering for Parsi weddings. I'll just ask her to manage it.'

'Catering… Exactly how many people are you inviting?'

'Around twenty-five or so, I thought,' Darius said, not noticing Mallika's horrified expression. 'The living room's big enough to hold that many, and if it isn't they can go and stand on the balcony.'

The intercom rang and he went to answer it, leaving Mallika to deal with her panicky reaction to meeting twenty-five of Darius's friends all at once. She always felt shy in large groups—while not agoraphobic, like Aryan, she still preferred meeting a maximum of three or four people at a time.

Darius came back after a short conversation—presumably with the security guard who screened visitors at the main gate.

'I bought a painting last week and it's on its way upstairs now,' he said. 'I was hoping I'd get a chance to show it to you before I left for Delhi again.'

Nidas had recently taken over a smaller firm, and Darius was travelling to Delhi almost every week to manage the merger of the two companies' assets. It was stressful, and Mallika knew he didn't enjoy the trips. She hoped it was because they took him away from her and the small amount of time they had left together...

'I didn't realise you had to go this week as well,' she said. 'When's the takeover going to be complete?'

'At least another two months,' Darius said, sighing as he pulled her close. 'It's crazy. There's so much to do. But it's a big acquisition for Nidas, and in the long term it will make a big difference to our share value. It's just a difficult process right now—especially since the need for greater efficiencies means some of their staff are being let go.'

He was silent for a while, and Mallika hugged him back without saying anything either. It was the first time he had touched her seeking comfort, she realised—so far everything had been about sex. In a way she felt closer to him this way than when they were making love, and it was an odd sensation.

The doorbell rang, and he let her go to open the door.

The painting was carefully packaged in layers of bubble wrap, and Darius had to use a knife to get it out.

'What d'you think?' he asked as he knelt to prop the painting against the nearest wall.

The painting had appealed to him the minute he'd seen it, tucked away in the corner of a little art gallery he patronised. A mass of swirling colours, it managed to capture exactly the feel of an Indian market—you could almost smell the spices and feel the dust and the heat.

Mallika looked at the signature at the bottom right-hand corner. 'This is a good example of the artist's work,' she said, sounding impressed. 'It would have been a brilliant investment if you'd bought it a few years ago.'

'I bought it because I like it,' Darius said, a puzzled look on his face. 'It isn't an *investment*.'

'That's a good reason as well,' Mallika said, sounding amused. 'I'm sorry—I guess I've been working on investments too long to remember that people sometimes buy expensive things just because they like them.'

'Different perspectives,' he said, laughing as he got back to his feet.

He came closer and slid his hands around her waist, making her shiver with longing.

'Stay for dinner?' he asked, nuzzling the most sensitive part of her neck.

'I can't,' she said regretfully. 'I need to get back home.'

'Stay this once,' he said, pulling her closer, and they kissed once more—a long, drugging kiss that left her with trembling knees and a blind desire to tug his clothes off and spend the rest of the day making love on the living room floor.

'Aryan...' she said.

Darius groaned. 'He'll be okay just this once,' he said. 'We've never spent a night together, Mallika, and I'm leaving soon—we mightn't get another chance.'

Put like that, she found it almost impossible to say no, and after another half-hearted protest she messaged Aryan to let him know that she was staying over at a friend's home.

It was around four in the morning when Mallika woke up with a start. She didn't know what exactly had woken her, but her pulse was pounding as if she'd just finished a gruelling race. Next to her, Darius muttered something in his sleep and put a heavy arm around her, pulling her close to his magnificent chest.

Gingerly, Mallika stretched a hand out to the bedside table to pick up her phone. Perhaps the message tone had woken her—she wouldn't put it past Aryan to be messaging her to come home quickly, or perhaps to pick up some exotic computer accessory on her way home.

The screen was blank, however, and there were no messages at all other than one from her bank offering her 'never before' rates on a loan. Puzzled, she checked the signal—it was at full strength, so that meant Aryan hadn't messaged her at all.

'Darius,' she whispered, and he woke up, blinking a little as the light from the mobile phone display hit his eyes.

'Something wrong?' he asked, sitting up as he took in her expression.

'There's not a single message from Aryan,' she said weakly, realising how stupid she sounded as soon as the words were out of her mouth.

Thankfully, Darius immediately understood what she was trying to say.

'Have you tried calling him?'

'He might be asleep,' she said, and to his eternal credit Darius reached across and put his arms around her.

'Do you want me to take you home?' he asked softly, and she nodded.

There were very few cars on the road, and it took less than ten minutes to drive to her flat. The watchman was asleep, and the lift had been switched off, so they had to climb the stairs to her flat. Mallika's knees were trembling by the time she got to the right floor and unlocked the door.

'Should I wait outside?' Darius asked.

She shook her head. 'Stay in the living room,' she said. 'I'll just check on Aryan—hopefully he's fine and I've dragged you all this way for nothing.'

But he wasn't fine.

When Mallika tiptoed into his room she found him lying stock-still in bed, his eyes wide open and feverish. For a few seconds he didn't seem to recognise her, and she sagged onto her knees in relief when he blinked and said, 'Mally…'

'Are you okay?' she asked.

He shook his head. 'I have a headache,' he offered.

She reached out to touch his brow. 'You're burning up,' she said, trying to keep the worry out of her voice. 'I'll get you a paracetamol…maybe you'll feel better after that, okay? Why didn't you call me?'

'I fell in the bathroom and hit my head. I'm not sure where my phone is.'

Mallika clicked on the light—sure enough, there was a huge purpling bruise on his forehead.

'Is he all right?' Darius asked softly as she came out.

She shook her head. 'I don't think he's eaten a single meal since yesterday,' she said. 'And he's got a raging fever. He's also fallen down and hurt his head.'

'I'm so sorry,' he said quietly. 'I shouldn't have pushed you to stay. Is there anything I can do?'

She shook her head angrily. 'It's not your fault,' she said, almost to herself. 'It's mine—for even imagining that I could have a life of my own. Will you get me some biscuits from the kitchen, Darius? I need to make sure he eats something before I give him a paracetamol.'

He nodded, and she went to the medicine cabinet to try and locate the pills. There were only three left in the blister pack, and she popped one out. Darius came back with the biscuits and a glass of water, and she carried them into Aryan's room.

'Eat these first, and then swallow the medicine with the water,' she said.

'I'm not hungry,' Aryan whispered.

Suddenly her control snapped. 'I don't *care*!' she said. 'I stay away for one night and you don't even take care of yourself! Sit up right now and eat—if you don't want me to call an ambulance and get you put in hospital.'

It was the first time she'd ever shouted at him and Aryan sat up in shock, blinking woozily as he took the biscuits from her. Mallika felt horribly guilty, but at least he ate them silently before swallowing the medicine.

'Try and sleep now,' she said, tucking him back into bed. 'I'll call Dr Shetty as soon as it's morning.'

'Stay with me,' Aryan mumbled, reaching for her hand as she got up, but she pulled away.

'I'll be back in a minute,' she said, and went out to Darius.

'I'm so sorry I dragged you out like this,' she said wearily. 'I should have just come home last night.'

'Do you need me to go and fetch a doctor?' he asked.

She shook her head. 'I'll call our family doctor in the morning,' she said. 'I think he'll be okay till then.'

'Right,' Darius said. 'I'll see you when I'm back from Delhi, then—okay?'

She nodded, and he dropped a quick kiss on her forehead before letting himself out.

'He's got an infection. His immunity levels have dropped, staying indoors like this,' the doctor said as he prescribed a course of antibiotics over the phone. 'I'll try to come and see him in a couple of hours, but if he doesn't start leading a normal life this is going to happen more and more often.'

'How's he catching an infection, then, if he isn't going out?'

'From *you*,' he said. 'You work, don't you? *You're* carrying the infections home, but because your immunity levels are normal you're not catching them yourself.'

She spent the next two days nursing Aryan. The doctor visited him, as he'd promised—he'd known both Mallika and Aryan since they were children, and he was as worried about him as Mallika was.

Aryan didn't react as the doctor spoke to him—he'd slipped back into silent mode, and he stared passively at the ceiling while the doctor tried to explain the harm he was doing himself by his self-imposed house arrest.

'The quicker you get him to a good psychiatrist, the better,' Dr Shetty told Mallika when she took him aside to ask what she should do. 'I can treat his physical symptoms, but I can't do much about his mental state. And you're just making it worse by humouring him.'

Perhaps he was right, Mallika thought wearily as she went back inside to persuade her brother to eat something and take his medicine. Perhaps she *was* making her brother worse. Only there was little she could do if he refused to see a psychiatrist—it had been difficult enough persuading him to see Dr Shetty.

She tried to get a psychiatrist to come and meet Aryan, perhaps by pretending to be a friend of hers, but that wasn't the way they operated, apparently. Or at least the reputable ones didn't, and she didn't want to trust Aryan to a quack.

'I mightn't be able to come for dinner on Saturday,' she told Darius when he called one evening.

'Won't Aryan be okay by then?'

'He's over the worst, but he's still a little weak—and he's still not eating properly.'

'Can't one of your relatives stay with him? That aunt of yours who lives nearby?'

'He doesn't want anyone else around,' Mallika said. 'I'm so sorry, Darius.' She was very tired, and her voice shook a little.

Darius immediately softened.

'I'm sorry too,' he said gently. 'Take care. I'll be back from Delhi tonight, and I'll come across and see you on Sunday.'

Mallika was too exhausted to tell him not to come—anyway, Aryan had probably figured out by now that she was dating him. And she wanted to see Darius badly. He'd become the one sane, stable thing in her world, and she knew she was growing horribly dependent on him.

'Are you going out?' Aryan asked on Sunday morning.

It was obvious why he'd asked—Mallika had changed the ancient T-shirt and tracks she normally wore at home for a peasant blouse and Capri pants, and she'd brushed her hair into some semblance of order.

'No,' Mallika said shortly. 'A friend's coming over, and I don't want to look like something from a refugee camp.'

'Is it that Parsi friend of yours? Cyrus, or something?'

'Darius,' she said.

Aryan didn't reply, and she felt a surge of annoyance sweep over her. She'd spent the last few days waiting on him hand and foot—he hadn't bothered to thank her, even once, and now he was behaving as if she didn't have the right to invite a friend over.

Hot words bubbled up to her lips, and she was about to say something when Aryan spoke again.

'Your hair looks just like Mum's when you tie it back like that,' he said, and suddenly Mallika felt tears start to her eyes.

She'd inherited her riotously curly hair from their mother, but while her mum had always carefully brushed her curls into a tight bun, she'd always kept hers short.

Darius gave her a brief kiss, full on the mouth, as he strode into the flat. 'For you,' he said, handing her a box of expensive-looking chocolates. 'How's Aryan doing?'

'He's much better,' she said, taking the chocolates from him. 'Thank you so much.'

He grinned at her. 'You don't need to be so formal,' he said. 'We missed you yesterday—especially Shirin. She's been dying to meet you again.'

'I wish I could have come,' Mallika said regretfully. 'I couldn't leave Aryan alone, though.'

'I'd have been all right on my own,' Aryan said petulantly, walking into the room, his eyes hostile as he looked at Darius. 'Hello,' he said, nodding briefly at him before sitting down on the sofa.

'She was worried about you,' Darius said as he settled his tall frame into the chair opposite Aryan. 'You were quite ill, weren't you?'

The boy looked a little thinner than the last time Darius had seen him, but otherwise he seemed perfectly healthy. And more than capable of looking after himself for one evening.

'I'm better now,' he said, his eyes dark and resentful. 'I can manage on my own if I have to. Anyway, she's hardly at home—whenever she can, she goes away without telling me where she's going.'

The unfairness of it took Mallika's breath away, and she could only stare at Aryan speechlessly.

Darius took one look at her, and took over the conversation. 'I think your sister stays with you for as much time as she can,' he said. 'She can't work from home *every* day, can she?'

Aryan bit his lip, but didn't reply.

Mallika jumped in to dispel the suddenly awkward silence. 'Which would you prefer? Tea or coffee?'

'Tea's good, thanks,' Darius said, and she got up to make it.

'Aryan...?'

'You should know by now that I don't drink the stuff,' he muttered.

Darius frowned.

'Did you have an argument with your sister?' he asked quietly once Mallika had left the room.

Aryan said nothing, but his eyes widened a fraction.

Darius leaned forward. 'I don't think that's the way you normally speak to her,' he said. 'She's completely devoted to you, and she wouldn't be if you were that rude all the time.'

For a second it looked as if Aryan would burst into speech, but then he got to his feet and left the room without a word. A door shut somewhere inside the house, and Darius assumed that he'd gone back to his room. He exhaled slowly, standing up and running a hand through his hair. He very rarely lost his temper, and the sudden surge of anger he'd felt had surprised him as much as it had upset Aryan.

He made his way to the kitchen, where Mallika was pouring tea into two delicate china cups. She looked up at him and smiled, and he felt immediately guilty.

'Sorry—did Aryan leave you alone?' she asked. 'His social skills are a bit basic.'

'I think I sent him away,' he admitted, leaning against the doorway. 'I didn't like the way he spoke to you and I called him out on it. It's not the kind of thing I normally do, but he got under my skin.'

He'd expected Mallika to be annoyed, but she just handed him his teacup, her brow furrowed in thought.

'What did you say to him?' she asked.

He told her, and she shrugged.

'That's pretty mild,' she said. 'Our family doctor spoke to him for a good fifteen minutes yesterday— I'm not sure Aryan even registered what he was saying.'

'How long are you going to manage like this?' Darius asked softly, his hand going out to caress her cheek. 'You need to have a proper life of your own—it just isn't fair to you.'

Mallika went into his arms, burying her face in his

chest. 'I don't know,' she said. 'I need to sit down and have a proper talk with Aryan—maybe I'm reading him all wrong, hovering over him when he could do with some space.'

'It's worth a try,' Darius said, bending down and brushing his lips lightly against hers, making her quiver with need. 'Will you be able to get away for a while in the afternoon? Varun really wanted to meet you.'

For a few seconds Mallika couldn't remember who Varun was. Then she realised he meant the schoolfriend who'd come over from the US.

'At your place?' she asked.

'Yes,' Darius said. 'I'm going down to his hotel to collect him—I'll see you in a couple of hours, okay?'

After Darius left, Mallika went and knocked tentatively on Aryan's door. There was no reply, and she knocked once more before pushing the door open. Aryan was in bed, his face turned towards the wall, and she went in and sat next to him.

'Are you feeling okay?' she asked, putting a gentle hand on his shoulder.

He flipped over onto his back—an abrupt movement that threw her hand off.

'Are you going to marry that guy?' he demanded.

Mallika took a deep breath. Clearly she'd been wrong about the conversation with Darius having had no effect on her brother.

'He's just a friend, Aryan,' she said. 'I'm not planning to get married for a long, long while. Perhaps never.'

Aryan stared at her, his eyes stormy. 'Because of me?' he asked.

She shook her head. She couldn't lay all the blame

at his door, however much she wanted to. 'Because I think I'd make a rotten wife,' she said, a little sadly. 'Don't worry about it, Aryan. Concentrate on getting better. Once you're back on your feet, maybe we could try going out together. Maybe for a walk to Hanging Gardens. Remember how much you used to love going there as a kid?'

'I don't want to go out,' he said, sounding like a truculent kid. 'You don't need to fuss over me, Mally. I'll go when I want to.'

'When will that be? You heard what the doctor said. You're making yourself ill like this.'

'I don't care,' he said, turning away from her again. 'And if I do get ill you can leave me here and go wherever you want. I'm not forcing you to hang around and look after me.'

'You're not,' Mallika said calmly. 'I feel like looking after you because you're my brother and I love you, even though you're perfectly obnoxious at times.'

Aryan didn't react, but when she got up to go he stretched out a hand and held her back without turning around.

Mallika sat down again, reaching across to smooth his hair off his brow.

'I do too,' he muttered under his breath.

She leaned closer. 'You do too, what?' she asked.

'I love you too,' he said, the words so indistinct that she had to strain to hear them. 'And I'm sorry if I'm obnoxious. It's just so hard without Mom.'

His breath hitched in his throat, and Mallika's heart went out to him. They had never been a very demonstrative family, and this was probably the first time she'd told her brother that she loved him since they'd both reached adulthood. Maybe that was part of the reason he was this way—he'd been only twenty-two when their parents had died, and it had to have been tougher on him than her.

'I miss her too,' she said softly.

Aryan said something under his breath that she couldn't hear at all.

'What was that, *baba*?' she asked.

He said in a whisper, 'It was my fault.'

'What was your fault?'

'The accident,' he said. 'I smelt the gas leak when I went into the kitchen to fetch some water. But I forgot about it and I didn't tell Mom.'

'You *knew* about the leak?' Mallika said blankly.

This had never occurred to her. She'd berated herself so many times for not having gone down to Alibagh with the rest of the family—if she'd been around she'd have gone into the kitchen with her mother and smelled the leak. The only reason her mother hadn't noticed was because she'd had a bad head cold and had completely lost her sense of smell. Her father, of course, never stepped into the kitchen, and normally neither did Aryan.

'I've been wanting to tell you ever since,' he said. 'I can't stop thinking about it.'

'Why didn't you tell me?' she demanded, but deep, dry sobs were racking his body now and he couldn't answer.

Mallika got up from the bed, too worked up to stay still. The last two years had been hellish. She still wasn't over the shock and grief of losing both parents together. Almost every day she wished she could have done something to make her mother's life easier—if she'd known about her father's unfaithfulness she'd at least have been more understanding with her mum. Every teenage tantrum she'd thrown had come back to haunt her, and every time she'd taken her father's side in an argument now seemed like a betrayal of her mother.

She looked at Aryan, huddled up on the bed. Aryan had always been petted and spoilt. Her mother had expected Mallika to grow up fast and shoulder responsibilities as soon as she could, but she'd been far more indulgent with Aryan. Her father had been equally indulgent with both, but it had been quite evident that he had valued his son over his daughter.

'Did you tell Dad about the leak?' she asked suddenly, but Aryan was already shaking his head.

'I didn't realise it was serious,' he said in a flat little voice. 'It was only when I heard her screaming... And by then it was too late to do anything.'

He'd been in the garden, Mallika remembered, studying for his college exams. She'd always felt terrible for him—actually being there and unable to help. A lot of her subsequent indulgence towards him had been because she'd thought he was dealing with the trauma still.

'I'm sorry,' Aryan said, his eyes pleading with her. 'I'd do anything to undo what happened...but I can't.'

'I know,' Mallika said. 'I know. I just wish...'

There were so many things she wished—that Aryan had raised the alarm, that he'd at least told their father... The accident hadn't been his fault, but the fact that he could have prevented it made it seem even more tragic than it had before.

Aryan bit his lip, tears welling in his eyes, and Mallika suddenly remembered him as a child, toddling around the kitchen one day and getting underfoot until her mother had picked him up and sat him on the kitchen counter. Mallika had protested at the unfair treatment—*she* never got to sit there—but her mother had laughed and picked her up as well, dancing around the kitchen with her to the tune of an old Bollywood song playing on the radio while Aryan laughed and clapped his hands.

It was one of the very few memories of her childhood she had where her mum was happy and smiling.

'Mum wouldn't have wanted you to torture yourself like this,' she said, going to Aryan. 'It was an accident, and we can't undo any of it. Come here.'

She held out her arms and Aryan crawled into them, hugging her back surprisingly fiercely.

'I'll try to be less of a pain from now on,' he said. 'I wish I'd told you earlier…but, Mally—you don't know how difficult it's been.'

'I can imagine,' she said. 'But it's behind us now. Let's try and get you sorted out.'

For the first time Aryan seemed amenable to the thought of getting help, and Mallika used the opportunity as best as she could. After an hour of coaxing and cajoling she'd managed to get him to agree to going with her to a psychiatrist, and she heaved a sigh of relief. Hopefully things would take a turn for the better now that she knew exactly what was bothering Aryan.

It was only when she went to fetch her phone to make an appointment that she noticed all the messages and missed calls from Darius. Her mouth dropped open in dismay—it was past six, and she'd agreed to meet him and Varun at four.

Fingers trembling a little, she dialled his number.

'I'm so sorry—' she said when he picked up.

'It's all right, Mallika, you don't need to apologise,' he said, sounding resigned. 'Is Aryan okay?'

'Yes,' she said. 'I should have called. I'll explain when we meet, but I really couldn't have come.'

'I understand,' he said. 'I'll see you around at work tomorrow, then.'

Darius was frowning as he put the phone down, and Varun raised his eyebrows. 'You've got it bad, haven't you?' he said.

Darius smiled reluctantly. 'Is it that obvious?'

'Pretty obvious,' Varun said lightly. There was a brief pause, and then Varun said, 'So what are you going to do about it?'

Darius shrugged. 'Nothing,' he said. 'I'm out of here in a few weeks, and I don't know when I'll be back. There's no point trying to do anything about it. In any case, she isn't interested in anything serious either.'

'You could be wrong about that,' Varun murmured.

Darius shook his head. 'I'm not,' he said, but he wondered if it was true.

There were times when he'd thought Mallika was close to admitting that she cared for him, but something seemed to hold her back. Perhaps the same thing that held him back—the realisation that they wanted very different things from life. He was going away, and for Mallika Aryan would always be her first priority.

'If you really care about her there's always a way,' Varun said.

Darius laughed. 'You sound like a soppy women's magazine,' he said lightly, trying not to show how much the words had affected him.

He *did* care about Mallika—in fact, there was a real

risk of his being completely besotted by her. But he couldn't give up his adventures—not when he was finally free to go.

Maybe there *was* a way, and all he had to do was convince her that it would work.

CHAPTER TEN

'I'M SORRY ABOUT YESTERDAY,' Mallika said guiltily. 'Aryan was very upset, and I completely lost track of the time.'

'Don't worry about it,' he said. 'I understand. Is Aryan okay now?'

'Yes,' she said, and before she knew it she was telling him what had happened. 'I think he'll be better now,' she said. 'The guilt was eating him up, and he hadn't told anyone.'

'Poor chap.' Darius's expression was sympathetic. 'That's one hell of a burden to be carrying around. But you're right—if he's talking about it, it's a turn for the better.'

'Let's see how it goes,' Mallika said.

She was being careful not to sound too optimistic, but it was clear to Darius that she was much happier than she'd been in weeks.

'In any case, I'm feeling a lot better about leaving him on his own now. There was a time when I was scared he'd actually harm himself…he was behaving so oddly. Anyway, let's not talk about Aryan—how was your weekend with Varun? Did you guys have a good time?'

'The best,' Darius said, thinking back to his last conversation with Varun. This was probably a good time to bring it up with Mallika, only he wasn't sure how to begin.

'You look very serious,' Mallika said teasingly. 'What are you thinking about so deeply?'

'Not thinking, really. Just…wondering.' He'd meant to lead up to the subject slowly, but his naturally forthright nature made it difficult.

'Wondering about what,' she asked. 'Global warming? Cloud computing? How to save the euro?'

He grinned in spite of himself—Mallika was so often serious that she was irresistible in a lighter mood.

'Nothing quite so earth-shattering,' he said. 'I was thinking about us.'

Her smile faltered a little, and she said, 'Oh…' before making a quick recovery. 'Serious stuff?'

'Well, kind of.' He reached across and took her hands in his. 'Mallika, I know you've had a lot to deal with since your parents died, and I don't want to put you under pressure. But I was thinking—perhaps we don't necessarily need to split up when I leave.'

'Not split up?' she repeated stupidly.

He leaned forward, his expression serious and intense. 'Come with me,' he said. 'If not for the whole trip, at least for part of it.'

Mallika stared at him as if he had suddenly gone crazy. 'What about my job?' she said. 'Aryan?'

'We'll work that out,' he said. 'You can take some time off—I'll square it with Venkat. And Aryan will be fine for a while—especially since it sounds like he might be on the mend now. I'm not asking you to come immediately, if that doesn't work for you. Take some time to settle him properly…maybe ask a relative to be with him. But you need to get away perhaps even more than I do.'

It was an incredibly tempting thought. Being alone with Darius, far away from the problems and complications of her day-to-day life.

Darius meant a lot to her, and if she'd been a little less cynical about life and relationships she'd have fancied herself in love with him. He was committed and caring, and so incredibly hot that she could hardly keep her hands off him. Any other woman would have kidnapped him by now and forced him to marry her—she must be certifiably insane to let the thought of splitting up even cross her mind.

He was still looking at her, the appeal in his eyes almost irresistible, but she slowly shook her head.

'I don't think it would work,' she said slowly. 'I'm not saying I don't want to, but it just makes more sense to end this before it gets too complicated.'

'Mallika…' He took a deep breath. 'How d'you *really* feel about me?'

'I like you,' she said, stumbling over the words a little. 'You make me laugh when I want to cry. You're honest and straightforward, and I can trust you with every secret I have. When you look at me I feel like I'm the most beautiful girl in the world—you're probably the best thing that ever happened to me.'

'I can sense a *but*,' he said softly, though he gripped her hands a little harder.

'But I'm not sure I'm the best thing that ever happened to *you*,' she said in a rush. 'I'm not good for you, Darius. We shouldn't drag this out.'

'And what made you arrive at that conclusion?' he asked.

'We're completely different,' she said. 'You're a straight-forward guy—everything's simple for you—you know exactly what you want. If you feel like doing something, you go ahead and do it. If you like someone, you tell them. If you don't understand what they want, you ask. Things are a lot more complicated for me. Especially when it comes to love and relationships. My parents had the most messed-up marriage ever, and the thought of anything serious or long-term makes me want to run.'

It was probably the most direct conversation they'd ever had, but Darius was beginning to have a bad feeling about the way it was going.

'So we're different?' he said. 'That doesn't mean it can't work. And we're not in the same situation as your parents—we're not even planning to get married.'

Mallika sighed. 'I know,' she said. 'But it isn't just about us being different, or about my parents, Darius. Aryan's better, but I don't think I can leave him for a long while. And I'm not sure if I believe in long-distance relationships. It'll be torture for me, and it might end up being a drag on you. What if you meet someone else? For that matter, what if I meet someone else when you're away?'

Darius took a deep breath. 'I'm just saying that we have a good thing going and we don't have to split up when I leave. If either of us meets someone we like better, we can deal with it when it happens.'

'It won't work,' she said unhappily. 'It might be years before you come back—what's the point of trying to drag things out? We'll just make each other unhappy, and when we do split up we'll hate each other. I don't think I could bear that.'

Darius took her by the shoulders and turned her to face him.

'Mallika, do you know how many reasons you've given for not coming with me?'

Mallika shook her head.

'Five,' he said. 'Or maybe six—I lost count after a while. Sweetheart, no one needs five reasons not to do something. One or two are usually enough. Maybe you're overthinking this? For once you should just go with what your heart tells you.'

'I stopped listening to my heart years ago,' she said wryly.

She hadn't been making up the reasons—they were all there, buzzing around like angry bees in her head, and the more she thought about them, the more confused she got.

'Okay, so let's do something less drastic,' Darius said.

He was still holding her by the shoulders, and he pressed on them lightly to make her sit down opposite him.

'Why don't you take a couple of weeks off and come with me for the first leg of my trip at least? We could spend some more time together. Aryan should be fine.'

But she was already shaking her head. 'I don't want to,' she said flatly.

Darius just didn't seem to understand, and she was done with trying to explain herself.

'I left Aryan for one night, and you saw what happened to him.'

'Yes—he had a breakthrough! Maybe the start of his recovery,' Darius countered.

Mallika clenched her teeth. He just wasn't getting it.

'If you want to spend more time with me, shouldn't

you stay here, instead of asking me to go with you? I have a perfectly good reason to want to stay here. Why should I leave my brother to traipse around after you just because you've got some quixotic notion in your head?'

Darius inhaled sharply as a whole lot of things suddenly fell into place for him.

'So *that's* the reason,' he said quietly. 'You're scared because I'm doing something that's a little unconventional and you don't know how to deal with it. All this stuff about not wanting to get into anything long-term is hogwash.'

'I'm not a risk-taker,' she said. 'So you're right—it bothers me. And if we're still in a relationship when you leave I'm not sure I'll be able to handle it.'

'Right,' he said, his expression tight and angry. 'So we stick to the original plan, then? It's over when I leave?'

'That would be best, I think,' she said.

She was so close to falling in love with him that she couldn't bear the thought of dragging out the end—pretending that they could sustain a long-distance relationship. There was only heartbreak at the end of it, but she couldn't bear to see him so upset either.

'Darius?' she said. 'I know you've tried to explain it many times, but *why* do you need to go?'

His expression relaxed a little and he said, 'I thought I *had* explained it. There's just so much more to life than this—so much to learn, so many places to explore, so many things to do… I don't want to wake up one day and discover that I've wasted most of my life. The world is such a big place, and I've only seen one small corner of it. I want to explore, have adventures, challenge myself—really see what I'm made of.'

'Right,' she said. 'I hear what you're saying, but I

guess my brain's just wired differently. I like the comfort of what's familiar…of doing what's expected of me.'

'It's wired just fine,' he said, reaching out to twine a lock of her hair around his fingers. 'I suppose I'm the one being unreasonable, asking you to stick with me when I'm not offering anything concrete in return.'

'It's not that,' Mallika said, and when he didn't reply, she added, 'I can't handle uncertainty, that's all. If it helps, I'm crazy about you.'

Darius's eyes darkened in response.

'How crazy?' he asked, and she pressed her body against his, nibbling at his throat and tugging his shirt out of his jeans to slide her hands over his hot bare skin.

'Moderately crazy,' she whispered. 'Actually, make that extremely crazy.'

He was moving against her now, lifting her so that her body fitted more snugly against his, and unbuttoning her top to get access to her pert, full breasts.

'I guess crazy will have to do for now,' he said, and she gasped as he finally got rid of her top and laid her down carefully on the nearest sofa. 'But I'm not going to give up on you.'

'I'll be moving out of the flat in a couple of days,' Darius said over lunch a few weeks later. 'The board's agreed to let me leave Nidas a little early.'

Mallika stared at him in dismay. While she was sticking to her decision, she hadn't realised how much it would hurt when he actually left. Unconsciously, she'd got addicted to him—to seeing him every day, hearing him laugh, running her hands over his skin and putting her lips to his incredibly sexy mouth.

Sometimes she thought that agreeing to go with him

for part of his trip would be worth the inevitable heart-ache—then all her old demons would came back to haunt her and she'd change her mind again.

'When are you leaving Mumbai?' she asked.

'Four weeks from now,' he said. 'But I thought I'd spend the last month or so with my parents and Shirin—just to make sure everything's settled for taking care of them while I'm away.'

Who's going to take care of me? Mallika felt like yelling at him, but she knew there was no point, so she tried to look as unconcerned as possible.

'Do you need help with moving?'

He hesitated. 'Not really. It's mainly clothes and some kitchen things—I'll be leaving most of it with Shirin anyway.'

'Finished packing?'

'No, I'll start tomorrow,' Darius said, wondering if he was being a colossal idiot.

He knew Mallika cared for him, and that if he pushed just a little harder he'd be able to break through her defences. But he'd planned for years to take this time off just for himself, with no work or family responsibilities, and he knew he'd regret it all his life if he stayed. And Mallika hadn't even *tried* to understand why he felt the way he did. If he stayed for her he knew he'd resent it—and her—after a while, and that would be the end of any kind of relationship.

He was halfway through packing the next day when the doorbell rang. Straightening up from the carton he was taping shut, he wiped a hand across his forehead. It was a hot day, and the number of cartons was growing alarmingly—he seemed to have collected a fair amount of junk in the few months that he'd lived in the flat.

'Oh, good, you're here,' Mallika said when he opened the door. 'I was worried you'd have already packed up and left.'

She was wearing skin-tight jeans and a peasant-style top that showed off her slender neck and shoulders, and Darius stood staring at her for a minute, his mouth growing dry with longing. Over the last few days he'd told himself over and over again that their relationship no longer made sense. He'd more or less bullied Mallika into giving it a shot, but now that his departure was imminent keeping the pressure on just wasn't fair. To either of them.

Wordlessly, he stood aside to let her into the flat. A whiff of her citrusy perfume teased his nostrils as she walked past and he bit his lip. Good resolutions were all very well, but he was only human.

Mallika stopped in the middle of the living room. 'Oh…' was all she said as she took in the cartons neatly lined up in rows and filling more than half the room.

'Shouldn't you have hired professional packers?' she asked. 'Do you have any help at all? Or are you trying to handle this on your own?'

'On my own,' he said. 'A lot of these are books and CDs—they take up more space than you'd think.'

But she wasn't listening to him any longer—her mouth was turning down at the corners and she put her arms around him abruptly, burying her face in his shoulder. 'I wish you didn't have to go,' she said, her voice muffled against his shirt. 'I'll miss you.'

'I'm leaving the country, not dying,' he said drily, though all he wanted to do was tip her face up and kiss her and kiss her, until there was no space for conversation or thought.

'Yes,' she said. 'But we won't have a place to be together for the next month. Unless….' She looked at him, her face lighting up. 'Oh, how silly—why didn't I think of it before? This flat'll be empty, won't it? I won't rent it out, and we can meet here whenever we want.'

Darius shut his eyes for a second. Mallika probably had no idea of what she was doing to him. All his life he'd prided himself on his decisiveness and self-control—it was only when he was with Mallika that he turned to putty.

'Don't leave India right away,' she said, stretching languorously on the bed a couple of hours later. 'Stay on in Mumbai for a few more weeks. You can start your self-discovery thing here just as well as in any other country.'

He shook his head, smiling at her. 'It won't work.'

She cuddled a little closer to him, pulling the sheet up to her chin. 'Don't move all your things, then,' she said. 'I'll cancel the lease agreement, so you won't need to pay rent, but you could come back to stay here whenever you want.'

Darius caught her close, pressing his lips to her forehead. 'Sweetheart, I need to do this *my* way,' he said. 'I need to work some things out, and I need a little space.'

The words stung far more than he'd meant them to, and he saw Mallika bite her lip to keep it steady.

'That's odd,' she managed finally, her tone as light as she could make it. 'I didn't have you pegged as someone who really got the concept of space.'

He gave her a wry grin. She had him there, and he

knew it. 'Perhaps you were right,' he said. 'Perhaps I never should have pressured you in the beginning.'

Mallika stared at him, a nasty, icy feeling gripping her heart. She'd been so close to telling him that she'd changed her mind—that she'd found she cared for him and wanted to give a long-distance relationship a shot. The last thing she'd expected was Darius himself having a change of heart.

'So you're saying that this is it?' she said, her voice still deceptively light. 'We don't stay in touch after today?'

'Something like that,' he said, and she nodded, not trusting herself to speak any more.

After a few seconds she slid out of bed, keeping the sheet wrapped around her as she collected her clothes from the floor.

'Be back in a minute,' she said, and slid into the bathroom.

For a few minutes she could only stare at her face in the mirror, feeling mildly surprised that it looked just as it usually did. Then, after splashing some water on her face, she quickly put on her clothes and flushed the toilet to account for the time she'd spent.

When she came out of the bathroom she looked as if she didn't a have a care in the world. Unfortunately Darius wasn't around to notice, and her lips trembled a little as she saw that he was already dressed and back to his packing.

'Got a lot to finish?' she asked, after watching him dump a big pile of clothes into a suitcase.

He shook his head. 'Another fifteen minutes or so. I'm sorry—I need to get this stuff done and then get back home. My mother has organised a family gathering and I promised I'd be there.'

She sat down on the bed, looking at him thoughtfully. One of the things *her* mother had repeatedly dinned into her head was to act with dignity. *'Apni izzat apne haath—* your dignity is in your own hands.' That had been one of her favourite sayings, along with, 'No one will respect you unless you respect yourself.'

'You should head off soon, then,' she said, getting to her feet with a brightly artificial smile on her lips.

It cost her every last ounce of willpower, but she walked across to him and leaned up to kiss him lightly on the lips.

'It was really good while it lasted,' she said. 'Thanks for putting up with all my whims and *nakhras*. Have a good life.'

'Mallika…' he said, and something indefinable flickered in his eyes.

She stepped back quickly, before he could touch her.

'I'll see you, then,' she said. 'Some time. Deposit the keys with the watchman, will you?'

And, leaving him standing in the bedroom, she hurried out of the flat, waiting till she was in her car before allowing a few hastily wiped away tears to escape.

CHAPTER ELEVEN

'I'M GOING OUT,' Aryan said.

He sounded oddly defiant—as if he expected Mallika to object.

It was almost a month since she'd broken up with Darius, and it had been tough. She missed him so badly that it hurt, and only the highest levels of self-control had stopped her from calling him.

Aryan hadn't said anything, but he'd been unusually well-behaved—probably sensing that she was very close to breaking point.

'Out?' she asked. 'Where?'

'Um…I thought I'd get a haircut. And maybe buy a couple of shirts.'

She should have felt pleased—Aryan was a lot better, but except for his trips to the doctor he'd stepped out of doors only once, for a walk around the garden with her. Wanting to go somewhere on his own was a first. He still ordered his clothes on the internet, and paid a local barber to come to their home and trim his hair once a month, and she couldn't figure out what had prompted the sudden decision to go to the shops on his own.

'D'you need the car?' she asked, trying to stall for time while she gauged his mood.

Aryan shook his head. 'Not today,' he said. 'I'll walk down Warden Road and get what I need. But if you could spare it for some time on Saturday that would be great?'

Feeling completely at sea, Mallika nodded. 'Yes, of course. You can have it for the full day, if you like.'

'I'm meeting someone,' Aryan volunteered after a brief silence. 'A...um...a girl. She's from Bangalore, and she's going to be here for a few days. I got to know her online,' he added a tad defensively as Mallika gaped at him.

'Figures,' Mallika muttered, once she'd got her breath back.

While she'd been obsessing about her little brother's lack of social interaction he'd gone right ahead and acquired an online girlfriend. Served her right for being so presumptuous, thinking he needed her help to get back to a normal life.

An unpleasant thought struck her, and she said, 'Aryan...?'

'Yes?'

'This girl—just checking—she's real, right? Not computer-generated or a...a...fake persona or something?'

Aryan laughed—a full-bodied, boyish laugh that made him look years younger. 'She's real, all right,' he said. 'I've video called her a few times, and I've done basic checks on her online profile. She's a computer engineer, and she's training to be a hacker. An *ethical* hacker,' he added hastily as Mallika choked on her tea. 'She's hired by corporates and governments to identify possible security breaches in their systems.'

'She sounds lovely,' Mallika said, wondering what kind of 'basic checks' one did on a prospective girlfriend. Finishing her tea, she got to her feet. 'Are you inviting her home?'

'I might,' Aryan said cautiously.

Mallika knew she had been a bit on edge ever since she'd broken up with Darius and Aryan was probably testing her mood. She turned her back to him now, and rinsed her tea cup with unnecessary vigour.

'You okay with me meeting her?' he asked.

'Yes, of course,' Mallika said, turning towards him with an overly bright smile on her lips. 'It's a good thing—you getting to know more people.'

She kept the smile plastered on her face until he left the flat, and then let out a huge sigh and flopped down onto the nearest sofa.

It was a relief, having the place all to herself to be miserable in. Aryan wasn't an intrusive presence, but he was around all the time, and sometimes she wanted to give full rein to her misery. Maybe scream and throw a few things, dignity be damned. She'd thought of going to the flat that Darius had vacated, being by herself for a few days, but it was too closely linked to him.

She'd gone back once, to get it cleaned and cover up the furniture, and the first thing she'd seen on walking in was the huge painting of a spice market that Darius had bought. He hadn't taken it with him, and it was still occupying pride of place on the living room wall. Walking closer to it, she'd noticed a little note stuck to the frame. *'Leaving this for you,'* it had said. *'Love, Darius.'*

It was the *'Love, Darius'* that had done it—she'd burst into tears, standing right there in front of the painting, and the skilfully etched heaps of nutmeg and chillies and cardamom had blurred into random blotches of colour.

Once she'd stopped sobbing she'd locked up the flat and never gone back.

Sighing, Mallika buried her face in her hands. She'd finally admitted to herself that she loved Darius, and that letting him go had been one of the stupidest things she'd ever done. She should have worked harder at their relationship instead of endlessly obsessing about her own troubles. But it was too late now—Darius had made it quite clear that he wanted a clean break.

After a while she pulled herself together and went out for a jog in a park near the sea. It had been a while since she'd last run, and she found the rhythm soothing—the steady pounding of her feet on the track helping her push everything to the back of her mind at least for a little while.

She stopped only when she was completely exhausted and the sun had begun to set. And when she got home she was so tired that she flopped into bed and sank into a blessedly dreamless sleep.

'It's the *annual party*!' Venkat said, in much the same tones that an ardent royalist might say, *It's the coronation*!

Strongly tempted to say *So...?* Mallika raised her eyebrows.

'You can't *not* come,' he said, looking outraged. '*Everyone* will be there.' He brightened up at a sudden thought. 'Darius will be there—he's still in town, and he's made an exception. We haven't told him, but we're holding a little surprise farewell for him at the end.'

Which was exactly the reason why she didn't want to go—but she could hardly tell Venkat that.

'I'll come,' she said. 'But I'll need to leave early. I have some relatives over.'

Well, Aryan *was* a relative, so technically she wasn't lying. And she could think of several things she would rather be doing that evening.

As it turned out, Darius was the first person she ran into when she walked into the party. *Of course*, she thought, giving herself a swift mental kick. She should have landed up there after nine, when the party would have been in full swing, said hello to Venkat and slipped out. Now she was terribly visible among the twenty or so people dotting the ballroom.

Darius found himself unable to take his eyes off Mallika. She was simply, even conservatively dressed, in a full-sleeved grey top and flared palazzo pants. The top, however, clung lovingly to her curves—and it didn't help that he knew exactly what was under it.

'Looking good,' he said, and her lips curved into a tiny smile.

'Thank you,' she said primly, hating the way her heart was pounding in her chest.

The people around them had melted away as soon as they saw Darius and Mallika together—even a blind man would have sensed the strong undercurrents to their conversation.

'Not too bad yourself,' Mallika added, just to prove that she wasn't shaken by his proximity.

It was true—in jeans and a casual jacket worn over a midnight-blue shirt Darius was breathtakingly gorgeous. His hair was brushed straight back from his forehead, and his hooded eyes and hawk-like features gave him a slightly predatory look. He'd lost weight in the last month, and his perfectly sculpted cheekbones stood out a little.

'Venkat said you mightn't come,' he said.

She shrugged. 'I don't like formal parties,' she said. 'But he made a bit of a point about it. So I thought I'd hang around until a quarter past eight and then push off.'

Darius glanced at his watch—it was barely eight, and most of the Nidas staff hadn't even arrived yet. In previous years the party had continued till three in the morning. While a few people had left earlier, even then, an eight-fifteen exit would set a new record.

'Do you really need to leave?' he asked. 'Dinner won't be served before ten.'

'I'll eat at home,' she said, giving him a quick smile. 'I'm not too keen on hotel food in any case.'

There was a brief pause, and then they both started speaking together. Somehow that broke the awkwardness, and when Darius laughed Mallika smiled back at him.

'You go first,' he offered.

'I was just asking how your parents are,' she said. 'And Shirin and the kids.'

'They're fine,' Darius said. 'Though my mum's taken to bursting into tears every time we talk about me leaving. It's driving my dad nuts.' His smile was indulgent, as if he was talking about a child and not a sixty-year-old woman. 'And Shirin's doing well. Her divorce hasn't come through yet, but we're hoping it'll happen by the end of the year. She's coping, the kids have settled and she's started looking for a job.'

'That's all good news, then,' Mallika said, smiling warmly at him.

He felt his heart do a sudden flip-flop in his chest.

'Yes,' he said stiltedly. It was tough enough, having to pretend that she was just like any other colleague. Having to actually stand here and carry on a superficial conversation was proving to be incredibly difficult.

'I'll…um…circulate a bit, then,' she said, indicating the half-full room. 'Now that I'm here I should say hello to as many people as I can before slipping out.'

He nodded, about to tell her that he'd like to see her before she left when the lights went out quite suddenly. A loud popping sound followed by the smell of burning plastic indicated a short-circuit.

Mallika stopped in her tracks as people around her gasped and exclaimed. A few women giggled nervously and Darius came to stand next to her, his features barely discernible in the dim light.

He took her arm and swivelled her around a little. 'Maybe you should wait till the lights are back on before you walk around and talk to people.'

'No, I'll just go now,' she said. She hated the dark, and the people milling around were making her nervous. 'I have a torch on my cell phone—hang on, let me put it on.'

The light from the torch was surprisingly strong, and he could see her quite clearly now, her brow furrowed in thought.

'Damn,' she said. 'This thing's running out of charge. I must have taken dozens of calls during the day, and I forgot to charge it before I left.'

'I'll walk you to the exit,' Darius said, taking her arm.

She thought of protesting, but her whole body seemed to turn nerveless at his touch—following him obediently seemed to be the sensible option.

'Shouldn't they put on a back-up generator or something?'

'They won't if it's a short-circuit,' he said. 'There's a risk of fire. Here—I think this is a shorter way out.'

He led her down a corridor that to Mallika looked exactly like the one she'd been in earlier. This was deserted, though, and it opened into a little *faux* Mughal courtyard with a small fountain in the centre. The fountain wasn't playing, but the pool of water around it shimmered in the faint light coming from the streetlights outside the hotel.

At that point the light coming from her phone flickered and the battery died. Mallika made a frustrated sound and shoved it into her bag. 'I can't call my driver now,' she said.

'D'you want to use my phone?'

'That would be very helpful,' she said drily. 'If only I remembered his number.'

'We'll page the car, then,' he said. 'Do you remember the car's number?

'Sort of,' she said. 'It has a nine and a one in it.'

'That helps,' he said gravely. 'Driver's name?'

'Bablu,' she said, so triumphantly that he laughed.

'We can page Bablu, then,' he said. 'That's assuming the paging system is working.'

She grimaced. 'I didn't think of that,' she said. 'Which way's the exit, anyway?'

He pointed to some glass doors opposite the ones they'd used to enter the courtyard.

'That way,' he said. 'Though we might as well sit here for a while. There's a bench over there, and it'll more pleasant outside than inside the hotel with no air-conditioning.'

She followed him to the bench, and he brushed a few leaves off it before they sat down. 'It's so quiet here,' she said. 'You'd hardly think we were in the middle of Mumbai.'

'The walls cut off the noise,' he said. 'But you can tell you're in Mumbai, all right. Look up—you can't see a single star because of the pollution.'

Mallika laughed. 'You're right, I can't,' she said. 'I should have known you'd burst my little fantasy.'

Darius went very still next to her. 'Why d'you say that?' he asked finally.

She flushed, thankful he couldn't see her in the dark. The words had slipped out, but she *had* been thinking of the happy bubble she'd been living in when they were still dating.

'It was just a stray remark,' she said, wishing he wasn't so perceptive. 'I didn't mean anything by it.'

'I think you did.'

'And I'm telling you I didn't!' Her voice rose slightly. 'Can't you just leave things alone, instead of digging around and trying to make me say more than I want to?'

'I'm sorry,' he said quietly, putting a hand over hers. 'I'm not trying to upset you.'

Mallika jerked her hand away. It was a childish gesture, but she was very near tears, and soon a few drops did escape and roll down her cheeks. She didn't wipe them off, hoping he wouldn't notice in the dark.

Of course she should have known better—Darius immediately leaned closer.

'Are you crying?' he asked, sounding so worried and concerned that her tears rolled faster.

'Of course not,' she said, trying to sound dignified and totally in control.

Unfortunately a little sniffle escaped, and Darius muttered something violent under his breath and swept her abruptly into his arms.

'Mallika—don't,' he said, trying to kiss the tears off her cheeks while simultaneously smoothing her curls away from her face. 'What's wrong? Is it something I did?'

Mallika fought for control and jerked away from him finally, scrubbing at her cheeks with her hands.

'It's all right,' she said. 'Moment of weakness. All better now.' She was feeling hideously embarrassed—crying all over an ex-boyfriend was the ultimate dumped woman cliché.

'It's *not* all right,' he said firmly. 'I know we're not together now, but I care about you still, and I'm not going away until you explain what's wrong.'

'*What* did you say?' Mallika asked, so stunned that she could hardly get the words out coherently.

'I'm not going away until I find out why you were crying,' he said.

'Before that, you dimwit!'

'We're not together now?'

'No, no—*after* that!' Mallika said, sounding outraged.

'I care about you still?' he asked, puzzled and amused in equal parts now.

'Yes, that's it,' she said, relieved that he'd finally got it right. 'Did you mean it?'

'Yes,' he said slowly. 'But you already know that.'

'You never told me!' Mallika said through gritted teeth. 'How the *hell* was I supposed to know?'

It was still dark, and Darius couldn't see her face, but he could sense the anger coming off her in waves. For the first time since he'd met her that evening he began to think that there might be some hope after all.

'Why else do you think I kept on trying to make it work for us?' he asked gently. 'Even when you kept sending me away?'

'I don't know!' she said. 'I thought it was general cussedness or something! And you lost interest as soon as your travel visas came in!'

He should have been annoyed at that, but right now what she was *not* saying was more important than what she was.

'I *do* care,' he said gently. 'In fact, I think I've been in love with you for a while now—only I kept trying to make myself believe that I was confusing attraction and affection with love. It was only after we split up that I realised how much I love you, and by then it was too late to do anything about it.

'You utter *idiot*,' she breathed.

He frowned. 'Does that mean…?'

'Of course it does,' she said, grabbing him by the shoulders and managing to shake him in spite of his bulk. 'I've been in love with you ever since you took me to meet your family that day. But after that you started to back off, and I didn't know what to think! I wanted to—'

What she'd wanted was lost as his arms came around her, crushing her against his chest.

'I've missed you,' he said, his lips hot and urgent against hers. 'God, so much.'

Mallika kissed him back just as hungrily, her hands gripping his shoulders as if she'd never let him go again. It felt so *right*, being back in his arms—she felt completely alive for the first time since he'd left.

'I missed you too,' she said, when she was able to speak. 'I'd think of calling you every single day, and then I wouldn't because I didn't want to seem desperate.'

'You couldn't have been more desperate than me,' he said wryly. 'I've been an idiot, Mallika. I was so sure I was doing the right thing.'

'By breaking up with me?' She shook her head, sounding confused. 'If you were in love with me, how could it possibly be the right thing?'

'I didn't know you cared for me too,' he said, tracing the delicate line of her jaw with one finger. 'It felt like I was forcing myself on you sometimes. Not physically,' he added as she made a sudden movement of protest. 'But you wanted to keep things light—and there I was, talking about long-distance relationships and making it work, when you clearly didn't want to listen... And you were obviously so uncomfortable with me giving up my job and leaving Mumbai that I thought the best thing to do would be to call a halt.'

'I've thought a lot about that,' Mallika said, sliding a hand up his chest to rest right against his heart. 'I think I finally do understand why you want to get away from the rat race—why you need to break away from what's expected of you.'

'So will you come with me?' he asked, capturing her hand in both of his and dipping his head to kiss it. 'At least for a while?'

The hidden lighting in the courtyard came on as if on cue, and he could see that her lovely lips were curled up slightly in a smile.

'I'd love to,' she said. 'Not right away—you should have the first few months to yourself, to do what you originally planned, and Aryan still needs me around—but I'll spend every bit of leave I get with you. And once you're back we can figure out what we should do.'

'Get married,' Darius said, and when she instinctively

pulled back he didn't let her go. 'I know all the reasons you have for not marrying,' he said. 'But if you think about it none of them hold if we're in love with each other.'

'I'm scared of marriage,' she admitted. 'Scared that things will go wrong and we'll end up being unhappy like my parents were. Even if we love each other now.'

'We'll be fine,' Darius said. 'Trust me.'

And suddenly Mallika knew that she did. She trusted Darius completely and absolutely, and she wanted to spend the rest of her life with him. Marriage still scared her, but she'd have plenty of time to get used to the idea.

'I love you,' she said softly. 'And you're right. We can make it work. Together.'

EPILOGUE

'*A GHAR JAMAI*—that's what these Hindustanis call men who marry their girls and move in with them,' Aunt Freny said with relish. 'That's what you're going to be. Not that we're not happy you're back. This gypsy-type living for a year might have been fun for you, but it drove all of us mad with worry. Hopefully once you marry you'll stay put. And as you've had your honeymoon before the wedding…'

'Freny!' Mrs Mistry said in awful tones.

Darius had been back for a month, tanned and leaner than he'd been when he left, but otherwise unchanged. Mallika had left Nidas and spent the last three months with him, travelling around Europe. After the wedding they would move into Mallika's flat in Parel, and then they had plans to set up a small company to aid NGOs with improving the infrastructure in rural areas.

'We're still going for a honeymoon, Aunt Freny,' Darius said mildly. 'It's just that it'll be in the villages around Mumbai.'

'It's his wedding day—you leave him alone, Freny,' Mrs Mistry said warningly as Freny geared up to retort. 'Come here, *dikra*, your collar's just a little crooked.'

Darius ignored her. 'Mallika's here,' he said, his eyes lighting up.

Aunt Freny snorted. 'Your son's a son until he gets a wife, et cetera, et cetera,' she said to Mrs Mistry. 'Though in your case your daughter really does seem set to be with you all her life!'

Luckily Mrs Mistry wasn't paying attention either, and she didn't hear Aunt Freny.

Mallika was walking in on Aryan's arm, dressed in a perfectly lovely red brocade sari with a heavily embroidered deep-red veil draped over her head. Her arms were loaded with gold bangles, and she wore a heavy gold *kundan* necklace around her slender neck. For the first time in years her curly hair was parted in the middle and tied back in a demure chignon, and she wore a red *bindi* in the centre of her forehead.

Darius was still gazing at her, spellbound, when she stumbled a little. She was quite close to him now, and he caught her by the shoulders to steady her.

'High heels,' she said, making a little face and laughing up at him. 'My aunt insisted.'

'You look lovely,' he said, meaning it.

She blushed a little. 'I don't feel like myself,' she said. 'If I could, I'd get married in my work clothes.'

'You'd look just as lovely,' he said, bending down to kiss her.

There was a collective indrawn breath from Mallika's side of the family, while Darius's smiled indulgently.

'Come on—let's get this show on the road,' Aryan said. 'Stop looking into each other's eyes, people.' His newly acquired, now *off* line girlfriend elbowed him, and he said, 'What? They'll miss the *muhurat* and Auntie Sarita will have a fit!'

It was a simple registered wedding, in spite of Mallika's interfering aunt's insistence on a traditional wedding sari and the actual signing happening at an auspicious time. Once they were done, both bride and groom heaved a sigh of relief.

'Any chance of us being allowed to skip the reception?' Darius asked hopefully.

His mother glared at him. 'Absolutely not,' she said firmly. 'How can you even suggest it, Darius?'

'Because I want to be alone with my wife,' he said in an undertone.

Mallika smiled up at him. 'We have the rest of our lives together,' she said, and he smiled back, putting an arm around her and pressing his lips to the top of her head.

'So we do,' he said softly as she slipped an arm around his waist and leaned in closer. 'Did I happen to mention how much I love you, Mrs Mistry?'

'You did say something about it,' Mallika said thoughtfully. 'But it wasn't all that clear. Could you explain it a little more clearly, please?'

* * * * *

A TANGLED ENGAGEMENT

TESSA RADLEY

For all my wonderfully wild writer friends.
You're all simply awesome!

One

Georgia Kinnear could barely contain her excitement.

Her father commanded the head of the long oval table that dominated the Kingdom International boardroom, a position that granted him an unobstructed view of all present for the Managing Committee's weekly meeting.

Norman Newman and Jimmy Browne had been her father's yes-men for almost three decades—more than Georgia's entire lifetime. Both men served as directors on the board of the luxury goods company, but gossip had it that they'd decided to retire and would not be reappointed at the annual general meeting later today. Not that her father had breathed a word. Showing his hand had never been Kingston Kinnear's style.

If the rumors that had been swirling around Kingdom's cutting rooms and stores all week were true, the annual general meeting due to start in an hour was going to change her life forever…

It was about time!

Her father glared down at his watch. "Where's Jay?"

Jay Black was the original corporate crusader—never late, always prepared, always dangerously well-informed. A rival to respect. Georgia was thankful that no one appeared to have noticed the tension and constant skirmishes she had with him. By unspoken agreement, they both preferred to keep it that way. Their private war. Yet, despite her wariness toward him, taking the opportunity to put the knife in behind his back didn't feel right.

"The copier jammed—he'll be here any moment," she told her father, and tried not to think about how good Jay had smelled when she'd crouched beside him, trying to fix the troublesome machine. Like Central Park on a sunny spring day—all green and woody.

Her father puffed, and Georgia tensed, steeling herself for an outburst.

"That thing has been giving problems all day. I'll get a technician to check it," Marcia Hall said calmly, and her father stopped huffing.

"Thank you." Georgia smiled across at her father's PA of more than two decades. The woman was a saint. Marcia knew exactly how to placate her irascible father, a skill Georgia had never acquired—despite growing up with him and working alongside him since leaving school.

Georgia wished Jay would hurry up.

In an attempt to steady herself, she focused on the larger-than-life photos of celebrities along the wood-paneled walls. Each wore—or carried—Kingdom goods. Totes. Clutches. Coats. Scarves. Gloves. Umbrellas. And, of course, the epochal luggage Kingdom was famous for. Each image was emblazoned with the legendary advertising slogan: "My Kingdom. Anytime. Anywhere."

Her father cleared his throat, and the room fell silent. "We'll start without Jay."

Switching her attention to her father, Georgia said, "Uh, no, let's wait—"

He quelled her interruption with a sharp sideways cutting gesture of his right hand, leaned back in the padded high-backed leather chair and rested his elbows on the armrests.

Her father took his time studying his audience, and Georgia's nerves stretched tighter than a pair of too-short garters. Her left hand trembled a little, and to occupy herself, she smoothed the yellow legal pad on the table in front of her and picked up her Montblanc pen, one of her most treasured possessions.

Norman Newman, the soon-to-be-gone Chief Operating Officer, was seated on Georgia's left, sandwiched between her and her father.

Chief Operating Officer...

She savored the sound of his title. By the end of today, it would be hers.

Together with her sisters, Roberta and Charis, Georgia already sat on the Managing Committee that was responsible for the day-to-day management of the company. An appointment to the Board of Directors would launch her career into the stratosphere. And then she'd join the inner sanctum of the Financial Committee—the ultra-secret FinCo—where all Kingdom International's real decision-making happened.

It was impossible to sit still.

She couldn't wait for her and Roberta to be appointed to the board, couldn't wait to implement the ideas they'd been talking about for years. New stores. New design directions. New global markets. Ideas their father—backed up by his pair of yes-men—had resisted. But that would change now...with the end of Jimmy and Norman's reign.

Kingston would finally have to listen to his two daughters...

Surreptitiously, she stuck her hands under the edge of the table and wiped her suddenly sticky palms down her skirt.

Where *was* Jay? The fashion house's financial analyst had already been appointed to the secret FinCo by her father, which had caused Georgia many sleepless nights. It was time for him to witness her triumph.

The boardroom door opened.

At last!

Even her father turned his head to watch him enter. Tall. Perfectly proportioned and elegant in a dark business suit, Jay moved with easy grace.

Georgia flashed him a wide smile. With his arrival, her over-stretched nerves eased a little. But instead of his customary taunting grin, Jay didn't spare her a glance; his dark head remained bent, his attention fixed on the sheaf of papers in his hand.

"You all know that I am not getting any younger," her father was saying, "but I've always been determined to give Methuselah a run for his money."

A ripple of laughter echoed around the table.

What was this? Georgia went still. Did her father also plan to announce his own retirement today? It was her dream to follow in her father's footsteps, her plan to one day be President and Chief Executive Officer of Kingdom International. But she'd never expected the opportunity to come so soon.

Too soon.

Even she knew that. He couldn't retire. Not today. She'd never be appointed...

She rapidly speculated about who he'd lined up to take his place.

Jay had seated himself in the empty chair to her father's left. She shot him a questioning look across the expanse of polished cherry wood. As the luxury fashion house's financial analyst, Jay was in prime position to have the best insight into her father's convoluted thought process—something that constantly raised disquieting emotions in her.

But Jay's attention was fixed on the stack of papers he'd set down on the table in front of him. Somewhere in that pile were documents that were about to transform her life forever. Yet, suddenly Georgia couldn't stop wondering what else might be in there.

One of her father's infamous surprises?

Did Roberta know something she didn't?

Meeting Georgia's questioning gaze across the board-room table, Roberta rolled her green eyes—glamorously defined with black-eyeliner—toward the ceiling while her perfectly manicured nails toyed with a pink cell phone. Clearly Roberta thought the comment nothing more than Kingston's idea of a joke.

"I have no plans to retire yet." Her father smiled, and Georgia's pulse steadied a little. "The corner office is far more comfortable than any in my home. My daughters will have to someday carry me out in a box."

There was more laughter. This time, Georgia joined in, the sound high-pitched to her own ears. Of course, her father had been joking. He wouldn't give up his position so easily…

Georgia's attention switched back to Jay, but from this angle, all she could see was the top of his head.

A rapid glance along the length of the boardroom table revealed the mood amongst the other members of the Managing Committee. Since the start of the rumors, Georgia had quietly set up one-on-one meetings with each of them to smooth the coming transition. She was satisfied she had them all on her side. Yet, right now, they all appeared mesmerized by her father.

With one exception…

At the foot of the table, her youngest sister doodled in a sketchbook, locked in a secret world of Kingdom's nascent designs. Charis didn't look like she'd registered a single one of their father's jokes. No surprise there. Meetings were her idea of hell.

Georgia knew her youngest sister would not be interested in an appointment to the board…or whether their father planned to retire. As long as Charis had a pencil and paper, she was in her element.

Again, Georgia tried—in vain—to catch Jay's attention. She willed him to look up so she could figure out what was going on inside that maddening, quicksilver mind.

But he remained stubbornly hunched over the documents in front of him, his espresso-dark hair falling over his forehead.

A wild thought swept into her head.

Was it possible…?

Had her father lined *Jay* up for *her* job?

Old insecurities swamped her. But she weighed the evidence. Only minutes ago, she and Jay had been engaged in a teasing exchange by the copier. Jay had even joked about buying her a cup of coffee when she got the appointment—

No, not *when*, but *if*—

Her breath caught.

He'd definitely said *if* she got the appointment…

Had Jay been trying to warn her?

She replayed that silly exchange. Despite the teasing, he'd seemed a little terse. She'd attributed it to his battle with the monstrous machine. But had it been guilt?

He'd said there was something he had to talk to her about. He must've already known he was getting the appointment she craved.

She stared blindly at the pen between her damp fingers as her thoughts whirled chaotically. *She* was the ideal candidate to replace Norman. She knew it, and so did her father. She'd proven she could do the job over and over in the past couple of years.

The pen slipped under the pressure of her fingertips. Her father couldn't possibly have decided to give *her* job to Jay.

Could he?

* * *

The faster Jay read, the more the words on the page in front of him blurred together. He shook his head, fighting to make sense of the cumbersome legalese.

What kind of prick had drafted this nonsense?

He speared one hand into his hair to push it off his brow. It needed a cut. But he hadn't had time. The past two weeks had flashed past as he'd fought to clear his desk of never-ending fires. And he still hadn't gotten to the bottom of the quiet niggling rumors about Kingdom on Wall Street.

He suppressed a groan as his focus on the black print sharpened. Kingston Kinnear had lost his damned mind. And he couldn't have picked a worse time to go nuts.

In three days' time, Jay was going on leave—his first visit home in years. And he'd made a vow to come clean with Georgia before he left. If he weren't such a goddamned coward he would've done it a long time ago.

Today was already too late…

He hadn't expected his orderly work existence to rapidly turn to crap.

Kingston's retention of a new firm of attorneys to handle "a special project" had seemed harmless enough. If Jay hadn't been so focused on fixing every last crisis before going on leave he might have suspected something clandestine was happening. And maybe talked Kingston out of this insane course of action.

Too late now.

He shuffled the papers back together into an orderly pile, then linked his hands together on top of it as though holding them down would stop the mayhem from escaping. Then he looked up—straight into the pair of Colorado-sky blue eyes he'd been avoiding.

Georgia was smiling at him. She lifted an eyebrow in question and his gut sank into the Italian loafers he wore.

Jay looked toward the head of the table where the cause

of all the trouble sat. Kingston placed his palms on the armrests of the chair and pushed himself slowly and deliberately to his feet. It was the only chair with armrests, giving it the appearance of a throne, which, no doubt, was exactly the impression he intended to convey. Finally, he straightened the lapels of his hand-tailored suit jacket with a dramatic touch of showmanship.

The boardroom went so silent that Jay could hear the whir of the state-of-the-art air-conditioning. At last, Kingston spoke. "While public stockholders own forty-nine percent of Kingdom, I have always enjoyed the comfort of holding a majority interest and I have been considering the future of the company for a while now."

Georgia sat straighter. Jay knew she was expecting an appointment to the board today...

On top of the tower of documents, his hands curled into fists.

A frisson of electricity zapped around the boardroom. Even Charis had stopped her frenetic sketching and was watching her father intently.

For the first time, Jay wondered whether Kingston had already secretly begun selling off his private stock—it would explain the recent, unexpected movements in the stock market.

The old bastard was stringing them all along...

Or did the youngest Kinnear daughter have any idea of what her father planned? Charis was, after all, the apple of her father's eye. Jay still hadn't worked out what Kingston had planned for his youngest daughter. So far, nothing in the documents he'd speed-read had dealt with her fate. But Jay had no doubt that Kingston had control of his youngest daughter's life finely outlined. He rather suspected that this time even Charis had been kept in the dark.

The tension in the boardroom had become palpable.

Georgia chose that moment to speak. "Roberta, Charis

and I have always been deeply involved in every facet of the company—we are all heavily invested in Kingdom's future."

What a miserable understatement! Kingston expected his daughters to live and breathe the company. And Georgia, even more than her sisters, had made Kingdom her life. There had been moments when her blinkered commitment to Kingdom had caused Jay to despair.

It was Charis who put what everyone was thinking into words. "The obvious thing, Daddy, would be to divide your fifty-one percent share equally among the three of us."

"That would be the obvious solution," drawled Roberta.

Jay braced himself for the firestorm to come.

Finally, Kingston spoke into the silence. "To do so would fragment the company. If I transferred seventeen percent to each of you, it would leave Kingdom extremely vulnerable to takeover."

So Kingston had heard the same rumors he'd been hearing—and hadn't mentioned a word. The first rumblings had surfaced a couple of months ago, but Jay's own investigations hadn't turned anything up. The market had settled down. Then this past week, the stocks had fluctuated, and yesterday the share price had been especially erratic.

"Not if we stood together—we'd still hold the controlling interest." Georgia's knuckles were white as she clutched the pen like a lifeline. Jay discovered that his own hands were clenched just as tightly.

"When have the three of you ever stood together?" scoffed her father.

At the other end of the table, Charis dropped her pencil, and the sound was loud in the large boardroom. "Daddy—"

"So what do you intend to do?" Roberta challenged the old tyrant, talking straight over her sister. "Give everything to Charis?"

"I have three daughters—I must take care of each,"

Kingston said with breathtaking sanctimony. Jay knew the wily old codger had never done anything that didn't serve Kingdom—and himself—best. "But naturally, I will reward my most loyal daughter."

"Don't you mean your favorite daughter?" The edge to Roberta's voice was diamond-hard.

Across the table, the gold pen fell from Georgia's fingers with a thud. "My loyalty to you is beyond doubt." The glitter of hurt in her eyes caused Jay to freeze. "I put in eighty-hour work weeks—heck, I don't have a life outside of these walls. I haven't had a vacation in over two years."

"That's your choice." Kingston shrugged away her plea.

Georgia's lips parted, but she must've thought better of what she'd intended to say. Eyes downcast, she picked up the pen and capped it, and then set it down on the legal pad in front of her.

"You have been unusually silent, Charis. What do you have to say, honey?" Kingston's chilly eyes defrosted as they rested on his youngest daughter.

Charis raised her chin and faced her father down across the length of the table. "Nothing."

"Nothing?" A freeze returned to the blue eyes so disconcertingly like Georgia's in color. "You will be more enthusiastic shortly, my daughter."

Jay felt the hairs on the back of his neck prickle as, taking his time, Kingston's gaze rested on each of his three daughters in turn. "The incentive will be straightforward," he announced. "Whoever proves their loyalty to me first will receive twenty-six percent of the total Kingdom stock—over half my share—and that should be a big enough block to give real power. The other two of you will split the remaining twenty-five percent."

Murmurs broke out around the table. But the three sisters sat like stone.

Jay couldn't bring himself to confront the bruised hurt

in Georgia's eyes. And he knew Kingston had barely gotten started...

Kingston should not have been permitted to torment his daughters in such a cat-and-mouse fashion. Jay forced his hands to relax, smoothing over the stack of papers that contained untold chaos.

"Before you ask, your father has devised a way for each of you to prove your loyalty." He spoke without inflection, not allowing his fury to boil over. "He has a plan."

Two

Georgia's throat closed. Murmurs of surprise swept through the boardroom and then subsided. Across the boardroom table, Jay watched her father through narrowed eyes.

"Jay is correct—but then I always have a plan." Satisfaction oozed from her father's measured tone. "That's how I grew Kingdom from the business my great-grandfather started in a back room into the billion-dollar brand it is today."

"What kind of plan?" Georgia finally found her voice.

Her father didn't even glance her way. "I'm concerned my daughters will be taken advantage of by the unscrupulous money-grubbing sharks that hunt the fashion waters. So I have prepared a shortlist of men able to protect—"

Georgia's breath caught. "A list of men?"

"Protect? Who? Us? *Why?*"

Their father ignored Georgia's and Roberta's squawks of outrage. "The first of my daughters to marry the candidate I have chosen for her will be deemed the most loyal and will be awarded the twenty-six percent holding in Kingdom."

"What?" Georgia and Roberta burst out in tandem.

He was talking as if they weren't even present.

What was going on?

Then it dawned on her. The answer must lie in the documents neatly stacked in front of Jay. He'd still barely spared her a glance.

Georgia had had enough.

Rising in her seat, she pushed aside the clutter of pad, pen, phone and empty take-out coffee cup, and reached across the width of the table. Her feet left the plush carpet and her skirt tickled the back of her thighs as it rode up against her pantyhose. No matter. Modesty was not a priority.

"Georgia!" her father thundered.

So he'd finally noticed her…

She blocked out the familiar angry voice and, with a final heave forward, snatched the block of papers in front of Jay and then slithered back into her seat clutching her prize, her heart pounding in her ears.

Commotion had broken out. But Georgia didn't allow herself to be distracted; she was too busy skimming the pages.

"What the hell is this?" Her eyes lifted to lock with Jay's in silent challenge. He flinched. So he should! "The shares are to be transferred to me and my husband on the day of my marriage…?"

"Marriage?" Roberta was beside her. "Let me see that! I didn't even know you were dating, you secret sister."

Not for the first time, Georgia wished she shared her sister's irreverent sense of humor. "I'm not dating anyone— and I have no intention of getting married." Ever. Georgia's knuckles clenched white around the pages. Not after Ridley. As always, she expertly blocked what she remembered of that disaster out of her consciousness while she did a rapid scan of the thunderstruck faces around the table. Jay's expression was flat, closed off in a way she'd never seen.

Then she appealed for a return to normality. "Jay, what on earth is going on?"

Before Jay could respond, Kingston said loudly, "Georgia, I have chosen a man for you who will do a fine job running the company when I retire."

Panic filled her. "But—"

He held up a hand. "I'm familiar with your dream, and the man I have chosen will match you perfectly."

As Georgia shook her head to clear the confusion, Roberta spoke softly into her ear. "He's about to graft his own vision onto your dream, and then he'll sell it back to you."

"What do you mean?" Georgia whispered.

"Just watch and listen, sister. The master is at work." Roberta sounded more cynical than usual. "Let me see those documents."

Georgia eased her death grip on the papers.

"He will mentor you," her father was saying. "Teach you what it takes."

"You think I need a mentor?" Georgia said faintly. "After all these years? I know the business backward. I know the products, and more importantly, I know the people. I'll head up Kingdom when you step down one day—it's my birthright. And that journey starts today—with the announcement of my appointment to the board."

But her father was shaking his head. "You may be my daughter, but you're not getting a free ride."

A free ride? How could he even think that? But she'd already read the answer in his eyes. He was going to make her jump through hoops—because he didn't believe she could do it. It wasn't just that she was a woman, that she wasn't the first-born son he'd wanted. He would never believe she wouldn't let him down again…

She'd hoped he'd forgotten. Shame suffused her. She should've known… Unlike her, he never forgot a thing!

Nor did he ever forgive.

He blamed her for both the humiliating breakup with Ridley, of which she remembered enough patchy detail to make her swear off dating for life...*and* the horrific car crash that had followed, of which she remembered nothing at all.

"Oh, my God! It even says who you're going to be marrying..." Roberta's voice broke into Georgia's desperate thoughts.

"What?" Her head whipped around.

"Look!" Roberta shoved the papers back at Georgia. "You're going to marry Adam Fordyce."

"Adam Fordyce?" Charis echoed from across the room. "You can't marry Adam Fordyce!"

"That's what it says here, in black-and-white." Roberta's perfectly manicured red nails jabbed at the paper. "That's who Kingston has picked out as your marriage mentor— or perhaps I should say merger mentor? Because that's what this is starting to sound like. I didn't even know you knew him."

This was crazy...

The splintering light from the giant chandelier overhead was suddenly too bright. Georgia touched her fingertips to her temples. Had she gone crazy, too?

A swift glance around the boardroom table revealed that only Jay hadn't reacted. He sat silent and watchful, the familiar gleam of laughter absent from his eyes.

It struck Georgia with the force of a lightning bolt.

He'd known of her father's plan all along...

The betrayal stung. She and Jay clashed often. He infuriated her. He taunted her. The close working relationship he shared with her father concerned her. But despite the rivalry and never-ending mockery, he'd always been honest with her—sometimes brutally so.

Jay had known...and he hadn't mentioned a word about it.

Georgia sucked in a deep breath. She'd deal with Jay—and the unexpected ache of his treachery—later. For now, she had to derail her father's plan. "Of course, I can't marry Adam Fordyce. I don't know him from Santa Claus."

"Unfortunately, he doesn't reside at the North Pole. He lives in Manhattan and he heads up Prometheus," murmured Roberta. "*Forbes* named him one of the top ten—"

"Oh, I know all that! But I've never met the man."

"And trust me—" Roberta was shaking her head "—Adam Fordyce is nothing like Santa Claus. He's the coldest-hearted bastard you'll never want to know."

Charis banged her sketchbook on the table. "That's not true."

Georgia suppressed the urge to scream. "I'm not marrying anyone, and when I do get married, you won't learn about it from a bunch of documents I had no part in drawing up." She shot a killing glare across the table at Jay. "Now, Kingston, why don't you take a few minutes to tell us all what you've been cooking up?"

Her father didn't hesitate. "Adam and I agree it's—"

"'Adam and I agree'?" Georgia repeated, staring at him in horrified dismay. "You've actually discussed this with Adam Fordyce?"

"Oh, yes, we've come to an understanding."

Of course, he had. Otherwise, it wouldn't already be reduced to black-and-white on paper. Jay had known all about it. Adam knew about it. Norman and Jimmy were probably in on it, too. Half the world had known what her father planned for her future…but no one had bothered to fill her in.

Hurt erupted into a blaze of fury she could no longer suppress; it flamed outward, until her skin prickled all over with white-hot heat.

She couldn't bring herself to look at Jay. So she focused

her anger on the one man who she'd worked to impress her whole life. Her father.

"How could you have arranged all this behind my back?"

"Easily!" Kingston's gaze sliced into the heat of her anger like an arctic blast. "You will marry Adam Fordyce."

But, for once, he didn't freeze her into silence. Georgia had had enough. "I told you—I haven't met this man, much less even been on a date with him."

"I've already fixed that." Kingston smirked with satisfaction. "Fordyce will escort you to the Bachelors for a Better Future Benefit on Friday night."

"You're joking!"

"I never joke about business. I've arranged the most important alliance you will ever be part of, Georgia."

He sounded so proud…so confident that she would go along with it.

Why should she be surprised? He'd pulled this kind of stunt before. Except that time, she'd fallen head-over-heels into his manipulative scheme.

Never again.

Even as Georgia reeled from emotions she couldn't find words to express, her youngest sister waded into the fray. "When did you and Adam get so cozy, Dad?"

Georgia finally found her voice. "Let me handle this, Charis. I'm the one he's trying to marry off."

"Not only you." Kingston gave Charis a fond smile. "I've found suitable husbands for all three of you."

A stunned hush followed his pronouncement.

"That's preposterous!" Charis was on her feet.

Her father's face softened. "Charis, the man I've chosen for you is the man I've come to regard as a son over the past two years."

Shock filled Georgia and her attention snapped back to Jay. "You…*you* are going to marry Charis?"

Jay's face was frozen.

Jay and… Charis?

Her sometimes ally, full-time rival…was marrying her sister?

Georgia's stomach churned.

Since Jay had come to work at Kingdom, they'd sparred and argued—or at least she'd argued, while more often than not, he'd simply needled her, provoked her…then laughed at her irritation. He'd unerringly turn up at her office with the take-out coffees she craved, arriving just in time for her to bounce strategies off him. He might excel at pushing her buttons, but Jay was insightful and very, very clever, and all too often his opinions were right on the mark. Despite her distrust, she'd come to rely on his cool level-headedness.

And he'd betrayed her.

Stupid!

She should've known better than to trust one of her father's sidekicks. At least this time, she wasn't infatuated with Jay—or engaged to marry him. Like with Ridley.

Everyone was talking at once. Roberta had drawn herself up to her full height. She looked like some lush goddess. "There's only one thing I want to know. To whom have you dared to barter me?"

But Kingston didn't spare her or Georgia a glance.

Charis's face was pale. She was saying something, but Georgia couldn't concentrate. The sound of her heart pounded fast and furious in her ears and she felt completely incapable of the clear, analytic thought that usually came easily.

All she could think about was that today was supposed to be the best day of her life.

"Father—" Her voice sounded high and thin. Alien. Like someone else's.

She hardly ever called him *Father*—and certainly never at work. It never helped to become emotional. Kingston detested tears, and she'd displayed enough weakness two years ago to last a lifetime.

And her father still held that against her.

She concentrated on the celebrity photos on the wall. Charis had designed most of those carefully crafted products. Roberta had dreamed up the advertising campaigns. And she herself knew the production process from start to finish—how to make sure they made millions from every product launch.

Did her father not understand how indispensable she was to the Kingdom brand? Did he never wonder why he and Norm could find time to play golf so often?

The only way to appeal to his sense of logic was to find a strategic or monetary angle that would make him pay attention.

She drew a breath. "Kingston—"

That sounded better. Stronger. But he didn't even turn his head; all his attention was focused on Charis.

"So, let me get this totally clear. Adam Fordyce is going along with this?" Charis demanded.

As Jay had already gone along with it…

"Oh, yes." Her father actually smiled. "Fordyce is a powerful man and he needs the right kind of wife. And Georgia will be perfect."

Georgia couldn't believe what she was hearing. That's what her father thought of all the years…her whole life… that she'd put into Kingdom? It qualified her to be…what?

The perfect wife?

It was the kind of label Jay, at his most provocative, might have used to needle her…but, tragically, her father was serious.

"And what if we're not prepared to go along with this… madness?" Charis picked up her sketchpad and held it like a shield against her chest.

"If any of you refuses to put Kingdom first—and fails

to show loyalty to me—you'll forfeit the right to stock in Kingdom and immediately have to clear out your desk and be escorted off the premises by security." Kingston's eyes were colder than the ice that covered the Hudson River in mid-winter. "You will no longer be welcome in my business, in my home…or in my life. You will cease to exist."

The air whooshed out of Georgia's lungs, as terror blinded her.

"I'm not going to be a part of this insane scheme, Father." Charis's eyes burned great dark holes in her pale face.

Georgia was startled by the sudden urge to give her sister a hug. Neither of them had ever been the touchy-feely type.

"You can split your stocks between Roberta and Georgia however you choose." Charis stormed past them to the door. "Because… I quit."

Georgia was aware of a ghastly hollow feeling of rejection in the pit of her stomach.

Nothing would ever be enough to make her father proud of her.

Even if she hadn't lost her mind, along with a chunk of her memory, on that disastrous night a little over two years ago when she'd discovered Ridley in bed with another woman.

Even if she'd been perfect.

Unable to help herself, she blurted out, "You don't believe I can run and manage the Kingdom brand, do you, Kingston?"

Roberta leaned forward to murmur, "He doesn't think any woman can run his precious Kingdom!"

But Georgia couldn't summon up a smile. There was only a deep, aching hurt—and endless bewilderment.

What about Jay's role in this? They spent all their working hours arguing, negotiating, talking about every single facet of Kingdom's business, but he hadn't been watching her back. He'd been in on her father's plan…and he hadn't tipped her off.

How could she have allowed him to render her so vulnerable? She'd grown lax and complacent. She hadn't even seen this ambush coming.

"What does Kingston think we've been doing all these years?" she said softly, for her sister's ears alone.

Roberta shrugged. "Who knows? He's always thought women are nothing but pretty decorations."

"That's not true!"

Roberta gave her a long look, and then shrugged again. "At least I had a break from working with him every day while I was in Europe. But you and Charis…" She flipped back her strawberry-red hair with her hand. "I don't know why the hell I ever came back to New York."

Georgia's gaze flickered to her father. But he wasn't paying them any attention. Already on his feet, his face scarlet, he headed toward the exit, chasing after their younger sister with Marcia tottering in his wake.

"Charis!" he bellowed through the open set of double doors. "Get Charis, Marcia. Fetch her back!"

Her father's PA scuttled to do his bidding, and he swung around. Georgia fell back at the ugly fury on his face. "After everything I've done for her!"

It hurt to acknowledge that Charis had always been her father's favorite…

A strange croak sounded.

Georgia stared at her father. Where his face had been red moments before, now it had turned ashen. He clutched at his chest.

Her breath caught. "Father…?"

As she watched, his knees crumpled.

"Jay, help him!" Georgia shoved back her seat and rushed around the table.

Jay got there first, grasping Kingston beneath his shoulders as he sank to his knees on the carpet.

"The resolutions…" her father gasped.

"Stop worrying about the company," Georgia said.

"Who's going to look after Kingdom if—"

"Don't. Don't say it." Fear caused her voice to crack. "Don't even think it."

Kingston Kinnear was immortal—a living legend. He couldn't die.

Her father was struggling to say something.

"Please. Don't talk."

"I'm not going to die." A groan. "I'm more worried about…a takeover."

Georgia bit back her response. She should've guessed he considered himself immortal. "There'll be no takeover. We'll take care of—"

His next moan struck terror into her heart.

"Oh, no!" She dropped down next to him, panic making her breathless. His pasty skin had broken into a sweat.

Then Roberta was beside her.

Their father lay on the carpet. Jay had helped him onto his side and was pushing his jacket open, ripping his tie undone.

"Oh, God, he's having a heart attack!"

Roberta's gasp rooted Georgia to the ground. Her brain stopped working. All she could think was that she hadn't done the first aid course she'd sent the rest of the administrative staff on—because she hadn't had time. She should've done it…then she'd have known what to do—instead of kneeling on the sidelines like some kind of lost soul.

"Roberta, can you get his cuff buttons undone and check his pulse?" Jay instructed her sister.

Jay looked as coolly competent as ever—which only made Georgia feel more inadequate. She was falling apart at the seams, and he was as steady as a rock.

She looked around wildly. "Can anyone help with CPR?"

"He doesn't need it yet—he's breathing." Jay's fingers had moved from her father's wrist to hover over his mouth.

"Oh." She hadn't even known that. Her sense of helplessness increased.

"Call an ambulance," Jay instructed, his hand still over her father's mouth.

Frozen, she couldn't take her eyes off Jay's fingers. Was he *still* breathing? Georgia didn't dare ask.

"Call now," Jay ordered.

Adrenaline surged through her. She shot to her feet and hurried over to where her cell phone still lay on the boardroom table beside the Montblanc pen her father had given her for her twenty-first birthday.

Daddy.

It was a silent scream. The shaking was worse than before, and her fingers fumbled as she attempted to grasp the phone. He hadn't been *Daddy* for decades. *Kingston* at work—which was most of the time. Occasionally *Father*. But never *Daddy*.

The glass face of her phone swam before her. She was crying. Dammit! A tear dripped onto the screen. Her hands were shaking so badly she could barely punch the emergency dial button.

She couldn't fall apart. Not now.

Not when Kingston—the only real parent she'd ever known—was about to die.

Three

Jay paused in the hospital lobby as he spied Georgia's unmistakable silver-blond hair. She was tucked up in the farthest corner of a space that doubled as a coffee shop and gift shop.

If he hadn't been so concerned about her, he might have chuckled. He'd known he would find Georgia in the coffee shop, driven by her craving for the mule-kick of caffeine. *Black gold,* she called it.

He took his time studying her. She'd pulled a short black blazer over that sexy saint-and-sinner vintage YSL blouse. The stark color made her hair look like sunlit-silver in contrast. A coffee mug sat less than three inches away from her right hand. It appeared empty. In front of her, her laptop stood open, and she was hunched down behind the dull silver lid.

Working…even in this time of crisis.

Then his gaze took in her motionless fingers against the keyboard.

No. Georgia wasn't working.

She was hiding, Jay realized. Using her computer to block out the world.

Pity filled him.

She hadn't spotted him yet, so he detoured to the counter laden with bunches of flowers to order a couple of double-espresso shots. He suspected it was going to be a long night.

She looked up as he wound his way through occupied tables, her normally clear sky blue eyes clouded by worry.

The unexpected air of fragility that clung to her tugged at Jay's heart. "May I join you?"

A range of complex emotions flickered in her eyes, including the animosity that often sparkled there. "Would it make any difference if I said no?"

Their intermittent sparring had been going on since the day she'd returned from sick leave after her car accident to find him ensconced in the office beside hers—the office that had belonged to Good-riddance Ridley. His predecessor had done him no favors. It had taken Jay less than a day to realize that she considered him the latest in a series of yes-men hired by her father to usurp the place she one day expected to accede to. A competitor. A threat. He should've handed in his notice and quit then and there, and let her legendary father hire someone else to drive her crazy.

But he'd never been a quitter.

"Tell me to leave, if you'd rather be alone."

She hesitated, and then let out a sigh. "Actually, I'm not sure that I want to be alone." Georgia shut the lid of her laptop and slid it into the black patent leather Kingdom tote perched on the seat beside her. "Roberta's taken Marcia home. And I haven't been able to reach Charis to let her know Kingston…um, father…has had a heart attack."

"We don't know for certain that it was a heart attack." Jay pulled out a chair, sat down and placed the two cups on the table between them, while he searched frantically for appropriate words of comfort. "The EKG looked good. And the first round of blood tests indicated that his enzyme levels were normal—let's wait for the next set of tests before we jump to conclusions."

"There's definitely something wrong." Her expression was bleak. "He collapsed."

Jay wanted to let her drop her head against his shoulder and pull her close into his embrace, until her face hid in the junction between his collar and his ear. There, he knew, she would find sanctuary. She would tremble, and the tears would come...as they had once before...and no one would ever know of her pain.

Except for him.

He'd held her during a night she'd never remembered, during a night he'd never told anyone else about—not even Georgia. On Jay's first day at Kingdom International, he'd promised himself he would never touch her...not until she remembered that night. But she never had. Jay had known he had to tell her about that night, but it had gotten harder to come clean with each passing day he spent working with her.

There was a permanent entry in his monthly task list: *Buy Coffee & Tell Georgia the Truth Today*. Yet, every month he moved that sole uncompleted task forward to the next month. He just couldn't bring himself to do it. Because he was a coward. So this last month, he'd added a second drawn-in-sand deadline to the daily deadline he'd avoided for too long: to tell her the truth before he went on leave. And now that deadline was almost upon him.

But how the hell was he supposed to burden her with the truth now? With her father's life still in danger?

Maybe tomorrow...*if* Kingston's prognosis was good.

Finally, he said, "He's going to be okay."

She glanced around and, apparently reassured that no one at the nearby tables could overhear, she responded, "We don't know that."

Jay nodded, acknowledging the emptiness of his clumsy platitude. "We'll have a better idea once the chest X-rays are done."

She let out a breathy sigh, despair darkening her eyes. She reached for the nearest cup and took a long sip of the richly aromatic liquid before setting it down. "Back in the boardroom, I thought he was dying."

He could tell that soft heartfelt admission to him had cost her.

"Your father is as tough as boot leather."

Jay couldn't bear to see her like this...hurting. She always took care to appear capable and in control. "He's a fighter. He's not going anywhere—and especially not until the annual general meeting has been held."

Georgia choked. "I hadn't even thought about that. When will—"

"Don't worry. Your father has." Back at the office, as the gurney had been wheeled past, Kingston had reached out from under his blanket to grab Jay by the jacket. "I've been tasked with making sure Jimmy and Norman are back at work tomorrow."

The smile he'd half hoped for didn't appear.

"Roberta and I—"

Jay halted her with the shake of his head.

"You're both under enough strain at this time." He thought better of telling Georgia to let up on being the control freak for once in her life. The mocking humor he normally employed to make her examine her decisions—and make sure he kept his distance—would be out of line. "Take whatever help you can get."

Her chin lifted, and she pushed back a silver strand of hair. "Kingston wouldn't."

"You're not your father."

Georgia gave him a narrow-eyed look. She prided herself on being a chip off the old block. It made Jay want to shake her. She was worth ten of the icy man who rarely noticed her—and who certainly never listened to her. She could be so goddamned blind!

Her father could learn a thing or two from her.

"I keep getting nightmarish flashes of what happened. He was ranting one moment, furious as only he can get. The next, he was on his knees. I've never felt so helpless." Georgia dropped her face into her hands. "I can't imagine going to work at Kingdom without him there."

Again, Jay ached to put his arms around her, draw her close. But he knew she'd hate that he'd seen her so vulnerable. So, he did what he knew worked best: he leaned back…and waited.

At last, her hands fell away from her face, and she straightened. Jay could see her silently lambasting herself for showing any weakness.

"Jay, what if he needs surgery?" The words came out in a rush.

"Whatever he needs, he's in the right place to get it." He forced a grin. "His recovery is going to be hell. He's going to be a first-class pain-in-the-ass patient."

"Oh, God." Georgia looked appalled. "You're no help."

"I'm a great help—you couldn't do without me." He winked at her.

That look of haunting helplessness faded to be replaced with a glint of irritation.

Much better. He could tolerate blue sparks of annoyance…anything was better than that desolate little-girl-lost look.

"If you wanted to help, you'd offer to take care of him yourself." She took another gulp of coffee.

"No, thanks. Kingdom couldn't afford the danger pay I'd demand."

She choked.

"But you could hire someone else to do it," he suggested.

She set the cup down. "Then they'd need danger pay!" A flush of shame slid across her face, dousing the spark of amusement that had lit her eyes for an instant. "I shouldn't be joking. Surgery always carries risks. What if…" Her voice trailed away.

Jay instantly stopped grinning. "We don't even know that he's going to need surgery. They're still running tests."

"I know. I know. I shouldn't be jumping ahead. But it's awful being so powerless. All that chaos and then…nothing. I detest this waiting."

Georgia was used to dealing with crises on a daily basis—and solving them. Sitting around like this would be driving her nuts.

"I know this is hard for you," he said softly.

Her eyes flooded with emotion. Jay glimpsed fury…and fear. For a brief moment, her bottom lip quivered. Then she squared her shoulders.

"I've just remembered." Her tone was brisk, the chink of vulnerability vanquished. "You wanted to meet after the annual general meeting. We could do that now. What did you want to discuss?"

He'd planned to tell her about the night that they'd first met.

Placing one hand on top of hers, Jay discovered her silken smooth skin was unexpectedly cold to his touch. Was she in shock?

"Georgia, it can wait." No way was he about to dump that on her now.

Beneath his hand, her knuckles grew rigid. "But—"

He laced his fingers through hers, and cupped his free hand over the top of their intertwined fingers. He'd just broken his promise to himself not to touch her. There was a tightness in his chest.

He gave her fingers a gentle squeeze. "Everything can wait until we have more definitive word on your father's condition."

"You're right." Her hand convulsed under his. "You've been a rock, Jay. Thank you for coming—for asking the doctors all the questions Roberta and I were too scared to voice. And thanks for the coffee."

Her eyes, naked and exposed, sought his; Jay felt the jolt of impact right to his toes. Her thanks made him feel like the worst kind of fraud. But he couldn't bring himself to lighten the mood, to joke about watering down her coffee. He was too hyper-aware of her hand cradled within his larger hand, of the silkiness of her skin, of her unexpected vulnerability—and the shame of his own deceit.

On a soft exhalation of breath, she said, "Most of all, thank you—thank you!—for saving my father's life. I can never repay that."

He didn't want her gratitude. He was a jerk. An utter jerk.

He looked at their hands, linked together. He should never have touched her. Not until she had all the facts. God! What would happen then? After that, who knew if she'd ever let him this close again?

And who would blame her?

Shutting that miserable thought out of his mind, Jay did what he always did—sought escape from a wretched situation in humor.

"I never thought I'd be using Kingston as a dummy model for my first aid refresher course." He cocked an eyebrow at her. "Another coffee?" But he didn't really want to get up, because then he'd have to let go of her hand.

Beep. Shaking her hand free of his, Georgia leaped for her phone, her eyes frantically scanning the text message. When she looked up, the wild panic had returned to her eyes. "He's back from X-rays. I have to go."

That too-brief moment of shared—Jay didn't know what to call it—intimacy? Hell on earth?—was over.

He pushed his unfinished coffee aside. "I'll come with you."

* * *

The following morning, Georgia discovered that Jay had already beaten her back to the hospital coffee shop. Wary, she idled at the entrance, wrinkling her nose at the sharp tang of antiseptic that she encountered everywhere in the hospital, even here.

Toughen up!

Georgia took a breath and approached Jay's table.

Yesterday, he'd betrayed her. *So what!* It wasn't the first time she'd been betrayed; it wouldn't be the last. Today, after seeing the cardiologist, they had business to take care of. Her father would expect nothing less. She was strong. Pure steel. That's how he had forged her.

"I knew you'd turn up here sometime."

Jay gave her an easy smile as he rocked back in the chair and folded his arms behind his head. His light blue business shirt pulled tight across his chest, revealing ridges of muscle Georgia had no business noticing.

"Is your father out yet?" he asked.

She unglued her gaze from his chest and shook her head.

In the bright light of morning, fear still tasted bitter at the back of her throat. The second round of blood tests had been reassuring. It hadn't been a heart attack. Though further tests were being performed right now as a precaution.

"Has Charis been in touch?"

She shook her head again, her stomach winding tighter than a spring. She'd left messages everywhere for her sister. On her cell phone. Her home phone. Her social media pages. At the beach house in the Hamptons. Nothing. And when she'd called Lissa—Charis's best friend—she'd learned Lissa hadn't heard much from Charis lately. Her sister had been too busy with preparing Kingdom's next collection.

All the pressure was getting to Georgia. Normally, she thrived under pressure. The challenge. The cut and thrust of deals and deadlines. But it was nothing like this gut-wrenching emotional tumult she was contending with now.

"She'll come," Jay said.

"I don't know. When she quit, it sounded pretty final to me." Then she realized Jay wasn't talking about Charis coming back to work at Kingdom, but about visiting their father. Perhaps he already knew her sister better than she did. He was going to marry her after all. That caused a maddening twinge in her chest, and made her to snap, "I hope she calls soon—we need her to finalize the spring collection." And Kingston must be missing her...

What if Charis never got the chance to say goodbye?

God. Her father had been so pale...

Georgia had been so angry with him...at his arrogant assumption that he could run her life...force her to marry a man of his choosing. And then he'd collapsed, and her world had fallen apart.

Distractedly, Georgia combed the fingers of her left hand through her hair, and the tiny diamonds on her Cartier watch glittered like dewdrops caught in the sun's first rays. Kingston had recently been talking about getting into watches. She and Roberta had argued against it...

How she wished she could have that time over. She would have been more cooperative.

She looked up to catch Jay studying her. His hazel eyes had taken on the watchful green glint that always meant his brain was working at full tilt. And this time, she was the focus.

"What?" she demanded, instantly on the defensive. She'd never liked feeling like a bug under a microscope. Any way, she wasn't the traitor here.

"Let me get you a coffee."

"Because coffee solves everything?" Despite the under-eye concealer she'd applied, she suspected last night's lack of sleep showed. "Sit—you already have one." She extracted her wallet from her Kingdom Traveler tote and headed for the counter.

She felt antsy this morning, hot and bothered as though her clothes were too tight. They weren't.

Less than two hours ago, she'd finally gone home for a change of clothes. For once, she'd given no thought to what she'd flung on. Clad in the boyfriend blazer she'd worn yesterday, a pair of black wool trousers bought in Paris and her favorite black suede boots, she might appear dismally funereal, but there was nothing wrong with her clothes.

The problem lay with her.

She could feel Jay's eyes boring into her as she waited in line. It made her uncomfortable. Despite his concern, she didn't trust his motives for one moment.

Deep down—or maybe not so deep down—she was mad at him.

Murderously mad.

She accepted that much of Jay's work was highly confidential—he was the in-house finance guru after all—but yesterday it had been her personal life…her future…that he'd colluded with her father about. Maneuvering so that he could marry Charis—to secure himself a major chunk of Kingdom stock. And under the weight of the eternal debt she owed Jay, she was hurt and disappointed and very, very angry with him—the cocktail of emotions was confusing and exhausting. How was she supposed to pretend nothing had happened? Business as usual? Pah! She didn't know how she and Jay were going to be able to work together.

Even though he'd saved her father's life, she was far from ready to forgive him.

It was an impossible situation.

Once back at the table, Georgia set the mug of coffee down and bent forward to slide her wallet into her patent leather tote. Kingdom, of course, but last season's stock, Jay noted as he rocked back in his chair.

Sitting down, she said, "You and I need to talk."

There was a cool edge to her voice and her eyes had an uncanny resemblance to her father's. Yet, something more human, something close to reproach lurked in the blue depths.

Jay winced.

How had she found out? His chest contracted. He was never going to be ready for this confrontation—that's why he'd kept putting it off.

Coward.

"Okay, give it to me with both barrels." He braced himself.

"Your involvement in my father's scheme—" Her voice broke.

For a moment, he failed to absorb the meaning of her words. Then the blood rushed out of his head. She didn't know! He'd been granted a reprieve.

"You should've warned me!"

"Wait—" he demanded.

She warded him off with both hands. "Don't, Jay. No excuses."

He leaned back in the chair, light-headed, his heart jolting inside his chest. "I never make excuses."

No, he only lied to her every damned day.

"I expected better of you, Jay." Her lashes fluttered down, veiling the flash of whatever emotion—anger? Frustration? Both?—that had flickered within, and her silver hair fell forward to hide her face. But Jay was too desperate to allow her to shut him out.

"Georgia!"

She lifted her head and swung her hair back. "What?"

To his horror, Jay saw that her eyes glistened. *Tears.*

That was why she'd looked away. Georgia hadn't wanted him to see how much she was hurting.

"I thought——" She broke off.

The bewilderment that clouded those beautiful eyes almost ripped his heart out. He suppressed the urge to reach for her hand. To touch her. To offer the comfort she didn't want from him.

"Look at me," he demanded.

The look she turned on him was scorching; the tears had been seared away. Jay infinitely preferred her anger to her tears.

Then with a jerky movement, Georgia lifted the mug and took a hasty sip, sputtered and started to cough. Black liquid splashed everywhere as the mug tilted precariously. He reached out and steadied the cup.

When he looked up, Georgia's eyes were streaming.

She glanced around frantically. "Oh, damn!"

Jay pulled a white linen handkerchief out of his pocket. "Here, take this."

"It will stain."

"It doesn't matter."

"Thank you." She took it, her hand brushing his for an instant. She appeared oblivious to his sudden stillness. She wiped her eyes. Quickly. Surreptitiously. As though she feared people might see her crying. When all trace of tears had been wiped away, she turned her attention to the table and dabbed furiously at the spreading pool of spilled coffee.

Head bent, she murmured, "Damn you! I thought there was some degree of respect between us."

The words ripped into his heart. He deserved them—but not for this.

"I didn't expect you to stoop to conspiring with my father to marry me off to Adam Fordyce. Under our rivalry, I thought—"

Jay didn't want to hear more.

He couldn't claim their competition was all in her mind. Hell, he'd provoked her often enough. It had offered great camouflage for his real feelings after all. But he'd *never* colluded against her.

He scooted the chair closer, leaned forward and lowered his voice. "Here's the truth. I couldn't have warned you about his plan involving Fordyce—because I didn't know anything about it myself."

She stopped blotting the tabletop and looked up. He'd never seen her eyes so endlessly blue.

"That's not possible. How could you not have known? He gets you to vet everything that might come back to bite him—"

"—in the ass," Jay finished for her.

Her mascara was smudged, and there was a spark of disbelief in her eyes. His heart clenched. She'd never looked more fragile. Or madder at him.

"I'm not lying to you. The first inkling I had was when I started reading those damned documents after they jammed the copier. I didn't get to see what your father was up to until the Managing Committee meeting was about to start." Jay paused. It was crucial that she believed him. "Your father outsourced his 'special project' to an external law firm he hired because he knew I wouldn't have the time. Because I've spent the past week clearing my desk." And fighting to gather the courage to confess his labyrinth of lies to Georgia. "I'm going on leave, remember?"

"Oh, God. After everything that happened yesterday…" She sighed. "I forgot about that."

Jay could see the wheels spinning in her brain.

"Trust me, had I known about his plan, I would've told your father it was a dumb-ass idea."

She made a choking sound. It was less than a laugh, but the tightness around her eyes eased a little.

"I'd have liked to have been a fly on the wall for that

conversation," she said. "Or maybe not. He hates being challenged. You'd probably have been out of a job."

Not likely. But Jay didn't argue the point. He was too relieved that she was still talking to him. It felt like the sun and the stars had come out…at the same time.

But the spell of brightness would be all too brief. Once he told her—

"Although when you marry Charis, your job will be secure."

His teeth snapped shut so hard at her words that his jaw hurt. "I'm not going to marry your sister."

Georgia took her time examining his every feature. Finally, she appeared satisfied. "And Kingston knows that?"

"We've never discussed it."

Now he wasn't being entirely truthful, though there had never been an explicit conversation. For months, the old codger had implied that Jay's advancement within Kingdom might be fast-tracked if he obeyed certain instructions. And for months, Jay had stubbornly ignored the not-so-subtle nudges to date his boss's youngest daughter. His long-term interest did not lie with the Kingdom, but with something—or rather, someone—else.

Clearly, he should've taken Kingston's ham-handed attempts at matchmaking more seriously—or at least found a way to mention them to Georgia over one of the pitiful cups of take-out coffee he brought her most days—but he'd had no desire to bad-mouth the most important man in Georgia's life. Besides, he'd already stumbled so far down the unholy path of silence that it had become a habit to say nothing at all.

So, here he was—once again—trapped in the quagmire of his own silent stupidity.

"Well, I'm glad to hear that you didn't know."

Like magic the shadow that had hung over him evaporated. "You believe me?"

"Why on earth wouldn't I?" She studied him as though she were trying to read his mind. "You have plenty of faults, but dishonesty has never been one of them."

Jay shut his eyes. All at once, the shadows closed back in, darker than ever. There were so many things he needed to confess. But Georgia was hardly in the right frame of mind to learn about his deception. She had enough on her plate. He'd had the best of intentions to tell her the truth. How he'd met her at a fashion trade show. How he'd comforted her after her fiancé's devastating betrayal, before the crash that took away her memory of their time together. But despite his monthly task list, his daily coffee deliveries, he'd allowed the days of silence to stretch into weeks, the weeks into months, the months into years.

Two damned years.

Too many years to have any excuse. It was unforgivable.

"Look at me, Jay!"

Weary and defeated, he opened his eyes.

"Although there are times I wish you were a little less… blunt," Georgia said as she crumpled his coffee-stained handkerchief in the palm of her hand. She reached for her tote and dropped it inside. "I'll get this laundered for you."

"Don't worry about it." He shrugged. "I've got plenty more."

"It'll come clean."

She'd set her jaw in that stubborn way he'd grown to know far too well.

"And if it doesn't, then I'll buy you another." She swung back to face him, suddenly animated. "Hey, you know what? We don't do handkerchiefs. We do scarves. But no handkerchiefs—not in any of our collections. But we should. And not small dainty female handkerchiefs, but larger man-size ones." Her eyes had taken on fire in the way that they did when she was totally consumed by work.

Always Kingdom.

My Kingdom. Anytime. Anywhere.

Jay suppressed a sigh of frustration as the marketing refrain echoed in his head. It all came back to Kingdom. Every time. Yet, yesterday everything had changed. The foundations of her world had been reconstructed, but Georgia didn't appear to have noticed.

Maybe she never would...

"They'd be white—or maybe not quite white. Ivory. And made from the finest cotton." She paused. "Or perhaps linen, a fine light-as-a-feather linen that both women and men would appreciate. I like that! What do you think, Jay?" Then without giving him a chance to retort that he didn't give a rat's ass about handkerchiefs, Georgia added in a rush, "Perhaps with the Kingdom crown motif printed in white. I like it! I'll speak to Charis. Let's see what she thinks."

Then the light went out in her eyes.

"If she ever comes back to Kingdom."

"Georgia—"

She rose in a hurry. "I hate hospitals. This waiting... this sterilized place...is killing me. I'm going to go check if there's any news."

Jay's heart ached for her. What was really killing her was her corrosive fear that the manipulative son of a bitch who was her father might actually die.

Four

Georgia hurried along the hospital corridor and stopped abruptly in a doorway.

Kingston was already back in his private ward. The luxurious suite belonged in a five-star hotel, not a hospital, with its super-sized television, dining table and chairs, not to mention a seating area complete with a pair of leather couches and a coffee table buckling under the weight of floral bouquets. Propped up on a mountain of snowy white pillows, her father was arguing with a nurse, as was to be expected.

"Give me that!" He struggled to sit up.

The nurse ignored the rude demand and calmly pointed the remote she held at the window. "Mr. Kinnear, you won't be comfortable staring into the glare all day," she said in a bright cheerful tone, even as the state-of-the-art blinds whirred shut.

"I want that blind open!"

Georgia rapidly discovered the reason for her father's disgust: he'd been refused discharge. It only took her a moment to get the cardiologist's number from the nurse and update herself, while her father bickered in the background. Although the tests had indicated nothing of concern, the cardiologist was firm about keeping him for a further twenty-four-hour observation period.

Once she'd terminated a second call to the concierge doctor her father paid a fortune to retain, Georgia cast the nurse an apologetic smile, then waded into the fray.

"Dad, give the poor woman a break!"

The nurse shot her father a long look, muttered something and wisely bustled out.

"Must've recruited her from the marines." Kingston's frustration was about to cause him to rupture a blood vessel. "She won't let me smoke, even tried to tell me it's against the rules. Rules? I've never followed any rules. Now open that damned blind."

Jay was right: anyone who had the misfortune of having to deal with her father while he was incapacitated deserved danger pay. "All the other blinds are open. She's only trying to make sure you're comfortable." Georgia told him. Yet, still she found herself pressing the button on the remote so that the blind lifted. The habit of obeying her father was ingrained bone deep.

He blinked against the bright influx of light. "That's better," he persisted. "The day I lie down and listen to some bad-tempered witch is the day I leave here feet first."

"Kingston!"

But he was already looking past her to the door. "Where is Jay? Call him. Tell him to get his ass up here, will you?"

"He's downstairs. I'm sure he'll be here in a few minutes." Moving to her father's side, she reached out and covered his hand with hers, relishing the warmth of living flesh beneath her touch. He might be impatient, bad-tempered and cantankerous, but he was alive. She stroked his hand. "I'm here."

He shook her hand away impatiently. "I need to speak to Jay."

The rejection pierced her, but Georgia pushed her feelings aside. "You've just had a health scare. Why don't you ease up on meetings for a couple of weeks and take—"

"Ah, good, here's Jay now." He cut her off mid-sentence and sat up.

A wave of energy swept into the ward along with Jay. After she'd been dealing with her father, Jay looked like a glimpse of heaven.

For the first time, she wondered what role he would play in her father's new vision of the company. As her father's confidant—especially if he managed to bring Charis back into the fold as his bride—he'd have untold power.

Would that satisfy him? Or would he want more? He was too clever, too knowledgeable not to know his own worth. She narrowed her gaze as she contemplated him. Tall. Dynamic. Confident. Ambitious. A force to be reckoned with.

"Did you bring the resolutions?" her father barked.

"What resolutions?" she asked Jay.

"Good afternoon, Kingston, glad to hear you're feeling better. Hello again, Georgia."

"What resolutions?" she repeated.

Jay's smile revealed a set of slashing dimples that she couldn't remember ever noticing before. But his smile didn't reach the hazel eyes that saw far too much.

He tapped the leather folio he carried. "Got them right here."

Georgia felt herself stiffen. "Those empower me to run the company while Kingston recuperates, right?"

Jay shook his head, and her blood ran cold.

"Then what are they for?" she demanded.

"They authorize a fresh annual general meeting."

For the board appointments. Nothing ominous in that.

She switched her attention back to her father. She'd had enough of the rumor roller coaster. "Norman and Jimmy are standing down from the board, aren't they?"

"You keep doing your damned job—let me worry about Kingdom," her father snapped.

What was that supposed to mean?

Something dark flashed across Jay's face.

Georgia bit back the torrent of curses that threatened to tumble out of her mouth. "I'm on the Managing Committee—and so is Roberta," she said calmly. "You've taught us everything we know." While they might never have served on the Board of Directors, they were heavily involved in the day-to-day executive management of the company—she pretty much did Norman's entire job already. "Allow us a chance to do what you've trained us to do."

"And where is Roberta now?" Kingston raised his eyebrows. "Shopping? Or preparing to jet off to flaunt herself in the fashion capitals of Europe again? She's certainly not here!"

"That's not fair!" Georgia balled her fists. "She was here most of the night. Then she took Marcia home."

Jay interjected calmly, "I've spoken to Roberta—she's on her way back."

Georgia smiled across at him in gratitude, and a little of her head-crushing tension eased. "I don't suppose anyone has heard from Charis?"

Kingston snorted. "Charis had better not set foot in the Kingdom offices or in any of my stores. She walked out. Call security the instant she's seen."

A chill spread through Georgia. But business was the only language her father understood. Rubbing her arms, she said, "We need Charis to finalize the spring collection designs."

"*I* do not need her. Kingdom certainly doesn't need her." Kingston's eyes blazed. "She's no daughter of mine. Never speak of her again!"

Shock and something close to horror filled Georgia.

He'd meant it.

She crossed her arms over her chest. She'd been so sure he'd get over yesterday's fit of rage. Although his blatant favoritism for Charis had eaten away at her for years, she was stunned at how easily he'd written her sister off without a backward look.

Fear seeped into her. She tightened her arms over her chest, guarding her heart. A quick glance revealed that Jay was watching her. She hoped like hell he couldn't read her terror.

She might be next...

The click of heels in the corridor outside caused her heart to skip.

What if it was Charis? How would her father react?

"About time you arrived," Kingston grumbled as Roberta breezed into the room in a cloud of French fragrance.

Georgia let out the breath that had caught in her throat and her arms fell to her sides.

"Good to see you're as easy-going as ever, Kingston." Bending over the hospital bed, Roberta blew an air-kiss at their father's forehead.

Roberta's makeup was flawless, her lush figure encased in a wrap dress that accentuated every natural asset she had. From the way Kingston was scowling, he'd noticed, too.

"That dress belongs under a streetlamp."

Roberta did a little pirouette. "You think? I think it's perfect."

Kingston's eyes had narrowed to slits. But instead of getting into an argument, he sat up and growled, "Did you bring that pack of cigarettes?"

Georgia opened her mouth to scold him, but Roberta only laughed.

"You need to take better care of yourself," Georgia warned him.

"The cardiologist said I'm as good as new—"

"Not quite! On the phone, he told me that you need some stress-relief strategies." In his fit of rage yesterday, her father had apparently begun hyperventilating. Both the cardiologist and her father's concierge doctor warned it could happen again. "Why not take it easy for a couple of weeks? It will be a good opportunity to test out the succession plan we've discussed—"

"Bah!" Kingston snorted, his tone full of disgust. "You're not running the company."

Georgia stared at him. "I'm more than capable—"

"I will be back in the corner suite on Monday."

The familiar knot started to wind tight in Georgia's stomach. She drew a deep breath, held it for a second and breathed out. One count at a time.

"Can't you at least activate the backup plan we agreed to, Kingston? For the company's sake? What if something really is wrong? What if you become ill over the weekend?" All the possible catastrophes that had been playing through her mind came tumbling out. "And what if they don't discharge you this weekend—and you can't be at the office on Monday?"

"Then I'll authorize Jay to act as interim CEO."

Jay?

Georgia's breath hissed out and she switched her attention back to where Jay stood silhouetted against the window, the Hudson River glittering in the distance beyond.

Her father *was* lining up Jay to take her place as his successor. She wasn't just being paranoid.

Her throat closed up. Had Jay been angling for this ever since his first day at Kingdom? She hadn't been there when he'd arrived. She'd been in the hospital. Being immobilized following the surgery to her ankle had been bad enough, but it had been the concussion and memory loss that had worried the doctors more.

Despite Jay's easy smile, she'd prickled with hostility from the first day she'd arrived back at work. Jay's competence had radiated from him; he made Ridley look like an intern. Slowly, stealthily, he'd become a greater threat than she'd ever imagined. But she wasn't about to let him oust her from the position that would one day be hers.

Jay finally spoke. "I'm afraid I'm not available to serve as interim CEO, Kingston."

Shock caused Georgia to freeze. Jay was refusing her father? He'd had her dream handed to him on a plate and he was turning the chance to run Kingdom down?

Wasn't this what Jay wanted?

Her father and Roberta both turned to look at Jay where he lounged with apparent unconcern against the window.

"What do you mean you're not available?" Kingston raged.

Jay's tone remained level. "I won't be here."

Georgia finally remembered. "He's going on leave."

"Cancel it!" Kingston was struggling to get out of the bed.

Georgia leaped forward. "Father, settle down."

He ignored her, all his attention on the man behind her. "I need you in New York, Jay."

"Kingdom will run just fine without me." The slight upward kink of his lips didn't change Jay's resolute expression. "I'll check my emails and take some calls while I'm away. But I'll be back before any of you notice I've been gone."

I would notice.

The thought caught Georgia by surprise.

Kingston sighed loudly. "Then I'll have to make sure I'm back at work on Monday. Georgia—"

Shutting down her thoughts, she replied automatically, "Yes?"

"Get Marcia to arrange for Bruno to collect me at the usual time, will you?"

Georgia started to object, but then shrugged. What was the point? "Yes, Kingston."

"Oh, and, Roberta, I'm still waiting for that pack of cigarettes."

"Anything else you need?" Roberta asked, her voice saccharine-sweet.

From under heavy eyebrows, he glared first at her, then at Georgia. "A little cooperation from both of you would be helpful."

Roberta didn't flinch. "Ah, loyalty I think you called it yesterday?"

Georgia tensed, waiting for her father to explode.

But the strident ring of Roberta's phone interrupted the storm. Her sister glanced down at the device and pursed her lush lips. Not for the first time, Georgia noticed the fine lines around her immaculately made-up eyes. Roberta was feeling the strain, too. She'd been…different. Distracted. Distant.

"Give me a moment. I've got to deal with this." Roberta was already on her way to the door. "It won't take long."

Abandoned by her sister, Georgia turned to face her father. But she wasn't alone—Jay still lounged against the window, and Georgia was tinglingly conscious of his narrow-eyed appraisal.

"Forget about your half-cocked succession plan. I need you, Georgia." Her father gave her a weak smile. "Fordyce is a damn fine businessman. He's prepared to do a deal— he needs a wife. And he's exactly what our business needs in the long term."

Our business.

Georgia felt her heart melt. Her father needed her. He'd never admitted that before. The urge to do what he wanted—to gain his approval—pulled at her. But she was uncomfortably aware of Jay witnessing their intimate family drama in silence from the window.

So she brought it back to business. "Kingston, you know my views on bringing outsiders onto the board. It's far better to build succession from within the company."

"That's crap!"

"It's absolutely not!" she argued.

"Georgia is right. Internal promotion means far fewer surprises."

Georgia shouldn't have been astonished by Jay's support. After all, her argument for promotion from within worked in his favor, as well as her own. But he'd just turned down a shot at interim CEO…

What did Jay want?

Was he an ally or a foe?

"We've tried developing internal candidates before." Her father's gaze bored into her. "Haven't we, Georgia?"

Shame stained her cheeks and discomfort crawled in her belly. She didn't want to talk about Ridley. Not now. Not ever. "That was different."

"How?" her father challenged.

She certainly wasn't discussing Ridley in front of Jay. "You're missing the point. I can easily—"

Kingston flapped a dismissive hand. "You're not up to running Kingdom."

"At this stage, it would only be for a few days—"

"A few days too long!" He gave a dismissive snort. "I'm not taking that risk."

Then he collapsed back against the pillows and flung a forearm across his eyes. For the first time, he looked old… and beaten.

"I'm only asking you to do one thing for me—put my mind at rest and marry Fordyce." His lips barely moved. He was asking for her help.

How could she say no?

A piercing pain stabbed behind her eyes. The one thing that she'd learned from the Ridley catastrophe was that she was terrible at romance. She'd sworn off marriage—she didn't even date.

Now, Kingston wanted her to marry Adam Fordyce.

No dating—and no romance—required.

Jay was still watching her from his position beside the window, his expression shuttered.

Her gaze slid away from his scrutiny.

Would marrying Adam Fordyce bring her closer to what she'd wanted since she was a little girl, who visited the Kingdom offices and sat and twirled around in her father's high-backed leather desk chair? Her head threatened to explode. Was her father right? Would Adam mentor her and ensure she got what she'd always wanted? Or would he snatch away her dreams forever?

She'd always obeyed her father. But this…? She needed to list the pros and cons the way she always did when she made a decision. But more than that, she needed space… and a shot of black gold.

Grabbing her tote from where it sat on the chair against the wall, she said, "I'm going to get a cup of coffee. Can I get you one, Jay?"

He pushed himself away from the window.

She didn't want him accompanying her. She wanted to think. Alone. "I won't be long."

For once, she didn't want Jay's perspective. This was too personal.

But he didn't take the hint. His smile was easy as he came toward her. "It will give me a chance to stretch my legs—and I need to make some calls."

As she reached the doorway, Kingston called out, "And don't forget to bring me back a goddamned pack of cigarettes!"

Georgia stalked out and resisted the urge to slam the door.

* * *

It didn't take long for Jay to catch up with Georgia. As he came up alongside her, she quickened her pace.

Ducking her head down, she said, "So tell me…honestly…were Norman and Jimmy really going to retire and stand down had yesterday's annual general meeting gone ahead? Was there ever any chance of Roberta and I being appointed to the Board of Directors?"

Jay wished he could give her the answer she so badly wanted to hear. "Who knows what's going on in your father's head—I suspect he'll persuade his golf cronies to stay another term."

They reached the elevator and the doors slid open, revealing an empty car.

Georgia stepped in. "For one glorious instant, I actually believed my father had recognized all the work I've put into the company. I should've known better." She laughed, but the sound held little amusement. "He never had any intention of letting me in—not even temporarily. He wants a man in control." She stabbed a button on the control panel. "Someone like you."

Jay moved in front of the elevator doors and spun around to face her, giving her no choice but to look up at him. He was overwhelmingly conscious of her closeness…the fine grain of her pale skin, the bright blue of her eyes, the familiar scent of her…all the intimate details he had no right to appreciate.

He found his voice. "Not me. I'm not available."

A frown pleated her forehead. "You can tell him that all you like. It's not going to stop him. He'll talk you into it once you get back from vacation—he always gets what he wants. And you'll be married off to Charis before you can say—"

"That's not happening, either!"

"Don't be so sure." Her gaze lifted to focus somewhere

above his head—the floor indicators, perhaps. "He's already convinced Adam Fordyce to marry me."

"But you're not going along with that."

Georgia gave no sign of hearing a word of what he was saying, whereas he couldn't think of anything but her...

"He'll have his way—just wait and see. He never gives up until he gets what he wants. God knows who he's lined up for Roberta. That's going to cause fireworks, for sure." Georgia's eyes returned to lock with his. "Three successors for his beloved company. Three daughters—who come with stock certificates pinned to their wedding dresses—to dangle as carrots."

Georgia was angrier than he'd ever seen her.

"Roberta and I will never have feet big enough to fill his shoes—" She broke off as the elevator car came to a halt. "And besides that, we have lady parts."

How the hell was he supposed to respond to that?

She didn't give him a chance. Brushing past him, she said over her shoulder, "And who can argue with him? He'll only fire anyone who dissents! He's the boss."

Jay strode after her. "Georgia—"

With increasing frustration, he listened to the rapid click-clacking of her boot heels along the hospital corridor. For all his talk, the old man wouldn't be stupid enough to fire her. Kingston's insane scheme had already cost him one of the most talented young designers in the business. Losing Charis was going to create havoc in the coming months. And it was the same with Georgia. She knew too much about the inner workings of Kingdom for her father ever to risk getting rid of her.

The coffee shop loomed up ahead with its racks of magazines, floral bouquets tied with ribbons and the aroma of strong coffee.

It was now or never...

Kingston was going to be fine. Jay hesitated mid-step.

No, not now. She was far too worked up.

Coward.

But he forced himself to commit to some kind of action, saying, "That talk you and I need to have—how about I buy you a drink tomorrow night?"

"What?" She swung around, eyes blank with confusion. "Careful!"

Jay pulled her to one side as an orderly pushed a patient past in a wheelchair.

"The Bachelors for a Better Future Benefit," he reminded her once the pair had passed by, his heart knocking loudly in his chest. He'd been talked into being auctioned off as a dinner date for the charity. "We can meet for a quiet drink afterward." That way, he'd keep the vow he'd made to himself: to tell her everything before he left for Colorado.

"Oh, my God." Her hands covered her eyes. "I'd forgotten all about that. I swear I'm losing my mind all over again. It's like after the crash." She took a couple of sideways steps and sagged limply against the wall. When she dropped her hands from her face, her mascara had smudged, accentuating the hollows beneath her eyes. "Tell me, Jay, do you think I'm crazy?"

It was the first time she'd ever brought up that period missing from her memory. The night they'd met—the meeting she knew nothing about and had changed the course of his life—and the blanked-out days that followed her subsequent car accident on the way to the airport.

"You're not crazy. You're the most sane person I've ever met." It was more than he could handle to see her wilting like this. But he knew better than to touch her, to offer any comfort. He forced a smile. "At least, most days...after you've had a cup of coffee."

Placing his forearm against the wall beside her head, Jay leaned in toward her.

"I need your help…" He kept his voice deliberately light. "I need you to bid on me tomorrow night."

Her eyes snapped wide. "Me? Bid on you?"

He made himself grin—a shark-like toothy grin, and her eyes narrowed suspiciously. *Good.* "Think of it as act of altruism."

"Altruism?"

"You'll be saving me from hordes of—"

She interrupted him with an unladylike snort. "I can't think of anyone in less need of saving."

His grin widened in appreciation. "Afterward, to celebrate your good taste in winning me, we'll share a bottle of French champagne." He lowered his voice suggestively. "Then I'll sweep you off for that incredible dinner you've paid for…"

He was rewarded with a glint of fire in the depths of her blue eyes, and Jay felt a corresponding flame light up deep in his chest. He held his breath. *Down, boy.* He had to tell her the truth tomorrow night.

"You don't need me to bid on you, buddy. You'll do fine and raise plenty all on your own."

"I dare you to outbid everyone," he murmured.

But instead of rising to the bait, Georgia pinned him with a glittery look full of suspicion. "I don't do dares."

"Too risky?" he taunted.

She shook her head, a couple of strands of hair almost whipping against his arm where it rested close to her head. "Too impulsive."

Jay knew he was pushing hard, but he couldn't stop. "Too scared to live a little?"

She froze. "I'm not scared!"

Gotcha. He raised his eyebrows. "You sure about that?"

"Of course!" Georgia gave a dismissive laugh that he might have thought was real if he hadn't made an art of studying her for the past two years. "Why should I be scared to bid on you?"

He let her question hang, watching her, letting it expand to fill the space between them. "Because you're too scared to be swept away on an incredible dinner date with me?"

Her eyes darkened to sapphire. "I definitely don't do dates."

A second later, she gave another careless laugh. She'd recovered so quickly that if Jay hadn't been watching her, he might have missed the flare of panic.

"Your ego is showing, Jay Black. What a hard life, being *such* an eligible bachelor in New York—and having the privilege to turn down an interim CEO position that I would give my right arm for. Why would you worry about a dinner date?"

Jay stared into her eyes which, despite being shadowed by confusion and antagonism, were still the most beautiful thing he'd ever seen. He wanted to tell her those eyes were worth infinitely more than the CEO position she coveted so highly.

"Oh, God. I'd better not forget to arrange where I'm going to meet Adam."

Suddenly, Jay was no longer in the mood to jest. "You're not seriously planning to attend the benefit with Fordyce, are you?"

Georgia stared at him as though he'd grown two heads. "Of course, I am. Kingston's already arranged it."

A primal, possessive response rocked Jay back on his heels. The hand he had propped against the wall curled into a fist.

"I'm sure Fordyce will have no problem finding another date," he said through gritted teeth.

"It's hardly a date. But I can't just dump the man—he's far too important of a player. And I can't let my father down."

"Can't let your father down?" Jay stared at her. "That's a habit you need to break."

"I don't dare, Jay. If he fires me..." Her voice trailed away. "I'm nothing without Kingdom."

Carefully, Jay pushed away from the wall and uncoiled himself, taking a step backward before he said—did—something that he might regret.

Keeping his voice even with great effort, he said, "Why don't we go get that coffee you wanted?"

Five

They took their steaming cups to a sheltered bench Jay had discovered yesterday tucked away in the landscaped gardens surrounding the hospital. Three nurses stood a distance away, clutching their coffees, while half a dozen sparrows tussled like young thugs on the footpath.

A gust of wind shook a drift of withered leaves from a nearby tree.

"Would you like my jacket?" Jay instantly started to slide it off his shoulders.

"No, no. I'm fine."

Dropping her Kingdom tote on the wooden bench, Georgia drew her jacket more tightly around her, and then took a sip of the coffee he'd bought.

"I could get used to this coffee," she said, as she sat down in the washed-out sunlight.

He hadn't brought her out here to talk about coffee. With his free hand, Jay raked his hair off his forehead and sat down beside her.

"The sooner you tell Fordyce that you're not going along with your father's crazy notions of empire-building, the better."

"Maybe it's not crazy. Maybe it actually makes sense."

"Sense? It's completely mad!" Disbelief took his breath away.

"It'll be business—more like a merger than a marriage."

"But you haven't even met the man," Jay protested, seriously rattled now.

She took another sip. Jay noticed how the morning sun glinted in her hair. "That will change tomorrow night."

Desperation pounded through his veins. He wanted to grab her by her shoulders and warn her that she was making the biggest mistake of her life. Leashing his inner turbulence, he sat still as stone. *Reason, not reaction.* "You'd never do business with a company you hadn't done substantial due diligence on."

She didn't even crack a smile. "I'm not stupid, Jay. I'll certainly weigh up every advantage and disadvantage." Her tone had cooled. She glanced down at her watch. "We can't stay long. Roberta will be wondering where I've gotten to—"

"Roberta will call if she needs you." Jay had no intention of allowing Georgia to run out on this discussion. "Forget the business advantages then, and consider the personal aspects. You can't possibly marry Fordyce."

She flicked him a quick sideways glance, then looked away. "I may not have a choice."

His shoulders grew more rigid from the effort it took to stop himself from leaping to his feet. "Of course, you have a choice. No one can force you into marriage."

"It's not that simple."

"It's exactly that simple. Just say no."

"There are plenty of merits to it—even on the personal level." She began ticking them off on her free hand. "One, I'm hardly likely to fall in love with anyone."

"Why not? You shouldn't allow one bad—"

"Two, I work too hard—you say so yourself." Her middle finger unfurled, as she continued to count out reasons he didn't want to hear. "Which leads me to the next point. Three, I don't have time to date...to meet men."

Jay started to panic. "But you don't want to meet men, do you?"

"Doesn't every woman want to find The One?" She raised an eyebrow. "Someone to love."

The One?

Jay lowered both his eyebrows in response.

"What?" She stared back at him. A fine wisp of silver hair blew across her eyes. She pushed it away, hooking it behind her ear. "Isn't that supposed to be every woman's dream?"

"I never thought it was yours."

"Jay!" She actually looked offended.

Holy crap! How had he misread her so badly? He'd listened so carefully to her no-romance protests that he'd missed the yearning hidden deep below.

"You haven't looked at a man in the two years I've worked with you."

She didn't look pleased with his observation.

"So maybe it's just as well Kingston's come up with this plan. I get the chance to marry someone I'll have business in common with—and I don't need to go through the drama of dating."

"You don't need to marry Fordyce to avoid that fate. You could marry me instead of settling for second best." He grinned, partly to irritate her, but mostly to give himself an out lest she realize how deadly serious he was. "We've got plenty in common."

She gave a snort. "Like what?"

For starters, they both spent most of their waking hours at Kingdom, but Jay decided she might not appreciate that reminder right now. He needed to proceed with care—and humor. He stuck out his thumb, mimicking her actions from moments before. "You like arguing with me—"

"*You* argue with *me*!"

"Two." He flicked out his index finger. "You think my opinions are fantastic—"

"I do not!" Then she relented. "Okay, maybe as far as Kingdom goes—I'll concede that."

"Three," he said, counting the point with his middle finger. "You adore my sense of humor."

She rolled her eyes skyward. "Can't you ever be serious, Jay? This is exactly why I would never marry you."

Ouch!

Before he could react, she blurted out, "Anyway, I'd hate for you to sacrifice yourself."

"But it's okay for you to sacrifice yourself?" he retorted.

She set her jaw in a way that he recognized only too well. "That's different. I'll be marrying Adam Fordyce to get what I want."

Even the wind stopped gusting in the taut silence that followed.

"All you ever think about is Kingdom," he said quietly.

She didn't say a word. Instead, she drained her coffee and carefully set the empty cup down on the sunlit bench between them.

"Georgia, I know you were hurt by Rid—"

She didn't allow him to finish. "Kingdom will never betray me."

This time, her smile turned his guts inside out.

Never betray her? What the hell did she think was happening? What did she think her father was doing?

"And marriage to Fordyce wouldn't be a betrayal?"

"Betrayal of what?" She sounded genuinely confounded.

Of yourself.

Jay suppressed the urge to yell it at her—he didn't dare show the terror that now churned inside him.

"You don't want to do this," he said, the calmness of his voice surprising him. "It would be a massive mistake."

Her careless shrug rattled him further. "Plenty of marriages have worked with less—"

"And plenty have ended in bitterness and acrimony," Jay interrupted her. "Don't you want more out of life than a billion-dollar divorce settlement?"

Georgia glared at him. "You don't understand what it's like to be a Kinnear."

It was his turn to shrug. "Not very different from being a Black, I'd imagine."

"Don't be silly!" Her lips curved up into a smile that held no trace of any real amusement. "You couldn't possibly understand."

"Try me." Jay bared his teeth in a feral grin.

"My life was mapped out long before my birth. From my father's perspective, it went wrong from the moment I was born." She paused. "I was supposed to be a boy."

"George." Jay supplied the name.

"You know?" The bruised look he'd hoped never to see again was back in her eyes. "He told you?"

Jay hesitated, debating with himself how to respond. He let his gaze drift around the landscaped garden. The nurses had vanished. Aside from the squabbling sparrows, he and Georgia were the only ones left.

Slowly, he shook his head. "It's not hard to figure out."

"Father was so sure I'd be a boy. He wasn't interested in hearing some medical technicians' determination of what my sex would be. Because he knew. He even had the christening invitations printed, inviting everyone to 'celebrate the birth of my son, George.'" Her face wore a strange expression. "Funny, huh?"

Even on the second telling, Jay found little amusement in Kingston's arrogant certainty that he could preorder his firstborn's sex. Even less did he like the notion that her father had made his disappointment so evident to Georgia from the day she was born.

"You want to please your father." He knew he had to proceed with caution. "You want his approval—but you don't need to go along with this…this—" *Insanity.*

"You don't understand. You asked what I want. Well, here's what I want. I want to be the President and CEO of Kingdom. I want it for me—not for my father. I want it because I've worked for it all my life. I want it because it's mine by right, my birthright. I want it because I deserve it."

The words were a death knell.

Hell, he'd known it…but he'd never understood how deep her desire went—nor how far she'd go to secure it.

But he couldn't walk away. He was fighting for her life—and his own.

"So you think by marrying Fordyce you can convince him to let you take charge?" The glitter in her eyes warned him he was on treacherous ground. "Fordyce is an ambitious bastard. What makes you think he'll step aside and let his wife be boss?"

Her chin went up. "I'll persuade him."

God!

Imagining what form her persuasion might take made him go hot…then very, very cold. Jay tugged at the knot of his suddenly too-tight tie. An icy knifepoint of fear cut deep into his heart.

"You deserve more!"

His anger burned a white-hot streak through him. Anger at Kingston for his callous indifference to his daughters. Anger at Georgia for her blind certainty that her father would honor her efforts. Anger at himself for his foolish hopes.

To give himself time to cool off before he blurted out anything he'd later regret, Jay raised his cup and downed the coffee in two gulps.

The heat scalded the back of his throat.

He set the empty cup down on the bench beside hers.

"I love Kingdom... It's everything," she said quietly.

The vulnerability in her eyes took away his breath, evaporating the sermon he'd been about to deliver. At last, he said flatly, "It's only a corporation, Georgia."

She was shaking her head. "Oh, no. It's much more than that. It's all I have. It's my heritage. My family. My life. My legacy. If I have to marry Adam Fordyce to keep that, I will."

"You shouldn't allow your father to dictate who you should marry." He drew a deep breath. "It wasn't successful last time—why the hell would it work this time?"

She went white. "You know nothing about what happened before!"

Jay winced.

He hated, *hated* to see her hurting. Guilt ate like hot acid at his gut.

But he couldn't keep silent...not anymore.

"Georgia, that night that you...that Ridley—"

"I don't want to talk about it," she cut him off. "And certainly not to you. It's none of your business, Jay."

The words were a punch in his chest.

But it was his business...

He wanted to look away, before she saw into his soul and read the truth that blazed there in ten-foot-tall letters of gold fire.

That she'd changed his life.

That after they'd met, he'd flown home and set the wheels in motion. That ten days later, he'd called Kingdom International looking for her. Only to learn that she'd been through surgery and was recovering from a head injury. He'd been on the next plane to New York. His first stop had been the Kingdom headquarters. Georgia had still been away on sick leave. There'd been little chance of convincing her staff to give him her contact details. But he'd caught a break. The busy receptionist had assumed he was there for an interview. And in that instant, Jay had taken brazen advantage of the woman's mistake and he'd made his next life-changing decision. It hadn't been difficult to smooth talk his way into Ridley's job.

If he told her the truth now, he'd drive her straight into Fordyce's arms—she was halfway there already. Then he'd lose all chance to win her back. Forever.

"I'd hate to see someone so smart and brave trapped in a miserable marriage," he finally managed. "I'm concerned about you, that's all."

Desperate, seeking to lighten the moment—hell, looking for any distraction—he bent forward, intending to kiss the tip of her nose in an amusing comic fashion.

But it didn't turn out that way.

Instead of brushing her nose, his lips planted themselves on hers. The jolt of the brief impact rocked through him. It wasn't a particularly sexy kiss, as far as kisses went. But his lips lingered longer than he'd intended, refusing to obey his command to back off. Now. Before he blew it all to kingdom come…

Yet, surprisingly, she didn't shove him away.

Her lips were soft beneath his. Then—more surprisingly— her mouth moved slightly, her lips parting a little—probably because she was in shock.

She tasted of strong hot espresso and a sweetness that was all Georgia.

Jay didn't dare press the advantage, nor did he deepen the kiss. Too much lay unspoken between them.

He shouldn't be touching her!

So he retreated, and gave an unsteady laugh, while silently cursing himself.

"Speaking of mistakes, that was a mistake," she said, much too quickly.

Who was she trying to convince?

Him?

Or herself?

But he didn't risk challenging her. His heart was thundering so loudly he was sure she would hear it reverberating around the empty garden.

Her hands came out, warding him off. "Don't move—stay there—I have to work with you tomorrow."

Picking up the empty cups, Jay rose and swung away almost treading on a trio of sparrows bickering amidst a swirl of fallen leaves. He retreated to the trash can nearby and tossed the cups in with barely restrained force. Then, fighting to keep his face from revealing anything of his feelings, he stalked back.

He refused to think of that sweet, gentle kiss as a mistake.

He came to a halt in front of her.

"You don't love Fordyce. It will ruin your life," he said softly, and shoved his hands into his pockets.

She said nothing.

"You'd marry a man you've never met, a man your father picked out for his ability to run Kingdom? *Why?*"

She raised her chin in that maddeningly familiar gesture. "I'll make it work."

Or die trying.

That was his Georgia. The blind tenacity. The pigheaded drive. Everything that made her the most maddening, most fascinating woman he'd ever met.

His eyes locked with hers.

"They call him Mr. Ice," he warned.

Cool, rational logic always worked better. Or provocation. Except, right now, in his desperation, he couldn't summon either...

"Don't give in." He was begging, dammit!

She must have sensed something of his black emotional maelstrom because she tipped her head to one side and considered him with eyes that had cooled to a clear light blue, so disturbingly similar to her father's that Jay was filled with a flood of dread.

"Jay, I'm not giving in. I'm compromising."

"You're damn right, you're compromising. You're compromising who you are."

This was her life—his life—she was talking about. He wanted to shake sense into her. But he kept his hands thrust deep in his pockets and watched the color leach out of her eyes and the wall go up.

Damn Kingston!

So he gentled his tone. "It's your father's loss that he doesn't appreciate you for who you are."

The smile she gave him was brilliant...and utterly fake.

"You're lucky," she said. "You were born the right sex. I'm sure your father is incredibly proud of you, his eldest son—and of your achievements. You've had freedom to carve your own life."

"I suppose you could see it like that," agreed Jay with little humor.

"I've always been expected to work for the family company. I can't leave."

"Do you want to leave?" Tension vibrated through him.

"No, of course not! Haven't you heard a word I've said? Kingdom is my life."

Kingdom.

That was all that mattered to her. All she wanted. What could he offer to match that? Except the freedom to carve out her own life.

The desperate determination in her eyes warned him that it was pointless to even try to negotiate.

Pivoting away, Jay drew a deep steadying breath.

It was perfectly clear. Pressure would only make Georgia dig her toes in further and push her faster toward the altar. The hell-bent desire to fill Kingston Kinnear's shoes consumed her. She would do anything to be President and CEO of the company she'd been raised to revere.

Even prostitute herself to a man of her father's choosing.

Six

Georgia had intended for her first meeting with the man who she was contemplating marrying to be in private—even if it was in the back seat of a limousine.

Instead, it was taking place in a marble-tiled lobby on New York's museum row in the midst of a high society affair.

Her father's driver, Bruno, had arrived on time to take Georgia to the benefit. But there'd been no sign of Adam Fordyce, apart from the exquisitely packaged corsage on the back seat with a handwritten note from Adam that he looked forward to meeting her at the party.

Now Adam Fordyce's narrow mouth barely moved as he said to Georgia, "I see you received my flowers."

"They're beautiful—thank you." She carefully touched the corsage on her wrist and silently reminded herself not to rub her eyes any time soon.

"Would you—"

"Should we—"

They both spoke at once, and Georgia laughed awkwardly and felt herself color. This had to be worse than being a teenager on a first date. Tonight had to go well. She couldn't afford to screw this up...

Then she sneezed. And worse, her eyes started to burn. Of all the bad luck!

Georgia set her cocktail glass down on a nearby pedestal and sent a prayer to the beauty goddesses that her expensive waterproof mascara would hold up.

"I'm so sorry," she sputtered, her vision blurring. She fumbled with the clip of her sequined clutch and dug frantically around inside for a tissue. Her eyes pricked and two more sneezes followed in rapid succession.

"Good evening, Georgia."

Jay.

He thrust a soft linen handkerchief into her hand.

She blew her nose and dabbed at her streaming eyes while Jay and Adam greeted one another. Then she opened her eyes and, to her relief, the world slowly realigned as the noisy chatter echoed around them.

Jay stood before her, immaculate in a black tuxedo and a startlingly white shirt. A black bowtie completed the ensemble. He looked fantastic. The bidding on him tonight was going to be insane.

For some reason, that did not delight her.

"Thank you." She grimaced. "This is becoming a habit." Fluttering his handkerchief between her fingers, she made a mental note to get both handkerchiefs she now possessed laundered and returned ASAP.

"It's the baby's breath," said Jay.

"What?" She squinted up at him.

He raised an eyebrow. "Those little white flowers in the corsage that make you sneeze."

"You're allergic?" Adam was all concern.

"Yes." Once again, Georgia felt awkward, her stomach knotting up. She could kill Jay for drawing attention to her weakness—even if he was right about the allergy. "It's the single-flowered version that's the problem. I'm fine with the double-flowered hybrid." The orchid in the arrangement would be fine—but it would be too difficult to separate it from the baby's breath.

"Here, let me remove it," said Adam.

"I'll do it." Jay moved in between her and Adam, blocking her date from view. His fingers were cool against her skin as he gently removed the corsage from her wrist. This close, his clean-shaven jaw was level with her eyes and she could smell his aftershave—that subtle fresh blend of greenery and wood—as he concentrated on her wrist.

"How did you know I'm allergic to baby's breath?" she murmured to Jay alone.

His head tipped up and his darkening gaze tangled with hers. Instantly, the memory of the last time he'd been this close flashed into her mind.

He'd kissed her.

It had been dizzying, disorienting. She worked with the man... She didn't want to be thinking of how safe, how comforted she'd felt when he'd brushed his lips across hers. Yet, there'd also been a prickle of high-voltage tension... something that had nothing to do with comfort...or safety. And she certainly didn't want to think about—

"I'm observant," Jay said flatly.

Georgia searched her plundered memory bank for an occasion when she'd had an allergic reaction that he might have witnessed and came up blank. But that meant little. There were so many holes where certainty had once existed. The knots in her stomach grew tighter, and she looked away deliberately, and tried to refocus on her date.

She caught Adam studying them.

"Let me fetch you a glass of water," he offered.

"I'll be fine."

The last thing Georgia wanted was for Adam to think she was some kind of freak. But he was unreadable. His dark remote face contrasted so sharply with the pale eyes that revealed no emotion at all. It was easy to see how he'd been nicknamed Mr. Ice.

"Is there anything else I can get you to drink?" Adam's voice interrupted her thoughts. "Another cosmopolitan, perhaps?"

Coffee…

Jay would have offered her coffee. Even on this rarefied occasion, he would've conjured up a paper cup of steaming black gold, and she wouldn't have needed to ask.

She almost smiled—and only just stopped herself from sneaking Jay a sideways conspiratorial glance.

Adam was still waiting for her response. Feeling guilty at the headspace Jay was occupying, she over-compensated with a thousand-watt smile. "Maybe a lime and soda?"

"Done."

She watched Adam disappear into the throng.

"So you're going ahead with this crazy plan to marry Fordyce?"

Georgia's heart sank. Since their confrontation in the hospital gardens, his accusation that she was giving in— and the implication that she was taking the easy way out— had gnawed at her. There was nothing easy about what she was doing. But she couldn't expect Jay to understand. How could he? He'd never been in her position…

She tipped her chin up. "The more I consider it, the less crazy it sounds."

"I've instructed Charis to bid on me if I fail to make the reserve."

"She's here?" The information came as a relief.

"Yes, I ran into her in the lobby—she'll be joining you at the table Kingdom sponsored."

All Georgia's bubbling questions dried up as she gave Jay a slow once-over. He'd make the reserve for sure. The formal evening clothes made him look breathtakingly gorgeous—and his slightly wayward hair only added to the appeal. Working with Jay every day, she'd never even thought of him as handsome.

Where the hell had her eyes been?

"We have a decent budget for this event." Georgia certainly wasn't going to feed his ego. "Charis will make sure you go for a respectable figure. Don't forget to talk up the raffle of the Kingdom trolley bag we're doing tonight. Make sure to slip in mention of the Kingdom brand as many times as you can so that we get some decent media attention. And get some photos with whoever makes the highest bid."

"Thank you!"

Was that a hint of irony she detected?

Before she could call him on it, she spotted the event organizer making frantic hand signals in her peripheral vision. She nudged Jay. "I think that's your cue—and I need to find the cloakroom to fix my makeup."

"The moment of truth—let's see what I'm worth." Jay's smile didn't reach his eyes as he took her in, from her hair styled in an updo to the dark sapphire dress and the diamond drop earrings she wore. "You look beautiful."

The mirror in the ladies' room lounge revealed that Jay had been delusional in his assessment.

After salvaging her eye makeup and repairing the damage caused by her sneezing bout, Georgia went back out and found Adam in the lobby, holding their drinks. Once she joined him, he made short shrift of the rich and famous glitterati crowd that surrounded him.

There was no sign of Jay.

To Georgia's irritation, there was little opportunity for the social let's-get-to-know-each-other-better chatter she craved with Adam amid waiters circling with platters piled high with canapés, the constant greetings from acquaintances and a never-ending stream of interruptions by Adam's business connections.

Finally, much to her relief, a bell sounded, summoning the crowd to a large triple-height gallery that had been set up for the benefit auction. Adam revealed flawless manners as he seated her at the table sponsored by Kingdom close to the stage, before taking his seat beside her.

Good. Finally they would get a chance to get to know each other.

Georgia smiled a greeting at the others at the table. Roberta was already there, accompanied by a heart-stoppingly handsome man. Then Georgia recognized him.

"Blake. Blake John Williams." She laughed as he rose to his feet. "How long it's been!"

He came from one of New York's wealthiest families. Was he the reason for her sister's recent surge in texting activity?

Marcia Hall was sandwiched between Roberta and Charis, who had—surprisingly—come alone. Charis looked amazing in a traffic-stopping dress covered with a riot of beaded flowers. It was nothing like the elegant garments Charis usually wore. Georgia had never seen anything like it. It definitely wasn't her sister's work. But Charis had discovered some exciting new talent. Once photos got out, the unsuspecting designer was going to be mobbed with orders.

Two other couples filled out their numbers at the table.

As the meal progressed, the conversation predictably turned to fashion. Adam was exchanging small talk with Roberta's date. Georgia's gaze strayed to the table where the bachelors were sitting. Jay was seated at the farthest end, head tipped to the side in a pose Georgia knew so well. Another of the bachelors leaned across and said something that made Jay smile, and he laughed as a third chipped in.

Georgia felt her own mood lighten.

When Jay laughed, he was utterly, irresistibly wicked. If he laughed like that when his turn came to be auctioned, he would have no problem winning a more than desirable figure.

Her glance flicked across to Charis. How far would Charis need to go? But her sister was staring fixedly at the floral arrangement in front of her. Whatever Charis was thinking about wasn't making her happy. Georgia's own heart ached in response. Their father's rejection must be killing her sister.

For the first time in years, Georgia wished she and Charis were closer.

"A glass of champagne?" Adam offered.

It reminded her of Jay's joke about sharing a bottle if she bid on him—and won—him tonight.

Georgia came back to earth.

"Yes, please." She smiled, and the wine waiter at her elbow filled her glass.

"Excuse me for a moment." Adam pushed his chair back. "There's someone I must talk to—I'll be back shortly."

As he left, Georgia glanced back to where Jay sat to one side of the stage. He was chuckling at the antics of the first bachelor getting ready to be auctioned off.

As though he felt the pressure of her stare, Jay turned his head and met her gaze. His laughter froze.

A sharp pang pierced her chest, causing Georgia to draw a quick breath. What was this? She couldn't be jealous of the woman who'd win him...

How ridiculous.

Jay was her rival. A perpetual thorn in her side.

Their relationship was...complicated. Confusing.

But he made her laugh.

And in those unguarded moments, she forgot about her fears. She even forgot about the terror of not being enough.

But Jay wasn't laughing now. His gaze was boring into hers. He alone knew the stakes that faced her tonight, and the magnitude of the decision she'd made. Tomorrow, her world would be different. She'd have Adam.

She'd no longer be alone.

And after tonight's benefit auction, some other woman would be sharing a dinner date and laughing with Jay.

Georgia acknowledged the truth: she envied the mystery woman that carefree, frivolous experience.

One of the other bachelors tapped his shoulder, and Jay's fierce focus shifted, breaking the bond between them. He got up and headed for the stage.

When Jay leaped up the stairs two at a time, and sauntered into the spotlight, Georgia found herself tracking his long strides. He finally stopped and turned to face the crowded gallery, dimples slashing his cheeks as he grinned and adopted a pose so typical of Jay: legs spread apart, hands on his hips, head tilted back. Confident. Arrogant.

Of course, it only served to show off the superb cut of his tuxedo—and the lean body beneath. A charge pulsed through the crowd as the female half of the audience swooned.

The opening bid came quickly from Georgia's left.

Xia. A top fashion blogger. She and Jay had dated a while back. The relationship had fizzled out, but it had led to some fantastic product exposure for Kingdom on Xia's blog. Roberta still raved about the Xia Factor.

"Come, ladies, get out those checkbooks." The auctioneer was extolling Jay's virtues. Cameras flashed.

This was Charis's cue.

Georgia glanced across the table—but the chair Charis had occupied only minutes before was empty. Roberta was no help, either—she was conversing with her date, their heads close together. Quickly, Georgia scanned the gallery. There was no sign of Charis's stunning dress anywhere. Where had her sister gone?

From the lofty height of the stage, Jay's gaze met hers. His eyes were narrowed in challenge.

Of its own volition, her hand lifted.

"Is that a bid?" the auctioneer asked.

Georgia nodded.

Somewhere at a table behind Georgia, a woman whooped with excitement. Her girlfriends giggled, urging her on. Georgia turned in her chair and watched as a gorgeous platinum blonde, poured into a glittering red dress and sporting heavily mascaraed lashes that were too long to possibly be real, raised her hand to place a bid.

An unfamiliar tension curled through Georgia.

She narrowed her eyes. The woman didn't look like Jay's type—too glamorous. Too blond. Then it struck her: as much as she and Jay snarked and argued, she didn't really know what Jay's type was. Xia was beautiful in an exotic kind of way. Then there'd been a willowy fashion model: Dominique, if she remembered correctly. And there'd been a couple of others who had lasted little more than a couple of months. Nic and Carrie. Georgia couldn't believe she remembered their names.

Jay's girlfriends never seemed to last long.

There were no photos of any women in his office. Come to think of it, there were no photos of any description.

She told herself that Jay deserved better. She told herself that Kingdom contributed to the Bachelors for a Better Future Benefit Auction every year. She told herself a lot of things. And she even told herself that it was irrelevant how much fun it might be to call a truce on their rivalry and to spend a carefree evening enjoying laughter and a little champagne.

All the while, Jay's grin taunted her, daring her to do it.

She'd make it quick. Georgia drew a deep breath. "Ten thousand dollars."

Satisfaction filled her at the sudden silence that followed.

Xia was undeterred. "Eleven thousand."

"Twelve thousand." The glamorous blonde in the too-tight dress.

"Twelve and a half." Xia again.

"Thirteen." Glam sounded smug.

Xia shrugged, graciously giving in. Glam grinned, certain of her win.

"Bids?" The auctioneer called. "Ladies! Spoil yourself. You owe it to yourself to have a great evening for a good cause with this fine specimen of manhood here."

Sounds blurred around her. Lights flashed. Adam rejoined the table, sinking back into the chair beside her, and she only spared him one glance—glimpsing his dark frowning face—before swinging her attention back to the stage. Jay was worth blowing the whole budget on. After all, it was for a good cause.

"Fifteen thousand." Her voice rang out, loud to her own ears.

"Sixteen," Glam came back instantly.

Fifteen thousand was the agreed budget. Georgia barely hesitated. She didn't want that woman winning Jay for the night.

"Twenty thousand."

On the stage, Jay stopped grinning, and his eyes locked with hers.

"Twenty-two."

Glam wasn't giving up.

"Twenty-five thousand dollars," Georgia said with grim finality.

"That's more than we allocated from the marketing budget for tonight's event," Roberta chided from across the table as the auctioneer crowed, "Gone."

Georgia didn't spare her sister a glance; she was too busy trying to read the unfathomable expression on Jay's face. Was that a hint of satisfaction? Or a fresh challenge? But she replied, without needing to think too much, "It will be worth it—and it should make a splash in the fashion magazines and the wider media. There are enough cameras here tonight—plus it's tax deductible."

"It will need a fair amount of press coverage," Adam broke in, "to recoup that kind of expenditure."

"Leave it to me." Roberta was grinning. "I'll make sure I organize photos of Jay and Georgia wearing plenty of Kingdom loot in an A-list dining location that will get us the best kind of exposure."

Before Georgia could respond, Adam said, "Georgia, I'd like a word with you. Alone."

Seven

Georgia was conscious of Jay's eyes boring into the back of her head as she picked up her clutch, slung its delicate silver chain over her shoulder and rose from the table. Adam's hand rested on the base of her spine, and a commanding pressure guided her forward.

A set of doors led to a glass-enclosed balcony that ran along the length of the gallery. Georgia knew that once she stepped over that threshold, her relationship with Adam would change forever.

But she told herself this was what she wanted. She could salvage what she'd worked so hard to attain by marrying Adam. She would be President and CEO of Kingdom one day.

Why should she allow Jay's cautions to spoil her vision of the future?

Drawing a deep breath, Georgia stepped forward.

Beyond the glass walls, the cityscape glittered.

Adam's hand slid down her bare arm and came to rest against her hand. His fingers were cool, his touch curiously impersonal, despite the skin-to-skin contact.

Mr. Ice.

Unbidden, Jay's description of Adam leaped into her

mind. Georgia fought to block it out. *Not now.* Not when she needed to focus on Adam, focus on building a rapport with the man.

They were going to be partners. Intimate partners. In business. In marriage. In everything...

"What a beautiful night," she said.

Adam got straight to the point. "Your father has spoken to you—you know why we're here."

She nodded mutely.

This was it, the moment when her life changed. Georgia half expected the earth to move.

"What exactly is your relationship with Jay Black?"

What? She goggled at him. "Jay and I work together."

Adam arched his eyebrow in response.

"We're colleagues. We... We're responsible for a lot of Kingdom's strategic planning," she found herself stuttering. The antagonism and secret rivalry between her and Jay was something she didn't care to share, but Adam needed to understand that Jay was central to Kingdom's success. "And he's my father's right-hand man."

"Women don't bid twenty-five thousand dollars on a colleague."

"You heard Roberta. It was nothing more than a PR stunt."

Except it had felt way more personal than that...

Before she could marshal her scattered thoughts, Adam was already reaching into the pocket of his dinner jacket.

"I've got something for you."

"Oh?"

He drew a small square box from the pocket of his suit jacket. "I think you'll like it." He flipped the box open. "It has all three *c*'s—cut, clarity and color. Four, if you add carat. It's as good an investment as a diamond can be."

Investment. The ring sparkled up at her.

"Try it on."

Georgia slowly took the ring from the box.

"It's impressive." Then, in case that sounded too clinical, she added, "It's magnificent."

The ring was magnificent…in an icy classic kind of way. Was this how Adam perceived her? Flawless and glittering? The perfect trophy wife?

As good of an investment as a woman could be?

And why not? Her father measured her worth in the same terms.

"We will be married next June."

A summer wedding…

But instead of a warm wave of pleasure, Georgia felt flustered at his haste. He was talking of wedding arrangements already. What had happened to courtship? To getting to know each other? He'd taken her assent for granted. Was that her father's doing? Had he assured Adam she would not object?

Anger started to smolder deep within her heart. *Fine!* She'd let Adam find out who she was through negotiations—nothing new to her about that.

"We'll need to hammer out a prenup first." She spoke carefully, giving herself time to think and get her emotions under control.

"Sure." He shrugged. "But we already have an agreement in principle."

He stepped forward and his hands slid around her shoulders. He was tall—well over six feet. And solid. His chest rose like a fortress in front of her.

Reaching out a hand, she placed it on the wall of hard muscle that blocked out the light around her. Adam tensed. Panic crushed her. For an awful moment, Georgia felt… trapped.

She fought the suffocating claustrophobia that had come out of nowhere.

Deep breaths, she cautioned herself. It was okay. She

was okay. Or she would be, as soon as she pulled herself together.

Adam was going to kiss her...

She couldn't afford to screw this up. It had to work. And it was up to her to make sure it did.

She turned her face up and closed her eyes, dreading what was coming.

When his lips landed, they were firm...and cool. Adam Fordyce kissed with technique. That, at least, was a relief.

Yet, instead of being swept away by lust, as she should have been, Georgia found herself waiting...

And waiting.

For what, she wasn't sure. Whatever it was didn't happen.

He slid his hands along her back and pressed her closer. Out of nowhere came a stab of stark terror. She went as stiff as a board.

He raised his head.

"Nice," she choked out.

Made of ice, she found herself thinking.

Damn Jay! And why was she thinking of Jay, anyway? Or the coffee-flavored kiss full of care and tenderness he'd bestowed on her yesterday...?

The memory of their too-short moments of warmth and comfort in the garden's pale sunshine contrasted with the darkness that surrounded Adam. She pulled away a little more.

"Yes."

It took Georgia a scattered moment to realize that Adam was agreeing with her assessment of that cold kiss as *nice*.

In the dim light, she couldn't read his expression. It might've helped ease the tension in her stomach, the thunder in her head. She drew a slow steadying breath.

Nice.

She'd lied.

And the earth hadn't moved.

Beyond the glass walls, the buildings dominating the skyline stood glittering and silent. Nothing had changed.

Only the hammering of her heart.

She immediately grew impatient with her own reaction. Why should the earth have moved? She wasn't some teen princess with grandiose expectations anymore. She was a grown-up woman, with a hotshot position on the executive team at an iconic fashion house. Hey, she knew that the earth didn't move because of a kiss. That fireworks and glass slippers and golden rings forever were nothing more than fantasy. She understood reality. Adam was a real man—not a fairy tale prince.

She and Adam shared a common vision: commercial success.

It was a start—they would build on it.

She couldn't afford to think about the urge to flee; she wouldn't think about Ridley…and she wouldn't think of Jay. She had to think of Kingdom.

"Very nice," she amended, trying harder. *Throw more heart in, Georgia.* They would both have to work on this. She'd do more than her bit. Like she always did.

Georgia tried to forget that moment of panic when he'd taken her into his arms, that sensation of being trapped and crushed, that terrifying spike of adrenaline. It had come out of the blackness at the bottom of her brain… It had happened before, when she thought of Ridley, of that moment she'd walked into the hotel suite and found him with a sales assistant on the bed. While the woman had struggled to get her dress back on, Ridley had lit into Georgia, telling her it was her fault. She didn't have what it took to hold a man.

And after that, a big dark blank…

Not now. Please not now.

So she filled her lungs with air, and tried to smile at Adam.

If she tried a little harder, if she invested some more enthusiasm, it might ignite some magic. But searching for the positive side was hard work.

Especially when she longed for Jay. For the barbs and banter that had become so familiar. At least she knew where she stood with him. Most of the time. She longed to use him as a sounding board to clear this confusion that kissing Adam had evoked. To clear the sudden doubt she was experiencing...

Grow up, Georgia.

This is your life. Nothing to do with Jay...

Another thought struck her. Had Adam's cold kiss been intended to seal the execution of an agreement? Had it been that calculated?

She was a person, dammit. Someone with emotions and dreams, who possessed a heart, as well as a brain.

"There are some..." *terms* was too unromantic a word, Georgia decided "...things we need to discuss before I agree."

"Things?"

She shrugged, feeling unaccountably foolish. *Negotiate.* She gritted her teeth. "How this marriage is going to work."

"It'll work like any other marriage."

From nowhere, Jay's voice flashed into her head. *And plenty have ended in bitterness and acrimony. Don't you want more out of life than a billion-dollar divorce settlement?*

"Really?" She arched her eyebrows. "Most people don't marry for the reasons we will be marrying." *Most couples are in love, actually.* But of course, she didn't say that.

"So what things do you want to discuss?"

Now she felt even more idiotic. But Jay's sweet kiss of comfort in the hospital garden yesterday had let a whole lot of emotions out of the box. What with her father's dramas, and now this.... Boy, over the past few days, she'd discovered emotions she hadn't even known existed.

"Uh…how we will communicate—"

She broke off. Adam was staring at her as though she were crazy.

"How we will communicate?" he repeated. "Like most people do, I should think."

She could feel herself flushing. She tried again, "I'm talking about…"

Sex.

Adam's face darkened.

For a moment, she thought he understood.

But then he swung away from her, presenting her with a broad shoulder. Half his face was in shadow. The ring she still clutched mocked her. She caught a flash of cold fire and glanced quickly away, reluctant to fit it on her finger yet.

Turning back to face her, he spoke again. "You're aware of my relationship with Charis?"

Georgia sighed a small sigh of relief. It was too soon to be discussing intimate details—his change of subject was a good idea. Rapidly, she reviewed which of Charis's current projects Adam might be involved with. She drew a blank. "I didn't know you and Charis had any business dealings."

"My relationship with Charis has nothing to do with business." There was a husky undertone to his voice, a smoky heat in his eyes that belied his nickname.

That caught Georgia's attention. On rewind, her sister's silence this evening played through her mind, and understanding dawned in a flash. "Oh, my God. You're talking about a personal relationship, aren't you?"

Adam stared back at her, unblinking.

There was an instant of disbelief.

Then the outrageous idea coalesced into certainty. "You're lovers!"

The silence stretched as she waited—in vain—for a denial that never came. Tightness bubbled at the back of her throat as she thought about the kiss he'd given her while her sister sat inside the ballroom.

"Uh…the relationship is over?"

Of course, it must be. She couldn't believe she was even asking.

Otherwise—

His silence took on the quality of cold forged steel.

Otherwise…how could he possibly propose to her? Or kiss her? Her stomach twisted, a sick sensation filling it as the silence grew colder.

Georgia held up the glittering diamond engagement ring he'd given her like a talisman. "It's over as of now. Right?"

Adam's head jerked back. "That ring changes nothing. You need to understand that our marriage will not change my relationship with Charis—that's non-negotiable."

"You mean…you're going to…" she broke off, seeking a sanitized way of uttering the unspeakable "…you're going to keep…" *sleeping with* "…seeing…my sister while you're married to me?"

"I'm glad you understand."

Understand? Georgia stared at him. Had she gone completely crazy? Or was he crazy?

"So," she drawled, her brain working overtime to catch up, "you've discussed this with my sister? She knows you'll be married to me, even while you sleep with her?"

He gazed at her through slitted eyes, his face an iron mask. "Charis will do exactly as I want."

What he wanted was to marry Georgia and sleep with her sister. Have his cake and eat it. Bile rose at the back of her throat. Georgia's heart ached. For Charis…and for herself. The situation was ghastly beyond anything she'd ever contemplated.

Finally, she said, "So I guess our marriage will be in name only."

Adam didn't reply.

A numbing emptiness invaded her. Was this what she wanted? A marriage that was nothing more than a business arrangement? Marriage to a man who was sleeping with her sister?

You deserve more...

Jay was right. This travesty wasn't what she wanted.

"I want children," she said at last. The thought uncurled out of the secret mists of her mind. It was something she'd never contemplated, but which had always been there. Except she hadn't known it existed.

Adam was saying something. She hadn't heard a word of it.

"What?"

He spoke again, slowly, as though she were simple. "A child is no problem."

"No problem?" She tried to grasp what he meant by that. "You mean IVF, right?"

"There are easier solutions." His voice dropped, each word softly clipped.

Her whole being rocked as the words sunk in.

"Easier solutions?" she echoed the heresy he'd uttered and stared at him, shocked. He didn't just mean to marry her and sleep with Charis—he meant to sleep with them both! "But..."

How would her sister feel about that?

Certainty settled in fast. Jay was right. Adam Fordyce truly was made of ice. There was no humanity in the man who stood before her, his eyes so dead. Nothing. Jay might be maddening and infuriating. But at least he still had feelings. Emotions. This man had none.

Amoral asshat!

Poor Charis.

No wonder her sister had looked so miserable.

But Georgia knew how she felt about it. And that made her decision easy.

She handed the ring back to him.

Damn. Jay had been right. Again.

"I can't marry you, Adam. I'm sorry."

Why was she apologizing?

"Your father—"

Georgia shook her head. "No. Not even for my father."

He stared icily down his long straight nose at her. "Sleep on it."

Nausea rose in her throat at his phrasing.

"Keep the ring." His confidence was staggering.

She shook her head and thrust it back at him.

"At least take the weekend to think it over. Once you've had a chance to think about it, you'll realize there's no point throwing away everything we'll have together." He smiled. But the thin smile didn't reach his remote colorless eyes. "Call me on Monday morning—we'll talk some more. This is going to work."

Georgia knew she was going to be sick.

"Shall we go back in?"

Unable to speak, Georgia nodded. She hitched the chain of her clutch higher up on her shoulder. His hand rested lightly on her hip as he escorted her toward the gallery filled with chatter and laughter.

A sideways glance revealed that he was smiling, a hard savage smile.

"I need to go to the cloakroom." And then she needed to find Jay. He was the one person she could rely on to help her.

Without a backward glance, she left Mr. Ice standing alone on the threshold of the crowded room.

Georgia slunk into the ladies' room. Beyond tall urns overflowing with fragrant lilies and a velvet-covered chaise, she spotted a familiar exquisitely beaded gown.

Charis.

Her sister had seen her enter and was watching her in an ornately framed gilded mirror.

Despite her inner upheaval, Georgia flicked her a quick awkward smile. But Charis didn't smile back.

"Your lipstick is smudged." Her sister's face was pale and tight.

"Oh." Georgia flushed, and humiliation crawled through her. Damn Adam for putting her in this situation! She extracted Jay's crumpled handkerchief from the clutch slung over her shoulder and rubbed frantically at her mouth.

"It's fine now." Charis's voice was flat.

Nothing was fine. God, this was awkward. "We need to talk."

Charis's gaze shifted to her own reflection. She pursed her lips into a moue. "Come hell or high water, I'm going to finish the spring collection if it kills me."

"Father doesn't want you in the build—"

"He doesn't need to know!"

Georgia started to argue, then thought better of it.

"Why didn't you say you were dating Adam Fordyce when Kingston made his announcement?"

"I don't want to talk about it."

"Charis—" Georgia broke off, searching for an easy way to say this. "Listen, I'm not going to marry him—"

"Have you told that to our dear father?"

"No." Georgia's stomach seized up at the thought. "But I will."

"Good luck with that." Charis tossed the soiled towel in the disposal slot.

Then, for the first time since Georgia had entered the cloakroom, her sister swung around to face her.

"He won't let you back out."

She wasn't sure whether her sister meant their father or Adam Fordyce.

Tonelessly, Charis added, "You're welcome to Adam."

Georgia said in a rush, "I don't want him. Adam Fordyce makes me sick!"

"Then that makes two of us." There was such savagery in Charis's voice that Georgia recoiled.

Jay's provocative question rang in her head. *You'd marry a man you've never met, a man your father picked out for his ability to run Kingdom? Why?*

It had seemed so clear-cut, so logical.

Until Adam had kissed her...and then, to her appalled shame, her body had taken over...and the reaction had not been good. She'd found herself thinking of Jay...

So she'd turned Adam down. For the first time in her life, she'd gone against her father's wishes.

Once Kingston found out...

Georgia shuddered with dread.

But her father didn't know what she'd done. Not yet.

She felt a flare of hope. There had to be a solution. A way to keep her father happy...and keep her position safe. An overwhelming desire to talk to Jay filled her. Jay always gave her perspective. He had the ability to ask questions that made the solutions to whatever was bothering her so obvious.

She glanced at Charis. Her sister was blotting her lips with a tissue. She looked composed...but ghostly pale.

"Are you okay?"

Charis's eyes were dark and distant. "Why wouldn't I be? I have a collection to finish. I'm going to make it the biggest success Kingdom has ever seen. Then I'm going to live my life—without all the never-ending drama that comes attached to Kingdom."

Georgia wanted to argue—to convince Charis that Kingdom was what kept them together. Kept them family. She ached for what might've been. For all the years that had been lost. But Charis was clearly in no mood for a heart-to-heart.

She touched Charis's arm. "I don't suppose you know where Jay is?"

Charis shook her off. "He went home."

"Home?" Georgia realized she didn't even know where Jay lived. No matter. Bruno would know.

"He's flying out on vacation." Her sister opened the cloakroom door.

"No he's not!"

Georgia grabbed her clutch. Jay wasn't going anywhere. Not until he'd helped her sort this mess out.

Eight

It was already after midnight.

Jay had just finished packing the last white profession-ally pressed T-shirt into his bag and was about to zip it shut in readiness for his early morning flight when the doorbell chimed. Before he had a chance to react, it sounded again.

"Hold your horses!" He strode through the apartment and yanked open the front door.

Georgia stood in front of him.

To catch his breath, Jay leaned against the doorjamb and folded his arms across his chest. Even as he examined her, he prayed she wouldn't detect the sudden drumroll in his chest.

Jay didn't bother to ask how she'd gotten past the door-man; Georgia on a mission could achieve anything she set her mind to.

Under her evening coat, she was still wearing the midnight blue couture slip dress she'd worn to the benefit auction—and she clung to the silver-sequined Kingdom clutch that Jay had recognized from last fall's collection. Her silver-blond hair was still drawn off her face in a stylish knot although several tendrils had escaped, adding to her air of fragility. The stark simplicity of the look was broken only by the stunning pair of art deco diamond drop earrings he knew were her sole legacy from her mother...and a stain of red on her lips.

His gaze narrowed. Her lipstick was slightly smudged around the edges, showing signs of hasty repair. Her lips were full, ripe. Kissed.

Jay suppressed the surge of raw emotion that shook him. He might not know where she'd been, but he had a damned good idea who she'd been with...

"What do you want, Georgia?"

"May I come in?"

Cocking his wrist, he glanced at his watch. "It's late."

"You promised to share a bottle of champagne with me if I bid on you—so here I am."

Too late for champagne now, too late for the intimate tête-à-tête he'd planned to soften her outrage. He thought of all the great intentions he'd had to tell Georgia the truth.

But now it was too late to confess that he'd lied from the outset. That he'd never been recruited to fill the position Ridley—her errant fiancé—had left vacant at Kingdom. While she'd been recovering from a car crash that had sheared away a portion of her memory, he'd taken advantage of being in the right place at the right time so that he could have second chance to get to know her better.

He risked another glance at her tempting strawberry-red lips as the dreams that had sustained him for two years turned to dust.

He should've told her the truth, instead of being such a damned coward.

But he hadn't—and now it was too goddamned late.

There was no point in discussing the night they'd first met—a night she'd long since forgotten. Why open an old wound that held so much trauma for her? There was no point in convincing her to give him a chance to start over. Georgia was lost to him.

She'd followed her father's orders.

Yet, still, Jay found himself unable to resist the inexorable force that caused him to step back, allowing her space to pass and enter his apartment, even though the tightness in his lower gut warned him this was a dumb idea. Despite an urge to slam it, he shut the door with a dull click.

She shrugged off her coat, and he hung it up on one of the coat hooks that lined the hall alcove.

He flat-handed a control panel on the wall as he passed by, and the apartment exploded into bright light. Now was not the time for dim mood lighting. He waved her into the living space ahead of him. At the island of Carrara marble that functioned as a dining table and divided the streamlined butler-style kitchen from the lounge, he stopped, keeping the slab between them.

He didn't want her anywhere near him—not now, looking so well-kissed by another man.

A man she intended marry…for Kingdom's sake.

"You want a drink?" He sure needed one. "Tequila?"

Her shoulders hunched. "Not tequila!"

Stop being an ass, Black!

"What about a glass of that champagne you offered earlier?" Her brightness sounded forced.

He was in no mood to celebrate. Instead, he said, "How about coffee?"

"Much as I'd love a cup, the caffeine will keep me awake."

Jay clawed a bottle of whiskey out of the liquor cabinet and poured two stiff fingers of amber liquid into a tumbler. The time had come for him to cut his losses. To leave Kingdom, the cold corporation that had chained Georgia's soul. To find some distant place to lick his wounds in peace—preferably across a wide stretch of ocean.

London. Paris. Sydney.

Whatever. He certainly had no intention of dancing at Georgia's high society New York wedding.

For the first time, he was grateful that he'd be out of town for the next couple of weeks.

The tumbler thudded against the marble. He reached for a second glass, poured in a shot and pushed it across the slab to her. "Why did you come here?"

She set her glitzy clutch down and faced him across the sleek black-veined slab, her eyes unexpectedly shadowed. "I need…advice."

"Has something happened?" Giving a silent snort of derision, he picked up his glass and swirled the whiskey around the glass when she didn't answer.

Dammit, he could see what had happened. It didn't take a genius to work it out.

Genius? He was an ass!

He contemplated her over the lip of his glass. "It's Fordyce, isn't it?"

She nodded. "He asked—or, should I say, expected—me to marry him."

No surprise there.

"Congratulations." Jay took a slug of whiskey, set the half-empty glass down and wiped the back of his hand across his mouth to stop himself from swearing violently.

His pain would go away. Someday. On his deathbed.

Georgia leaned toward him and spread her hands out on the marble countertop. "Do you see a ring?"

He stared at her fourth finger.

It was bare.

The breath left his lungs, and his gaze skittered across the marble before rising to her face. "You turned him down?"

"Stone cold."

Stepping around the cold sleek slab, all he could see was the fullness of her bottom lip. "But you kissed him."

"*He* kissed *me*."

Under the stain of strawberry-red lipstick, her mouth

was trembling. The tip of her tongue slid along the inside of her lip, and he wrenched his eyes away.

"I couldn't go through with it."

She was pale, her eyes stricken. What the hell had caused her to look so wounded? Instead of a surge of triumph, Jay quelled an overpowering desire to go and hunt Adam Fordyce down. To pummel the tycoon to a pulp with his bare fists. Leashing his rage, he asked levelly, "What happened?"

Georgia wrapped her arms around herself and rubbed her palms over her bare shoulders. "You say he's made of ice. You're wrong—he's colder than ice."

Jay clenched his hands into fists at his sides. There wasn't a trace of ice within him. Only a raging molten heat.

"What did he do?"

"Nothing. He didn't hurt me—at least not physically." She shivered and goose bumps rose on her arms. "Sticks and stones—it's not true."

What the hell?

"Tell me!" Jay insisted.

She shook her head and winced. Uncrossing her arms, she smoothed her hands over her face, over her hair, coming to a stop as she encountered the topknot. "My head hurts too much."

Restraining his impatience to know what Fordyce had said to rattle her so deeply, Jay murmured, "Your hair is tied too tight. Take out those pins."

He moved so close that he could see the flecks of silver in her bewildered eyes. His fingers were already unclenching to help her. Her hair came down in a swath of soft silk. Jay's fingers tangled in the silver mass, threading through it, combing it until it fell around her face.

"Better?" he asked as gently as he could.

She nodded. "Jay, I'm so glad you were home."

Unexpectedly, she leaned forward to rest her forehead against his chest.

Jay went rigid with shock. He forced his hands down to his sides. She nestled against him, tucked against the white fabric of his dress shirt, while his heart rattled an erratic tattoo beneath. It was hard to remember that Georgia never liked being touched, that she held herself separate, distant. But not now. Not tonight.

If he bent his head, his lips would touch the fine silver hair—

Fool!

One. Breathe in.

Two. Out.

All Georgia wanted was a confidant. A little comfort. She'd had one hell of a week. He needed to keep reminding himself of that simple fact, until his moronic body got the message.

She lifted her face. "Can I ask you something?"

His hands wrapped into fists to stop himself from touching her.

"You can ask," he said warily.

"Is…is—" she stammered. "This is harder than I thought it would be."

Uh-huh. "What?"

"Um—"

"Spit it out!"

She bit her lip, and a pink flush warmed her cheeks. "Do you have a dream woman?"

He felt himself flush in turn. Saw her eyes register his discomfort.

"Oh," she said.

He felt awkward and exposed. "What nonsense is this?"

"Charis is your dream woman?" she asked.

"Charis?" It was the last thing he'd expected her to say. "My sister."

"I know who Charis is," he growled.

Jay held back a curse. The woman he wanted was far from a dream. She was real. Flesh and blood. And she was cuddled up against him. Yet he didn't trust himself to touch her.

"Jay?"

There was a strange expression in Georgia's eyes. Was that yearning he read there? Or was he indulging in another futile fantasy?

"No," he finally said, "Charis is not my dream woman."

"I'm so glad to hear that."

His heart thumped in his chest, and he silently cursed the leap of hope. "What's this about?"

"So there's no chance that you might want to marry Charis?"

"I've answered that before." He knew he sounded terse. "Why all these questions?"

"Adam and Charis are lovers." She dropped her head down, and her voice was muffled by his shirtfront again. "I didn't want you to get hurt…if you felt something for Charis."

Jay almost laughed. Jesus…what a royal screwup Kingston had made.

"Did Fordyce tell you that?"

"It was obvious—and he didn't deny it when I blurted it out. It gets worse." She sucked in a deep shuddering breath. "I thought he was telling me their affair was over. He'd just proposed to me—if one could call it that. Whatever it was, he'd given me a ring. Stupid me." Her whole frame shook against him. "God, I was wrong. So wrong." Another shiver went through her, and she buried her face deeper against him. "Adam told me he would continue to sleep with my sister…that it wouldn't interfere with our marriage."

Damn Fordyce!

"I didn't even know Charis was seeing him."

Georgia's hurt and bewilderment hung between them, and Jay couldn't think of a single platitude that might ease her pain. Finally, he allowed his fists to uncurl and let his arms steal up around her. Bowing his head over hers, Jay couldn't escape the soft feminine scent of her. To his horror, blood rushed to his groin.

"How did you respond?" His voice was husky.

Georgia's head came up so quickly that his lips brushed across her forehead. She pulled back a little, putting space between them, and his arms fell away.

Had she felt his arousal? God, he hoped not.

"What do you think I did? I told him I couldn't marry him." Her chin came up. "I told him I needed the bathroom—I felt sick."

Jay forgot his own dilemma. He snorted. "You actually told him that? That he made you sick?"

"Not quite." For the first time, a spark of her familiar feistiness showed through her anguish. "Trust me, there was nothing funny about it."

"I'm not laughing." But he felt a rush of very male satisfaction. In all their barbed exchanges, he might have annoyed her, frustrated her, but he'd never made Georgia sick…

"I ran into Charis in the ladies' room." Her words tripped over each other. "I don't understand her. I don't think I ever have."

The pain that underpinned her confession made Jay swallow. God help Fordyce when he found the man…

"She told me she intends to be part of the launch of the spring collection—and to hell with whether Kingston lets her or not."

"Well, I suppose that's one bit of good news."

His response didn't help.

"It's not! I don't think she intends to stay at Kingdom. She didn't even want to talk to me. She's always been as stubborn as a mule. She even told me I was welcome to Adam—and then she picked up her purse and walked out." Georgia gulped in a deep breath. "I couldn't bring myself to go back into the ballroom, but Adam was waiting for me in the lobby. That's when I got really scared because he looked so terrifying. He said I had to marry him, it was all arranged—" She broke off.

The wild despair in her eyes tore his heart out.

Under his intense scrutiny, Georgia colored. "So I ran."

"To me."

"It was run to you...or throw up that five-hundred-dollar-a-plate dinner onto his highly polished handmade shoes."

That was his Georgia!

Something like euphoria made him feel as high as a kite. He stepped forward and took her into his arms. It felt...right.

"You don't have to do anything you don't want."

She sighed. "Just hold me, Jay. Please?"

God.

Torn between the need to give her the comfort she craved and his fear of what might happen next, Jay shuddered. There was no way he could disguise the effect her closeness was having on his body. But there was no chance that he'd resist her request.

Even if it cost him his peace of mind.

When his phone buzzed in his pocket, Jay cursed silently at the sudden tensing of Georgia's body.

"Is it Kingston?" she whispered, her fear tangible. "Charis?"

The spell was broken.

Jay moved away and pulled his phone out.

"It's my mother."

"Answer it—something may be wrong."

He bit down on a tide of four-letter words. Against his better judgment, Jay accepted the call.

His mom was loud and enthusiastic. He made himself wink at Georgia as he waited for his mother to run out of steam, and as soon as she slowed down, he said, "Mom, I'll call you back later. I'm in the middle of something."

"You work too hard, Jay. You should consider coming home. Permanently."

He didn't intend to have that discussion right now—not with Georgia watching, and a hard-on to end all hard-ons filling his pants. "Mom—"

"It would make your father so happy. And Suzie is looking forward to seeing you again. We all are. You've been gone too long."

He was relieved to hear that Suzie actually wanted to see him again. Georgia shifted from one high-heel clad foot to the other in obvious discomfort. Before he could smile at her, she drifted farther into his apartment, clearly intent on giving him some privacy.

"Mom, I have to go. I have someone with me." He cut off her rush of questions. "I'll see you tomorrow."

Jay killed the call and went in pursuit of Georgia.

Through an open door, Georgia spotted what had to be Jay's bedroom.

The enormous windows on the opposite wall framed the brightly lit city skyline.

Wow!

Fascination drove her into the room. It was decorated in shades of navy and dull gold brightened with an ivory knit throw draped across the bed. Over the headboard hung an abstract canvas full of stormy movement, dominated by midnight blues and inky grays, a narrow shaft of light piercing the dark turmoil.

Then she spotted the open steamer bag beside the bed. The sight drove all other thoughts out of her head.

She heard footsteps behind her.

Without taking her eyes off the bag, she asked, "When exactly do you leave?"

"First thing in the morning."

Georgia wished she could escape like Jay. Fly away. Go home to a family where everything was simple and uncomplicated. Before she could stop herself, she found herself saying, "Can I come with you?"

"What?"

Trying not to feel foolish, she considered pretending she'd been joking—as Jay had been when he'd invited her to marry him. But the impulsive idea wouldn't go away...

In a rush, she said, "I could check online and see if there are still seats available..." Her voice trailed away when she got no response. Maybe it was a stupid idea. "We don't even need to sit together."

"Why?"

At last, she turned to him.

He stood a couple of feet behind her. The dark intensity in his eyes unsettled her.

"Why don't we need to sit together?" By deliberately misunderstanding his question, she tried to inject some humor into an exchange that had grown astonishingly awkward.

For the first time, she became aware that it was well past midnight...that she was standing in his bedroom...that several buttons of his rumpled shirt were undone, revealing the chest she'd buried her head against. And his feet were bare. It was intimate. They were asking for trouble.

Yet, she wasn't the least bit afraid.

This was Jay...

Although she had to admit, after the auction earlier tonight, she was seeing him in a different light. He was a very attractive man. It would be all too easy to fall for him.

But Jay had never had any interest in her. She simply wasn't his type.

Jay still hadn't smiled. "Why would you want to come with me?"

"I need a break."

God, she hoped she didn't sound like she was begging, but she was at the end of her tether.

"You want to avoid your father," he said slowly.

"No," she denied too fiercely. She looked down, away from that penetrating gaze. "I just need to leave." Escape. Her father was going to kill her when he found out she'd turned Adam down.

The air vibrated with her desperation.

Jay blew out a breath in an explosive gust that sounded loud to her ears. "Georgia, you have to tell your father that you're not going to marry Adam."

"I know. I know. I will." *Someday.* "Just not yet."

Jay went silent again. From under her eyelashes, Georgia watched him, trying to read his thoughts. He must be thinking she was the biggest coward on earth.

As the seconds passed, the mounting tension started to get to her. Even taunts and rivalry were better than his silence.

Well, she'd better get used to it. Jay was going to be gone for two weeks.

It would mean two weeks without his heckling. Without his laughter and lame jokes. Without that crooked smile at her office door each morning…and two take-out coffees in his hands. Without someone to argue with and bounce her ideas off—and share the triumph of success with. The place was going to be dead without him.

She swallowed, stunned at how forlorn she felt.

Somehow, Jay Black had become so much more than

a threatening rival. More than a colleague to collaborate with.

An astonishing realization struck her.

Jay had become a friend.

A friend she could turn to for support...and comfort. She remembered the electric brush of his lips against hers. That had been something more than friendship...

No!

She couldn't afford any disturbing thoughts about Jay. He was her friend. Better to have him as a friend than a lover who would betray her at the first opportunity.

She gazed at him, silently imploring.

Jay thrust his hands through his hair, causing the espresso-brown strands to stand up untidily. "Georgia, it's my parents' wedding anniversary—"

"You're right. I'd be party-crashing." Embarrassment seared her.

"It's nothing like that." He gave her a long look. "But you'd be better off facing up to your father."

Watching Jay cross the room and hunker down to zip the steamer bag shut, she tried to imagine his parents' home in some pretty, small town. It would be modest. With a white picket fence. No doubt, his mother and father loved Jay to death. She seemed to remember that his family had visited him over the past couple of years. Jay had taken them to shows on Broadway, done family stuff. Not that she'd given it much thought; she'd been focused on work. Now she wished she'd paid more attention...even asked to meet his family. She thought of how fondly he'd smiled a few minutes ago while he'd spoken to his mom. A wave of something close to envy swept her.

It had been a long time since she'd had a mom.

Only a dad. Her mom had driven away one day and she'd never come back. It had been left up to Kingston to tell them weeks later about the helicopter crash that had claimed the life of their cheating mom and the boyfriend she'd loved more than her daughters.

What would it be like to have grown up in a safe, secure environment like Jay's family? To be loved for oneself? To have no expectations placed on you from the moment of birth? To have a mom—and a dad—who loved you?

To her surprise, Georgia discovered she wanted to find out. She wanted to feel what it was like to live in the warm surroundings of a normal family.

If only for a week…

Except she had to be back at work by Monday. Kingston would be there—supposedly taking it easy.

But if she could escape for the weekend…

"Jay?"

He looked up, his eyes unfathomable.

Hauling in a deep breath, she said with raw honesty, "I haven't taken a vacation in years. I'm not coping well with the decisions I've had to make this week. Going away for a couple days will give me a chance to get some perspective. Please, may I come?" Laying herself open like this was hard. She tried to smile but her bottom lip trembled. "I won't stay long—only until, say, Sunday night."

"What about your father?"

She fought the claustrophobic fear of her father's displeasure when he learned she'd left without a word. Even worse would be his rage when he learned she'd turned Adam down. She couldn't face him. Not yet. He'd steamroll her to change her mind, to go prostrate herself to Adam.

"I'll make sure Marcia and Roberta take care of him until Monday."

"You know that's not what I mean." Jay's eyes didn't leave hers.

Beneath her apprehension about telling her father that she'd turned Adam down lay the haunting terror that her father was going to disown her. Abandon her. Just like he'd done to Charis…

Without Kingdom, she had no family.

No future…

"Putting it off never makes it any easier. Trust me on that." Jay's smile was crooked. "I speak from experience."

"I know. I know. I'll do it. I won't put it off indefinitely. I'll do it on Monday."

"You don't want Fordyce telling him first—"

"Adam's so sure I'm going to change my mind that he told me to take the weekend to reconsider. He won't say anything to my father. Please, Jay. I need this time away to think about how I'm going to handle Kingston's reaction when I tell him that I've turned Adam Fordyce down." Just thinking about confronting her father caused her stomach to churn anxiously.

Jay's face softened, and her frantic fear eased a little.

Finally, he rose to his feet and placed his hands on his hips. He studied her in a way that was a little too calculating.

"What?" she demanded.

"Okay, if there's a seat, you can come."

She gave a squeal of relief and delight and rushed toward him to throw her arms around him.

"Wait!" He warded her off with one hand, and gave her a ghastly grin. "There's one condition."

"Anything!"

"You should know better than to agree before hearing the terms." His grin grew feral. "Haven't you learned that much this week?"

"Better the devil I know," she teased, back on familiar territory. "What do you want?"

There was an abrupt shift in his expression, and he stopped grinning. "You'll come along as my fiancée."

"What?" She hesitated, uncertain now. "What do you mean, your fiancée?"

"Don't worry. It won't be the real deal."

Were his parents really so conservative? "Uh, surely you can tell your parents we work together…that we're colleagues? We don't need to be engaged to spend a weekend together."

Jay's expression lightened as he gave a chuckle. "My parents haven't spent the past couple of decades buried in the woods. But they're hoping to persuade me to return for good. A fiancée with a career and a family in New York would convince them that's not going to happen."

Georgia was so relieved she would've promised anything. Besides, she couldn't wait to meet Jay's small-town family.

"Oh, I can do that. And I can tell them how indispensable you are to Kingdom, how much Kingston relies on you and what a great future you have ahead of you. They'll be even more proud of you when they find out what a hotshot you are in the Big Apple."

She gave him a smile full of eternal gratitude.

"Thank you, Jay. You're the best—the very best friend I could ever have!"

Nine

Aspen, Colorado.

Jay had collected a sporty black SUV rental at the airport, and now, as they drove through the town bustling with Saturday morning activity, Georgia looked about with interest. Last night, when Georgia had begged Jay to take her home with him, she certainly hadn't expected their destination to be one of the premier ski resorts in the country.

She'd never been to Aspen—clearly, a big mistake. There certainly weren't many towns that boasted Louis Vuitton and Prada stores—Kingdom ought to have had store presence here, too. Georgia made a mental note to follow that up as they left the heart of the town behind, and Jay swung through a roundabout onto the picturesquely named Castle Creek Road. She wondered how far away from Aspen his parents lived. She'd love to come back for a look around the town.

"I thought you might like to see some famous Aspen Gold," said Jay, tossing her a quick grin.

They passed under a bridge, and the road opened out ahead. Georgia bit back a torrent of questions and sat back to enjoy the ride.

The road snaked upward as the dark blue-green mountains rose steeply around them. In the distance ahead, snow-capped peaks jutted out against the Colorado blue sky. The beauty was breathtaking. Her heart soared as they sped into a tunnel of ghostly silver-white trees topped with clouds of golden foliage. Too soon, they emerged on the other side. Seconds later, they swept through a bend, and the next flurry of slim silver-and-gold aspens flashed by. Georgia smiled in delight.

About ten minutes later, Jay slowed and pulled over.

"Why are we stopping?" she asked, turning away from the awe-inspiring landscape.

Jay killed the engine and swiveled to face her. "You'll need an engagement ring."

That brought her swiftly back to reality.

"It's not necessary—it's not a real engagement."

"It is for this weekend. My parents will never believe our engagement is real without a ring." Jay's eyes glimmered. "They'll be annoyed enough that I didn't let them know before."

"But they know I'm coming?"

He shook his head. "It'll be their anniversary surprise."

"You didn't call ahead to let them know you were bringing a guest?"

"You worry too much."

He leaned toward her and she caught a whiff of the delicious woody notes of his aftershave as he reached for his shearling jacket in the back seat. From one of the pockets, Jay extracted a small velvet-covered box and flipped it open.

The ring inside made her gasp.

A gorgeous round art deco diamond—the biggest blue-white she'd ever seen—blinked up at her. Set in white gold, with four diamond-studded petals folded back down the sides, it looked like a flower smiling up at her.

Georgia's heart sank. "My God. What if I lose it?"

"In one weekend?" Jay lifted a brow. "Unlikely. Anyhow, it's insured. Do you like it?"

I love it.

She controlled her impulsive response, but honesty compelled her to say, "It's the most beautiful ring I've ever seen."

Part of her was horrified. Jay earned a very good salary, but he wasn't wealthy...at least, not compared to her family. What he must've spent on that ring wasn't worth a one-weekend charade—unless he had it on loan. But even then, the insurance premiums would be horrific. A ring like this hadn't come from a last-minute foray into one of the airport shops. By some magic, Jay must've pulled strings to have it couriered to him this morning.

His attention to detail left her gasping.

Georgia's lips parted, but when Jay took her hand, all her questions scattered.

"Here, let me put it on." Cradling her hand between both of his, he stroked the length of her fingers. Her skin started to tingle. Then he slipped the ring onto her finger.

A perfect fit.

Adam had never even gotten his as-good-an-investment-as-any-diamond-can-be ring onto her finger. The memory of another engagement ring—Ridley's—crowded in. Shuddering, she blacked out those disastrous associations.

Thank God, this time it was only a pretense.

Because she truly wasn't any good at this engagement stuff...

Jay's ring winked up at her. She thought of her mother's art deco earrings, which were all she had of the woman who had walked away from her three young daughters. She stared at the exquisite ring for a long moment, wishing, wishing... For what? She gave up trying to figure out what she yearned for, and lifted her gaze from the most beautiful ring she'd ever seen to the man beside her.

"Jay, it feels like it's never going to come off."

He was smiling at her, his hazel eyes warm and amused.

Georgia took in his features. The firm chin and angled jaw, dark with rough stubble. The good-natured curve of his mouth. Her gaze lingered. Why had she never noticed until recently the deep slashes beside his mouth that gave his face such rugged masculine appeal? Or the spark of bright green in his eyes? Like moss in the depths of a dark pine forest.

She worked with the man every day and all she'd ever allowed herself to focus on was their rivalry. For good reason. Every secret, silent SWOT analysis she'd ever done had convinced her that Jay was her biggest threat.

Yet, when offered the chance to usurp her place in her father's life, he'd turned it down.

He did her head in.

"Good," he said easily. "I'm glad it fits. Now you don't need to worry about losing it."

Unexpectedly, he lifted her hand and brushed his lips across the backs of her fingers.

Her heart bumped in her chest as the moment stretched between them, oddly intimate...and so very sweet.

It was friendship, Georgia told herself firmly. That's what the warm glimmer in his eyes signified. No point making more out of it.

So, instead of leaning across the space between the seats and seeking the shelter of his arms as she had last night, she simply smiled at him. "Thank you, Jay."

She was thanking him for the surprising comfort she'd discovered in their friendship—and the opportunity he'd offered for her to be part of a loving family for a brief time, giving her time to heal, to become whole again. It was friendship. She needed to keep reminding herself of that. Because there were other unfamiliar yearnings be-

neath the warmth of gratitude, yearnings that felt nothing like friendship.

As she studied him, his expression grew serious. "There's something we need to talk about."

The sudden intensity in his eyes caused her to still. "What is it?"

Georgia might not be aware of it, but she wanted him to kiss her.

The dewiness in her eyes, the lush, ripe fullness of her pink mouth told Jay all he needed to know.

Even as hope fired up within him, he suppressed it. He understood her hunger. That desperate desire to seal lip against lip. But he could no longer be satisfied by kisses. He wanted more. Much more. Just for starters, he wanted to slip his hands under the soft sweater she wore, strip it away and touch her skin. He wanted to shuck off his clothes. He wanted her naked against him.

But he had no right to any of those things.

The moment he'd put the ring he'd inherited from his grandmother on her finger, he knew that he couldn't leave any unspoken deceit between them. He had to face his fear...and tell her the truth.

Even though it meant he risked losing her.

Forever.

So don't screw it up this time, Black.

Jay hauled in a deep breath to steel himself against the terror.

Cupping his hand under her jaw, he tipped her face up to his. Looking into dark-lashed eyes, he said in a rush, "What if I told you that we'd met before?"

As always, the beauty of her eyes, clearer than Colorado summer skies, enthralled him. Right now, they glistened softly.

"This is going to sound...weird. Sometimes I feel I've

known you all my life, Jay." Her throat bobbed. "You understand me—almost better than I understand myself."

"That's not exactly what I mean."

She blinked rapidly. "Then I don't understand."

Jay decided to sidestep the thorny issue of that powerful sense of connection he, too, knew so well. It had hit him the very first time he'd seen her in the hotel bar. Bam! Between the eyes. He hadn't understood it, either. So, for now, he was sticking to what could actually be explained.

"I'm talking about two years ago," he said softly, his heart pounding against his ribs.

"Two years ago?" she repeated slowly, her eyes never leaving his.

Jay nodded, watching her, his chest tight. Georgia—of all people—wouldn't have missed the significance of the timing. "Before I came to Kingdom."

"No!" She pulled back and laced her fingers together. His hand fell away. "I don't believe you. I would've remembered meeting you."

The interior of the SUV closed in on him.

To escape the sudden claustrophobia, Jay thrust the car door open.

"Let's walk," he commanded gruffly. Without waiting for an answer, he climbed out, dragging his jacket with him.

He led her down a short track between the quivering aspens to the edge of the bubbling creek. The wind blew off the distant peaks with a snow-chilled edge so typical of the Rockies, and Jay slung his jacket around her shoulders to block out the worst of it. The jacket was long enough for Georgia to sit down without getting her jeans damp. She did so, and then he settled himself on a tussock beside her.

A splash in the water caused her to jump.

"Trout. Brown trout," he told her.

Her profile was etched against the silver tree trunks that surrounded them.

"Where?"

Jay didn't pretend to misunderstand. She wasn't asking about the trout, and he knew he'd run out of time... and distractions.

"Las Vegas. I was attending a conference—you were there, too. With your fiancé." *Good-riddance Ridley.*

Georgia went very, very still.

The creek babbled busily in front of them as he waited for her response.

An aspen leaf drifted past on the surface. The current swept it between two rocks and it spun into the eddies below and down toward the deep rocky overhang where he knew lazy fish loved to lurk. All the courage he'd summoned threatened to drown along with the golden leaf.

She pushed her hair—paler than the silver bark of the aspen trees—off her face, and finally she looked across at him.

"When, exactly, did we meet?"

"On the Friday night." He waited.

There was an explosive silence as she absorbed that.

"I don't remember."

Jay had to ask. "How much do you remember about that night?"

"I don't want to talk about Ridley." Her tone was flat. There was no emotion in the words. He'd heard far more enthusiasm in her voice about the rising costs of Italian leather for next season's totes.

Tipping his head back, Jay stared at the blue sky visible between the gold leaves above. Hell, she never ever talked about the damned man. Why had he thought she would now?

Her eyes were bright with accusation when he glanced back at her. "You should've told me we'd met."

"I...tried."

He told himself he had. When she'd returned to work

on crutches, her broken ankle encased in a moon boot, she hadn't shown any hint of recognition. That had been when he'd learned what hell was. It had been blisteringly clear that Georgia didn't remember him. The concussion she'd suffered in the car crash had wiped out several days afterward…and parts of the time just before. Jay hadn't realized how much he'd been banking on her favorable reaction to finding him in the office next door. She'd refused to discuss the car accident, her injuries, any loss of memory and her ex-fiancé. And Jay hadn't wanted to rub her nose in whatever she remembered of her humiliation.

"Not hard enough!"

At her stony expression, the ache in his chest swelled.

He hesitated, loath to confess that he'd been afraid. Afraid of exposing himself to her ridicule as their relationship settled into habitual snark and rivalry. He was still afraid. But now, at least the past was out in the open—she knew they'd met before.

"I thought it would be better if you remembered by yourself."

"What do you know that I don't?" She shook her head and her hair swirled around her shoulders. "Dammit, Jay. You kept this from me, every day. For two years."

Anger and distrust cooled her eyes; he'd expected that. Hell, he deserved every bit of it.

"I'm sorry," he said.

"You're sorry?" She glared at him. "You think that's enough?"

"I know it can never be enough, but I'm very sorry—I shouldn't have kept it from you."

What he badly wanted was her forgiveness. Day after day, he'd held stubbornly on to the hope that she would remember. One day. How could she not? The bond that had linked them from the moment they'd met had blown him away. She had to remember it.

So each morning, he'd resolved that he would tell her the truth, while secretly hoping she would remember him. Each morning, he'd brought her a cup of coffee.

Each day, she'd greeted him with a wide smile, a clever quip and suspicious eyes filled with fear that he was trying to edge her out of Kingdom.

And each day, it had nearly killed him. And he'd put it off for another day.

Two years of his life—and hers—had ticked by. He'd hidden his desires by playing the fool. He'd made her laugh. He'd driven her crazy. But he'd also worked to help her chase the dream she wanted—a dream of a future that every day took her further away from him.

But Jay wanted more than a dream woman. He wanted Georgia. He loved her mind. He loved her spirit. And he wanted his ring to stay on her finger.

More than anything, he wanted her love.

A wave of self-disgust at his own impatience swept him. He was pressing her too hard. He'd harbored a selfish hope that telling her that they'd met before might jog her memory. It hadn't happened. And it was probably for the best. While she might get to remember him—the first time he'd held her, comforted her—on the flip side, she'd also get to remember everything else about good-riddance Ridley that she'd so carefully blocked out.

He sucked in a deep breath. "Do you want to call this off? Do you want to go back?"

"Back?" Her eyes were dazed.

"Back to New York."

Georgia stared at Jay. His normally smiling lips were pressed into a grim line and there was no laughter visible in his eyes.

"No, I want to stay!" Despite the shock he'd delivered, she wasn't ready to face her father. At least not until she'd decided how she was going to appease him without giving in to his wretched demand.

Jay gave her a long considering look and got to his feet. He stretched out a hand to help her up, but she ignored it, brushed past him and marched back up the trail. All too soon, they were back in the SUV. He restarted the vehicle and spun it around to head back the way they'd come— back to Aspen.

Thoughts tumbled through her head as she tried to make sense of what Jay had told her, what it meant for her. For them. For their working relationship.

Jay had lied to her.

Turning her head away, she looked out the window. Around them, imposing mountains dominated the vast landscape. But this time, instead of driving through the town, Jay headed into the surrounding hills. She caught a couple of the road names as they climbed higher and higher through the switchbacks and the homes became increasingly more exclusive.

Hunter Creek Road.

Red Mountain Road.

When a pair of stone gateposts set with heavy black wrought-iron gates came into sight, Jay slowed. He pressed a code into a keypad beside the gate, and the heavy gates swung swiftly and silently open.

As the SUV purred along a driveway lined with aspens that shimmered in the sunlight, she realized her assumptions about Jay's family might have been a little off. The driveway ended in a spectacular sweep in front of a house.

No, not a house. Forget that. A luxurious Colorado lodge rose out of Red Mountain to a haphazard height of at least four stories. Not even the warm rays of the morning sun could soften the craggy lines of the stone structure that had been built to withstand storms and snowfall in the harshest of winters.

Georgia stared. "*This* is where your family live?"

So much for a white picket fence…

And what about the party tomorrow?

Any chance that it would be a low-key family affair went out the window. She thought frantically about the casual selection of garments she'd tossed into her Kingdom carry-on for a small-town family visit. She'd deliberately dialed it back, not wanting to arrive with a mountain of luggage looking like some super-spoiled big-city fashionista.

Aside from the French blue jeans and turtleneck sweater that she was wearing with a pair of flats, and her Kingdom coat with its distinctive crown-pattern lining on the back seat, there wasn't much in her carry-on.

Mentally, she listed the contents. Fawn riding-style pants that never creased. A white shirt—not silk, because she'd foolishly decided silk would be too over-the-top. A plain wool cardigan—not cashmere. A white long-sleeved T-shirt. Apart from her Kingdom coat, her favorite pair of well-worn Chelsea JJB boots was the only recognizable brand she'd packed. One pair of modest heels—nothing like the sublime skyscraper works of art she wore most days to work. One dress. God. The dress! It was an ode to understated mediocrity.

Her confusion and shock crystallized into anger.

She could kill Jay for not warning her!

Before she could give voice to it—or the million questions bubbling in her head—a small crowd spilled out of the lodge's enormous wooden front door and tumbled down the stone stairway.

Later, she promised herself. She would kill Jay later. He'd die a slow death. A very slow death…

She was out of the vehicle before he could come around and open the door. More shaken than she would ever have admitted by the discovery that Jay didn't come from some average small-town home, Georgia hovered beside the SUV

as a woman wearing Western-style jeans, a pale pink cashmere sweater and a pair of black suede Jimmy Choo boots
rushed down the stairs to fling her arms around Jay and
kiss him soundly.

A moment later, the woman turned to Georgia and examined her. She had Jay's hazel eyes. It was his mother.
There was no doubt about those eyes.

Georgia smiled hesitantly at Jay's family.

The people who loved him. The people to whom she
and Jay were about to pretend they loved each other and
intended to marry…and live happily ever after.

For the first time, the stark reality of the deception they
were about to enact struck Georgia. If there was one thing
she was worse at than engagements, it was telling lies.

Unlike Jay…

How would she convince anyone that she was a besotted bride-to-be? Aside from that fiasco with Ridley, she'd
never had much practice.

Her palms grew clammy.

There were two more women and a man behind Jay's
mother. The younger woman was more casually dressed
than Jay's mother in a pair of JJB boots—newer than those
Georgia had packed—along with black jeans and an oversized white linen shirt. Once again, Georgia thought of the
sorry contents of her overnight bag.

Jay moved closer. When he took her clammy hand in
his, it eased her fluttering nerves. The sense of relief she
felt further confounded her.

He gave her hand a gentle squeeze. "Mom, Dad, Jennifer, Betty…meet Georgia Kinnear. My fiancée."

Everyone appeared to freeze.

"Did you say fiancée?"

As Jay might have expected, his mother was the first

to speak, even as his father's face grew tight-lipped with disapproval.

"Kinnear? Isn't that the name of that man you work for?" His father's dark brown eyes bored into him.

Here we go, Jay thought. His father knew the industry inside out. J.J. knew exactly whom Jay worked for. This was simply the next salvo in a long running battle. Their relationship had gotten no easier with absence.

Georgia was smiling at his father, a careful, charming little smile. Jay noticed she hadn't offered her hand. Clearly, she feared his curmudgeonly parent might choose to ignore it. He rather suspected she'd read the situation correctly. Sometimes, she could be the most astute woman he'd ever known—yet, at other times, she remained as blind as a newborn mouse.

"I'm Kingston Kinnear's eldest daughter, Georgia." She was still smiling. "Nice to meet you."

Her hand had gone cold in his. Jay gave it another gentle squeeze.

"Georgia, this is my family. My parents, J.J. and Nancy, my sister, Jennifer…and Betty, who has looked after our family for decades. You'll meet more of the extended family and plenty of friends at the anniversary celebration tomorrow." Turning his attention to his family, he said, "I'm fortunate that Georgia has agreed to marry me." Jay raised the hand he held and kissed it.

He heard her breath catch. He froze, too. The slanting sun caught the ring on her finger, causing it to glitter with fierce blue fire. He felt Georgia jerk, and looked up.

Their eyes caught…tangled…held.

He forgot everything. His family receded. His whole awareness centered on the pair of clear sky blue eyes.

The moment shattered as a furry body barreled into his legs.

A golden Labrador grinned up at him, and he heard Georgia laugh.

"I see I forgot to introduce Zeus," he said ruefully.

She rubbed the dog's head.

Jay looked up. Everyone appeared to be transfixed at the sight of the ring on Georgia's hand as she caressed Zeus's ears. No one could have missed what he'd known the moment he met Georgia: the ring was perfect. The blue of the diamond reflected the brightness of her eyes, while the silver setting glittering with pavé diamonds matched her hair. With his grandmother's ring on her finger, Jay had sent a message: he expected his family—every one of them—to honor his choice.

"Don't let Zeus jump up—his feet are all muddy."

His mother was the first to step forward, gently kneeing Zeus out of the way. She kissed Georgia, first on one cheek, then on the other.

"This is such happy news," she said, her voice thick with emotion.

Thank you, Mom. A wave of love for his mother filled Jay.

His sister hadn't moved. She stood beside his father, a question in her eyes. Jay read it as easily as though his sister had yelled it at him.

What about Suzie?

Dammit!

The old guilt stirred deep in his gut. He pushed it away. He'd deal with Suzie later. Tomorrow. She'd be at the anniversary celebration. Unlike the old man, Jennifer would reserve judgment—even though her loyalties would be torn.

Jay headed back to the SUV. It only took a moment to heft their bags out of the trunk. Georgia, thank God, had traveled light. He retrieved their coats from the back seat. His mother had finally released his brand-new fiancée, who looked a little dazed as he dropped her coat over her shoulders.

"Let's go inside," Jay said brusquely. For now, she had endured enough. There was more to come—her weekend escape was the beginning of his purgatory. There was little hope of forgiveness: he'd left it too late for that.

"Give me one minute. I need a word with Betty to sort out a few last-minute details." Nancy Black touched her husband's arm and fixed him with a look that Georgia guessed held a warning. "Darling, prepare Jay and Georgia something refreshing to drink—I'm sure they're parched after the trip."

"I'll get Zeus cleaned up." Jay's sister grabbed the Labrador by the collar.

Georgia's desire to murder Jay escalated another level.

He hadn't been joking. He'd given his unsuspecting family no warning that he was bringing a guest—much less a fiancée. His mother's need for time to consult with the housekeeper revealed that much. Not that Nancy had made her feel like an interloper; to the contrary, Nancy's welcome had been the warmest of all.

Nor had Jay been joking when he'd said his parents would expect her to be wearing an engagement ring, although she hadn't anticipated that they would be quite so riveted by the sight of the ring on her finger.

This was far from the modest, ordinary family she'd expected.

Jay's mother exhibited the easy style of a woman comfortable with wealth, while his father wore jeans, a Western jacket and, once again, the ubiquitous JJB boots—although his were the scuffed cowboy kind.

And then there was the house…

Once inside the heavy front door, Georgia found herself standing in a double-height—or was it triple-height?—

foyer. Never-ending living spaces unfolded before her, with fabulous mountain vistas visible through the surrounding windows. In the distance, a curved staircase in black wrought iron with a carved wooden bannister rose to the upper floors. From the marble-tiled lobby, two steps led down to a spacious living area arranged around a stone fireplace. Wooden floors—walnut, she suspected—were scattered with large handwoven rugs. On the far side of the fireplace, Georgia glimpsed a dining space surrounded with vast floor-to-ceiling windows that framed more spectacular views.

She wanted nothing more than to get Jay alone. To demand some answers. Why had he never said a word about his family's wealth? In all the time she'd known him, all the time she'd worked head-to-head with him, he'd never discussed it. He'd mentioned parents and a sister in passing. But nothing had prepared her for this—this—

Words failed her.

Murder might not be enough…

As she and Jay trooped down the two stairs behind J.J., Georgia tried to fathom the family dynamics that were swirling around them. There was clearly a bond of deep affection—love—between Jay's parents. But the relationship between Jay and his father was not as easy to decipher. Jay gestured to a leather sofa. Once she sat down, Georgia glanced around with interest, taking in the pewter chandelier overhead and the pair of bronze elk statues beside the hearth. But when Jay settled beside her, his thigh close to her own, any curiosity instantly evaporated.

All she could focus on was the pressure of Jay's thigh against hers.

"So, you want to marry my son?" J.J. had taken the leather armchair directly across from where she and Jay sat.

Before she could respond, Jay spoke from beside her. "I proposed—I want to marry Georgia."

But J.J. appeared deaf to the warning note in Jay's voice as his bitter brown eyes drilled into Georgia.

J.J.

The name nagged at her. Jay's father looked vaguely familiar. But she'd swear they'd never met. Georgia took her time studying him. The broad shoulders and head of gray hair. The heavy brows over measuring eyes. He was the picture of a successful, wealthy man comfortable in his skin right down to the scuffed Western boots he wore. JJB boots. Like hers.

J.J. Black?

As in JJB Boots? Iconic Western boots. She and Roberta both loved them. She'd had a vague idea that the company was based out west. In Colorado?

Oh, my God!

Jay was one of *those* Blacks.

And he'd never told her?

JJB Boots!

Deep inside, something twisted painfully at that thought. Despite all their skirmishes, despite her fears that Jay was after her dream job, she'd always known he shared many of her own visions and values. She'd spoken the truth down beside the creek: Jay understood her better than anyone she'd ever met, and that only intensified the hurt she was feeling. He'd confessed to lying to her about the past. Now she'd discovered he'd chosen to tell her nothing about his family business—yet he knew everything there was to know about Kingdom.

How had he come to work for Kingdom? How had he learned about the post Ridley had vacated?

Jay had risen to his feet. A dark wood unit opened to reveal a liquor cabinet and a fridge. "What would you like to drink, Georgia?"

A destructive impulse to demand a triple tequila before noon overtook her. Georgia stifled it. Jay might be amused, but she doubted J.J. would appreciate it. Getting off on the wrong foot with the man would only make what was starting to look like a challenging weekend more difficult.

"May I have some water, no ice, please?"

"Sure." Jay took a bottle of mineral water out of the concealed bar fridge, then twisted the top off and poured it into a tall glass.

Georgia felt ridiculously obtuse. Part of it was Jay's fault—he'd never given her any hint. How could she have guessed? It wasn't as if Kingdom ever had any business dealings with JJB Boots.

Although that wasn't such a bad idea…

"—and I'll cut down on my working hours once you're back. Your mother will be pleased."

What? Ripped out of her thoughts, Georgia's sudden movement caused the ring on her finger to flash blue fire. All at once it no longer mattered how or why he'd come to work for Kingdom.

Her gaze meshed with Jay's.

"You're planning to leave Kingdom?" she whispered.

"Of course, he's going to leave!"

She blocked out J.J.'s loud voice and kept her eyes on the man who had become her rock. Jay's expression was unfathomable. It had been bad enough to think about him leaving her for a vacation, but for Jay to leave Kingdom forever…?

"My son was never going to stay at a New York luxury label when he has the solid family tradition of JJB Boots waiting for him back home."

There. If she'd needed confirmation, she had it in J.J.'s contempt. Anger, hurt, a raw pain contracted her chest.

But Jay's eyes remained steady on hers. "My fiancée would be the first to know if I were considering such a drastic step."

Fiancée. His warning was clear: she'd better not give the game away.

Even as he handed her the soda and sat down beside her, a frantic desire to slip into the bracing chill outside overcame her. Anything to get away from the suddenly oppressive mood in the room and to clear her thoughts.

Jay was part of JJB Boots. He had a career—a life—waiting for him here. A life he'd said he didn't want to be pressured into going back to. But someday, he would realize the value his family and the JJB Boots brand held.

Someday, he would leave Kingdom.

All Georgia's anger at Jay evaporated as a greater dread set in.

They made a great team. How often, during the worst moments of her day, when she was bogged down with stress and deadlines, would Jay arrive brandishing a cup of coffee just as she liked it and flash that lazy grin, his eyes glinting with devilry. Tension would seep out of her. Life would instantly become simpler, more fun for a few moments. Solutions to all the problems plaguing her would fall into place.

What would she do when Jay decided to leave?

A shocking realization struck her: she didn't want him to leave. Ever.

Really rattled now, Georgia couldn't hide her relief when light footsteps sounded, and Nancy reappeared.

"Ah, good. J.J., I see you got Georgia a drink." No one disabused her of the notion. "Everything is sorted out, Jay. The guest suite is ready for both of you."

The guest suite is ready...for both of you?

Georgia blinked. Twice. Her lips parted. "Um—"

"Thanks, Mom." Jay was already on his feet. "I'll take our bags up."

Georgia was left with no choice. Flashing a polite, vacant smile in the direction of her hosts, she abandoned her untouched drink and dashed after him. He took the wooden stairs two at time, his black boots thudding against the wooden stairs.

Black leather boots…

JJB Boots.

How could she have been so blind? She could've screamed. Had Jay been laughing at her all the time that he'd had her fooled?

"Wait," she called out as he reached the top.

"We're just through here." Without slowing, Jay vanished through a stone arch.

Ten

"You have some explaining—"

Georgia came to an abrupt stop under the arch. Through the rustic doorway, she could see Jay setting their bags down on an antique blanket chest at the foot of the bed.

She did a double take as she took in the size of the sleigh bed that dominated the guest suite. It was ginormous.

"—to do." Her voice fizzled out.

And just like that, Jay's relationship to JJB Boots became the least of her worries.

One bed… Two people.

And not another bed in sight. Tension gripped her belly. Refusing to acknowledge it, she reminded herself that she and Jay were colleagues.

No, they were friends.

Only friends. Nothing more…

She thought of the skimpy lace and satin pajamas in her trolley bag and drew her brows together.

"I am not sleeping here, Jay." She fought to keep her voice from rising. "Not in one bed."

"And if there were two beds? Would that make a difference?"

Georgia narrowed her gaze. She was starting to suspect

that the lazy mocking smile, the good-humored teasing masked a more intense, far more complex man. This Jay was all too familiar. Maddening. Provocative. Engaging. Amusing. But not even an invitation to debate the matter was going to distract her. Not this time.

"That hardly solves the problem," she said firmly.

The corners of his mouth kicked up into a crooked smile. Oh, she knew that smile…

Except this time, her reaction was different. More complicated. For once, she didn't rise to the bait. Instead, her eyes flickered to the undone top button at the neckline of his white shirt and the sliver of bare skin revealed at his throat, then quickly away…back to his face.

From the light in his eyes, she knew he'd recognized the heat she'd felt.

"We don't even have to sleep, you know." He followed that smile up with a wicked growl. "Not if you're so dead set against it. That should solve the problem, right?"

She swallowed hard.

Suddenly, she was finding it hard to breathe.

While that magnificent maple bed behind her was simply waiting…

Georgia's heart started a slow thud in her chest.

He was coming closer. The wickedness in his widening smile caused her throat to tighten further and her skin began to tingle.

How had she never noticed the sensual ease with which he moved…or the sexy slant of his cheekbones? The catalog of her oversights was growing longer by the hour.

"Hey." She struggled to laugh.

Too late. Way too late. It came out breathy and expectant, and the awful sound hung between them.

Nice work, Georgia!

Warmth flooded her face. Striving for firmness, she

channeled her most businesslike boardroom voice. "Don't tease, Jay."

His smile was all teeth, and his eyes gleamed.

"Whatever makes you think I'm teasing?"

At the low husky note, a pang of yearning—just short of pain—stabbed at her heart. A memory of that instant she'd uttered the reckless bid that had won her Jay at the Bachelors for a Better Future Benefit Auction swept over her. His stunned expression and the surge of triumph that had seized her in that moment came sharply back into focus.

When his gaze dropped to her mouth, the tingle flared into heat, shocking her with its intensity. Georgia resisted the urge to run the tip of her tongue over lips gone suddenly dry.

But she couldn't stop her heart from slamming against her ribs.

"Stop it!" she croaked.

"Okay." He looked up from her mouth and met her gaze full-on. "So what do you want?"

That huskiness in his voice—her heart recognized it. Even though she could've sworn she'd never heard it from Jay before. She backed up a couple of steps. The drumbeat against her ribs grew heavier.

"Your parents will be wondering where we are." Desperation called for desperate measures.

"My mother knows we'll be taking time to freshen up a little."

She took another step back. The big bed banged into the back of her legs, and she stilled in surprise.

"So, you never did answer my question."

She was aware of his intent gaze, of his lean strength, of the heat of his body in front of her. *Oh, dear heaven.*

"What question?" She shuddered inwardly at the squeakiness of her voice.

"What do you want?"

Her heart jolted. His closeness—

The rustle of denim, the smell of suede and the fresh mossy, woodsy scent of his aftershave filled her senses.

"Georgia…"

At last, she lifted her gaze. The final traces of a smile still lingered. But as their eyes connected, it vanished. The diamond hard-edged intensity in his expression caused her heart to splinter painfully.

Jay wanted her.

In the absence of his teasing smile, the hard slash of his cheekbones and the tight line of his mouth were a revelation. Again, that Alice-down-a-rabbit-hole sense of not knowing, not seeing the real Jay filled her.

Her breath caught in the back of her throat. She placed her hands on his forearms, the suede jarringly rough beneath her touch. "I don't think we should—"

"Don't think," he ordered.

His head came down.

"Feel," he whispered against her mouth.

Her heartbeat went through the roof.

Excitement tore through her. This kiss was nothing like the sweet, chaste kiss of friendship they'd shared in the hospital courtyard. This time, there were no preliminaries. His mouth was hard and hungry. His tongue lashed into her mouth, tasting her…scorching her.

Digging her fingertips into the thickness of his jacket, Georgia made a little sound in the back of her throat.

It was part surprise. Part something…darker, far more frightening.

Then she released her grip on him to edge her hands down around his hips. As he groaned and pushed closer, she clutched at his jeans, the ridge of the pocket edges rough against her fingers. Beneath the denim, she felt the tight butt she'd so covertly admired on the stairs only minutes before, and arched up against him.

He felt hard and unmistakably male against her.

Panting, she tore her mouth from his. Instantly, he eased back so that her hands slid from his buttocks to his hips.

Her hands tightened on the waistband of Jay's jeans.

Did he know what he was doing to her? Did he know about the desire that pulsed through her veins? She flipped him a quick upward glance from under her lashes. He was watching her, disconcertingly composed, his gaze steady. No glint of mockery in sight.

"Are you okay?" he asked, utterly serious for once.

"Of course!" She tried to smile.

But was this a good idea? They worked together. She was terrible at romance. And worse at reading men's intentions. Now was the time to tell him that the only thing they had in common was business. The fashion industry. Work. Kingdom.

Only...

That wasn't true. Not anymore. Something had changed. *She* had changed.

And Jay had changed, too.

He desired her.

Despite his level gaze and apparent calm, the evidence she'd felt pressed against her had been unmistakable.

Maybe she had it all wrong...

Maybe she *was* his type. Maybe he really did want her, Georgia, the woman she was under the Kinnear veneer.

Beneath the churning uncertainty and confusion, it was as if a dam wall had broken and a torrent of emotion had been released. For the first time in years, she no longer felt shamed by what she felt. By what she wanted.

Or by doing something about getting it.

So what did *she* want?

Right now, she wanted to be kissed by Jay...

A real kiss, not some sweet innocent kiss between friends. A real rip-my-heart out kiss, wherever that led.

"Oh." The sound burst from her in frustration.

Releasing his hips, she brought her hands up, sliding them over the rough suede past the buttoned edges until they closed on the lapels of his jacket. His eyes blazed as she gave a little tug. Then he laughed and twisted around, leaving her holding the abandoned jacket. She flung it onto the bed behind her.

His hands came down on her arms as she plunged forward, grasping a fistful of his shirtfront.

He steadied her. "Slowly, sweetheart."

"Don't you dare laugh!"

He didn't want her. The heat of all-too-familiar doubt rose through her. The fear of humiliation, of making a fool of herself all over again seized her gut. She swallowed.

Jay's hazel eyes were unexpectedly serious as they searched hers.

"Do I look like I'm laughing?"

His mouth was at eye-level. It was a beautiful mouth. It spoke to her in ways her heart understood. And it wasn't laughing.

Georgia wanted to sob with frustration, even as her grip on his shirt tightened, her emotions seesawing wildly between desire and betrayal. She twisted her hand. A button threatened to pop.

She didn't want it to be like this.

Forcing herself to look away from that mouth that was driving her crazy, Georgia released her grip on his shirt, and smoothed down the creased fabric.

The hurt that had been festering since she'd put two and two together about JJB Boots spilled over.

"Why didn't you tell me, Jay? About JJB Boots? Why the secrecy?"

Lifting his hands away, he speared them through his hair. She felt bereft at the loss of his touch.

"It was always on my résumé."

Which she'd never seen because she'd been convalescing when Jay had been hired. And why bother when every frenetic day, Jay's actions spoke louder than any testimony ever could? He'd proven himself an excellent hire. "You never talk about your family."

"You never ask," he countered.

Silently, Georgia acknowledged her blinkered absorption in all things Kingdom.

"I told you a couple of times that my mom and sister were visiting New York. You didn't show interest in hearing more."

"Your dad didn't come?"

His mouth tightened. "No." He ran his hands through his hair again and hunched his shoulders. "Who my family is doesn't change who I am. JJB Boots—and J.J. Black for that matter—do not define who I am." He looked up, his gaze direct. "I'm sorry. I screwed up. I hurt you."

His hair stood up in spikes where his fingers had mauled it. Without laughter, he looked older, resolute, disturbingly serious.

The maddening rival was nothing like the man who faced her now. He'd withheld so much of himself. She couldn't dismiss that. But the man hidden behind the mocking mask was so much more. Her apprehension lifted, causing her to blurt out, "You're my rock, Jay. I never want to lose that."

"You won't. I promise."

It was enough.

"What do I want?" She tipped her head. "More than anything, I want you to kiss me again."

The fingers that brushed against her chin, cupping her cheek, shook a little. His free hand came up to her shoulder. With a jerk, he drew her closer.

Caught in his embrace, held against him, despite everything she'd discovered about him today, despite everything he'd withheld, Georgia felt safe. She leaned into him and his arms tightened fiercely around her. He nuzzled her, and his breath warmed her neck. She needed that warmth. *His* warmth.

Then his lips were on hers, her lips parted and he sank in.

His leg shifted forward, sliding between her thighs. One hand closed on her breast, and his fingers stroked. Slowly, deliberately, he caressed the tightening peak under her sweater, causing bursts of arousal. Georgia's knees almost gave way again.

She closed her eyes, lost in the fresh flare of desire.

A little gasp escaped against his mouth.

A loud knock shattered the hot daze, and the bedroom door flew open.

"Georgia, we don't dress up fo—" Nancy stood in the doorway, her mouth a perfect *O* of surprise. "I'm sorry. I thought you might need some towels."

Flushing wildly, conscious of his hand on her breast and the solidness of the big bed behind her knees, Georgia tried to extricate herself from Jay's hold. But he held her close, refusing to let her go, his body shielding her from his mother's view.

Over Jay's shoulder, Georgia could see Nancy clutching a pile of towels.

Jay's mother cleared her throat. "Uh. Dinner will be ready in less than half an hour—we don't dress up. Please join us for a drink."

"Thanks. And, Mom…" Jay said as his mother paused "…wait a little longer after you knock next time, okay?"

Nancy's eyes were wide with shock. She dropped the towels on the tallboy just inside the door, nodded and fled.

Eleven

Jay's frustration knew no bounds.

After retreating to take a shower so cold that his skin still stung, there was no relief to be found back in the bedroom where Georgia stood in front of the dresser, brushing her hair. He pretended not to watch—all the while itching to run his hands through the soft silver strands as he had last night.

Hell, he'd need another cold shower if this carried on.

She'd swapped the sweater she'd been wearing earlier for a snowy white shirt tucked into her jeans and a wide woven belt. She didn't spare him a glance as she secured her hair in a loose knot at the nape of her neck. He wanted to rip the pins out.

"Are you ready?" His voice was husky.

She nodded and moved to the door.

Jay slung an arm across her shoulders once they exited the guest suite. Downstairs in the dining room, his mother and Betty had their heads bent over a piece of paper on the dining table, while Jennifer watched them approach from across the table.

"That's the final list?" he asked the women.

"The final-final list." His mother peered at him over

her reading glasses, revealing no sign of the awkward moment in the guest room as she smiled at Georgia. He loved his mom!

"More like the final-final-final list." Jennifer grimaced. "Between Mom and Betty, tomorrow is going to run like clockwork."

"They're a pair of dynamos—they wear the rest of us out." Jay tipped his head toward Georgia, allowing himself the surreptitious pleasure of inhaling her perfume. He pulled out the chair at the table for her.

"We kept it small," his mom was saying to Georgia. "Only a hundred and eighty guests. That way, we can enjoy ourselves."

"Is there anything I can do to help?" asked Georgia.

"Yes, you can help with all the last-minute details after dinner. Jennifer, I'll need you, too, please."

"With pleasure." Georgia sounded a little more relaxed.

He could tell that his mother already liked Georgia. How could she not? Jay felt a swelling of warmth in his chest as he sat down beside Georgia.

"So long as I'm excused from the flower arranging." His father's gruff voice interrupted his thoughts. The last to arrive, J.J. took his customary place at the head of the table.

Jay didn't register his mom's response because Georgia chose that moment to turn her head and give him a small smile, slashing his guts to ribbons. He slowly smiled back, and instantly the sizzle of awareness reignited between them. Then color rose in her cheeks and her gaze fell away, breaking the connection.

The meal passed in a blur.

"That was delicious." Georgia's knife and fork clinked together as she set them down on the plate.

"Betty is a marvel," his mother responded with pride in her voice. "What do you say, Jay?"

"The fish was good," he managed, scrambling to remember what he'd eaten. He'd been too conscious of Georgia's denim-clad thigh beside his own, his shoulder brushing against hers as he reached for the salt, her scent drifting across, intoxicating him.

"Of course, it is. Freshly caught by your father." His mother caught his eye and smiled.

Jay felt himself reddening—something he couldn't remember happening since he was a teenager. Was his enthrallment with Georgia so obvious?

"You used to come with me, Jay. Remember the bighorns in the high country pastures? The water holes where we'd find fish under ledges no one else knew about?" His father grimaced. "But these days, you have more important fish to fry."

"Jay and Georgia could visit over the winter. We could all go skiing." His mom looked hopeful. "And Georgia might even want to tag along next time you and Jay go out fly fishing."

"What would a New York fashion plate know about tying a fly?"

Jay winced at his father's rudeness, even as Georgia flinched beside him.

Georgia spoke before he got a chance, her chin rising a notch. "I can get by on a pair of skis—and I can certainly learn to fly fish."

His father snorted. "You'd get wet."

All Jay's muscles went rigid. His father was spoiling for a fight. With barely concealed anger, he said, "Dad, there's no need for—"

A chair scraped as his mom rose hurriedly to her feet. "Betty is sorting the cutlery and linen for tomorrow's party. I need to check on the apple pie and make sure it's not burning. J.J., you can come and help me."

His father clambered to his feet, pointedly ignoring Georgia.

Jay opened his mouth to blast his father, but was stalled by the touch of Georgia's hand on his thigh.

"Let it go," she murmured so only he heard.

"Suzie makes some of the best flies in Colorado." J.J.'s truculence sliced through the distance between them. "You should be marrying her."

"J.J.!" His mother's voice was sharp. "Now!"

"Uh, I think I might go help, too." Jennifer shot to her feet.

The moment his family disappeared, Georgia swiveled her head and Jay received a hard stare.

"Suzie?"

She began to remove her hand from his leg. He brought his hand down, enfolding hers, forestalling her withdrawal. He rubbed the back of her hand, luxuriating in her soft skin under his palm. "I apologize for my father's rudeness."

She didn't acknowledge his apology. "Is there something else you've forgotten to tell me?"

Jay didn't want to talk about Suzie. Not with his parents and sister about to return at any moment. "Let's discuss this later."

"I think you need to fill me in now."

The tilt of Georgia's jaw warned him that she was not about to be deterred.

"Who is Suzie? Your girlfriend?" she persisted, picking up the paper napkin laid across her lap and tearing it in half.

"Ex," he muttered.

Georgia narrowed her eyes until the flash of blue through the cracks of her black lashes glittered brighter than the diamond on her finger. "How ex?"

"I haven't seen her in years."

Georgia's look of relief caused the oppressive weight in his chest to lift a little.

Crumpling the shredded napkin into a ball, she dropped it onto the table. "Well, I suppose I should be thankful you haven't put me in the unsavory position of being the other woman."

Jay winced.

The sound of his mother's raised voice chastising his father wafted from the direction of the kitchen.

Georgia drew a breath. "My presence here is causing friction."

Damn the old man! "This friction between my father and me is nothing new."

"I feel so guilty for misleading your family. Your mother is so lovely. She believes I'll be back to visit with you. She's already including me in future skiing trips. I can even understand your father's hostility—he resents me because he believes I'm keeping you away. I shouldn't be here."

It was all his fault that Georgia felt like an outsider. By convincing her to agree to a sham engagement, he'd created this situation—not his father.

But the alternative was to lay his heart on the line...and have her stomp all over it. Because of his own male pride, he'd made it harder for her, not easier.

Tightening his hand around hers, he said, "The truth is, my father finds it hard to accept I'm a man, not a boy any longer. I'm not coming back. He knows that—but he refuses to accept it."

"He wants you to take over the legacy he's built," she said softly. "It's his dream."

The irony of that wasn't lost on Jay. Georgia craved most what she thought Jay had walked away from. Families could be hell.

He drew a deep breath and said, "But it's not my dream."

"He loves you, Jay." The sparkle in Georgia's eyes had gentled. She turned her hand over, threading her fingers through his, and Jay's heart contracted. "He wants what's best for you."

Jay shook his head. "No, it's not what's best for me that he wants. It's what's best for him. And that's not love."

"You need to talk to him." There was concern in her eyes.

Her compassion loosened a tightness deep within him. But he concealed his vulnerability by arching his eyebrows and saying with pointed irony, "*I* need to talk to *my* father?"

Georgia shifted in her seat, her cheeks reddening. "I'll talk to Kingston on Monday. Honestly, I will."

Instantly, Jay felt bad. Georgia's relationship with her father was far more complex than his with J.J.

He squeezed her hand, then released it and rose to his feet. "Okay, I'll go talk to J.J."

"Be gentle," she murmured so softly he had to strain to hear the words. "For both your sakes."

From the doorway of the den, Jay shook his head and smiled at the sight of Zeus sprawled across the leather chesterfield, snoring.

Wooden bookshelves packed with books on fishing, business management and the craft of boot-making lined the walls. A box-frame filled with the first flies that Jay had tied under his father's tutelage still held pride of place, and the almost-buried memory of that long ago time tugged at Jay.

"So the prodigal son has returned."

His father rolled the leather executive chair away from the window and set his whiskey glass down on the antique walnut desk next to a box of carefully crafted flies. The eyes that inspected Jay were filled with a critical glint that was all too familiar.

"About time, my boy."

Jay shoved Zeus to one side to make space on the couch. Settling himself beside the snoring dog, he crossed an ankle over his knee and strove for calm.

"Dad, we need to talk."

"This nonsense about an engagement must end." Already, his father was hijacking a conversation that hadn't yet begun. "I want you back home."

Slowly, Jay shook his head. He allowed a slight smile to tilt his mouth as he rocked his boot-clad foot back and forth.

"I'm not coming back."

His avoidance of the word home was deliberate.

Home was where the heart was, and his heart had taken up residence elsewhere.

"Of course, you are!" His father gave an impatient snort. "You've had enough time away. It's time for you to come back and marry Suzie."

Once again, his father was treating him like a boy, rather than the man he'd become. Keeping his voice steady, Jay said, "I'm not going to marry Suzie."

There was only one woman he planned to marry.

"You're engaged—"

"That's over. You know that, and Suzie knows that."

"Suzie still wants to marry you—she'll jump at the chance."

Jay doubted it.

Some of the residual guilt about his old friend stirred. He forced it down. Guilt was the last thing Suzie—or he—deserved. "What Suzie really wants is to be a permanent part of JJB Boots—marrying me would've secured that."

"That's not the point. Suzie needs you—she needs a husband," his father insisted. When Jay refused to respond, J.J.'s hands balled into fists. "The business needs you, too, Jay."

They'd finally gotten to the crux of what his father really wanted.

The old tightness was back in Jay's gut, winched tighter by the steel chain binding him to dreams that had never been his.

This time, when he shook his head, it was with finality. "You're looking at the wrong Black."

"What the hell is that supposed to mean?"

His father's bull-headedness was as frustrating as always. Colorado would never be big enough to hold them both. Jay felt his hard-won calm slip. "You know what it means, Dad. Open your eyes to what's in front of you. Jennifer—"

"Jennifer has done her best to help hold things together while you've been gallivanting around New York. You've gotten the qualifications we decided you needed, and I've given you enough time to gain the necessary industry experience to run our business."

Jay steeled himself not to react. Zeus pressed up against Jay's thigh. Absently, he scratched the dog behind his ears.

"I need you here running JJB Boots! Jennifer will get married someday—"

Jay's hand stilled as he cut his father off. "I'll be married first."

"It's not the same, Jay."

If Georgia had been here, she would've have accused him of being deliberately provocative. She would have probably been right. But his father's stance would have infuriated her, too. J.J. was almost as bad as Kingston.

Dinosaurs, both of them.

Zeus's nose nudged at his hand. Jay recommenced rubbing the soft feathery ears and the dog settled his muzzle onto his paws.

"The world has changed, Dad. There is life after marriage. Jennifer and Suzie will make fine business partners in JJB Boots—even if both of them decide to get married someday."

"Don't be flippant, boy! You're my son. My successor. Your place is at the head of JJB Boots."

Jay didn't allow his rising annoyance to show. "I'm not coming back. It's not what I want."

They lapsed into uncomfortable silence.

He'd promised Georgia that he would be gentle, so he searched for words to soften the blow. "Dad, I'm a man, not a boy anymore. I will visit you and Mom. And I hope you take time out to come to New York next time Mom visits." But Jay wasn't holding his breath. It hadn't happened in two years.

With a violent kick of his foot, his father swung his chair away to stare out the window into the darkness that had settled over the jagged peaks. "I will cut off your allowance."

At his father's raised voice, Zeus whimpered. Stroking the dog's head in reassurance, Jay almost smiled. J.J. was using the same tactics Kingston had used so successfully on Georgia. But it was an impotent threat—and J.J. was enough of a realist to know it.

"You will find I haven't touched that for years." It had been longer than five years since Jay had spent a cent of the quarterly allowance he received from the trust fund set up by his grandfather. Nor had he touched the parcel of stocks his grandfather had left to him—as the sole grandson. "I'm quite capable of fending for myself."

"And what of your fiancée?" The chair spun back. His father's mouth was clenched as tight as a trap.

His fiancée…

A vision leaped into his mind. Of Georgia grabbing his shirtfront, pressing up against him, careless of his clothes or hers. Of the wild kiss that had followed. Of her hot little gasps against his mouth…

Whoa! He had to crawl into bed beside Georgia tonight…and sleep. He'd be awake all night if he started to think about the wild little sounds she'd made in the back of her throat.

"I wouldn't be so sure that little lady agrees with your

high moral stance, my boy. She's accustomed to the best in life. Luxury labels. High heels and charity balls. Not hiking boots and wading in mountain streams. That high society lifestyle, it doesn't come cheap. Will you be able to fend for her and keep her happy?"

His father had no idea what would make Georgia happy. But Jay rather suspected he might. If only she gave him the chance.

"I think I'll be able to keep my fiancée happy."

"Don't be so sure. Her father will expect—"

"Now that brings me to what I came in here to talk to you about." Jay's voice lowered as he lifted his foot from where it rested across his other ankle and set it firmly down on the rug. He sat forward on the chesterfield. "Why don't you tell me about the mission you've been on to buy up stocks in Kingdom?"

Twelve

With the heady scent of gardenia soap clinging to her, Georgia stepped out from beneath the shower and quickly wrapped herself in one of the soft luxurious bath towels that Jay's mom had left. The last thing she wanted was for Jay to walk in and catch her naked.

It was absurd to feel so nerve-rackingly aware of him.

They'd worked together in adjacent offices for years. But that was before that sizzling kiss. And now, the treacherous tingle that prickled along her skin refused to be doused by the rough rub of the towel.

Clothes, she needed clothes.

Back in the bedroom, she shimmied into her pajamas, covering up her shower-dampened body. Catching sight of her reflection in the armoire mirror, Georgia quivered. Pale aqua satin clung revealingly to her hips and bottom. The V-neckline of the flagrantly feminine cami top gaped wide, while lace side panels revealed still more skin. It looked like she was doing her best to stage a deliberate seduction.

What she needed was body armor, Georgia decided grimly. The corporate kind. A smart no-nonsense big-name jet-black designer pantsuit would work just fine. But she was stuck with what she'd packed.

She rolled her eyes. Of course, there was an alternative!

Ever conscious that Jay might stroll in at any instant, she sped to the armoire and emerged—triumphant—with a long-sleeved white T-shirt. She whipped it over the cami, and then scrutinized her image critically.

Not quite boardroom armor, but an enormous improvement.

Deciding that the chairs grouped by the glass door presented a better option than waiting in the bed, she made her way across the room. The damned satin pajama bottoms whispered against her sensitized skin with every step. Perching on one of the straight-backed slipper chairs, Georgia picked a fashion magazine off the coffee table. Her fingers trembled as she flicked through the glossy pages. Not even an interview by one of her favorite fashion feature writers could hold her attention as her stomach twisted into convoluted knots.

So much had happened today. The ring. Jay's confession that they'd met before he'd come to Kingdom—and she didn't remember. Meeting Jay's parents—and finding out that they owned the iconic JJB Boots brand. Then there'd been the discovery that his family expected Jay to marry another woman.

And the cherry on top: the shock that Jay actually desired her.

Restlessly, Georgia shut the magazine with a snap and shoved it aside. Once on her feet, she started to pace.

Jay wasn't engaged to Suzie; he was free to kiss whomever he pleased.

Georgia chewed her lip. Did it matter that he hadn't told her about his family's business? The JJB Boots brand held no threat to Kingdom. Did it even matter that Jay had never mentioned the first time they'd met? He'd done her a favor. It was a day she never talked about—she didn't even remember most of it. The little she did remember, she'd worked hard to forget.

If there was one thing her experience with Ridley had proved conclusively, it was that she was useless at relationships. She certainly wasn't expecting love and commitment from Jay. But she wouldn't mind another one of those knee-weakening kisses.

Shock caused her to stop in her tracks. She wanted—

Even more than kisses, she wanted to sleep with Jay.

She closed her eyes.

What was she thinking?

God, it was hard to admit. She wanted pleasure. The kind of mind-blowing pleasure that kiss earlier had promised. Opening her eyes, she stared blindly at the carpet. They were two consenting adults with no reason not to indulge in a no-strings fantasy for a night.

Maybe even two nights...

She could change her flight—and fly back early Monday morning. Excitement and nerves churned in her stomach.

Even as she considered the possibility, footfalls sounded on the wooden stairs and the door handle rattled. Her heart jolted, and the tension inside ratcheted up another notch. Georgia hesitated for only for a fraction of a second before diving into the big bed, sinking into the indulgently soft linen as the door swung open.

Jay had arrived.

The wooden door shut behind him with a heavy clang, causing the drapes that framed the glass doors leading to the terrace to flutter. Georgia's pulse rocketed from zero to a hundred when Jay strode in. Determined not to let the sudden intimacy rattle her nerves, she drew a deep breath to ask him how the talk with J.J. had gone.

But as he strolled forward and began to unbutton the tiny buttons at the cuffs of his shirt, the unspoken words dried up.

After shaking the cuffs loose, Jay started on the buttons down the front. Georgia could only stare as the shirt's edges parted to reveal an impressively muscled chest and a washboard stomach, both of which confirmed he was no stranger to a sweaty workout.

Georgia's fingers played frantically with the corner of the sheet as she watched him shrug off his shirt. With his hair mussed and his shirt billowing, he looked deliciously disheveled.

She tingled as acres of male skin were laid bare.

How had she missed that he was simply gorgeous for so long? Was she completely blind?

"You were right that I needed to talk to J.J." Jay fished into his pocket and dropped his wallet on the nightstand.

Then, to her relief, he walked across the room, giving her plenty of opportunity to admire the surprisingly well-developed laterals sloping to a narrow waist. With a flick of his wrist, he tossed the shirt over one of the chairs beside the glass doors.

He headed for the armoire. "Plenty of positives came out of it."

Jay lifted an arm, and Georgia couldn't help noticing the rounded peak of the bicep and, below, the bulge of his triceps as he rubbed his hand back and forth over the back of his neck. Somehow, he'd found time in his awful work schedule to do a fair amount of serious curls. A flush of warmth came with the discovery that the man who walked in and out of her office every day had a body worth lusting after—had she been given to lusting.

The sound of a zipper severed the sudden silence. Then he kicked off his boots and shucked off his jeans, and her brain stopped working.

Georgia tried—unsuccessfully—not to gawk at the muscled ridges on his chest. The taut, tight abs. Was she the only one who had never noticed? He'd certainly aroused enough feminine interest at the benefit auction. She discovered she didn't care for the memory. She didn't like the idea of Jay being pursued by every Dom, Nic and Carrie. She didn't like the idea of his being engaged to another woman—any woman!

Except her.

She was jealous.

Even as the realization dawned, her stomach clenched. After a final wide-eyed gawk, she forced her gaze away from his lean, taut body and bare muscled thighs, his snug-fitting black briefs—all that kept him decent—and fought to concentrate.

But she had to ask. "Your family clearly regard Suzie as much more than an ex-girlfriend."

He shot her a quizzical look. "Suzie and I had an understanding."

"Understanding?"

The word was jarring. It reminded her of her father, and that terrible, distasteful confrontation with Adam which, in truth, she hadn't understood at all. Dread weighed down her stomach.

"Exactly what kind of understanding?" she prodded.

"Suzie wanted children—and so did I. One day." He shrugged one beautiful bared shoulder. "Neither of us had found anyone better. We'd been friends—and work colleagues for years—she was Jen's best friend. There was no good reason why marriage between us shouldn't work," he said, his voice growing muffled as he bent down to pull off his socks. "It was convenient."

Jay disappeared into the bathroom, closing the door with a click.

As she stared at the closed door, Georgia wrestled with the uncomfortable emotions coursing through her. Jay wasn't in love with Suzie. He wasn't in love with anyone. He'd told her himself he had no dream woman. She slowly let out her breath and felt her tension ease. Her jealousy was unfounded…and simply silly.

By the time Jay reappeared a few minutes later, his hair damp and his jaw smooth, with a thick white towel slung low across his hips, Georgia had recovered her composure.

Raking a hand through his hair, he came toward the bed.

He sat down on her side of the bed, and the towel slipped a little lower.

Georgia sneakily side-eyed Jay's mouth to see if he was grinning. Only to discover that his lips were firmly pressed together, the bottom one full and surprisingly sensual.

"What Suzie and I shared…wasn't enough. Something was missing." He planted one hand one either side of her shoulders and leaned toward her, the fresh tang of soap mixed with the woodsy smell of him surrounding her. "There wasn't any chemistry," he murmured.

Excitement started to spiral in the pit of her stomach. She ached to touch the rough dark stubble on his jawline, to run a finger over that unexpected bump on his otherwise straight nose.

"I wanted more," he whispered, his eyes smoldering like molten embers. "I wanted this."

He cupped her cheek, his fingers gentle, and her heart contracted. And then he kissed her.

The hunger of it seared her.

This was hot and burning. This was a flame igniting potassium. She saw flashes of lilac. White. Silver. Burning.

A frightening emotion shifted deep in her chest. A new shivery, painfully raw pleasure. If this was chemistry, well, she couldn't get enough of it.

Drawn by the unnamed need, she confessed, "I've never felt anything like this before."

Summoning all her courage, she wound her arms around his neck and tugged him close, closing the gap between them. Maybe Jay was right. Maybe chemistry was worth everything.

"Do you want to do this?" he asked against her lips.

"Oh, yes!"

He moved his hips. "Are you sure?"

Georgia moaned and arched against him. "Very."

She wanted to see if she could lose all sense of time and place like that again or whether she'd imagined it. She wanted to experience the excitement, the rightness of his mouth against hers. For a moment, she thought about where they were, in his parents' home, then discovered she didn't give a damn.

Her breath caught, freezing in her throat.

She'd always worried about doing the right thing, about what people thought, about the consequences. But she wanted this more. Much more. She wanted Jay.

All of him.

Body. Heart. And soul.

She reached up and stroked her index finger along the blade of his nose, curiously exploring the jagged ridge where he must've have broken it at some stage. He'd gone very still, watching her.

His pupils flared. In retaliation, he trailed a fingertip along the sensitive skin of her neck, along her jawline. Her head fell back, her lips parting.

Then he touched her mouth.

"You have a beautiful mouth. Made for kisses." His voice held a dark deep edge, as one finger outlined her lips.

They felt full and swollen. His face was at an angle, throwing his cheekbones into sharp relief. No vestige of humor remained in his intent eyes. Only heat.

"So kiss me," she invited.

With a hoarse groan, Jay hauled her closer and licked her open mouth. His mouth sealed hers shut and their legs tangled, the satin of her pants slippery between them.

"How have I managed to resist you?" he murmured.

She didn't think she'd ever get enough of touching him. Her arms crept up around his broad shoulders. She reveled in his skin, sleek and supple, beneath her fingertips.

His hand smoothed over her shoulder and traveled down until it rested, strong and steady, on the curve of her breast. His fingers stroked, and she gasped.

He kissed with fierce intensity, and Georgia responded kiss for kiss. When his hand edged under the T-shirt, she aided him, lifting, twisting, breaking the kiss, impatient to get the garment off, craving the caress of his hands on her bare skin.

When he touched her, she transformed into someone else.

Someone more than Georgia Kinnear, daughter of Kingston Kinnear, gifted student and hotshot executive. Jay made her feel like the most amazing, tempting woman in the world. Sexy. Desirable. Special.

He was nothing like any other man she'd ever known. Her father. Ridley. Adam.

He made them all look like greedy, controlling jerks.

No wonder she loved him.

She *loved* Jay?

Georgia's breath caught, freezing in her throat.

But he allowed her no time to ponder the discovery. He ran two fingertips along the lacy neckline of her camisole, his lips following the invisible tracks he'd traced. Then the camisole, too, was stripped away.

He tasted her. The soft hollow at the base of her neck. The valley that lay between her breasts. And finally, when she thought she might go mad, he tasted her taut nipples.

Then he returned to her lips and kissed her with a passionate intensity born of desperation.

They only had tonight. Or maybe, if she got very lucky, two nights…

When he shifted again, and his hands sought the waist-band of her pajama bottoms, she was quick to help him, dying to feel her bare body against his.

His fingers stroked. Heat scorched her. Her breath hooked in the back of her throat, then hissed slowly out as his fingers retreated. A heartbeat later, they slid forward again, teasing her nub with sure purpose. Her hips twisted. She bit her lip to stop the squeak that threatened to erupt.

She'd never considered herself vocal. Jay had discovered a side of her she hadn't even known existed.

Two—God, she thought it was two—fingers slid into her. Deep. She arched off the bed and her breath caught on a sob.

"Jay!" It wasn't a protest.

"What do you want?"

She cast around for words. Polite words. Words that wouldn't make her blush. "I want you. There. In me."

Jay seemed to know exactly what her jumbled words meant. He shifted to rummage on the nightstand. Then he was back. He moved over her, above her, resting his weight on his elbows as he nuzzled her neck. Then his hardness found her.

Georgia gasped at the tightness.

There was a moment when she thought it would be impossible. Then he slid a little deeper. The tightness expanded into a painful tautness. She tensed.

"Relax," he whispered.

The sensual tickle of his tongue against the sweet groove beneath her ear caused her to shiver, then convulse into giggles. And the tension drained out of her.

When Jay moved again, her arms closed around him, pulling him deeper. She walked her fingers down his back, adoring the way his body stiffened, and dug her fingers into the mound of muscle on either side of his spine. He groaned. Her fingers crept lower…lower…

"Don't touch," he managed to say. "Or I will come."

The threat—if that was what it was—caused her to raise her hips a couple of inches off the bed, arching against him, then sinking down onto the mattress again. It was Jay's turn to gasp as the friction notched a turn tighter.

"Do. Not. Move."

"Yes, Jay."

She whispered the obedient words against the curl of his ear. Then her own tongue snuck out and she experimentally licked the edge. He hissed.

The friction of his body quickened against hers. Georgia felt the edge of tension rising. Hot and tight. Her feet came off the bedding, her knees hugging his hips, deepening the pleasure. Her eyes shut tight and she focused blindly on the driving desire. Then, unexpectedly, she came apart.

Georgia gasped.

Sheer delight rippled through her.

His body jerked. Once. Twice.

Then he fell forward, and buried his face in the crevice where her neck met her jaw. With a groan, he murmured, "Georgia, you are the most unforgettable joy of my life."

Thirteen

Jay stared down at the woman asleep in the bed.

She lay on her side, knees bent, her cheek resting on her palmed hands. The diamond he'd placed on her fourth finger winked at him. Jay wanted nothing more than their engagement to be real. For the ring that Georgia said fit so perfectly to stay on her finger. Permanently. With another simpler gold band beside it.

And he was determined to make her happier than she'd ever been.

Dark eyelashes lay peacefully against cheeks flushed with sleep. Unable to resist, he bent down and brushed his lips across hers.

She opened her eyes, stretched languorously. Then her eyes widened.

"Jay?"

"Good morning." He set two cups down on the nightstand. "I brought you some coffee."

"You must've read my mind."

He gave her a slow smile.

Leaning forward, he kissed her again. This time, she was fully awake and her lips parted beneath his. Placing his hands on either side of her, Jay braced himself against the onslaught of desire that rushed through him.

Lifting his head, he groaned. "We can't afford to get distracted. It's almost time for the party."

Georgia wound her arms around his neck. "Thank you for my coffee."

"Any time."

The mood in the room was imbued with an intimacy and sense of promise, filling Jay with a surge of renewed hope. Yesterday, he'd come clean with Georgia. And last night had been incredible. Now he simply had to convince her they belonged together.

Forever.

Then her phone rang.

Where had she put her purse last night?

Catching a glimpse of it buried under Jay's shirt on one of the chairs by the window, Georgia slung her legs out of bed, remembering too late that she was naked.

Flushing, not daring to look at Jay, she grabbed a throw off the bed and pulled it around herself. When she reached the chair by the window, she clutched at the throw and clumsily dug the now-silent phone out of her purse, glancing at the screen.

Roberta...

Panic instantly had her wide awake.

She frantically hit the redial button and stared blindly out over the private terrace to the mountains beyond, counting the rings and silently urging Roberta to answer.

When, at last, she heard her sister's voice, she said, "Please tell me Kingston is okay."

"He's fine." Roberta sounded loud and comfortingly familiar. "Breathe, sister. Be very grateful that you're not here. He's making everyone's life miserable."

"Oh." Georgia shut her eyes as the waves of panic subsided. "I'm so glad."

"Glad that we're suffering?"

Georgia stifled a sob of laughter. "Glad that he's back to his normal self. Glad he hasn't had a relapse."

"I'm still not sure there was much wrong with him to start with," Roberta said tartly. "But the stock price at markets' close on Friday? Now that's a different story."

Hunched over her cell phone, Georgia felt the familiar anxiety rise. "What do you mean?"

"Someone is buying up Kingdom stock." Roberta's voice took on a hard edge. "And that is enough to give our beloved father a real heart attack."

Georgia's grip on her phone tightened. "I'll fly home immediately."

"Don't bother to reschedule." Roberta's sigh came loud and clear over the miles that separated them. "There's nothing you can do—certainly not until Monday. But I called to tell you…" Roberta's voice trailed away.

"What?"

There was a pause, then Roberta said, "I just wanted to remind you that I'm not in the office for the next few days. You're flying back tonight, right?"

Georgia hadn't gotten around to changing her flight to the morning. "At this stage, yes."

"The sooner, the better. With the weather closing in, the airports may close."

So it was done. There would be no second night with Jay. The disappointment was crushing.

Georgia ended the call and turned to find Jay watching her from the bed, his arms linked behind his head.

How would she react when he breezed into her office bearing cups of coffee after he finally returned from vacation? She froze. Would she ever forget how he'd kissed her, licked her, loved her last night?

Would they be adult and pretend it had never happened? Or would they revert to the snarky, energetic rivalry they'd shared before? Would they still be able to work together? Or would awkwardness take over?

Georgia faced the reality of loving Jay. She wasn't dumb enough to pretend to herself that Jay felt the same about her. He wanted her. Sure. He liked her—she was pretty sure about that, too. They had their shared work ethic in common. She simply had to keep her emotions under control. It shouldn't be difficult; she'd had enough practice.

"Is everything okay?" he asked.

She slipped her phone back into her purse. "Kingston is giving everyone hell, the weather's terrible in New York and Roberta reminded me that she won't be in the office tomorrow."

"Sounds like business as usual."

About to tell him about Roberta's concerns about the stock price, she hesitated. There was nothing Jay could do about it until tomorrow. For now, she was going to enjoy the rest of her escape with Jay. Tomorrow, she'd be back in New York—and back to reality.

She flashed a smile at him. "Time for us to party."

The celebration was in full swing.

Tall stands of exquisite flowers and masses of colorful balloons filled the airy space. A quartet played, and there was a roaring fire in the fireplace.

Everyone had been so welcoming, so pleased to meet Jay's fiancée. In addition to family friends, plenty of Aspen's well-heeled crowd were present. Georgia had taken the opportunity to add several valuable contacts to her network.

Yet, with Jay's arm hugging her to his side, the feeling of being a total fraud swamped Georgia.

"This is awful," she whispered to him after the dozenth time his mom had excitedly dragged another of her friends over to introduce her only son's fiancée. "Your family doesn't deserve this, Jay."

Jay tilted his head closer. "Let's talk about this later—"

"That was your mom's best friend—your mom told her I'm her new daughter. I can't do this, Jay. We need to tell your parents the truth."

"Okay. But after the party. I'm not going to ruin this occasion for my mother. There's not long left, people will start leaving soon."

"Sorry to interrupt you lovebirds." Betty's arch tone caused Georgia to start. "Jay, can you give me a hand moving some of the anniversary gifts into the den? They're almost spilling out the front door."

"Of course." He shot Georgia a brooding look. "I won't be long."

He wound his way through the crowd with the housekeeper bustling behind him. Georgia watched him pause to respond to a greeting from a multimillionaire who'd made his fortune in retail. Then Jay turned to kiss a renowned actress on the cheek, before shaking hands with another couple. Georgia watched how the faces of men and women alike lit up. Jay was well-respected, and an easy authority radiated from him.

How had she ever missed that authority?

Shifting from one foot to another, casting little glances in the direction where Jay had disappeared, Georgia felt like a teenager in the throes of a crush, hyper-aware of Jay's every move.

She slipped outside.

On the covered terrace that faced the majestic Rockies, the guests had broken up into groups. Some stood clutching tall glasses bubbling with the best champagne, and others congregated on built-in seating around the edges of the terrace, while waiters circulated with trays still piled high with food.

Jennifer was chatting with a group of beautifully dressed women.

As Georgia approached, Jay's sister rose to her feet and came toward her. In a low voice she said, "That's Suzie in the red dress."

Georgia glanced past Jay's sister. A jolt of shock caused her to catch her breath.

"But she's—"

"Yes. And, in case you didn't know, Suzie also worked with Jay and me at JJB Boots." Jennifer bent her head closer and lowered her voice. "Mom had already consulted with a wedding planner. The caterers had been booked. The dress and the bridesmaid's dresses had been ordered when Jay dumped her for you."

"Jay jilted her?" Georgia knew she was gaping. How could Jay have done that to Suzie?

"You didn't know?"

She shook her head. "No."

"Don't feel sorry for Suzie—she'd hate it. I was so pleased they were getting married—my best friend and my big brother. Everyone was thrilled. We all knew it was only a matter of time before Dad retired and Jay stepped into his, uh, boots."

Despite the joke, there was real anxiety in the other woman's face. Jennifer honestly believed that Georgia had been the cause of her brother's breakup with her best friend.

"Jay had never done anything unexpected in his life. Sure, he and Dad fought, but we all knew they'd hammer their differences out eventually. But then he met you and broke off his engagement to Suzie. He walked away from JJB Boots and he hasn't been back since. Dad wants him in the business…but Mom and I would settle for having him come home from time to time. We hope you'll persuade him to visit—even to spend Christmas."

"You think Jay will do what I want?" breathed Georgia. The idea was so preposterous she almost laughed out loud. Only Jennifer's set expression stopped her mirth from spilling over.

"My brother is so in love with you that if you asked him to mortgage his soul to buy Kingdom International for you, he would."

In love with *her*?

Georgia nearly admitted that Jay didn't love her at all, that this engagement was one big sham. But she came to her senses just in time. Of course, Jennifer believed Jay loved her—after all, they were engaged, and she had a great big glittering rock on her finger to prove it.

Georgia curled up a little more in shame at the charade she and Jay were perpetrating on his family. It needed to end. And she needed to leave. She didn't belong here.

She itched to reassure Jennifer, to tell her that she was no threat, that she would never keep him from his family…that she didn't have the power to break his heart. She wanted to tell her that she and Jay were only friends.

But that, too, had become a lie.

She realized Jennifer was still waiting for a response.

"I'll talk to him," she said lamely.

"You'd better come and meet Suzie—you'll be seeing plenty of her when the two of you visit."

There was no way out.

Suppressing her own discomfort, Georgia approached the pretty blonde in the red dress. An uncomfortable silence fell as they reached the group. After the introductions, Suzie gave her a sweet smile. Georgia could only admire her.

To break the ice, she smiled back. "I understand you work with Jennifer at JJB Boots."

Suzie's eyes lit up. For the next few minutes, Georgia forgot her discomfort and listened with interest to Jennifer and Suzie kidding around. When a break came in the conversation, Suzie glanced around and said easily, "Ladies, why don't you give Georgia and me a chance to get acquainted?"

The women in the tight-knit group looked at each other and then rose to their feet in unison.

"Come, sit." Suzie patted the cushion beside her.

Georgia sat, smoothing the skirt of her simple pink knit dress around her knees.

Suzie touched her hand. "Don't worry. J.J. is not going to get his way. Jay finds working with him stifling—they fight like bears. J.J can be quite something and he's never understood what makes Jay tick. But he's never worried me. I love it here. By taking over JJB Boots and marrying me, Jay would've done what he considered his duty. But then he met you. If we'd gotten married, it would have ended in divorce at some stage. Jay did us both a favor."

Georgia stared.

How could the other woman not have been in love with Jay?

But then relief surged through her. Under different circumstances, she would have liked to have been friends with Suzie. A pang stabbed her heart. Deep down, she knew that when this charade was over, she would never return to Colorado.

How on earth was she ever going to be able to face Jay every day at work?

"J.J. believes that the end always justifies the means. That's why he's blackmailing Jay."

Suzie's words jerked her back to the present. "Blackmailing Jay?"

"Manipulating is probably a better word. Jay hasn't told you?"

Slowly, Georgia shook her head.

Suzie rolled her eyes. "Jay's always been protective. J.J.'s not going to get anywhere, but Jay should have told you. You're a big girl—and he can't play the knight in shining armor forever. Honestly. Men!"

"I'm sure Jay will tell me," Georgia defended Jay, despite an inner twinge of unease.

Suzie's gaze moved to a point behind Georgia. "Speak of the devil."

Jay guided Georgia down a set of steep stone stairs to the pool deck below. Inside the stone pool house, the distant chatter of the guests dimmed and all that could be heard was the tap of her heels.

"The water is heated—my parents swim most days," he said, leading her to a pair of oversized wrought-iron chairs with plump overstuffed cushions set amidst a forest of greenery.

But Georgia didn't take the time to study her surroundings—or to sit down. Instead, she impaled him with suspicious eyes. "Jennifer tells me you jilted Suzie practically at the altar."

Jay winced.

"Is J.J. blackmailing you?"

"Who told you that?" he demanded.

"Suzie."

Jay drew a deep breath and sat down. "My father has been buying up stock in Kingdom—"

"J.J.'s behind the erratic stock prices?" Georgia interrupted him. "How long have you known?"

"I noticed the shifts in the stock a few months ago—"

"A few months?" She frowned down at him. "When did you plan to enlighten me?"

"At first, the movements were irregular…with no obvious pattern. It could have been a variety of factors. Last week, an earlier sequence of patterns was repeated. I confronted my father. He admitted he was responsible. I've dealt with him." His father had miscalculated—and he would not be doing so again.

"You've dealt with him?" Georgia still hadn't sat down. "You should've told me."

"I only spoke to Dad last night, after dinner." Jay knew he was on thin ice. He'd intended to tell her last night...but once he'd gotten to the bedroom and found Georgia in his bed, all good intentions had flown out the window. He'd abandoned his strategy of playful patience...and given in to desire.

"You've been keeping me in the dark. You're supposed to be my—"

"What? Colleague?" He raised an eyebrow, suddenly tired of watchful caution. "Friend?"

"No! Yes. You're both of those. But you're more." Her expression shifted.

Jay held his breath, waiting.

"You're my lover." At last, she answered his silent question.

Somewhere deep in Jay's chest, a warm glow ignited.

"Georgia—" He reached forward and snagged her fingers between his. "I'd never let my father harm you. Believe that."

She resisted. "I need to call Roberta—"

Jay tightened his grip on her fingers, restraining her. "Listen to me. I've sorted it out."

He yanked her hand; she lost her balance, toppled over and landed sprawled across his lap. Her blue eyes blazed up at him. He pulled her close, securing her in his hold. However much he stood to lose, there would be no secrets between them. Never again. "Hear me out. My father has sold the stock he purchased to me."

"To you?" She stared up at him, emotion shifting in her eyes. "Why would you want to own Kingdom stock?"

Why indeed?

He'd been asking himself the same question.

"I don't," he said tersely. "I did it—" He broke off.

For you.

But Georgia was frowning. She was adding up the limited pieces of information she had at her disposal and coming to God only knew what conclusion. In his arms, he could already feel her stiffening. She moved restlessly in his lap and against his will, his body reacted to her abrupt movements.

"Sit still," he growled.

"The takeover—"

"Listen," he said roughly, determined not to be distracted by the dictates of his body. It was imperative for them to talk. "My father has no ambitions to stage a hostile takeover."

"How can you say that?"

"Dad had some mad scheme of using his newly-acquired stake in Kingdom to force me to do what he wanted—return to JJB Boots."

Her frown had deepened. "He thought that would work?"

He shrugged. "He thought if he had a decent block of Kingdom stock, he could lean on the Kingdom board to fire me."

"Why did you resign from JJB Boots?"

Jay hesitated. "When I went to that fashion trade show I was seeking…something. I thought I was looking for a new challenge…but I couldn't crystallize what I needed. All I knew was that I no longer knew where my life was headed—or what I wanted." There was no harm in admitting any of that. "I was in danger of becoming one of those sad sons who can never make a decision without running it past Dad's master plan first. One of those men who never stand on their own two feet, and live out their lives as sad shadows of the men they might have become."

Georgia shifted. "Sometimes it's easier just to be swept along with the current."

"But it's harder, too." Jay wanted her to understand. "You lose yourself—and finding that inner certainty again takes strength."

"And Kingdom offered a bigger and better challenge?" Her voice was as brittle as glass. "One that would make you strong again?"

He didn't respond as she wriggled in his lap, and he loosened his grip so that she could sit up to face him.

Pulling the hem of her pink dress straight across her knees, she said, "Was that first meeting that Friday night really a fortunate coincidence, Jay? Or did you—and J.J.—plan that, too?"

"My father had nothing to do with it. Our meeting was nothing I'd ever planned for." But it wasn't the whole truth. There was more. "I didn't come to Kingdom to apply for a job. I came looking for you."

"Oh, God." Georgia stiffened in his arms. "Let me go."

Let her go? Anything but that!

But she was so tense in his hold, so rigid, it was clear she didn't want to be anywhere near him. The battle inside him was fierce, and the familiar fear was consuming. If he let her go…he was going to lose her. Forever.

But he was out of alternatives. He had no choice but to release her. So Jay opened his arms, and she scrambled off his lap.

Her chest rising as she drew a breath, Georgia pushed her hair off her face and finally looked at him.

"That Friday night did we…?" Her throat bobbed. "Did I know you were engaged?"

"No."

There was a sudden spark in her eyes. "Did you take advantage of the situation...? Did you take me to bed?"

"What do you take me for?" The ache in his chest deepened. "I was engaged... You were in a state of distress. We didn't sleep together—at least not in the way you're asking."

The tough, determined set to her jaw was one Jay knew all too well.

"What's that's supposed to mean?" she demanded.

"In the interests of full disclosure, you should know that we stayed together that night. You shared my room. And I held you—until you fell asleep."

Her hands came up to cover her eyes. "Oh, my God."

"You didn't want to go back to your room because your fiancé and his—"

Georgia's voice cracked. "You know about that?"

Her hands dropped away from her face, and she stared at him, flushed deep, deep red with a humiliation that made him want to draw her into his arms.

"That you caught your rat-shit fiancé in bed with another woman? Yes, I know about that. You told me."

"*I* told you?"

He nodded.

"So you thought it might be a good idea to take me back to your—"

"There were no other rooms available. The hotel—and the adjacent hotels—were jammed to the rafters with conference goers. You were distressed. You had nowhere to go. You slept in the bed. And once you were asleep, I moved to the couch. A very uncomfortable two-seater couch, I might add, but I'll forgive you for not thanking me for my gallantry."

A little of the tension went out of her. "Well, thank God for that."

"I'm not that much of a bastard. You were very shaken after breaking up with Ridley."

"How I wish my memory about him had been blanked out." She stared at Jay bleakly. "That…incident…has replayed in my mind over and over, thousands of times."

He'd been so sure the traumatic memory had been suppressed that he'd never dared bring it up to her. "Georgia, none of it was your fault."

Her expression didn't change. "My father doesn't agree. He blamed me. Ridley was the perfect son-in-law as far as he was concerned."

Jay gave a snort of disgust. "Then you had a lucky escape."

He was tempted to tell her that Fordyce would've been a far worse mistake, but managed to bite the barb back.

He'd never given up hope that Georgia would remember him. But she never had, not even now when he'd filled in the gaps she deserved to know.

"What is it, Jay? What's wrong?"

"You were gone when I woke up on the Saturday morning," he told her.

Slowly, she shook her head. "I don't remember. Days… that entire weekend…is simply gone."

"I know. I tried to contact you—only to learn that you'd crashed the rental on the way to the airport. You'd been hospitalized. I was worried." Nothing as mundane as worry. When he'd heard that she'd been in an accident and was awaiting surgery…he'd been truly terrified. He'd sweated bullets. "I wanted to see for myself that you were okay."

"I was fine."

The sound he made was not pretty. "I got to see you several weeks later, and you were not fine! You returned to work far too soon, hopping around on crutches—"

She shrugged. "Kingdom needed me. Besides, I'd heard Ridley's position had been filled, and I was eager to meet his replacement."

Jay knew she'd been worried her place in her father's

life…in Kingdom…might be usurped. The day she'd met him, she'd been bristling with suspicion.

Even though he doubted Georgia would ever admit it, the period after her accident had been one of crisis. Her faith in herself must've been badly shaken by her memory loss, by Ridley's betrayal and her father's angry disappointment. Hardly surprising that she'd turned, as always, to work.

Kingdom had always come first, and Jay knew it always would. The company pulled at her…even as her father pushed her away. And it saddened him to see how hard she worked to try to gain her father's approval and love.

"You should've been resting, keeping your ankle elevated." He didn't want to nag, but he couldn't help himself. "That's what non-load bearing means."

"Well, you certainly reminded me of that often enough."

He had. He'd tried his best not to hector her, and had taken refuge in the taunting rivalry that had grown between them.

"And you brought me coffee…" her voice softened at the memory "…whenever I needed it."

But bringing her coffee was never going to be enough.

For him.

Or for her.

Despite everything, he couldn't help her attain what he knew she really wanted: to prove herself by getting the top job at Kingdom and winning her father's love. And Jay was in danger of doing what his father had done to him: smothering her with protection and expectations.

If he loved her, he had to give her the freedom she needed.

Even if that meant losing her forever.

Fourteen

Fake.

Their engagement was fake. She was an imposter...a fake. She, who worshipped at the altar of honesty, had lied. To Jay. To herself.

She'd been so scared of becoming lovers with Jay, so fearful of jeopardizing their working relationship, so terrified of risking the tentative friendship between them, that she'd been blind to the fact that she was falling in love with him.

Forget blind. She'd been asleep.

For years!

What if she took a chance and told him how she was starting to feel?

As Georgia stared at Jay, a vision of all the possibilities filled her mind. They were dynamite together. She wanted to share her slice of Kingdom with him...the plans and projects and shining success she'd plotted for years.

But before she could get up her courage, he spoke. "Do you ever think about what you want? Deep down?"

She was shaking inside when she said, "I want to be someone people respect and—"

"People? Or your father?"

Jay's interruption jolted her.

"Are you sure that's what you want?" He tipped his head to one side, studying her. "What you really want most?"

She wanted more than one night… She wanted a future with Jay.

Georgia drew up her shoulders and let them drop. "There are other things I want."

"Like what?"

The impossibility of Jay falling in love with her made her hesitate…

Her mind veered away and she thought of her weariness. "Well, a vacation would be nice." Not running away or avoiding, but simply a time to relax and reflect.

"What else?"

"I've been meaning to spend more time with Roberta. I missed her when she lived in Europe. Yet, since she's returned to New York, we haven't spent much time together." All they seemed to do was work.

"You two are close." His voice had dropped.

"Very. It's quite strange because when we were children, she was much closer to Charis."

"Did you resent that?"

"No. I don't know. Maybe."

"Perhaps much of the tension between you and Charis comes from your father's dominance and manipulation?"

"What's this? Psychoanalysis 101?" But she had to admit that her father had always made it clear that Charis was his favorite—even when she pretty much killed herself to be everything he'd ever wanted from the son he'd never had.

"No. I have no desire to fix you—you are perfect the way you are."

She blinked in disbelief. Had she heard right? Had Jay actually told her she was perfect? With no gleam of mockery in his eyes…eyes that were already glancing away at the watch on his cocked wrist.

"What time is your flight?"

Her heart contracted. She told him, even as she tried to fathom what he was thinking.

But his face gave away nothing.

"The guests will be leaving soon, and then I'll give you a ride to the airport."

She'd half expected him to ask her to stay.

But he hadn't. Something inside her withered.

"I suppose you've got what you want all figured out?" She flung the words at him, feeling curiously defenseless.

If it hadn't been for his stillness, and the slight narrowing of his eyes, she would've thought he was quite at ease.

"Yes, I know exactly what I want." His lips curved up, but his eyes remained watchful. "Two years certainly gave me plenty of opportunity to work that out."

The fears that had always been so much a part of her everyday life bubbled up. She hesitated, and then said in a rush, "Is Kingdom part of it?"

"If you have to ask that, you don't know me at all." He took a few steps away, making her feel more alone than ever. "Come, we need to go back to the house."

What did Jay really want? There were so many more questions she wanted to ask, but Jay was waiting, his body tense.

So, she would be leaving…

There was the confrontation with her father that lay ahead. Her heart plummeted. She was dreading it. But she couldn't prevaricate anymore; she had to tell her father the truth that she'd turned Adam's down proposal. But she was not going to allow him to banish her from Kingdom as he had Charis. And before she left Jay's parents' home, she owed them an apology for the sham engagement. She wasn't much looking forward to that, either; but at least then her conscience would be clean. She wanted Jay's parents to remember her as someone with integrity. Even though there was no reason she would meet them ever again.

"Come on." Jay had paused on the stone stairs. He held out a hand to her. "Let's go say goodbye."

All the guests had finally left, and the anniversary party had been a stunning success.

While Georgia packed her bag, Jay had disappeared to check his email and make a couple of calls. Once she was all packed up, conscious that she would be leaving very soon and that she still had to undo some of the damage she'd done this weekend, she made her way downstairs.

In the den, J.J. was at his desk and Nancy sat on a couch with Zeus asleep at her feet. J.J. narrowed his eyes over the top of his spectacles as Georgia entered.

Once again, the shame about lying to Jay's parents washed through her. So much for her high principles. "I've come to say goodbye," Georgia announced.

"No doubt we will be seeing more of you, for those ski-ing trips at the very least." Nancy rose to her feet. "The snow will be here soon."

J.J. removed his spectacles and set them down on the desk. "You do know that Jay is only marrying you because you're your father's right-hand man, don't you?" He paused. "Jay has always wanted to call the shots."

"Stop it, J.J."

Georgia gave Jay's mom a grateful smile, before turning her attention back to J.J. "Jay could've taken over JJB Boots, if that's all he wanted, and he would've gotten total con-trol far more easily." Suzie was right. J.J. had no idea what motivated his son. "But that's immaterial, and you have no need to worry about me keeping Jay away, because I won't be marrying him. Our engagement was a facade. Fake."

There was a gasp. Then Jay's mother was at her side. "What's this nonsense about a fake engagement? The two of you are perfect for each other. We—I—would welcome you with open arms."

Bemused, Georgia stared at Jay's mother. For the first time in years, the yearning for a mother flared. Then she threw her arms around Nancy and hugged her. A real warm hug. Tears pricked at the back of her throat. "I'm so sorry for deceiving you. Thank you for being so welcoming. Whoever gets to be your daughter-in-law is a very lucky woman."

Nancy hugged her back. "Georgia—"

From behind her, she heard a curse.

Georgia let go of Nancy and spun around. Jay stood in the doorway, her trolley bag at his feet. Now that it was finally time for her to leave, Georgia felt a lump in her throat.

It was time to finish what she'd started.

She hurried to Jay's side.

"This belongs to you." She tried to wrest the beautiful ring from her finger, but it refused to budge.

"Don't," said Jay, his jaw tight.

"I've already told your parents that our engagement is not real—and that I'd never stop you coming back."

"I'm not coming back to JJB Boots. My father knows that."

J.J. muttered something Georgia decided it was better not to hear.

"Your father can come along to New York next time Jennifer and I visit," Nancy said quickly.

This time J.J.'s muttering was louder.

Nancy rounded on her husband, her hands on her hips, her eyes flashing. "It's time we traveled together. Why, I was speaking to Joyce earlier, she and Bill have been wanting to go on a cruise for years, but they've never gotten around to it. She invited us to go along."

"Wait a minute." J.J. looked concerned. "I can't simply leave our business—"

Nancy tossed her head. "If you want, you can stay here and run JJB Boots, but I'm going on a cruise."

"You can't expect me to leave the company for months—"

"One month, that's all." Nancy brandished her index finger at J.J. "I intend to go once a year. While I certainly don't expect you to do anything you don't want, I've been dreaming about this for a long time. Now I'm going to do it."

"Go, Mom!" Jennifer's voice rang out from the doorway. "Make your dreams happen."

"Dad, you could always leave JJB Boots in Jennifer and Suzie's more-than-capable hands." Jay's suggestion broke into the cacophony. "Who knows? You might even find they do an outstanding job."

It was the baffled expression of blank shock on J.J.'s face that caused Georgia to interject, "Don't make the mistake my father made two decades ago. He was married to his business. He put Kingdom ahead of my mother's needs. He drove my mother into another man's arms. And then she died—they both died—and she never came back."

And her father was still putting Kingdom ahead of his daughters...

She thought about Jay's reasons for walking away from JJB Boots. He'd said something about needing to become his own man...not a boy in the shadow of his father. Was she in danger of having her growth stifled by her father?

She'd always held her father up as an ideal—a role model. He worked hard, he'd built a successful brand, he struck fear and awe into the hearts of everyone who knew him. She'd long ago decided that the only way to gain his respect was to rise to the top in the family business.

J.J.'s astonishment had turned to real horror, bringing Georgia back to the present. "Nancy would never leave me. I doubt she'll even go through with this cruise nonsense, either."

"Oh, I'm going through with it. I'm booking that trip first thing tomorrow. I'm going to have fun!"

Jay crossed to hug his mother. "Way to go, Mom!" Then

he straightened, and said to his father, "Georgia's right. You should think about having some fun, too. Before it's too late." Then he added, "Now, Georgia has a plane to catch."

"Don't let her get away," his mother called from behind them. "Keep that ring on her finger."

In the doorway, Jay paused, and said over his shoulder, "I have no intention of letting her get away."

The SUV swept down Red Mountain, and Georgia felt like part of her heart would remain behind. This was the place where she had first realized how deep her feelings for Jay went...how much she loved him. This was where they had first made love.

Her thoughts were interrupted by the vibration of her phone.

"Leave it!"

Irritated by Jay's peremptory tone, she ignored him and hauled the phone out of her purse to check the screen.

"Oh, no! My flight's been canceled. I'm going to have to call the airline to rebook." Another thought struck her. "I'll have to book myself into a hotel, too."

"You're welcome to stay with my parents."

"I don't think so—not after dropping that bomb that we're not really engaged."

Jay steered the SUV toward the town center and threw her a mischievous look. "Maybe we can finally share that bottle of champagne I promised you if you bid on me."

"Never mind a bottle of champagne.... You still owe me the fantasy date I won." Then she had second thoughts. "We'd better not do that today. Roberta would go nuts. She'll want to leverage every PR angle. She'll make sure our *date* takes place in some A-list restaurant and that we're appropriately dressed in all things Kingdom with a photographer of her choice on hand to document it."

"God help us both." Jay gave a theatrical shudder that

had her laughing, even as he pulled the SUV into the fore-court of one of Aspen's luxurious hotels. Within minutes, they were ensconced on a terrace with the mountains loom-ing all around.

Once the sommelier departed after a lively discussion with Jay, he turned to face her. "There's something I need to discuss with you," he said quietly.

The energy that came off him in waves made Georgia feel decidedly on edge. "What's wrong?"

"I've resigned from Kingdom, Georgia."

"Resigned?" The bottom dropped out of her stomach. This was worse than anything she could have anticipated.

A mix of emotions swamped her. Complex feelings of bewilderment, betrayal and a sense of being utterly aban-doned when she'd least expected it. Her worst fears had come to pass. She'd known this would happen. Now it had.

She was losing Jay...

"Does Kingston know yet?"

"I emailed him my resignation before we left my par-ents' home."

Then on the heels of her inner turmoil, she said, "Does that mean you're going back to JJB Boots?"

He shook his head. "I think you know better than that. JJB Boots does not—"

"Define you? Own you?"

He nodded. "It took a while to break those bonds."

"Was it worth it?"

He nodded, his eyes intent. "I will never regret it."

"Will you stay in New York?" She asked the question, though she dreaded the answer.

"I don't know yet."

Georgia had never considered leaving New York, never considered leaving Kingdom. But if Jay was not there...

Something inside her shriveled up.

Raising her chin a notch so that he wouldn't see how

devastated she was, she asked, "So what's next? Another journey? Where to this time?"

He gave her a smile that was all too familiar…and more than a little wicked. "Now, that rather depends on you."

"On me?"

He nodded. "A couple of hours ago, you asked if I knew what I wanted. I do. I want you, Georgia. I would like to ask you to marry me—to spend your life with me. That's what I most want."

Her throat closed. She had to choose between Jay…and Kingdom. She couldn't have both.

"You don't need to give me an answer right now. Take all the time you need."

"I have to go back to New York—"

There was a slight change in his expression, a tension in his body. Did he think she was trying to escape?

"I have to tell my father I can't marry Adam," she said.

Jay hadn't asked her to choose, of course. But she knew she had to be clear in her own mind about what she wanted. She didn't ever want to feel regret. Or to feel she'd been coerced into making a choice she wasn't ready to commit to.

Could she do it?

She didn't even have to weigh up the pros and the cons.

Because she wanted Jay more than she wanted Kingdom. The contentment, the laughter, the feeling of being valued that Jay brought to her life.

It was a shock to acknowledge. And it had happened slowly, so slowly that she'd never even noticed he had become more important to her than her very reason for being.

The sommelier came back, bearing a bottle of champagne and two flutes. He filled their glasses with a flourish before retreating.

Jay lifted his glass to her. "Here's to you, Georgia."

"And you." Her glass chinked against his. "I—"

Her phone rang. She set her glass down to pick it up and glanced at the screen.

"Bingo." She glanced across at Jay as illumination struck. "It's my father. Do you want to guess why he's calling?"

She didn't wait for an answer but pressed receive.

Her father's voice was loud in her ear. "Jay has resigned."

"I know," she said.

"You know?"

"I'm with him right now. And Kingston, there's something I need to tell—"

"So what are you doing about it?"

The look she shot Jay said it all.

"Kingston—"

"Roberta says you've been in Aspen. What kind of crazy, irresponsible move is that?"

She rolled her eyes at the interruptions. "Think of it as business."

"Business? What do you mean?"

"We should open a store here."

For the first time, there was a pause.

"Do a cost analysis," her father commanded.

Georgia remembered saying something similar that first day they'd driven through the town. It made her feel distinctly uneasy. She was nothing like her father.

"Kingston, I'm not going to marry Adam Fordyce."

"I'll hire someone first-rate to manage—" There was an abrupt pause. "What did you say?"

"I'm not going to marry Adam."

Her father actually snorted. "Of course, you are—we've agreed to it."

"*I* haven't agreed. And as the bride, I'd say I have some choice in who I marry."

"Don't be silly now, Georgia."

He was still treating her like a child. But then she had

never fully stepped out of that role. She'd kept him on a pedestal as a way to avoid having to create an intimate relationship. She was no longer a girl, it was time to become her own woman.

"I'm not being silly at all. I'm perfectly sane. Probably for the first time in my life. And I'm going to marry Jay."

At that, Kingston exploded. Georgia held the phone away from her ear.

There was a wild joy in Jay's face. He threw his head back and laughed, then raised his glass to her in acknowledgement.

Finally, when her father paused to draw a breath, she said into the phone, "My mind is made up. And I'm taking a week's vacation—maybe even two weeks."

She shot a look at Jay to assess his reaction.

He just grinned.

She was done arguing with her father. "Disinherit me if you like—I'll only quit. Then you won't have as much time to play golf."

Georgia's heart was pounding in her chest as she killed the call and smiled across at Jay. "That was far easier than I thought it would be. He needs to face reality. He can't run my life anymore—because I'll be spending it with you."

Jay raised his champagne flute, his face alight with admiration. "To you, Georgia. My fiancée."

But he hadn't finished yet.

Leaning forward he brushed his mouth against hers and murmured, "I knew from the moment I met you that there was no one else like you. How I love you."

There was so much pride in his voice that her heart melted like honey in the sun. She wished she could remember that first moment they'd met. But it didn't matter, because she'd grown to love the man who challenged her more than any other, who understood her, who matched her. He was her future.

Epilogue

It had been an hour since the crash of the phone hitting the desk told Marcia Hall the call had come to an end. It had been awfully silent in the massive adjoining corner office since then. Marcia was starting to feel a little concerned about her boss.

From the parts she'd overheard, the call had not gone well.

She rose to her feet and made her way to the water-cooler beside the group of sofas across from her work-space. Through the wall of glass windows, the predicted storm clouds were closing in, darkening the sky outside. She was a little worried about Roberta and Georgia flying in these awful conditions. She poured a glass of water— chilled to the exact temperature her boss demanded—and made her way through the adjoining door into his office. It was more than an office. It was the archive of his life. The photos on the walls documented his meetings with stars and fashion icons.

He sat there, staring at the blotter. His gaze lifted as she stopped before the desk.

"That stupid girl turned Adam down!"

When he spoke of any of his daughters like that, it upset

her. "Don't work yourself up, Kingston. We don't want another trip to the hospital."

"Bah."

She set the glass down on the leather mat in front of him. "Here, have a sip of water."

He glared at the glass.

"She's taking a vacation." He looked dumbfounded. "She's not coming back to New York tomorrow. She doesn't even know how long she intends to be gone."

Marcia suppressed a smile of glee at the news that Georgia wouldn't be flying in this weather. "Kingdom is not a prison. She's allowed time off."

Kingston let out a growl. "Her refusal to marry Fordyce puts me in a goddamned uncomfortable predicament."

Marcia couldn't have stopped the smile that split her face if her job had depended it.

Had Georgia finally realized what had been there in front of her all this time? She hoped so. No point telling her boss that his predicament was one of his own making. Instead, she said, "Kingston, she's a grown woman. Let her go… Let her make her own decisions."

"I need her here. With me. With Kingdom."

"If you don't let them go, you may have no Kingdom." Nor any family, either.

He laid his head back. "Marcia, this isn't how my plan plays out."

"Sometimes life has a way of upsetting those rigid plans." Then more softly, she said, "You need to learn to let go, Kingston."

His eyes were closed, and he gave no sign that he'd heard her.

"What the hell am I supposed to tell Fordyce? How will I ever face the man over the negotiating table again?"

So, this was about loss of face rather than about the loss of another daughter. "I'm sure you'll find a way."

From the outer office came the sound of a ringing phone. She glanced toward the door, and then back at the man she'd worked with for almost three decades. The man she knew better than anyone else in the world. He was as deaf to reason as he was blind to the truth.

Marcia Hall shook her head and went to answer the phone that wouldn't stop ringing.

The show must go on.

* * * * *

BETWEEN MARRIAGE AND MERGER

KAREN BOOTH

One

Lily Foster delighted in the *idea* of a wedding—two people so in love they vow to be together forever. The *reality* of a wedding, even as an observer, made Lily break out in hives. There she stood in the New York City Clerk's Office, without the usual trappings of organ music or a minister or the bride in a flowing gown, and the nuptials still put her on edge. Her skin felt clammy. She couldn't stand still. Her instinct was to run out of the building as fast as her pumps would carry her. But she couldn't do that. She had to stay put. She'd been generously invited to the impromptu nuptials of her boss's sister. Lily would've done anything for her boss, Noah Locke. To her own detriment, she adored him.

Still, for Lily, watching anyone get married was like unpacking a dusty old steamer trunk of miserable memories of her dream day that never was. When a woman has been left at the altar, no matter the reasons for it, she doesn't forget it. Ever. And Lily's world seemed hell-bent on dredging up the memory today.

"By the powers vested in me by the state of New York, I now pronounce you husband and wife."

Tamping down her jealousy and choking back a sob of sentimentality, Lily watched as the bride and groom—Noah's sister, Charlotte, and her new hubby, ridiculously handsome Michael, got lost in a passionate kiss. For that instant, she could feel the love between them. It was a life force that hit her from five feet away. Tears silently streamed down Lily's cheeks. Charlotte, in a knee-length white dress that hugged her five-month baby bump, popped up on one foot, kicking the other into the air. It was like the cover of a fun contemporary romance. That was enough for Lily. She couldn't watch anymore.

She pulled a tissue from her bag and dared to look at Noah, who was standing up for the groom. Noah wasn't watching the kiss either. His hands were stuffed in the pants pockets of his slim-fitting gray suit. He was staring at his shoes, probably because they were beautiful and expensive, like everything in his life. Noah was a notorious playboy, so much so that the New York tabloids loved to play with him the way a cat bats about a mouse. Weddings were undoubtedly not Noah's scene. Lily didn't even need to ask.

It was no surprise that Noah chose to play the field. He was perfect—tall and trim, athletic but not muscle-bound, with expertly tousled sandy brown hair that was tidy around the ears and back, but a bit long on the top. His moss green eyes were hypnotic, or maybe it was the sum total of Noah that made Lily lose her words or her memory of what she was supposed to be doing. Noah was *that* guy. The one you can't stop looking at. The one you can't help but think about. Thankfully, Lily was beyond that for the most part. She'd spent the last two years training herself to ignore Noah's beguiling features. She'd had no choice. As her boss, Noah was off-limits. Her job was too important. She was good at it, and even better, Noah and his brother, Sawyer, knew it.

Charlotte turned to Lily and Noah. Her newlywed smile took up nearly all the real estate between her diamond stud earrings. "Thanks for being our witnesses. Michael and I really appreciate it. I don't know what to say. We just got a wild hair and decided today was the day."

Michael leaned down and kissed the top of Charlotte's head. These two were so adorable together it made Lily's cheeks hurt. It also bruised her heart a little bit. She'd had an impossibly romantic love like that once. Or so she'd thought, but it had slipped right through her fingers, groom and all.

"Happy to do it. Congratulations." Noah stepped in and kissed his sister on the cheek, then shook Michael's hand.

Charlotte's phone rang and she squealed, grabbing Michael's arm and rushing out into the hall. Probably some famous well-wishers. The Locke family was known for their extensive connections.

"Want to grab a drink? It's nearly five o'clock. No point in going back to the office." Noah extended the invitation to Lily as if it were no big deal, as if she were just one of the guys, a role she suspected she would always have in his mind. He and Lily had done a few social things together, and they were always fun, but they filled Lily with pointless notions like hope and left her with sexy dreams, the kind where she'd wake up at 4:00 a.m. drenched in sweat and gasping for air. The sort of dream where you couldn't bring yourself to open your eyes or get out of bed. You wanted to languish in it forever.

"It's sweet of you to ask, but I think I'm going to head home, get out of these shoes and maybe do some reading."

"Friday night. Headed to that bookstore you like? What's it called?"

Lily's favorite spot in the city was a bookstore specializing in romance novels. "Petticoats and Proposals. You know all my tricks, don't you?"

"I try. I pay attention. It's a long-lost art, you know."

Their gazes connected and Lily's heart took up residence in her throat, pounding like crazy. *Boom boom. Boom boom.* It was as if Noah's eyes were magnetized, pulling on her, not allowing her to look anywhere else. She wanted to put the world on Pause and simply stare into them for a few hours. In between kisses of course. If she was going to slip into a fantasy world, she might as well make it exactly what she wanted it to be.

"It's because I can't stop talking about it."

"I'm sure that's not the reason." Noah cleared his throat and looked away for a moment. "Thanks for coming today. Charlotte couldn't deal with the wedding and the baby on the way. I'm actually happy for her. I wouldn't want to deal with all of those plans either. It seems like such an ordeal and then it's all over."

"Yeah. Me neither." Noah didn't know the half of it. And no amount of paying attention was going to get Lily to talk about it. Some things were better left buried.

"Okay, then. See you Monday."

"Yep. Have a good weekend." Lily smiled and walked away. Exactly like it didn't hurt at all to distance herself from Noah Locke.

Working with Lily, Mondays were always the hardest. Noah had endured a few days away from her, and his ability to keep himself together had worn off. Today seemed like an especially difficult start to the week. He couldn't even look at her.

"You're in early for a Monday," she said, with her usual happy singsong. She was standing in his office doorway, undoubtedly stunning.

"Some emergency meeting about the Hannafort Hotels deal. Charlotte's coming in for it, too. Not sure if she told you, but we've cut her in since she made the initial introduction." Noah still hadn't raised his sights, but he could see in his periphery that Lily was wearing her blue sweater. *The* blue sweater. The one that not only showed off every beguiling curve she possessed, but the one that really brought out her mesmerizing sapphire eyes.

"Oh. Okay. Let me drop my things, check email and I'll be right in."

"Sounds good." As if the sweater weren't bad enough, he couldn't avoid her heavenly scent. The faintest trace of it floated in the air when she left the room—sweet and sunny, just like her. His iron will was going to have to work doubly hard today.

"Unless there's something you need right now," she added.

He could hear her drumming her fingers on the door casing. For a moment, he imagined those delicate hands unbuttoning his shirt, touching the bare skin of his chest. He had to stop that train of thought right there or he'd lose it. "I'm good. Take your time."

With that, Lily disappeared from view. Noah sat back in his chair and a heavy exhale rushed from his lungs. *This is becoming impossible.*

Even after two years, Noah's love/hate relationship when it came to working with Lily wasn't getting any easier. He loved seeing her face every day, the way she lit up the office and managed to diffuse tense situations, but he hated how she could turn him into a blithering idiot. He hated being in enclosed spaces with her, like the elevator, where it took superhuman strength to keep from telling her how badly he wanted to kiss her. He hated having this all bottled up inside him. It wasn't how he operated with women.

But if ever a woman was off-limits, Lily was. She was a dream employee, clever and capable, a quick learner who was also organized and meticulous. She was too valuable to Locke and Locke, the company Noah owned and operated with his brother, Sawyer. As Sawyer had said many times, Lily might be uncommonly lovely and smart and kind, but Noah needed to keep his tongue in his mouth and his eyes in his head. To compensate, he'd been letting his eyes and his mouth wander elsewhere. It helped, but only a little.

"Okay. I'm back." Lily waltzed into his office and started straightening papers on his desk. She knew exactly how he liked things, and he'd never even had to tell her. She'd simply picked up on his preferences.

"Good weekend?" he asked, making small talk and sneaking a single glance. Her golden blond hair in a low twist brought attention to her lithe and graceful neck. He loved the naughty librarian aspect of it. He wanted her to peer at him over reading glasses and tell him to be quiet.

"The usual."

"Friday night at the romance bookstore?"

"I can sit there for hours and get lost in love stories."

He found it adorable that Lily was a bookworm. He, too, loved to read, but preferred nonfiction—history and biographies. He was not an incurable romantic like Lily, which was probably a big part of his attraction to her. He longed to shed at least some of his pessimism about love. Case in point, Lily had teared up at Charlotte's wedding, even when the civil ceremony had none of the sappy buildup of a traditional wedding. Noah was happy for his sister, but he did not get choked up. The very notion of a wedding unnerved him.

Charlotte's voice rang out from the hall beyond Noah's office walls.

"Sounds like my sister is here." *Back to work.* Noah stepped out from behind his desk and only allowed himself the smallest of glimpses of Lily in her black skirt. Studying the sway of her hips was a luxury he couldn't afford.

"Morning." Noah greeted his sister in the reception area, aka Lily's domain. Charlotte came by the office now and then, especially since involving her in the Hannafort Hotels deal, but she usually only came at lunchtime. It wasn't normal for her to be here first thing. She was always too busy running around doing real estate agent things, and lately, mother-to-be things.

"Did Sawyer talk to you about the video?" Charlotte's voice had a frantic edge to it as she swished her long blond hair to the side and unbuttoned her wool coat.

"Sawyer's on a call with Mr. Hannafort," Lily chimed in, buzzing around the office, running the photocopier, answering phones. "He left a note on my desk and said he was not to be disturbed. I'm not sure when he'll be done."

Sawyer's door opened and out he marched. His suit coat was off and his shirtsleeves were already rolled up like he'd been working for hours. This was not a good sign. It was hardly ten minutes after nine. "Charlotte, did you tell Noah about the news story?"

"I haven't had a chance," Charlotte said.

"She just got here." Noah felt as out of the loop as could be. "Does somebody want to tell me what's going on?"

"Hannafort saw it. He's not happy," Sawyer said.

"Oh no." Charlotte bustled into Sawyer's office with

all the dramatic urgency of a lawyer about to declare "I object!"

"Do you want to sit in on this?" Noah asked Lily. He was unsure what "this" he was about to walk into, but he and Sawyer were making a point of including Lily in high-level discussions. She'd earned the opportunity and it made everything in the office run more smoothly.

"I do, but I'm almost done with the Hannafort projections. You guys will want those for the meeting." She smiled wide—a flash of bright white framed by full, pink lips. Noah savored that instant. He had a feeling the rest of his day was about to tumble sharply downhill. "You go ahead. I'll be there in a minute."

Noah wandered into Sawyer's office. "Does somebody want to tell me what's going on?" He took one of the two seats opposite Sawyer's desk. Charlotte was in the other. The morning sun streamed through the tall, leaded glass windows of their office in the Chelsea neighborhood of Manhattan. It was a bright late March day, a bit brisk for Noah's liking, although the mood in Sawyer's office was even colder.

"Charlotte called me early this morning," Sawyer started.

"I tried to reach you, Noah, but I got voice mail. Why do you never answer my calls?"

Noah hated his phone. He often turned it off or simply left it in another room. There was something about being available to everyone at all times that he detested. It made him feel trapped. "Sorry. So what?"

Charlotte pulled out her phone. "I have the link saved."

Sawyer held up a hand and turned his laptop around so Charlotte and Noah could see it. "Let me save you the time. I have it pulled up on my computer. Lyle Hannafort sent it to me."

The webpage Sawyer had opened looked to be a spot for online gossip. Not Sawyer's usual fare. If he was online, he was watching the markets or sports, particularly college basketball this time of year. "Now I'm really lost," Noah said.

"You won't be." Sawyer scrolled down and clicked on the icon in the center of the screen. The video began to play.

Noah only needed to hear his name, purred by a woman with a sultry voice, to feel like the ground had fallen out from under him.

Big Apple businessman, Noah Locke, of the Locke hotel family, has been busy with the ladies over the last several months. And do we mean busy.

All warmth drained from Noah's body. His hands went cold. He'd been in the tabloids before, but this was different. These were moving pictures—shot after shot of Noah walking into and out of bars, restaurants and apartment buildings all over the city. A different woman on his arm in every picture. With a number counting them off. One... two...three... They stopped at fifteen. Noah felt sick.

Although his brother, Sawyer, and sister, Charlotte, have both settled down, it seems Noah is rallying to keep that trademark Locke wild streak alive. His father, James Locke, has not only been married four times, he's been romantically linked to hundreds of New York socialites over the years. Perhaps the middle Locke child is patterning himself after dear old dad.

Noah had a real talent for shrugging things off, but right now, he wanted to put his fist through a brick wall. "I'm calling our lawyer. This is defamation of character."

"Is it? Did they lie about a single thing?" Sawyer turned his computer back around to Noah's great relief. That final voice-over line and slate in the video was already permanently burned into his brain. *Perhaps the middle Locke child is patterning himself after dear old dad.* That was absolutely *not* the case.

"Well?" Charlotte asked. "You didn't answer the question."

Noah sat back, kneading his forehead, trying to think of anything they'd said in the video that was untrue. He would've asked to see it again if it hadn't made him sound like such a miserable excuse for a human being. Was he terrible? He didn't want to think he was. "Well, no. I mean, yes, I dated all of those women. That's true. But the last time I checked, this is a free country and a single man is allowed to have dinner with a single woman."

"Or fifteen," Charlotte quipped.

"I don't really see the point of this. Is it the slowest news day in the history of the world?" Noah's jaw tightened. He hated this.

"People love gossip. Especially about rich men who like to spend time with pretty women," Charlotte said. "You should know that by now."

Noah did know that, but in the past, Sawyer had most often been the target if there was anything tawdry to be said about the three siblings. A few times Charlotte had been busted for her party girl ways, but that had been a while ago. Now that both Sawyer and Charlotte were hitched, and both sets of wedded couples had babies on the way, apparently Noah was left to be the top of the dubious Locke family heap.

Noah then remembered what Sawyer had said before they'd come into his office. "Hold on. Hannafort has seen this? How in the hell did that happen?"

"It's the internet, Noah. This stuff spreads like wildfire. He's not happy about it, either." The deal they were working on with Lyle Hannafort, founder and CEO of Hannafort

Hotels, was massive. A real game changer. There was a mountain of money to be made. "He's a straight shooter. He doesn't mince words. And he's already predisposed to thinking badly of anyone named Locke. You know how hard we've worked to convince him we're not like Dad." Lyle Hannafort hated Sawyer and Noah's father and the feeling was mutual. They were bitter competitors. As much as that might have been one of Lyle's reasons for doing this deal, it was also a reason for calling it off.

"I'm very aware of how hard we've worked."

"He said he's not sure he can do business with a man who doesn't treat women as they should be treated," Sawyer said.

Noah sprang from his seat and jabbed his finger into the top of his brother's desk. "Now, hold on a second. Taking a woman out to dinner does not equal treating her badly. I'm always a gentleman. Always."

"You're just a gentleman a *lot*." Charlotte cocked a judgmental eyebrow at him, bobbing her foot. Noah could've easily fought back—Charlotte had once dated half of the men in Manhattan—but he couldn't be mean to her. Plus, she was expecting, and if he was worried about being seen as an ass, lashing out at his pregnant sister would not be a good move.

"I know that you're a good guy, Noah," Sawyer said. "Charlotte knows that, too. But Hannafort has built an empire on being a family man. He has five grown daughters, so I'm sure he's seen his fair share of men behaving badly. He totally owns up to being old-fashioned. He and his wife were high school sweethearts."

Noah had been impressed to learn that little factoid about the Hannaforts. That was a long time with one person. How did they make it work? In Noah's family, they didn't. Their dad had burned through each of his marriages, and there had been many serious girlfriends in between. There was a difference between Noah and his dad, though, and it was plain as day—one man a serial monogamist, carrying relationships to a cherished place only to destroy them. The other man, Noah, knew his limitations. He never led a woman on. Never. He was always clear about where and when things were ending.

"So what is Hannafort saying?"

"Let's say that we've gone from a place where both parties were head over heels to a place where one side is thinking about leaving the dance."

This deal had been in serious discussion for only a month, so things were still fragile. After months of convincing Lyle to talk to them, they were just starting to get comfortable with each other. This was supposed to be the honeymoon phase, but that seemed to be over. "Seriously? It's that bad?"

"As he put it, he has no patience for negative publicity that could have been easily avoided." Sawyer rocked back in his seat.

"How was I supposed to avoid this? No one could've predicted this." Noah had been looking forward to a quiet day in the office. He had no meetings, only a few phone calls, and he and Lily were supposed to have a discussion about some new projects. He'd been looking forward to that, however hard he'd have to try to concentrate on work.

"I think his point was that it never would've happened if you weren't the guy who dates dozens of women."

"What he really means is that if I wasn't like Dad." *Which I'm not.* Noah grumbled under his breath, frustrated beyond belief. He would never admit it to anyone, but part of the reason he'd been going out so much was because of Lily. The nights when he went home alone were awful. He couldn't watch TV, he couldn't read a book. His mind kept drifting to Lily, everything she'd done or said at work that day, replaying in his head like a never-ending movie. There was something about her that stopped Noah dead in his tracks.

But Sawyer had been crystal clear about it—all of that was too bad. *Lily is the best employee we have ever had. She is perfect. Don't mess this up. We need her and all you do is break hearts.*

Noah got it. Lily was forbidden fruit.

"How do we convince Mr. Hannafort that Noah's not that kind of guy?" Charlotte asked.

Sawyer snickered. "By finding him a wife. Or a fiancée."

Charlotte stifled a grin. "But it would have to be right away. Preferably before we go to Hannafort's daughter's wedding."

"Ideally, yes." Sawyer stared off into space like he was brainstorming. Charlotte was doing the same. Noah wasn't about to contribute to their ludicrous meeting of the minds. There was no woman in his life he'd consider asking to marry him. No one was even close.

A knock came at the door. Noah turned as Lily walked in with four black binders in her arms. "I have the revenue projections from Mr. Hannafort's team. I cross-referenced them with our own, which are considerably more conservative."

"Great. Thank you," Sawyer said.

Lily doled out the presentations while Noah remained standing.

"Lily, you can take my seat. I'm happy right here."

She settled in, rocking her hips from side to side. "You got it all warmed up for me."

He sucked in a sharp breath. Good God, she was going to be the death of him.

Noah opened his binder. There was no time to absorb all of the information in this report, but one quick glance at a few spreadsheets told him one thing—they were going to make a lot of money if this deal went through. And his actions, which had been perfectly innocent at the time, could end up taking it all away. Charlotte, and Sawyer in particular, would never forgive him. Or if they did, it would take a very long time. There was already enough acrimony in his family from their dad. Noah refused to be the cause for this blowing up in their faces.

"Wow." Sawyer flipped through the pages. "These numbers are impressive."

"They are." Charlotte closed her folder and chewed on her nail. "Can't let this get out from under us."

"No, we can't." Noah racked his brain for a way to make himself seem less like a Lothario.

Charlotte narrowed her vision on him, then her sights drifted to Lily. She sat a little straighter and turned in her chair. "Lily, can I ask you a question?"

"Of course."

"Would you have any interest in going to a wedding with all of us? This weekend. I don't know what sort of personal obligations you have, and I know it's short notice."

As the words out of Charlotte's mouth found his ears, Noah quickly realized what she was doing. She was setting him up. With Lily. The woman who he'd been fighting to keep in the friend zone. Noah bugged his eyes at Charlotte, but she shot him a steely look right back.

"A wedding? Do you mean Annie Hannafort's wedding?"

Charlotte smiled effortlessly, like this all made perfect sense and would not cause a single problem. Noah already had a dozen reasons not to do what Charlotte was about to suggest. The reasons were already stacked up and waiting, and he'd only been living with this realization for less than a minute. "Exactly. It's just that we would need you to be Noah's date. Well, more than his date. We would need you to pretend to be his fiancée."

Two

Lily mustered the strength to hold her smile, but only because she was fairly certain her face was frozen. She managed to blink, so her eyes were working. That was good. Her mind, meanwhile, was frantically running around like a chicken with its head cut off. Had Charlotte Locke just said those words? Pretend to be Noah's fiancée? At a wedding, no less?

Lily's worst nightmare and her most closely held fantasy had decided to make sweet love to each other.

"Are you serious?" She realized how terrible the question must sound to Noah, but she needed clarification and she needed it now. This felt an awful lot like the moment her biggest high school crush asked her out in front of his friends, only to burst into peals of laughter. That was the day Lily learned how apt the word *crush* was when it came to love.

"I know it seems a little strange, but there's a reason behind it and you would be helping the company immensely."

Noah stepped closer and sat on the edge of Sawyer's desk, crossing his long legs, facing her with a look that could only be described as raw embarrassment. His expression was difficult to endure, which spoke volumes about how real it was. Noah was ridiculously easy on the eyes.

"You don't have to do this," Noah said. "This is not part of your job."

Lily couldn't decide if he was saying that because he desperately wanted his own out, or if he was simply being kind. She hoped for the latter, if only to save her pride.

"We would pay you, of course," Sawyer said. "We'll have to come up with a number. Maybe you should sit down and think about what you would need for three days away from home."

"Acting as Noah's fiancée." Lily wanted to be sure she'd heard that part right.

"Yes. There was a very unflattering video of Noah that turned up on a gossip website and we're trying to curb its effects. Mr. Hannafort wants to know that the Lockes aren't a liability when it comes to publicity."

"Unflattering video?" Lily could only imagine what Noah's sister was referring to.

"Do you want to see it?" Charlotte asked.

Noah grumbled. His straight shoulders dropped. "Don't show her the video. It's demeaning. Lily and I need to work together. I don't want her to think of me that way."

Charlotte leaned over the arm of her chair. "It's about the stable of women he's been dating lately."

Lily could feel her lips mold into a thin line. Oh, she knew plenty about Noah and his dates. A few women had come by the office, all intimidatingly beautiful. And she'd heard him talk to them, as smooth as could be. Lily would've done anything to have a man say one-tenth of what Noah regularly said to women he apparently hardly cared about. "I see."

"So as I said," Sawyer interjected. "We would need to come up with a number, but I promise we'll make it worth your while. This isn't normally something I'd consider, but desperate times call for creative measures."

Lily crossed her legs, her mind mired in the business of deciding whether or not this was a good idea. She loved working for Sawyer and Noah, so it would be next to impossible to say no. It wasn't in her DNA to let them down. But one downside of being employed by Locke and Locke was the limited opportunities for advancement. Lily had already worked her way well beyond the parameters of her title of Executive Admin. Sawyer and Noah had given her more and more responsibility, they'd even given her a few raises, but she was capable of even more. If the payoff was there. She was a hard worker, but she wasn't an idiot. She wasn't going to kill herself if they were just going to take advantage of her.

"If I do this, I don't want to be compensated with cash. I want a piece of the company." Lily was impressed with herself. She'd come out with it, no hemming or hawing. She sat straighter, fighting back any concern over how her proposal might be met. "A small piece, but a piece. I believe I've demonstrated that I'm a valuable asset to the company, but I want to do more."

Sawyer nodded slowly, as if he was still taking it all in.

"This isn't my call. I'm in on this Hannafort deal and that's it." Charlotte looked at her phone. "I'm also going to be late for my doctor's appointment if I don't leave now." She got up from her seat and shot both of her brothers a very pointed glance. "Don't screw this up. And Lily, don't let them screw this up."

Lily grinned as Charlotte excused herself and left. She did love the way Charlotte put her brothers on notice.

"What do you think?" Sawyer asked Noah.

"You've said it yourself a thousand times. Lily is by far the best employee we've had. She's irreplaceable. If she's willing to put up with me for a weekend, we should give her what she wants."

Sawyer chuckled quietly, and that made Noah laugh, which filled Lily with happy flutters in her chest. She was overcome with pride, knowing that she'd been a frequent subject of conversation between the brothers and in such a positive light, no less. It reaffirmed her decision two years ago to focus on her career and let romance and her personal life take a back seat. This might actually end up paying off.

"I think one percent is fair," Noah said.

"Agreed," Sawyer quickly added. "It might not sound like a lot, but if the Hannafort deal goes through, it will be sizable. And it should be income that comes in for years and years. Not bad for three days' work."

Lily was a bit of a whiz with numbers, so she knew exactly how big 1 percent of Locke and Locke could end up being, especially after having worked on the Hannafort projections. A nest egg to last her a lifetime? All for one weekend pretending to be enamored with gorgeous, unattainable Noah? This was a no-brainer if ever there was one. Even if the part about Noah did make her stomach flip-flop. Yes, she struggled at weddings, but she'd just endured one. What difference could another one possibly make? "I'll do it."

"That's great news. Thank you." Sawyer's eyebrows drew together. "I hope you know this is not something we would normally ask you to do."

"I've been here two years. I know this is not the way

things work around here. Sometimes things have to be done for appearances."

"Exactly."

"I should probably get back to my desk. I have lots of other stuff to do. Emails to answer." Lily rose from her seat, but something about this was still leaving her unsettled. Was this the right thing to do? Would it ruin her working relationship with Noah? They got along so well. She didn't want it to be awkward later. "I do want to clarify that this is for show, right? We're pretending. That's it."

Noah's eyes found hers and she felt naked, like he was looking right through her. "That goes without saying."

She smiled and nodded, like the loyal employee she was. But inside, all she could think was *of course*. Noah Locke was *that* guy and he always would be.

Noah closed the door when Lily walked out of Sawyer's office. "I don't think you've fully thought this out." He paced back and forth, between the chairs and the window. "We're talking about pretending to be engaged to each other. Do you know what engaged people do?"

"Um, I'm pretty sure, but why don't you fill me in." Sawyer was still poring over the Hannafort reports, dismissing this conversation as if it was nothing.

"Hugging. Holding hands. Kissing."

"Sounds about right. I know you remember how to do all of those things." Sawyer flipped to another page.

"But am I not supposed to be staying away from Lily? You were the one who wouldn't stop going on and on about how I needed to pretend that she was my sister. Don't mess things up, Noah. Stop making up excuses to be around her, Noah." He planted both hands on Sawyer's desk and stared him down. "This could easily mess things up with her. Then what? We lose our best employee because of some stupid stunt?"

"Now you see the validity of my original argument? When we're being forced to set it aside?" Sawyer closed the binder and looked him square in the eye. "I think the one thing that video proved is that you have no problem with walking away, so I'm certainly not worried about your feelings. As for Lily, she's being rewarded handsomely and she seems completely comfortable with the idea. She's a very strong person. I'm a little concerned, but I'm not overly concerned. How confused can two people get over the course of three days?"

"Honestly? I have no idea. I've never been fake engaged before."

"And that's the important thing to remember. This is fake. It's not real. It's not the same as if you had actually pursued her. That would have hurt her feelings when you decided to end it. Or…"

"Or what?"

"Or maybe she would've ended up ending it. Maybe she would've turned you down. I'm sure it's hard for you to imagine, but it could've gone down that way."

"You think I don't worry about that every time I ask a woman out? Because I do." Noah had thought about that a lot when it came to Lily, if only when he was trying to convince himself that going there in the first place would be a huge mistake.

Surely Lily dated a lot. She simply never mentioned it. In fact, she rarely talked about herself. He could only assume that she didn't have a serious boyfriend right now. She never complained about working late and she was always doing her Friday night visit to the bookstore she liked so much. It was silly, but a few weeks ago, Noah had been dateless and bored on a Friday night, so he'd gone for a run and accidentally on purpose ended up there. He'd peeked in the window, but couldn't see the corner she'd talked about. He'd also been too embarrassed to walk in. So he'd pretended his shoelace was untied and jogged back to his apartment, realizing how stupid the whole thing had been in the first place. What would he have said if she'd seen him? *I always go for runs in neighborhoods that are totally out of the way from where I live.*

"And don't forget, Lily's a tough cookie," Sawyer said. "I'm not as concerned about it as I was when we first started working on the Grand Legacy project and you couldn't keep your eyes off her or your tongue off the floor."

"You act like I'm the horniest guy you've ever met. Have you not noticed how stunning she is?"

"I noticed. Believe me. I've noticed. As have lots of our clients."

The worst part…or the best part, Noah couldn't decide, was that Lily didn't seem to know it. Or if she did, she didn't seem driven by it or obsessed by it. She simply seemed comfortable in her own skin, which Noah found very sexy.

"Okay. Well, I guess I'm going to go back to work with my fake fiancée. This is officially the craziest thing I've ever done, just so you know."

"I don't want to be a jerk about it, but this was your own doing. I appreciate your willingness to make it right. It'll all be fine. We'll do the deal with Hannafort and you and Lily can quietly break up. I doubt it'll even be on his radar at that point. But we need to remove any doubt he has now."

"Got it." Noah reached for the door.

"Wait. There's more. We need word of the engagement out before we leave and Lily is also going to need a ring. Everyone will want to see the ring."

Noah groaned in frustration. "How do we go about announcing an engagement? Do we call the society page?"

"I don't think we have time for that. I'll talk to Kendall. We'll figure out a way to leak it to the press." Sawyer's wife, Kendall, was a PR master. She'd done a brilliant job on the reopening of the family's historic hotel, the Grand Legacy.

Noah stifled another sigh. "Let me know." As he walked down the hall, he noticed that Lily was not at her desk. He rounded into his office. She was putting things away in his filing cabinet. He came to a dead stop. He didn't say a thing. Lily had this habit when she was standing, but concentrating on something—she'd step out of one pump and balance on her opposite leg, rubbing the back of her calf with her bare foot. Up and down, over and over until she was finished with the task. It was one of the many inexplicably sexy things she did.

Maybe this fake engagement had a bright side. Maybe this was the chance to get Lily out of his system. His brother couldn't say a thing about holding hands, long embraces, or kisses now. And if those things continued behind closed doors, and Lily wanted him, too, clothes could come off and he could finally know what it was like to make love to her, to have her hands all over him, and at the end of the weekend, they could part ways on the romantic front. It was perfect.

A little too perfect.

Noah couldn't escape the notion that his plan sounded like something his dad would do. He was not his father, and he would do anything he could to prove it. That meant he would have to be doubly careful and keep things especially chaste between them, all while trying to create the illusion that they were hopelessly in love. He had no idea how he was going to pull this off.

Lily whipped around, surprise in her eyes. She dropped down onto her bare foot and pressed her hand to her chest. "You scared me."

"I'm sorry. I didn't want to startle you, but you were so deep in concentration."

Lily worked her foot back into her black pump. "You could tell?"

"Yeah. You do that thing with your foot when you're focused."

Her cheeks turned the most gorgeous shade of pink, like cherry blossoms in spring, except brighter and more vibrant. It made him want to embarrass her more often. "I do?"

Noah swallowed hard. He hadn't had time to get used to the fact that it would be okay for him to say something about this now. Before, a topic like this was best avoided. "I did. I've noticed it for a while now. I'm sorry if that bothers you."

She shook her head. "No. Of course not. It doesn't bother me at all." Was that a hint of flirtation in her voice? If so, he liked being fake engaged to her, even if the clock hadn't yet started ticking on their charade.

"So, are you okay with our arrangement? There's still time to back out if you want." He didn't want to come off as unsure, but it was important to him that she not feel as though she'd been cornered. There had been three Lockes in that room and only one Lily Foster. It wasn't entirely fair.

"I'd be lying if I said that I was completely comfortable with the idea. I'm not much for faking something."

"Yeah. Me neither."

"But I'm also smart enough to know that people do all sorts of things in business to make a deal happen. And maybe if you aren't willing to be daring with something, you'll miss out. This would be a big thing to miss out on."

"The Hannafort deal."

"Of course."

It was good to have clarification, if only to keep things straight. "Well, our next step is for me to take you shopping for a ring."

"Wow. A ring." Lily looked down at her own hand as if she were trying to picture it. "I guess that's a must-have, isn't it?"

"Can't be fake engaged without a ring." He smiled when she shot him a knowing glance. "Except the ring will be real. I'm not putting a fake ring on your hand." Lily absolutely deserved a real ring, but he did have to wonder if this harebrained plan was going to end up ruining any fantasies she'd had about getting engaged. He didn't want to make assumptions based on her gender, but she did prefer books with happy endings.

Noah had zero fantasies about marriage. Or engagement. He'd never imagined the moment when he'd get down on one knee. He'd never thought about what it would feel like to love someone so much that the only thing that made sense was to be with them forever. It had always seemed, at best, unlikely and, at worst, doomed. Would he ever be in love? Would he ever feel as though he couldn't live without someone? Seventy-two hours or so and he usually knew that the woman of the moment wasn't the one. Or, admittedly, he'd gone into it with the assumption he would not find love. It wasn't the best attitude, but time and again, things played out that way. It was hard not to assume that the common denominator—his heart—wasn't built for love.

"Good to know that you're not going to force me to be excited about a cubic zirconia. Not that I wouldn't be happy with whatever you gave me. But, you know. A girl wants a diamond if she can get it."

"The only thing about the ring shopping is that we have to plan it out in advance. Sawyer's going to have Kendall leak it to the press so it will hopefully make its way back to Hannafort. And if not, we will at least have countered the bad publicity with good."

She nodded. "So the video was that bad?"

The thought of it made his stomach sink yet again. He hoped Lily never saw it. He hoped she never looked it up on the internet, although if the roles were reversed, he definitely would have done some due diligence. He truly didn't want her seeing him in that light. Even if it was biased, and pulpy, it wasn't a lie. There was a whole lot of truth in it. "It wasn't my best showing, that's for sure."

Lily patted him on the shoulder. When she moved her hand, it felt as though she'd marked him for life with her touch. "Hopefully we can make it go away. We should probably start tomorrow."

"Do I have a hole in my schedule?"

"No meetings from eleven to three. A nice big window."

"Perfect. Tomorrow at eleven we have a date to buy that ring." Noah could hardly believe the words after they'd left his lips. For a guy who'd sworn he'd never get engaged, he'd said it like it was no big deal, when he knew for a fact that it was.

Three

Lily did her best to stay busy at work the next morning, but knowing where she and Noah were going at eleven made it tough to focus. A mere twenty-four hours into their fake engagement and Noah was about to take her to buy the ring. She'd be lying if she said she'd never thought about stepping into a fancy jewelry store with a sweet, handsome, romantic guy. Her broken engagement had come with a ring that was a family heirloom, no shopping required. She'd had no idea that Peter wouldn't be able to go through with the promise that accompanied that ring, but returning it had been a simple process. She'd thrown it at him in a quiet room just outside the nave. He'd cursed her, scrambled on his hands and knees for it, nearly ruining his tuxedo pants. She'd cried and braced herself for what followed—telling a church full of invited guests that they were welcome to enjoy the reception, but there would be no wedding.

The events of that dreadful day were precisely why her fake engagement to Noah, although fun in premise, was about business and nothing else. She'd never had financial security in her life and that became her top priority after the love part went south. She had to take her chance to secure her future. It would be one fewer thing to fret about, in a world fraught with things that could make a woman worry, like whether or not Mr. Right would ever come along.

Out walked Noah from the confines of Sawyer's office. "So we're all set with the photographer or whoever is supposed to be outside the jewelry store?"

Sawyer followed his brother. "According to Kendall, yes. As to who it is and where they'll be, I have no idea. You'll have to be as convincing as possible. These people are very good at sniffing out a fake. And, honestly, you need to act like someone is watching, even when you don't know for certain that they are. The video should have taught you that much."

Noah cast his sights at Lily. It was as if he was saying *Can you believe what we're doing?* To which Lily would have replied *No*.

"I don't want any obvious signs that this is a Locke and Locke purchase, so put the ring on one of your personal cards instead of the company's. We'll find a way to reimburse you for it," Sawyer said. "I don't know if they'll let us return it when it's all said and done, but I suppose we could always sell it if we had to."

This was all too strange, an unromantic transaction. Lily dug around in her purse for a piece of gum, just to distract herself from this deeply uncomfortable subject.

"Sawyer, listen to yourself. We're not doing that." Noah grabbed his coat and slipped it on. The man had incredible shoulders, but the black wool brought out the strong line of them, enough to make her stifle a sigh. "If I give Lily a ring, she gets to keep it. I'm not asking for it back, even if this is fake."

Lily's heart broke out in a gallop, fierce and strong, like a young horse discovering it could run for as long and as far as it wanted to. That might have been the most romantic thing a man had ever said about her.

Even when his sweet sentiment was tied up with a satin bow called "fake."

Sawyer stuffed his hands into his pockets. "You're right. You're absolutely right. Lily, whatever you choose today, it's yours to keep."

"Oh. Well, thank you. I guess we'll call it combat pay?"

Sawyer laughed. Noah did, too, but it was far less convincing and came only after his brother had started it. He seemed so tortured over this whole thing, it was impossible to feel good about it.

"I'm kidding. Of course. If I wanted combat pay, I'd ask for cash." She smiled sweetly and got up from her desk, wishing there was a protocol somewhere for interactions with your fake fiancée and your fake future brother-in-law. She felt a bit like she was failing right now.

"You two have fun. Try not to get into too much trouble," Sawyer said, heading back into his office.

"No promises," Noah muttered. "And we're going out to lunch afterward."

"On the company dime?" Lily asked.

Noah unleashed a devilish smile. "Of course." He then offered her his arm, which he held in midair while Lily struggled to keep up with what she was supposed to do. "Remember what Sawyer said. We need to act like someone is watching at all times."

"Right." She hooked hers in his and he snuggled her against his body, sending a lovely shock right through her.

One touch, through layers of coats no less, and she felt like her shoes might shoot right off her feet.

They took the stairs down to the street. Noah's driver was waiting for them, standing outside the sleek black town car. He opened the door as they approached and Lily struggled to stay in the moment, to not let her consciousness become too detached from what was happening. This was a fantasy brought to life, and she should embrace the good parts. There would surely be bad moments when she would end up with flickers of regret over doing this crazy thing. For now, Noah Locke, Mr. Unattainable, was taking her to buy an engagement ring. She wanted to soak up every minute.

They got settled in the back seat. "Warm enough?" Noah asked.

She nodded. "Yes."

"Good."

"Yes." *Wow. So this is what the world's worst small talk is like.*

"I was thinking…" He looked out the window and shook his head.

"What? You were thinking what?"

He turned back and looked at her so earnestly she thought she might disappear into his green eyes. "What do people do after they buy an engagement ring?"

Have sex? Lily thought for a second about putting it out there, but decided there were only so many inappropriate jokes she could make. That would not be professional. "I don't know. Kiss?"

"Yes. Exactly." He nodded a little too fast, almost as if he was nervous, which seemed impossible. She'd witnessed more human moments out of Noah in the last day than she'd ever seen before. It was nice. "And, obviously, we haven't done that yet. I don't think it should be awkward. It should seem natural, especially if anyone is taking a picture."

She put her hand on his. "Right. Like Sawyer said."

"Following orders."

"He needs us to put on a good show. We should practice. At least once." The instant she said it, the air crackled with electricity. She'd pushed things to the next level. With the help of some convenient excuses, of course.

Noah's clever half smile crossed his lips, and his eyes swirled to a darker shade. The city whizzed by outside the window. Lily was overcome with the freeing feeling of being given permission to do something you shouldn't. Kissing Noah was such a bad idea, but when you'd thought about a bad idea for two whole years, it was hard not to be excited by it. His hand slipped under her hair and around her neck. She sat straighter. She angled herself closer. Every nerve ending in her body was cheering him on. His thumb settled in the soft spot under her ear. His touch was more than warm. It was a superhuman zap of heat. It might turn her into something she'd never been before.

His lips parted ever so slightly and she raised her chin as he lowered his head. His hair slumped forward. She loved that. She'd fantasized a million times about running her hands through it, feeling the thick strands between her fingers and smoothing it back. She wanted to stare at him forever, but she also wanted to savor every delicious heartbeat of anticipation. Her eyes fluttered shut. When his mouth met hers, she waited for it to change her life, but it was a soft brush of a kiss. A first date kiss. An *oh hi nice to meet you* kiss. It was nice. So nice. But nice wasn't going to cut it. Her body didn't merely tell her so, it was screaming it in both ears. She slanted her head and pushed up from the seat, aiming her shoulders straight for his. He pulled back. Her eyes flew open. Their gazes connected, both of them searching. It was an entire deliberation about their next kiss, wrapped up in two seconds. He smiled. She swallowed. He was coming in for the real thing.

The next thing she knew, she had all ten fingers working into his hair. Her arms landed on his shoulders. His hand was molded around her hip, squeezing like he was trying to get down to the bone. Their lips were in a mad scramble, parted, making way for tongues to roam. In under two seconds, they'd gone from zero to sexy sixty. The kiss was flat-out reckless now, like neither of them cared about ramifications. She was a woman and he was the hottest man she'd ever set her eyes on. One well-placed rub and they might as well be dry tinder. A fire was inevitable.

Lily dropped one hand and worked her way inside Noah's coat, which he'd been kind enough to leave unbuttoned. She palmed his firm chest, and even through layers of clothes—his suit coat, his shirt—she could feel the frantic pounding of his heart. She wanted nothing more than to experience that with bare skin against bare skin. Noah's hand traveled down to her knee and under the hem of her skirt. Lily felt like she might burst into full flame. He didn't waste a second, heading north, his palm caressing her stocking. Her heart was beating like a kid dragging a stick across a picket fence. He came to a dead stop when his thumb reached the top of her thigh-highs. Noah pulled back, breaking their kiss, breathless. Thankfully, his hand hadn't moved.

"Are those?" His eyes were dark with a brew of lust and curiosity.

She nodded, her lips floating back to meet his and steal one more kiss. "I can't stand regular panty hose," she murmured against his mouth. She took a soft nip of his lower lip.

A low groan escaped his throat.

The divider between the driver and the back seat started to lower. Lily scrambled to find a more demure position. The driver, most likely accustomed to this scene, didn't look at them. "Mr. Locke. We're here at Tiffany."

Noah gawked at Lily. Maybe he hadn't expected her to go for it. *Carpe diem, Mr. Locke. Carpe diem.* "Um. Ready?" he asked.

For what? she almost answered. *For you to tear off my clothes?* "Hold on a sec." She reached out and combed her fingers through his silky hair, which was just as tangled as her thoughts right now. "Your hair." It was even softer than it had been a minute ago. Maybe it was because she wasn't wholly distracted by his lips and chest.

"Thanks for looking out for me." He then scrutinized her hair and smoothed back one strand that was grazing her cheek. "You weren't nearly as disheveled."

Embarrassment crept over her, shrouding her from head to toe. She hadn't merely gone overboard, she'd behaved like a teenager who'd spent her adolescence locked up in an all-girls school. Lily made a mental note: *practice some damn decorum.* At least this was probably the norm for Noah, women going crazy for him. He didn't seem particularly fazed by it at all.

Noah was quite frankly shocked that he could climb out of the back seat and straighten to his full height. It felt like his pants had shrunk two sizes and *not* in the waist. Thank goodness for unseasonably cool weather, as well as his long wool coat. It could hide a multitude of sins. And stiffness.

He took Lily's hand as she stepped out of the car. The flush in her cheeks filled him with an unavoidable sense of accomplishment. He liked knowing that had been her response to him, but even better was having experienced it firsthand. She'd gone for far more than a practice kiss, which had honestly surprised him. She was always so businesslike in the office, never showing any interest in him outside the professional. Which was fine, and as it should have been. But it had disappointed him from time to time, for sure. Was there more there? Or was she amped up because her whole financial future was about to become so much sunnier?

Either way, it didn't matter. He wasn't going to be his father. He couldn't go overboard like that again. He had a professional relationship to maintain with Lily. Kissing like they just had was a one-way ticket to ruin.

They stepped inside Tiffany & Co., the beautifully appointed showroom with a maze of glass cases filled with jewelry, towering displays of crystal bowls and the ever-present flashes of their signature blue. Lily squeezed his hand a little tighter, which only made him want to reassure her that they were in this together. As unorthodox as their arrangement was, they had each other. For a few days.

An older gentleman at the first counter stepped out from behind it. "Mr. Locke?" His British accent made him even more distinguished than his appearance. His silvery hair was impeccably groomed.

"Yes. You must be Mr. Russell." Noah turned to Lily. "I made an appointment. I didn't want us to have to wait."

"Absolutely not. I understand you are a very busy man, Mr. Locke." He then turned his attention to Lily. A warm grin crossed his face and he stood even straighter. "And this must be the future Mrs. Locke." He reached out his hand and shook hers, regarding her as if she were made of fine china.

"Yes. That's me. Won't be long and I'll be Lily Locke." Mr. Russell let go and Lily smiled nervously at Noah. He got it. He hadn't thought about it in terms of her married name yet either.

They followed Mr. Russell to a counter in the middle of the store. He pulled out a velvet-covered board with at least a dozen engagement rings on it. "I took the liberty of picking out a few things to start. You had said platinum, right? And something larger than a carat? But you also wanted something ready-made. Not a custom ring, correct?"

Noah nodded. He didn't much like the idea of something right off the sales floor, but thus was their timeline. "Yes. Correct. We don't want to wait." He put his hand on the small of Lily's back. "What do you think?"

Lily leaned down, perusing them, but didn't touch a thing. When she turned back to Noah, there was a decidedly panicked edge to her expression. "These all seem really big."

"Yes…" His mind went blank as he tried to decide what sort of pet name Lily might like. "Honey. We talked about this before. Remember? I want you to have a beautiful ring. A ring that's just as gorgeous and amazing as you." That was the sort of thing a romantic guy would say, wasn't it?

"But aren't these a little extravagant?"

He shook his head as sweetly as possible. "No. I don't think so."

Mr. Russell cleared his throat. "Oh, dear. A few of these aren't quite as clean as they should be. Let me polish them up and I'll give you two a chance to chat." He'd obviously been doing this for a very long time. He seemed quite practiced in the art of ducking away when a couple was about to have an argument. "I'll be right back."

As soon as Mr. Russell was gone with the rings, Lily started in. "They're too much, Noah. It doesn't seem right that I would get that on top of the one percent. I want to be compensated, but I also don't want to take advantage of you or Sawyer."

"I hear what you're saying. And it's sweet, but you need

to think about me and my family. People are going to expect Noah Locke's fiancée to have a huge hulking ring.
Did you see the rock that Sawyer gave Kendall?"

"It all seems very superficial. A man's love should not
be demonstrated by the size of an engagement ring."

"And it isn't. The size of a man's wallet is demonstrated
by the ring. The love part people will have to figure out
on their own." That last thought gave him a sour stomach. He and Lily both deserved better than to be picking
out engagement rings with someone they weren't head
over heels for. "You're going to have to trust me on this
one. When we get to the wedding this weekend and you
show off that ring, we want people to be blinded by it. If
it's small, it'll just cast suspicion on the engagement and
that's one thing we can't afford."

Lily blew out a long breath through her nose and looked
around the store, shaking her head the whole time. "You
know, I'm surprised the grand Locke family doesn't have
a cache of heirloom engagement rings tucked away somewhere. Surely you guys have been handing down jewelry
from generation to generation. Maybe that would be easier.
Then I could give it back when we're done."

He didn't like that she was making assumptions about
his family or their history. There might have been many
Locke fortunes made over the last century, but there had
been a lot of sadness and heartache, too. They weren't
all spending their days rolling around on piles of money.
"There's no cache of rings. There is one family ring in
the mix, and that's all I know of. It was my mother's. The
sapphire engagement ring my father gave her. He gave it
to me when I turned eighteen."

"It sounds pretty."

"It's beautiful. A big oval surrounded by diamonds."
Noah almost choked on the words. More than twenty years

later and he still missed his mom. Plus, all he could think about was what his dad had said when he'd given him the ring. *If you ever manage to find the right woman, you should give this to her when you ask her to marry you. I'm just not sure you have it in you to be like me.* "I didn't really think that was appropriate for today."

The expression on Lily's face fell. "Oh. Of course. I'm so sorry. I wasn't thinking."

Noah understood how bad it sounded, but Mr. Russell was only a few feet away. "Wait. I didn't mean it that way."

She waved him off, not looking at him. "No. It's fine. I get it, Noah. Really."

"Right, then," Mr. Russell started. "Have we had a chance to have the 'size matters' discussion?" He winked at Lily and she laughed quietly. Thank God for Mr. Russell.

"Yes. We have." She leaned down, her thumb resting on her lower lip. "I think I'd like to try that one."

Mr. Russell picked up the ring and placed it gently on Lily's left ring finger. She slid it into place and held out her hand so Noah could see. "What do you think?"

The ring was stunning. And it looked lovely on Lily's hand.

"It's a square solitaire, just under two and a half carats. Platinum setting, of course, and approximately another two carats of small diamonds in the band." Mr. Russell watched Lily closely. "I'll get you the exact carat weight if this is the one you decide to take."

"It's a gorgeous ring. No question about that," Noah said. This was Lily's decision. Not his.

"Okay, then. We'll take this one."

"Are you sure? You don't want to try any others?" Mr. Russell asked. "How does the size of the band feel?"

Lily shrugged. "No. I'm good. I like this one. It seems like it fits fine."

"Okay, then. You have to appreciate a woman who knows what she wants." He smiled wide at Lily. "Truly. Some couples are here for hours."

"I bet." *At least we're efficient.*

"I'll get the paperwork together." Mr. Russell didn't leave, though. He seemed to be waiting, perhaps for the moment he'd undoubtedly witnessed many times with countless other couples.

Lily leaned into Noah and showed him the ring again. "I love it, darling. Truly."

Noah then remembered the show they were supposed to be putting on. He gazed into her eyes, but it wasn't the same as things had been when they were in the car together. Alone. This version of Lily was all business. "Good. I'm so glad." He leaned closer and they kissed. It was sweet and soft, but only an echo of the passion they'd shared mere minutes ago.

Mr. Russell smiled, seeming satisfied. He left for a moment, and returned with a packet of paperwork certifying the diamonds, along with a blue Tiffany box for Lily to keep the ring in, and the final bill. Noah pulled out his credit card, hoping that at some point, this might all start to seem at least a little more normal. Mr. Russell presented him with the receipt, Noah signed on the dotted line.

And just like that, it was done.

They bid their farewell and walked out of the store, hand in hand. As soon as they were in the car, he had to say something. "I'm sorry about what I said about my mom's ring. It didn't come out in a particularly kind way."

"No. It's fine, Noah. I get it. Our arrangement isn't real. We both knew that going into it." She held out her hand and wiggled her fingers. The chunky diamond sparkled. "And now I have the ring to prove it."

Four

It didn't take long for the photos of the Tiffany & Co. engagement ring kiss to end up online. In fact, it took less than an hour.

Noah's phone beeped with a text soon after they ordered their lunch at a restaurant he'd suggested. "It's Sawyer. Kendall just sent him a link to the photo of us picking out your ring. I'm not sure whether I should be happy or not, but we are now officially tabloid fodder."

Lily scooted closer to him in the half-round booth. It would be so easy to become accustomed to being near him, breathing in his citrusy cologne and putting her hands on him anytime. He showed her the evidence of their dubious newfound fame. There they were on a gossip website, locking lips in the most famous jewelry store in the world. It was so surreal. That was Lily Foster from an average family in Philadelphia, doing something distinctly not run-of-the-mill. "Yikes."

"Are you not happy with this?"

"It just…" Lily's stomach was filled with all sorts of uncomfortable feelings. She did not like the loss of control. She disliked the scrutiny of her private life. She hated feeling as though other people's opinions of her could boil down to this. For the first time, she understood how deeply upsetting it must have been to Noah when the tabloid video was released.

"Just what?"

"It's strange. Why would anyone care about this?" She winced at how unworldly her words might make her seem. She didn't want to be naive, but she couldn't escape the feeling that a person's love life should not be entertainment for perfect strangers.

"Now you know how I felt when that video ran. At least we knew this was going to happen. That's a big improvement over the way things happened for me."

Lily sighed and looked at the pixelated photograph again. This was the new cost of doing business, the price she'd be paying for securing her future with her small piece of Locke and Locke. This was the new normal. "Do you think this will be the extent of being in the tabloids? We won't have to keep doing this, will we?"

Noah took a sizable gulp of the Old-Fashioned he'd ordered to go alongside his steak sandwich and fries. "This should be enough to do the trick. We just needed Hannafort to buy the idea of us as an engaged couple before we show up at his daughter's wedding."

She smiled thinly and nodded. His words pointed to one truth—the notion of Lily and Noah as a couple was indeed something that needed to be sold. It needed the help of smoke and mirrors. "Okay."

The expression on Noah's face softened. "Are you just

saying okay? I have the feeling this is really bothering you."

She didn't want to make a stink. She wasn't someone to complain, but it did bother her. At least Noah was being thoughtful about it. That she appreciated. "I don't want to sound like a hopeless romantic, but it's a big deal to get engaged. It feels like we're tempting fate by doing it for show."

Worry crossed his face, a look she disliked. Noah was too perfect to stress. "Think of it this way, it's helping you build a nest egg, right?"

"Yes. That's important."

"And, hopefully, there are worse people you could be fake engaged to."

I'm not sure there's anyone better to be fake engaged to. "Of course. Don't be silly."

"More than anything, do you have any idea how many people get stuck with super unflattering pictures of themselves in the tabloids? This photo of us is pretty hot. We look good together." He smiled, seeming like he was desperate to reassure her everything would be okay. It was so endearing.

"True." Lily gnawed on her lower lip. She *had* noticed that. "Can you get Kendall to email me that link? So I have it?" She might be upset by the newspaper story, but she might also have that photo blown up and framed. She could hang it on the wall in her bedroom. Oddly enough, the kiss in the jewelry store hadn't been particularly hot. It had been sweet and nice. She hadn't noticed when it was happening that Noah had not only rested his hand on her hip, he'd curled his fingers into her coat. Even with the graininess of the photograph, she could see him pulling on her. Like he wanted her. Like that moment in the car when his hand slipped under her skirt and he'd discovered her stockings. There was a good deal of feminine pride wrapped up in being able to surprise a man like Noah. Very few women had likely made such an impression.

Noah's phone rang. "I'm so sorry. I should get this. It's Charlotte." He pressed the button on the screen and jabbed his finger into his ear. "Hey. What's up?" He nodded and popped a French fry into his mouth. "Okay. Hold on." He handed the phone to Lily. "She wants to talk to you."

"About?"

"Something about shopping."

"Hello?"

"Lily, it's Charlotte. I'm wondering, and I'm not totally sure how to ask this, but do you have the right clothes for this trip?"

Lily had no clue what that might entail. Did she have nice clothes? Of course. She made a point of being impeccably dressed at work. Did she have fancy, expensive clothes? No. "I'm not sure. Noah hasn't told me anything about what we're going to be doing."

"I'm not surprised. I'm sure it's the last thing on his mind. Thankfully, it's the first thing on mine. I do not want you feeling unprepared. You should feel comfortable in the Hannaforts' world of big money and luxury. I'll take you shopping to be safe. Plus, Noah's paying."

"Does he know that?"

"Not yet."

Lily snickered. "Okay. When?"

"Now? I had a client cancel on me this afternoon and Michael is working late."

Lily glanced over at Noah. How anyone could look so smoking hot eating a sandwich was beyond her. And the way his lips curved around the glass? She'd never wished so badly to be an ice cube, to slide down and crash into his mouth. "You sure? You don't have to do this."

"Are you kidding? I live for stuff like this. Meet me at the Saks in midtown in thirty minutes?"

"I'll have to clear it with Noah first, I guess."

"I'm clearing it. If my brother says a peep, remind him that he's on thin ice with me right now. Plus, if you're going to be my pretend sister-in-law, we should spend more time together, don't you think?"

"Good idea." It was nice to think that Charlotte could be Lily's ally in this. She needed someone on her side who wasn't an impossibly handsome man. Noah wielded too much power as it was. "I'll see you in a bit." Lily returned Noah's phone. "Your sister's taking me shopping for clothes for the wedding, but she wants me to meet her in a little bit. Can you and Sawyer manage if I'm out of the office this afternoon?"

"I don't have much choice. When Charlotte decides something is going to happen, it does. Case in point, our engagement."

"She does seem like a force of nature."

"She's always been like that. Even when we were kids."

Lily had often wondered what it must've been like to grow up on the sprawling Locke estate out on Long Island. "What about you? What were you like?"

"Quiet. Uncoordinated."

"You're lying."

"I'm not. I was always the one in the background. Sawyer was the star. He was the better athlete. He had more girlfriends. He did better in school. Charlotte was the one who was in crisis or kicking up trouble." Noah sat back and draped his long arm across the back of the booth. Lily hadn't moved back after scooting closer, so they were only inches apart.

Lily sat there and stared at Noah, his admission still

plain on his face. "I can't even imagine you like that. It seems impossible."

"I assure you it's more than possible, it happened that way."

Lily was seeing Noah in an all-new way and she wasn't sure what to make of it. Noah always seemed like the cocky golden boy of the Locke family, while Sawyer was the strong type A oldest sibling. Maybe she'd read it all wrong.

Noah got yet another text. "This is why I hate my phone." He picked it up from the table, shaking his head when he read the message. "Sawyer needs me to get back to the office. You should take the car to meet Charlotte and I'll hop in a taxi." He flagged down the waiter and handed over his credit card to pay the check.

"You don't have to do that. It's only eight or nine blocks for me."

"What kind of fiancé would I be if I let you walk in those shoes?"

Lily had strong thoughts on the answer. Peter had once left her to walk to a gas station two miles away when her car broke down. She'd called and asked for his help, but he'd been at the gym and wanted to finish his workout first. Noah probably had no idea how impossibly sweet he was being right now. "I want to walk. But I sincerely appreciate the offer."

"Okay, but I'll pay for a cab if you change your mind." He signed the bill when the waiter returned it, then plucked the card from the leather folio and handed it to Lily. "Shopping is on me, too."

"You don't have to do that either. I have money."

"You never would've been in this situation if it wasn't for me."

Lily couldn't forget it. It was omnipresent in her brain. It would be interesting to see where exactly the idea resided once she was back from the Hannafort wedding and all was back to normal.

Noah walked Lily out to the car and opened the door before the driver had the chance. "Tell you what. I'll send my driver to Saks after he drops me at the office. Then you won't need to worry about getting back."

Again, he was being so sweet. "That would be great. I'll try to be quick."

"As much as Charlotte likes shopping, she does not dawdle. I predict you'll be done pretty fast."

"Good to know." Lily was about to head up Fifth Avenue when Noah grasped her elbow and pulled her closer. Her heart sprang into action, beating double time.

"I need to kiss you goodbye," he whispered. "Or else it will seem strange."

She nodded, her brain as fuzzy as could be. His words were saying one thing, while his lips were telling her yet another. The kiss was soft and sensuous. Much hotter than the first acquaintance kiss in the car or even the one at Tiffany. Had that really been that morning? So much had happened today and it was only two o'clock.

"Bye." She wished the tone of her voice didn't contain such longing.

"Bye, honey." Noah cocked an eyebrow and climbed into the back seat of the car.

Lily stood on the sidewalk for a moment, processing. She'd kissed Noah four times today. Not bad for a day's work.

She began her short trek up to Saks, winding her way through the continuous stream of pedestrians. The air was crisp and cool, but the promise of spring was in the air. It filled Lily with sunny optimism. Despite her strange arrangement with Noah, things weren't bad.

She approached Saks Fifth Avenue, with its stony facade

and procession of American flags flapping high above the famous windows. The displays, like the weather, were harkening the start of spring with flashes of pretty pastels and flowers. Lily marched through the door and nearly walked straight into Charlotte. "You're here already."

"I don't like to be late."

Lily pulled back the sleeve of her coat to consult her watch. She was still five minutes early. "Where to first?"

"Follow me." Through the sprawling cosmetics department, avoiding salespeople threatening spritzes of expensive perfume, up the escalators they went.

Lily had never even been in this store before, although she had been to the outlet a block or two away. It wasn't that Lily was averse to spending a lot of money on clothes. It was more the product of growing up in a very middle-class family. It wasn't something that was done. And she'd always acted accordingly.

Lily followed as Charlotte got off on one floor and started tooling around like this was a time trial. Even more than five months pregnant, Charlotte was hell on wheels. "For the record, we should not be doing this on such short notice. We leave in three days."

Lily hadn't thought of it in those terms, but Charlotte was right. They'd be leaving for the Florida Keys Friday morning, flying on the Locke private jet, no less. Talk about being plucked from one world and landing in another.

Lily trailed along as garments flew off the racks in the department of every classic high-end designer you could imagine. Escada. Chanel. Louis Vuitton. Each item was handed to a salesclerk named Delia, whom they'd acquired along the way. Delia smiled, but she was definitely struggling to keep up. It would've been hard for most people to stay on pace with Charlotte, even without being loaded down with an armful of clothes. Lily herself was testimony to that fact, shuffling along as Charlotte explained her thinking behind each wardrobe choice she made. A dress for this, a skirt and blouse for that.

"Are you sure you don't want to pick anything out?" Charlotte asked. "I don't want to take over your fashion life."

"I'll let you know if I see anything I love. I trust that you know what you're doing."

"I've been to weddings like this before, and you will end up needing several outfits each day. Plus, I don't know about you, but I feel better when I travel if I have a lot to choose from."

Lily nodded. She'd had a modest upbringing, but her parents had loved to schlep her and her brother on weekend trips when she was growing up. "Yeah. I get that. It seems like a lot of clothes. I don't want to go overboard when I'm not paying."

Charlotte's eyebrows popped up into high peaks. "For what you're doing, you deserve to be compensated well. Noah backed us into this corner in the first place."

"The video itself wasn't really his fault. How could he have known that would happen?"

"He couldn't. The tabloids aren't known for giving their prey a heads-up. But still. He's the one who decided he needed to date half of the women in the city."

"I suppose he wasn't doing himself any favors." Lily sighed. What exactly was Noah looking for? A good time? If so, it was working. He always seemed very content— lots of women, and plenty happy about it.

Charlotte took another gander at the department she'd upended. "Anything else?"

"I trust you. Completely." Charlotte had classic taste. Everything was fresh and modern, but not overly trendy.

Lily went into the dressing room while Charlotte waited in an adjacent lounge, chatting away on the phone while Lily tried on outfit after outfit, parading about and seeking Charlotte's two cents.

"That is gorgeous on you," Charlotte said when Lily stepped out in a flowing royal blue gown with skinny straps and a bit of a plunging neckline. "That's perfect for the wedding. A definite yes."

Lily turned in front of the large dressing mirror. "You think it works?"

"Yes. Just be careful when you're wearing it around Noah."

Lily felt good in this dress, but thinking about it in the context of Noah seeing her in it made her extremely nervous. "You think he won't like it?"

"I think he'll like it a little too much, but that's his problem." Charlotte shooed Lily back into the dressing room.

A half hour later, Lily had five new dresses, three pairs of pants, six or seven blouses, and a raging headache from being under fluorescent lights for too long. Delia took everything to the register. "Now what?" Lily asked.

"Shoes," Charlotte answered flatly.

"Seriously?"

"I promise it'll be quick."

Sure enough, as soon as they arrived in the shoe department, an enthusiastic salesman named Roger was waiting for them. Charlotte kissed him on both cheeks and introduced Lily. Charlotte had apparently called him ahead of time, because he presented Lily with some carefully curated options. "These are for travel. Can't go wrong with classic black pumps."

Talk about an undersell. Lily had never imagined she'd own a pair of Christian Louboutin shoes. "Gorgeous."

"These are some fun beachcomber sandals you can wear

with a sundress or going to the beach." He set aside the first two boxes and pulled out a third pair—sky-high, sparkly and strappy. Two-thousand-dollar Jimmy Choo heels. "Absolutely gorgeous."

"Well? I'm thinking you can wear them for the wedding," Charlotte said. "And before you say a thing about the price, that's not the question. I want to know if you like them."

"I love them. All of them. But especially the silver ones."

"Perfect. Let's get your size and we'll get out of here. Roger, can you bring these to Delia?"

"Absolutely."

Five minutes later, it was time to pay. Lily nearly fell over when she saw the total. "I still feel weird about this." She pulled Noah's credit card out of her purse and presented it to the clerk.

"Don't. This is part and parcel of your job this weekend. Not that you couldn't with your own clothes, but I think you'll have more fun if you have some new things."

"Okay. Thanks." Lily might have to wait for her guilt to subside. She wasn't an extravagant person.

They took Lily's packages and hopped on the escalator. As they rode down, Lily couldn't help but notice that Charlotte was studying her. "Is something wrong?" Lily asked.

"I think I should warn you ahead of time that my brother is almost guaranteed to try something this weekend."

"Try something?"

"Make a move. When you're alone."

"I'll be fine. I can handle Noah." Or so she hoped. The one time they'd been truly alone, in the back of his car, things got very hot and she'd lost her mind in no time at all.

"I'm sure you can. And I'm not saying he won't be a

gentleman, because I know he will. But I also know that he's the king of smooth. He'll be all smiles and kind gestures and compliments."

"Isn't that what all women want?"

"Precisely why he's so good at getting them. I don't see any way he passes up the chance to be with you, especially when you're staying in the same hotel room. I want you to be prepared."

Lily imagined herself as the most willing sitting duck in history. "It'll be fine. I'm not worried about it. We've been alone lots of times in the office and he's never been anything but professional."

Charlotte nodded, but there was skepticism behind her eyes. "I know. He's handsome and all that. It's fine if that's what you want. But know that whatever happens, it won't last. I don't want to see you get hurt."

They stepped off the escalator and rounded to descend to the ground floor. Lily was torn. There were a million reasons why Noah making a pass would be a bad thing—the sanctity of their working relationship, closely followed by the fragility of her own heart. She only wanted to believe in happy endings, and since she'd never had her own, it made her more gushy than most when it came to romance. A guy who only skirted it? He was a terrible idea.

But there was this part of her that was so drawn to Noah and his magic—his smile, the way he made her pulse race when he walked into a room. It was impossible not to want more of that. She couldn't help but want him, even when all logic said he wasn't attainable. The thought of one night with him was incredibly tempting. And after their one passionate kiss? When he'd run his hand up her skirt and they'd both lost all sense of decorum? Her most base impulse was to throw caution to the wind when it came to Noah.

But ultimately, she had to preserve not just her job, but her stake in Locke and Locke. Another job she could get. But if she wanted to make the most of that 1 percent? She needed to keep a very close eye on it. Anything less would be reckless and irresponsible.

Five

Ever organized, Lily was packed and ready to go thirty minutes early on Friday morning. She was dressed in a brand-new outfit, a wrap dress in coral pink, the new black pumps with the signature Louboutin red bottom and a sparkly necklace, bought on Noah's dime. If ever there'd been a time when she looked confident and felt nothing of the sort, today was the day. Expectations galore had been foisted upon her for this trip. She had to appear as if she were a woman befitting the handsome and wealthy Noah Locke. And good God it made her nervous.

After her chat with Charlotte at Saks, she forced herself to reframe her expectations. At that point on Tuesday, a day into her role of fake fiancée, she'd started relishing the part where she got to kiss and touch Noah a little too much. She needed to remind herself why she had no business getting her hopes up about Noah, but she hadn't figured out how to shock herself into the right frame of mind. Then it came to her that morning in the shower. She needed to watch the video. She needed to see firsthand what was not only horribly embarrassing, but painfully true.

With twenty more minutes until she had to leave, she sat down at her home computer. An internet search quickly produced what she needed. Since it had first run, the video had been picked up by a spate of gossipy websites. Noah's dirty laundry was everywhere.

She pushed Play, sat back in her chair and crossed her arms over her chest. The voice-over started right away. *Big Apple businessman, Noah Locke, of the Locke hotel family, has been busy with the ladies over the last several months. And do we mean busy.* Then came the barrage of images. Noah's taste in women was hard to pin down—she'd give him that much, but there was no question that he was indeed a ladies' man. Some were curvy, some were rail-thin. Some were statuesque, others petite.

Lily took each image as it came. She was tough. The women in Noah's life were a fact. She'd known this about him all along. Still, being confronted with the visual evidence created a stabbing sensation in her chest. It's one thing to hear about a disaster, like a tornado ripping its way through a town, and quite another to see the footage of the actual devastation.

The worst of it was everything they said about him—that he was just as much of a womanizer as his dad and that he treated women as if they meant nothing. Lily was certain the former wasn't true, but she wasn't so sure about the latter. Judging by the breadth of Noah's female companions, it seemed safe to say that he saw no point in settling down.

Lily powered off her computer. Why should Noah have to decide anything? Handsome, single and wealthy afforded him the freedom to do whatever he wanted. Why should anyone deny him what was his to have if he so chose? The women in Noah's rotation had to have known what they were walking into when they agreed to go out with him. The rumor mill in the city was fierce. They had to know that Noah Locke was not the guy you get serious with. He was a fantasy, and a stunning one at that, but he wasn't for keeps.

Lily's phone beeped with a text.

We're here. Do you need help with your bags?

She replied to Noah.

I'm good. I'll be right down.

However rattled she might be by having watched the video, she was glad she'd done it. It was a solid reminder of what this weekend was about—a business transaction designed to convince Lyle Hannafort that Noah could be trusted. Lily was a prop, and nothing more.

She opened the door and reached for the handle on her roller bag when Noah appeared.

"Morning." Everything about him—his deep voice, his penetrating gaze and his casual confidence—stopped her dead in her tracks.

Prop, meet your date for the next three days, Mr. Tall, Suave and Smoking Hot. "How'd you get into the building?"

"One of your neighbors was coming out. I didn't want you to have to carry down your own bag." Noah reached for her suitcase, his arm brushing her shoulder. "Ready?"

Was she ready? An entire weekend of getting to look at him, hold hands with him, kiss him in front of other people, all while knowing it wasn't real? There was no way this wasn't going to leave a dent in her sense of self. "Yes."

"Got your ring?"

She presented her hand, which seemed like the normal response, but he had to go and cup her fingers, lifting them for further inspection. "It really is stunning. It suits you."

As to whether he was inferring that she was also stunning or merely that it did its job in giving her the appearance of a woman of substance, Lily was unable to determine. She knew only that her heart pinged around in her chest. "It's gorgeous." *You're gorgeous.* "Thank you."

Noah took her bag, Lily locked up and they made their way downstairs. His driver rushed over to them, taking Lily's suitcase and placing it in the back of the car. She climbed inside, followed by Noah.

"Won't take us long to get out to Teterboro," Noah said, referring to the small airport in New Jersey popular for private and corporate planes. "I hope it's okay, but I need to make some work calls."

"Please. Go ahead." This was perfect—he'd work and so could she. Lily sat back in her seat and opened her email on her phone. Her job was her ace in the hole. She didn't question herself when it came to that.

She responded to messages about several Locke and Locke projects, all commercial properties, one a renovation and the others new construction. One of Lily's primary responsibilities was to communicate with the general contractors and make sure they were on schedule and on budget. It was the nuts and bolts of the entire operation and freed up Noah and Sawyer to focus on long-term strategy, including deals like Hannafort Hotels.

She didn't take Noah's and Sawyer's trust lightly. Crucial and sometimes sensitive information came across her desk every day. She appreciated that they had no qualms about trusting her with it. Now that she had a stake in the company, her job was even more important to her. If ever there was a reason to stay on the straight and narrow this weekend, that was it. Being Noah's fake fiancée was simply another part of her job. Unconventional for sure, but if she looked at it like that, in three days, she'd have her nest egg, and an even bigger chunk of Noah's and Sawyer's confidence. As long as she kept her heart and her libido out of it, she'd be fine.

They arrived at Teterboro and the driver pulled through the security gate back to where the Locke private jet was waiting. Charlotte and Michael were climbing the stairs to board. Lily had arranged for the jet a few times, but she had yet to go anywhere on it. Scenes like this had never been part of her life, although she'd sure read about them in books. As much as most stories came alive in her mind, living it was surreal. Everything was moving in slow motion.

"Anything we need to go over before we get on the plane?" she asked, if only to keep herself wedged in reality.

"About?"

"You know. Us. We never had a conversation about getting our stories straight. You got called to that meeting after we bought my ring and I went shopping with Charlotte. Things in the office have been crazy the last few days. We haven't talked about it at all."

"It's pretty straightforward, isn't it? You came to work for us and we became close and there was an attraction and one thing led to another."

This was *not* helping Lily keep her head in the game. Her mind was too drawn to the many memories of times she and Noah had flirted at work. He'd flash his green eyes at her and make a joke. She'd laugh and smack his arm. And then next thing she knew, she was fantasizing about ripping his shirt off. "That works."

"We know each other so well, I think we can fake our way through it pretty easily."

"Of course."

The driver opened the door and Noah climbed out. Lily scooted across the seat and looked up to see Noah put on his sunglasses. He turned and offered his hand. Her skin touching his instantly put her off her game. It led her mind in too many hopeful and delusional directions, but she would've been lying if she'd said she didn't enjoy it. They walked across the tarmac, a stiff breeze blowing her hair from her face and rustling her coat. It was run-of-the-mill brisk weather for early April in New York, but she was glad for it. The crisp blast helped keep her wits about her. Noah kept rubbing the back of her hand with his thumb. He stopped at the bottom of the airplane stairs, letting her go first. Taking each step, she reminded herself to relax. She'd be fine once she was settled in her seat.

The interior of the plane was straight out of a movie—pure luxury with white leather seats, white carpet and chrome accents. A flight attendant was hanging coats in a closet. The chairs were clustered in fours, pairs facing each other with a table in between. Charlotte and her husband, Michael, were seated across from Sawyer and Kendall. They all waved and said hi, but they quickly returned to their conversation. That left Lily and Noah to sit together across the aisle.

The flight attendant breezed over. "Please, let me take your coats." The woman hardly looked at Lily, her eyes were so trained on Noah. Lily was used to his effect on women. She endured it every day, although before they'd become fake engaged, she'd tried to think of it as a perk, not a test.

"Want the window?" Noah asked.

"Oh, sure."

Lily took her seat and Noah settled in next to her. Charlotte leaned across the aisle. "How's the happy couple this morning?"

"Great," Noah responded. "Couldn't be better."

Charlotte smiled. "Perfect. You look amazing in that dress, Lily."

Noah turned to Lily and in the light streaming in from the window, his eyes were especially entrancing. "Better than amazing. You look perfect."

Out of the corner of her eye, Lily could see the look on Charlotte's face. It was exactly the same one she'd given her on the escalator at Saks. Noah was doing everything she'd said he would and Lily needed to prepare herself. At some point this weekend, Noah was going to make his move.

The flight time from New York to Key West was just under three hours—long enough for Noah to gain a full understanding of exactly how challenging this weekend was going to be. He not only had a front row seat to Lily in that mind-blowing dress, he had his siblings and their spouses watching. He could tell they were scrutinizing everything he and Lily did—talking and drinking champagne, chatting about work, Noah leaning closer to Lily when looking out the window on their approach into Key West. He hated it. They were all in love, they'd all found their soul mates, and they all knew he was faking it.

The instant Noah stepped off the plane in Florida, the humidity and tropical breezes wrapped around him, and he had the most unexpected response. He relaxed. His spine got a little looser, and as he put on his sunglasses, he warmed his face in the sun. They weren't in New York anymore. Noah hadn't realized how much he'd been hating the city until the salt air filled his nose and his view became nothing more than palm trees rustling in the wind. He took Lily's hand as they walked down the stairs, an action that had already become second nature. The timing was perfect. It was showtime.

A black stretch SUV emblazoned with the Hannafort Hotels logo was waiting on the tarmac to take them for the hour-long drive to Key Marly, the private island where the newest Hannafort resort was located. Lily and Noah sat next to each other on one of the long cushy black leather seats.

"I can't wait to see Key Marly. It's supposed to be incredible." Charlotte folded up her sunglasses and placed them in their case. "Private cabanas with plunge pools and everything."

Sawyer eagerly nodded in agreement. "This wedding is a prime example of why we need to be working with Lyle. The man is a marketing genius. He rolls out his brand-new resort with a private sneak preview weekend for his closest friends and business associates."

"All while his daughter gets married on the company dime, I'm guessing." Michael put his arm around Charlotte and tugged her closer.

"Exactly," Sawyer added.

All Noah could think as he looked over his shoulder at an outside landscape of funky shops and restaurants, with peeks of pristine ocean stretches, was that Lyle might be a genius for an entirely different reason. This was paradise.

When they arrived on Little Torch Key, they were taken to a gated dock where a gleaming white cabin cruiser was waiting. Luggage and passengers transferred, they skimmed through the calm crystal-blue water inside a luxury cabin with 360-degree views. The air-conditioning was a nice break from the heat and they were offered all manner of drinks and snacks by the attentive staff, but Noah was itching for a less contained experience.

"Do you want to go stand out on the deck and look at the ocean?" he asked Lily.

She nearly sprang out of her seat. "Yes."

As soon as they walked through the cabin doors, the sights, sounds and smells of untamed ocean took over, and Noah couldn't have been any happier. "It was driving me crazy in there."

"Me, too. It's way too beautiful to be sitting inside. I don't know how anyone could stand to sit in there and listen to that horrible elevator music they were playing anyway."

"Yes. The music. Terrible." Lyle might be a genius, but some aspects of his operation could stand some refining.

Noah and Lily both leaned against the railing, wind and sun in their faces as the boat approached Key Marly, a dot of an island straight ahead, a thick stand of tropical trees and foliage atop a sliver of silvery sand. Noah couldn't help but fantasize about Locke and Locke moving away from high-rises and into resorts. He could imagine an office on the beach, where he could take his laptop outside whenever he wanted, curl his toes into the sand and set up shop on a lounge chair. The best of both worlds. Of course, if he was working, he could only imagine it with Lily there, perhaps sitting right next to him, where they could discuss work and they could enjoy each other's company as much as they did now.

But could there be more between them? Could that dream scenario include things like love and romance? In his head, he wasn't sure. He wanted to see himself like that, but his mind refused to make the leap. The whole thing seemed like nothing more than a fantasy. The risk of their romantic involvement was too great. Forget that his own brother and sister didn't trust him not to break her heart, Noah didn't trust himself. He knew that panicky feeling he got when things started to get serious. He had no idea how to ever ward it off and Lily deserved better.

"It's so ridiculously beautiful." Lily peered down at the water as it rushed by.

Noah watched her instead, unable to keep from noticing how sexy it was when she tucked her hair behind her ear to tame it. *You're so beautiful.* He wanted to say it. He should say it. But he couldn't toy with her heart. He couldn't explain later that yes, he'd meant it, but he wasn't capable of following through. "It really is, isn't it?"

"I can't wait until we get there and I can take off these shoes and run around in my bare feet and stick my toes in the water."

"We're supposed to have our own plunge pool if you want to cool off." He suspected how ill equipped he was for the moment when he'd first see Lily in a bathing suit, but he couldn't take the suggestion back now.

"I vote for both ocean and pool if we can."

"I couldn't agree more."

A few minutes later, the boat pulled up to the Key Marly Resort dock. A line of uniformed bellmen were on hand to take their bags. At the end of the gangway, Mr. and Mrs. Hannafort were waiting. Even from a distance, Lyle Hannafort was an imposing man. He was about as tall as Noah, who was six feet three inches, but Lyle's broad frame was nearly twice as wide. He had a bowling ball bald head and a dark mustache. Lyle's wife, Marcy, was hardly five feet tall, and slim. With a thick mane of raven hair and her signature bright red lipstick, in many ways Marcy made just as much of an impression as her husband.

Noah and Lily were so excited to get to their cabana that they were first off the boat. He took her hand as they traversed the wood-planked surface, but her enthusiasm had turned to trembling. He leaned closer and whispered in her ear, inhaling a heady mix of her sweet perfume and ocean air. "We're in this together. It'll be okay."

She smiled up at him, sunglasses glinting in the sunshine, and squeezed his hand a little harder. "The dynamic duo."

Lyle Hannafort held out his hand to shake Noah's. "Nice to see you, Noah. Is this the young lady I've heard about?"

Noah didn't particularly like the idea of presenting Lily as if she were some sort of prize, but that seemed to be what was warranted. "Yes, Lyle, I'd like you to meet Lily Foster, my fiancée."

"Good to meet you, Lily. This is my wife, Marcy."

Marcy glommed right on to Lily, grabbing both of her hands and craning her neck to make eye contact. "Lily, darling, I am so happy to meet you. Let me see that ring. I heard about it in the newspapers, you know. Lyle showed me the picture. We were so glad to hear your happy news. I told Lyle that I really hoped that awful tabloid story about Noah wasn't true. I'm so glad to know they were just spreading rumors."

Noah wanted to hate that this had all started over a misunderstanding, but the truth was that if it hadn't happened, Lily would be home right now and he'd be attending this wedding stag while he watched his siblings carry on with their happy coupled lives. Every time he looked at Sawyer and Charlotte, he wanted to think that it meant he could find that kind of partner someday, too, but it felt too much like confirmation that two of the three Locke kids had cheated their family's marital curse and he'd better not press his luck.

"Mrs. Hannafort, that was not the real Noah. I hope you know that."

Lily's voice was as emphatic as could be, but Noah was stuck on her words. He *was* the guy in that video. They hadn't said a single untrue thing. And maybe he was like his father, which he didn't want to be. That left him even more convinced that he must be an absolute gentleman with Lily this weekend. They would put on the show of doting couple when they were in public, but in private? He would keep his hands to himself. He would sleep on the couch. On the floor, if needed. Lily would know exactly how much he respected her as a partner in Locke and Locke. She would know he revered her as a business-person and a friend. He would suppress his more lustful feelings. He wouldn't think about what it was like to kiss those petal-soft lips. He would try very hard to erase all memory of his hand on her thigh and his thumb rubbing across the lacy top of her stockings.

Marcy patted Lily's hand. "Of course that's not the real Noah. And it doesn't even matter, does it? You're getting married. That's all you need to think about right now."

Lily smiled thinly. "Yes. I know."

Married. Funny, but Noah had only thought about their arrangement in terms of being engaged. After this weekend and the deal was done, they'd quietly call it off.

"I want you both to know that we've taken extra good care of our newly engaged couple for this weekend," Marcy said.

"Indeed we have," Lyle added. "The staff knows to give you two the royal treatment. We don't want you to miss out on a single romantic moment."

"That really isn't necessary." Noah cleared his throat when he realized how quickly he'd blurted his response. "I mean, thank you, but don't go out of your way."

Lily elbowed him in the stomach. "It sounds truly lovely. Thank you so much."

Sawyer and Kendall walked up behind them and Noah took the chance to get away. They followed a bellman along a circular wood-planked walkway, which had paths spoking off to the individual thatch-roofed bungalows. Off in the distance, in a clearing, was the larger main building of the resort, which was presumably where much of the wedding would take place.

Noah and Lily were in bungalow eight. They entered a stone-tiled foyer that opened up into an expansive sitting room with high wood-beamed ceilings and a fan whirring overhead. On the coffee table in front of the sofa was a bottle of champagne on ice and a beautiful arrangement of tropical flowers in purple, orange and pink. There was even a note.

Don't forgot to put out the Do Not Disturb sign!
Love, Marcy.

"What does it say?" Lily plucked the card from his hand.

It says that I'm in deep trouble. He only wished that he could put out the Do Not Disturb sign and leave it there for days. *That* would be a vacation.

She smiled and put it next to the champagne bucket. "That was very thoughtful of her."

"Yes."

"Let's check out the rest." Lily led the way into the master bedroom. They both gasped when they stepped inside—through a full wall of accordion doors open to the ocean air was a small black-bottomed plunge pool surrounded by a lush garden. Beyond it was a full view of the stunning turquoise sea. The bedroom had a sprawling king bed with crisp white linens and mosquito netting draped overhead. "It looks like something out of a magazine or a movie. We can sleep with the windows open."

Noah nearly laughed. This place was perfect. If he were to take Lily somewhere to seduce her, this would be the ideal place. They wouldn't even still be wearing clothes right now. The special allure of hotel sex was too great and in a setting like this? It would be impossible to not be in the mood. Too bad that wasn't going to happen.

"I can sleep on the couch out in the living room." He stared at the bed, trying not to imagine Lily lying on it, waiting for him.

"No. It's too small. I'll sleep there."

"I'm not letting you sleep on the couch. That hardly seems fair. I'm the one who got us into this."

"We can't call the front desk and ask them to bring in a rollaway. Then they'll know the jig is up."

Noah sat down at the foot of the bed. Lily sat right next to him. They were inches apart, both staring out at the water. He glanced over at her, noticing for the one hundredth time that day how exquisite she was in that dress. He would have emptied his entire bank account to kiss her. He racked his brain for any lame excuse to revisit the notion of practicing.

"Compromise," Lily said. "We're both adults. It's a big bed. We sleep together. I will keep to my side. You won't need to worry about me."

Why was fate being so delightfully cruel to Noah? "Are you sure?"

"Absolutely." She patted him on the thigh, sending a sizzle straight to his groin. "Now let's change into our swimsuits and get into the water."

Six

In her aqua-blue bikini, Lily stretched out on the chaise lounge next to the plunge pool. She soaked up the day's fading rays, running her hand back and forth across her bare stomach. From behind her sunglasses she kept one eye peeled on Noah. He was floating in the plunge pool, resting his arms on the side with his back turned to her. She was pretty convinced by now. Something was up. There was no way she was the one woman on the planet Noah did not find attractive.

Still, he'd had a zillion opportunities to make a move and he hadn't taken the bait. Not when she'd asked him to put sunscreen on her back, not when she'd splashed him playfully in the pool, not when she'd made a comment about how good he looked in his black board shorts. If anything, it felt like he was trying to keep her away, which made no sense. Charlotte had said he was guaranteed to make a pass. And Lily would never forget the curl of his fingers in the paparazzi photo of them at Tiffany. He'd wanted her in that picture. She'd seen the evidence.

She propped up on her elbows and watched him. This view of his shoulders was nothing short of spectacular—every sexy contour and rounded muscle you could imagine. Noah was not overly built, but he was in excellent shape. "You're going to prune if you don't get out soon," she said, invoking a seductive inflection. This was the perfect opportunity for him to turn and get an eyeful, but he only made a cursory glance before diving under the water. That was it. He was practically daring her to make the first move. But he was her boss. If only she wasn't so concerned with keeping her job.

He broke the water's surface, planted his hands on the edge of the pool and hoisted himself out. He was a dripping wet Adonis. Every firm inch of him was glistening in the sun. They'd been in Florida for only a few hours and he was already tan. He grabbed a towel from a stack near the patio doors to their room and ruffled his hair. Lily had an irrational desire to walk over and help him with everything else that was in need of drying, especially that spot on his lower stomach, right below his belly button, where the narrow trail of hair led beneath the waistband of his board shorts. There were only two words to describe that part of him: *Yum. Oh.*

"We should probably get ready for dinner, don't you think?" he asked. "I'll hop in the shower first if you want a few more minutes out here." He wouldn't even look at her. And it was driving Lily up the wall.

"You go ahead. I need to figure out what I'm wearing anyway."

"Sounds like a plan." With that, he disappeared.

Lily flopped back onto the chair and groaned. This frustration was impossible. She wanted Noah so bad she could spit. But it was a terrible idea. She'd thought this trip might give her an out—he could make a pass, she could enthusiastically acquiesce, they could give each other a few amazing memories, and then they'd go back to the way things had been before. She already knew Noah was capable of that. As for herself, she wasn't certain she could pull it off, but she'd lived with far worse heartbreak. She'd been dumped at her own wedding. Nothing would ever be as horrendous as that.

Lily got up from her chair, put on her cover-up, traipsed back inside and flipped through the dresses in the closet, choosing a gauzy black maxi dress with skinny straps. It was the perfect sexy beach dress and she could wear flats with it, which would be nice and comfy.

Noah came out of the bathroom, wearing one of the white waffle-weave towels the resort provided. Lily was far too aware of what else he was wearing. Nothing. "The bathroom is all yours."

Lily decided another test was in order. She pulled her cover-up over her head and walked right up to Noah, planting her hand on his cheek. His stubble scratched her palm as she peered up into his eyes. He was so beautiful it made her chest ache. "I think your scruff could use some neatening up. It's getting a bit scraggly."

"Really?" His eyebrows drew together.

"You want to look your best for the Hannaforts. You can use the bathroom while I shower." Maybe a trial like this would be enough to push him over the edge.

"I really don't think that's appropriate. The shower has glass walls."

Sure enough, he flunked the test. Or passed with flying colors, depending on which side you were on. "Fine. Go ahead and finish up. I'll wait."

She plopped down on the end of the bed, resigned to

her fate. There would be no fun between her and Noah. At least she could triumphantly tell Charlotte she was wrong.

A moment later, Noah was done, looking as perfect as could be. "Better?"

No. "Much." She snatched up her dress and the rest of her clothes, and breezed past him into the bathroom. She took her shower, deciding to focus on the night ahead. It was better to worry about impressing the Hannaforts, rather than the endless cycle of Noah sex thoughts rifling through her brain.

Hair up in a towel, she slipped into her dress and turned in front of the mirror. Like Noah, she'd gotten a good amount of sun today. Quite frankly, she looked amazing in this dress. Such a waste. Noah wasn't even going to notice.

Noah put on a pair of black dress pants and a French blue dress shirt. *Keep it together, buddy. You can do this.* Only he was sure he couldn't do this. Being around Lily wasn't merely a test of his willpower, it was the Iditarod of chastity. Spending the morning with her on the plane was one thing, but he had not been prepared for the moment she'd stepped out onto the patio in her bikini and he'd had no choice but to jump straight into the plunge pool with no warning.

"Really wanted to go swimming, huh?" she'd asked.

"It's way too hot out here." He'd looked at her for a few seconds too long, his eyes traveling the length of her body, up from her feet to the swell of her hips and the gentle nip of her waist, to the round lusciousness of her breasts. He would've given up a year of his life to have had the chance to kiss her and press against her while she was wearing that bathing suit, but he knew where that ended—both of them naked in that beautiful bed under the mosquito netting. If he was going to ruin everything, he might as well go down in a blaze of glory, but no. He had a lot to prove to himself. He wasn't like his dad. He had to be strong.

"Noah?" Lily called from the bathroom. "I need help. I can't get this necklace clasp."

"Sure thing. Two secs." Maybe she'd be wearing a frumpy Hawaiian muumuu to dinner. *Please be frumpy. Please be frumpy.* He stepped into the bathroom and got his answer. Her dress was flowing and delicate, with a low back and a slit up one leg. She had her hair pulled to one side, and was holding the ends of the necklace at the nape of her neck.

"I hope you can get it. The clasp is tiny and so is the link it's supposed to go into. Your fingers might be too big."

He stepped behind her, taking the silvery chain, fumbling like a fool as he drew in her sweet smell and wished they didn't have to go anywhere tonight. Again and again, he missed with the hook of the clasp. His hands were slick with sweat. His pulse was thumping in his ears. His knuckles grazed the velvety skin of her neck, drilling electricity right into him. Finally, he hooked the clasp. He dropped the necklace like it was on fire, stepping back abruptly.

"Thanks," she said, shooting him a quizzical look via the mirror.

"No problem." He ducked out of the bathroom, thinking of icebergs and blizzards. That was the only way he'd make it through his evening with Lily.

They left their room and headed down the walkway, under the canopy of palm trees down to the main resort building. This was no high-rise hotel but rather three sprawling stories of exclusivity, containing a mere eight suites. Along with only twenty individual cabanas on the island, guests could enjoy a quiet and tranquil stay.

Noah and Lily followed the signs for the rehearsal dinner, which led them down a crushed stone path through a lush tropical garden to the pool area behind the hotel. The multilevel expanse of stone, water and plants seemed to go on forever, with waterfalls, spas and places to swim. A few folks were still partaking of the pool. Everyone else was milling about, enjoying a cocktail and the balmy night air. Noah took Lily's hand and they walked over to where Lyle and Marcy were chatting with a small group of people. Still no sign of Charlotte, Michael, Sawyer or Kendall.

"There's my favorite newly engaged couple." Marcy practically squealed with delight. "Did you enjoy the champagne I sent to your room?"

"We haven't had a chance to drink it yet," Noah answered. It had been his call to stick the bottle in the fridge. Popping that cork could've led to any number of poor choices. "But thank you so much. It was very thoughtful."

"Anything to make you all feel comfortable and welcome. I hope you enjoy what the staff has for you when you get back to your room tonight. I think you'll find it very romantic." Marcy nodded with a conspiratorial grin.

Lily looked at Noah, her eyes sweeping across his face as if she were trying to gauge his reaction. He had no idea how to respond to this revelation. He could only imagine what Marcy had in store, but one thing was certain—everything about their circumstances was made to sexually frustrate the hell out of him. "I can't wait to see it."

"I'd ask you to report back tomorrow, but I don't think I need to know the details." Marcy smiled wide. "Now if you'll excuse me, I need to visit with some of my other guests."

"I wonder what the surprise is," Lily said. "Chocolate-covered strawberries?"

"Probably. The usual clichéd trappings of engagement."

Lily's mouth formed a thin line. "You might think it's clichéd, but I think it sounds quite nice. Plus, there are worse things than someone leaving chocolate-covered fruit in your room."

"I know. You're right." *It's just that I'm going to want to feed it to you and take off your clothes and that was not part of my plan for this wedding.* "Let's go mingle."

Over the course of the next several hours, Noah and Lily met nearly every member of the extended Hannafort family. Lyle's parents, then Marcy's, as well as cousins and aunts and uncles. They had a lovely tropical-themed meal served poolside. Lily was a big hit, making sparkling conversation with the other guests and impressing everyone with her knowledge of everything from real estate development to romance novels. She even told Lyle's uncle a few off-color jokes that made him belly laugh and declare Noah the luckiest son of a bitch he'd ever met.

As the sun set and the sky turned darker, torches blazed and flickered. The waterfalls were lit with dramatic effect. The ocean breezes blew, and although the air cooled, it never lost that warm and humid feeling.

"I'm really tired. Let's go back to the room," Lily said.

It was ten o'clock and most of the guests had left. Noah had been putting off their departure, going back for seconds on key lime pie and ordering one last drink. He couldn't stomach the thought of what their romantic surprise might be. Surely something that was only going to make his charge that much more difficult. "You sure you're ready? It's so beautiful out tonight."

"Fine. You stay. I'll go back by myself." Lily got up from her chair.

"No. No. I don't want you walking by yourself." He reached for her hand, and she turned back, stealing his breath from his chest. She was so breathtakingly beautiful in this light, with the wind blowing her hair across her shoulders and her skin glowing with a gorgeous peachy tan.

"I couldn't possibly be in a safer place. And it's pretty obvious that you'd rather be here and not alone with me."

His stalling had been transparent, probably a little too much so. There was a very hurt edge to her voice that he disliked greatly. "I was enjoying myself with you tonight. That's all." He smiled. However much he wanted to create distance between them, he didn't want her to think he didn't enjoy her company. He did. He simply enjoyed it too much. He got up from his chair and took her hand. "Come on. Let's go see what over-the-top thing Marcy has waiting for us."

They took their time on their walk, listening to the birds in the trees and the gentle lap of the ocean off in the distance. Lily dropped his hand and traced her fingers along the inside of his arm, snugging him closer. He knew he should've ignored it, but he didn't want to. He put his arm around her shoulder and let her lean into him as they took the final steps to the front door.

When they walked inside, there was no sign of romance in the seating area where the bottle of champagne had been left earlier. "Huh. I wonder if they forgot."

Lily walked ahead of him into the bedroom. "Oh my God, Noah. In here. It's unbelievable."

He braced himself and followed her. The lights in their bedroom were off, but a warm glow came from the glass doors to outside. Hundreds of candles were lit out on the patio around the plunge pool. Even more were floating in the water. The bed had been turned down, and purple orchid blossoms were strewn all over the duvet. Another bottle of champagne was on ice next to the bed, and a tray was next to it with coconut massage oil. He couldn't have arranged a more romantic, sexy setting if he'd wanted to.

"Marcy wasn't kidding," Lily said.

"It's going to take forever to clean this up." He felt like

such an ass the instant the words left his mouth. Lily deserved every romantic delight before them and he was raining on her parade.

She cast a disappointed look at him. "We can't really call housekeeping and ask them to take care of it. Anyone who knows this is here thinks that our clothes are off by now. They think I'm giving you a sensuous massage. They think we're making love."

As imagined visions of Lily naked, her hands all over him, wound through his consciousness, desire and determination battled inside him. He wanted her more than he'd wanted any woman. She was right there. Mere inches from him. What if he took her in his arms right now and kissed her? What if they did everything that logically came out of this quixotic setting? Would it really hurt anything?

"You know," Lily started.

Noah held his breath. Was she about to give him an out? Tell him that they had to go through with it, lest housekeeping rat them out?

"Charlotte would be laughing her butt off if she saw this right now. She told me you were going to make a pass at me. She said you couldn't help yourself. This whole thing with the candles and the flowers and the champagne seems like they're practically daring you to do it."

And there he had his answer. Charlotte expected him to do that because he'd always done that, and their father had always done it, as well. He wanted no more assumptions made about him. His thirst for Lily only felt so potent because he'd been tortured for two years. What was another night or two? "My sister thinks she knows me, but she doesn't. You said it yourself that I'm not the guy in that video. I am not only capable of being a gentleman, it is my full intention to be exactly that."

Lily walked over to the head of the bed and lifted a corner of the duvet. "Fine. But we still have to make it look like you aren't." She grabbed the edge of the duvet and with a dramatic flick of her wrists, the orchid blossoms popped into the air, most of which fluttered to the floor. "I'm going to wash my face and brush my teeth. It's been a long day and I'm tired." She sauntered into the bathroom, leaving Noah to wonder how this all got even more messed up than it had seemed in New York.

He flopped back on the bed, staring up at the ceiling. Lily was going to be back soon. To sleep in the same bed with him. And he had to make sure absolutely nothing happened. Even if it killed him.

Seven

Lily made it through the night. She made it through waking up next to Noah, and having breakfast with him. She'd lived through an entire morning and part of the afternoon together, ignoring his good looks and the lack of passes made. She'd taken it all in stride, but now that she was dressed for the wedding, in the royal blue dress that Noah probably wouldn't even notice, she needed to take the edge off. She simply had too much baggage when it came to "I do."

There were three bottles of champagne in their fridge—one from yesterday, one from last night after the rehearsal dinner and a third that had shown up with that morning's room service alongside a beautiful tropical fruit platter and some omelets. They hadn't ordered the bubbly, but Marcy and Lyle had sent it anyway. They were apparently highly invested in Noah and Lily's engagement. At least someone was. Noah had shown no interest in at least enjoying their odd predicament in paradise.

And Lily was sick of it.

Pop. She waited until the wispy mist had trailed out of the bottle before pouring herself a glass of glorious golden bubbles.

"Oh. You decided to open one," Noah said, walking into the room all dressed for the wedding. He looked perfect, of course. Whomever had designed the modern-day men's suit had clearly had Noah in mind when they'd come up with the idea. He was straight out of the pages of a magazine.

"Can't let all this champagne go to waste."

"We could pour it out before we leave."

Lily took a sip. The effervescent sweetness was delightful on her lips and tongue. It was quite frankly the first blip of pleasure she'd had in the last several hours. Being around Noah was killing her. "We are not pouring this out. It's way too good. In fact, I'm pouring you a glass right now." She didn't bother to wait for his response. Maybe it would loosen him up a little bit.

"Fair enough." He took a sip and nodded. "Okay. You're right. It's delicious. We should drink every drop."

"That's the spirit." Lily felt so much better. This was the Noah she adored. If he was going to make her crazy, at least he could be a little more fun about it. Still, his strange attitude yesterday and that morning was eating at her. "Can I ask you a question? Did I do something to make you mad? You haven't been yourself at all since we got here. We're in paradise, but you don't seem like you're having any fun."

He took another sip and stared down at his shoes, his hair slumping forward. "I'm stressed about the Hannafort deal. I feel like so much of it rests on our shoulders and it doesn't really seem fair. It also doesn't seem right. He wants to do business with us because he thinks I'm the sort of guy who wants to get married. How messed up is that?"

"It's very messed up, but it's his call. So we go with it. But the part I don't understand is that you said we were in this together. It doesn't feel like that anymore. You're avoiding me and it's really starting to hurt my feelings." It felt so much better to get that off her chest. Even if Noah told her she was overreacting, at least she'd said her piece. "If there's something else going on, please tell me."

He downed the last of his champagne and bunched his lips together. He was clearly deep in thought. "It's hard to be around you sometimes, Lily. You're a very beautiful woman. I like you a lot. But you're also extremely important to our company. Sawyer would have my head if I touched you. And quite frankly, I'd be more than a little disappointed in myself. So, yeah. There have been a few moments in the last twenty-four hours that were more than I'd bargained on."

Lily wasn't sure she was still breathing anymore. Her brain was sucking up all the oxygen her body needed. That wasn't quite the response she'd been expecting. "Wow."

He shook his head. "I shouldn't have said anything. I'm sorry."

Lily reached out and grasped his hand. Touching his skin felt as though she'd completed a circuit and electricity was now free to zip back and forth between their bodies. "No. Noah. I'm glad you said something. I'm just taking it all in. I was starting to wonder if you found me unattractive."

"No. Quite the opposite."

Heat rose in her cheeks. "If it makes you feel any better, I'm just as frustrated. You're way too hot to be fake engaged to."

He laughed, and unleashed his megawatt smile. "You're funny."

She would've done anything to kiss him right then and there, but she knew she wouldn't be able to stop if she started something. "Not really what I was going for, but thanks."

Noah's phone beeped with a text, pulling them both out of the moment. He fished his cell from his pocket. "It's Charlotte. She and Michael are saving us seats. We should probably go."

Lily slugged down the last of her champagne, jammed the cork back into the bottle and put it in the fridge. "No matter what, you and I are sharing the rest of that bottle later tonight. Out on the beach."

The surprise on Noah's face was priceless. She should catch him off guard more often. "Yes, ma'am."

They held hands during the short walk to the ceremony, which was in the garden on the far side of the pool area. White chairs were set up in orderly rows with sprays of tropical flowers hanging from the back of each seat. A satin runner ran up the aisle between the two sections, nearly filled with guests, and at the very end sat a beautiful bamboo archway covered in orchids and lilies with a waterfall behind as the crowning touch. It was a gorgeous sight, picture-perfect, and everything a bride could ever want. Lily decided to start pricing everything out in her head, to keep her mind from wandering to bad memories. She'd planned her own wedding right down to the guest favors and the fondant icing. She knew exactly how much all of this cost or at least she knew the ballpark. Lyle and Marcy Hannafort were sparing no expense.

Noah and Lily found Charlotte and Michael. "Where are Sawyer and Kendall?" Noah asked.

"Kendall hasn't been feeling well since dinner last

night. I don't know if they're even going to make it for the ceremony."

"I hope everything's okay," Lily said.

"I think so. She said the baby is kicking like crazy and Mr. Hannafort had a doctor friend check on her this morning. They're making sure she gets lots of fluids and some rest," Charlotte said.

Noah grumbled and crossed his legs.

"Everything okay?" Lily muttered into his ear, taking her chance to inhale his cologne.

"Yeah. It just irks me when Sawyer doesn't let me know what's going on. I hate that Kendall is sick and I didn't know anything about it. What if it's something serious?"

There was the evidence of how close the three siblings were and just how easily they could set each other off. Lily took his hand and laced her fingers in with his. "It's okay. I'm sure he didn't mean anything by it. And maybe it was a guy thing. You know, like he didn't want you to see how upset he was. It's probably easier for him to be vulnerable with Charlotte."

Noah looked at her and smiled softly. "Yeah. You might be right. Thank you."

"Anytime."

The music started and the groom and his groomsmen took their places up near the archway. The minister stood at center stage, hands folded in front of him. Lily tried to ignore the way it felt to hear the strains of Pachelbel's Canon in D. Like a zillion other brides, she'd chosen this song for her own wedding as a prelude to her big moment. She'd stood at the back of the church and listened to it, a little bit nervous, a little excited, a whole lot of ready to get her show on the road.

Today, every note grated. They picked at the memory of standing in the back of the church and having her cousin run out and proclaim that there was no groom. Peter had not come into the church with his groomsmen. This exact music had sent Lily scrambling to find him. Later, she would find out from the church organist that he'd played it seven times before Lily made her way into the chapel and announced to everyone that there would be no wedding that day.

The music changed to Wagner's "Bridal Chorus" and the guests all stood. When Lily turned and looked at Annie Hannafort on her father's arm, her heart plummeted to her stomach. Annie was wearing almost the exact same dress Lily had worn on her day from hell. Matte satin in winter white, strapless, empire waist with a full tulle skirt. Lily watched in shock and awe as they marched past. Noah put his hand on Lily's shoulder and she panicked for his fingers, squeezing them as the tears began to stream down her face. She closed her eyes, willing herself to keep it together. Her broken engagement was in the past. It didn't hurt anymore. The trouble was Annie Hannafort was living her dream day right now. And it made Lily want to run away.

Lily forced her eyes open and faced the altar. Annie had joined her husband-to-be and Lyle had taken his place with Marcy. Everything was as it should be. But Lily felt queasy. And uneasy. Why couldn't they have been invited to a Hannafort funeral? At this point, it would've been better. As the guests all sat, Lily sucked in a deep breath, trying to ward off persistent images threatening to make her cry again. Her father's anger with Peter over dumping his baby girl and causing him to waste a pile of money. Her mother's face as she tried to be brave for Lily, all while she was obviously crumbling on the inside. The worst was her grandmother, who had never seen such a spectacle in all her life. She passed away two months later. It had been the last time Lily ever saw her.

"You okay?" Noah whispered into her ear.

She could only nod, looking straight ahead. She didn't want Noah to see how badly this hurt. Let him think she was the girl who choked up at weddings.

He then did something for which Lily was ill equipped. He put his arm around her and pulled her close. He stroked her arm with the backs of his fingers. He leaned closer and kissed her on the temple. "It's a wedding, Lil. It's okay to cry if you want to."

A small smile broke through her tears. What would she do without sweet Noah right now? Sweet, sexy Noah was going to make her lose her mind by the time they left Florida and their fake engagement was over. "I'm fine." She trained her vision straight ahead.

The minister spoke his first words. "Dearly beloved, we are gathered today to join this man and this woman in holy matrimony."

Lily choked back the tears. She didn't want to think about how much she had once hoped to be standing up there listening to those words.

Two hours later, Lily was doing much better, but it was all because of Noah. She pushed the remaining bites of wedding cake—vanilla layers with a sublime mango mousse filling—around her plate. She didn't care about food right now. Noah was too entertaining, a few yards away, crouching down and letting two of the flower girls put a flower crown on his head. He stood straighter and the girls giggled, then took his hand, and they turned in a circle in time to the music. Noah was being so charming and adorable right now, it hardly seemed fair.

Lily eyed him as he returned the crown and said goodbye to the little girls, making his way back to her. He was a vision to be sure—all long limbs and swagger. The smile on his face showed nothing but complete relaxation, a glorious change from the previous twenty-four hours. Lily was sure that every single woman at this wedding was jealous of her engagement to him. She hardly cared that it was all a charade. She could count the number of times she'd been in such an enviable position on one hand.

Still standing, Noah reached for his glass of wine and took a long drink, looking down at Lily while he did it.

"Thirsty?" She was unable to disguise the flirtation in her voice. Between enduring the buildup of the last two years, and the sheer exhaustion from keeping her hands off him over the past two days, she wanted him more than she ever had. Logic said that they might as well give in to it while in a setting where it was called for, but as Lily had learned, their arrangement made little sense. Soon they would head back to their room where the kissing and hand-holding would be cast aside in favor of their chaste and platonic real-life dynamic.

"Dancing with flower girls is exhausting."

"I bet. Probably all tuckered out, huh?"

He crinkled his forehead in that adorable Noah way. "Doesn't matter. I have yet to take my fiancée out on the dance floor for a spin. That needs to be rectified right away."

His fiancée. If only.

Noah held out his hand. He even winked at her, but Lily reminded herself this was all about appearances. This wasn't about wanting to dance with her. It was because Lyle and Marcy Hannafort were out on the dance floor. Noah and Lily needed to finish selling the idea of the two of them as a couple. It was yet another instance where these odd circumstances at least afforded Lily the fulfillment of a fantasy. Dancing with Noah, being in his arms, was one thing Lily had dreamed about more than once.

She slipped her hand into his and he quickly wrapped the comforting warmth of his fingers around hers. She rose to standing and he held his hand at the small of her back as they walked out to the dance floor. It was like stepping into another world, where white lights twinkled, soft breezes blew and romance was unavoidable. There was no tension, only happiness and celebration of love all around them. Noah pulled her into his arms and tugged her closer. Her breath left her lips in a rush. An arrogant off-kilter smile crossed his lips. If Lily could've done anything, it would've been to trap the magic of that moment in a box and keep it forever.

Marcy glanced over at them and smiled. Lily returned the expression, watching Marcy with Lyle. They were in love. You could see it in the way they clung to each other, the way they gazed into each other's eyes.

"What are you looking at?" Noah didn't look to see what had her attention. He remained focused on her.

"The Hannaforts. They're so in love."

"How could you possibly know that?"

"I can tell by looking at them. You can feel it."

"Whatever you're seeing is probably just as much of an act as we are."

The statement hurt. She hated the pessimism in his voice, made even worse by the reminder of their arrangement. "How can you can say that with such conviction?"

"I've seen my dad look at lots of women the way Lyle looks at Marcy. Trust me. It doesn't last."

"My parents look at each other like that and they're still in love. Happily married for nearly thirty years." She didn't like the pleading nature of her voice, but if she believed in anything, she did believe that some people found true love.

"I don't even see how it's possible to keep a spark for that long. It has to die out. Then what do you have to look forward to?"

Lily shook her head. "That's the excuse every affirmed bachelor uses. You don't have to rationalize your life choices. There's nothing wrong with being single. Look at me. I'm single, too. And I'm basically happy being that way."

"Why is that, exactly?" His eyes swept across her face. "Or more precisely *how* is that, exactly?"

"I don't understand the question."

"Well, you clearly believe in love and romance. You got all choked up at the wedding today. And at Charlotte's wedding. So why wouldn't you find some guy and jump in feetfirst?"

If only he knew it wasn't as simple as that. She wasn't about to tell him now. "Maybe the right guy never came along."

"Ah, the elusive right guy. The guy who doesn't worry about things like the spark dying out. He doesn't date dozens of women. Am I right?"

"The guy who was in that tabloid video is the wrong guy." She hoped that he would draw the logical conclusion from that. He wasn't like the Noah in the video. Not really. She refused to believe this story he kept telling himself about how he wasn't capable of more.

"So you watched it." His entire body tensed.

"I did. Yesterday morning."

"And now you know I'm a total ass."

She shook her head. "I've never thought that about you, ever. The guy in that video skims the surface. He doesn't care about anything deep or meaningful. I don't believe you're that guy. I know you're capable of more."

He scanned her face, but it was difficult to gauge his

reaction. Was he upset? It didn't seem that way. "What makes you think that?"

"I see how much you care about your job. I see how close you are to Sawyer and Charlotte. It really made you mad that Sawyer didn't tell you Kendall wasn't feeling well. Anyone who cares that deeply about anything is capable of love and commitment. I'm thinking that in your case it comes down to you not wanting to be like your dad."

His lips molded into a thin line. "It's more complicated than that."

"It always is. Emotions are tricky. You're not the only one who struggles with them, Noah. That's part of why I worry about what we're doing."

"Our arrangement?" he whispered.

There was so little reward in the admission she wanted to make, but at least it would be off her chest. Tomorrow, they'd fly back to New York and she could disguise her embarrassment for a few months and it would hopefully fade away. "Walking around holding hands and kissing all the time, I can feel myself getting attached to you. And I know I'm not what you want."

A low groan left his throat, and even though the song changed, Noah kept them moving on the dance floor. "Why would you say that? Why would you ever say that?" There was an angry and restless edge to his voice.

"And why are you acting so frustrated?" Lily looked up into Noah's face. His eyes darkened.

"Frustrated doesn't begin to cover it."

"Is it something I did or said?"

"It's not your fault. You're being honest. You're just being you. Which has been the source of my frustration over the last few days."

It felt as though Lily's breath had been stolen from her chest. Her mind raced, especially through the last few hours. "I don't understand. I've done everything you wanted me to do."

He looked away for a moment, surveying the crowd on the dance floor, then returned his attention to her. His gaze put her on notice, but as to what she was supposed to glean from it, she had no idea. He pulled her closer. The arm he had around her waist was tight. If she'd done something wrong, and this was what she got as punishment, she hoped he would tell her so she could keep doing it. He lowered his head. He was coming in for a kiss. Was this another part of their charade? Or was there something more? Here they were in this romantic setting, swaying on the dance floor at an extravagant wedding. If ever there was a time to kiss one's fake fiancée, this was it.

Lily tilted her chin up, making her lips into as seductive a pucker as she could. She closed her eyes and locked her knees—every time he kissed her, it was a challenge to remain standing.

The next thing she knew, Noah's lips were at her ear. "It's this. It's impossible to be around you and not want more. I thought I could make it through this trip without admitting it, but I can't."

Lily's pulse was pounding in her throat. She opened her eyes and looked at him, hoping for clarification. Was this the inevitable move that Charlotte had warned her of? Or was this something different? "More?" Lily had spent a whole lot of time wanting not only Noah's kiss, but the more part, as well. She had to be sure of what he was saying.

"You're so sexy, Lil. I don't know how I could not want more. I want you. If you want me."

Goose bumps popped up on her skin. She looked around at the other guests on the dance floor. No one was paying a lick of attention to them. Toasts had been made. Cake had been served. She returned her sights to Noah. He was so adorable right now, tentative and unsure. She'd never seen him like this before. "Do you want to get out of here?"

"Seriously?"

"Yes, seriously."

"Yes. A million times, yes." He took her hand and they beelined off the dance floor as stealthily as they could. Out of the reception hall, through the pool area they raced. Noah set the pace with his long legs, but even in heels, Lily had no trouble keeping up. She was highly motivated.

Noah pulled his key card from his wallet and swiped it to get them through the gate to the private cabanas. The wind always picked up the instant they were out of the safe confines of the pool area, where high walls helped to keep the two worlds separate. The night air was warm and soft against her skin, but it was nothing compared to Noah's hand as he pulled her along eagerly. He was a man on a mission and she loved that about him. It made her feel good. He wanted her.

They wound along the walkway to their cabana. The heel of Lily's shoe dropped between two planks. She stopped. Noah yanked on her arm, then rounded back.

"I'm stuck." She tugged on her leg, twisting her foot back and forth, but it wasn't going anywhere.

Noah dropped to his knee and wrapped both hands around her ankle, tugging on her leg.

"Ouch. Ow. Stop it."

"Sorry. I can't pull you loose." He looked up at her. The wind blew his floppy hair all over the place, making it an even sexier mess than usual.

"Damn. And I love these shoes. Charlotte convinced me to get them."

"Don't worry. We'll save your shoe. Let me figure this

out." Noah looked down at her foot again, but as he was assessing her plight, he started caressing her calf.

Lily sucked in a breath sharply. His fingers on her bare skin felt impossibly good. How was she going to handle it when there was even more touching? She might never recover. Which, right now, was perfectly okay with her. "Unbuckle it."

"Good idea." He freed her foot, then tried to pull the shoe out. "If I pull too hard, it's going to ruin the heel. Are you okay with that?"

"No. Don't do that. You paid a fortune for these shoes."

"Then what do you want me to do? Call maintenance and get them to remove the board?" Noah dropped his shoulders. He was frustrated again.

"Leave it. We'll get it later."

He straightened to his full height. "Really?"

Lily loved those shoes, but she'd waited an awful long time to be with Noah. This might be her only chance. "Yes." She stooped down and unbuckled her other shoe. Before she could take a single step in her bare feet, she was no longer standing. She was in Noah's arms.

"I'm taking zero chances. You get a splinter out here and it'll ruin everything."

She wrapped her hands around his neck and he headed straight for their cabana. This was a much faster way to travel. They arrived at their door in under a minute, easy. Noah put Lily down and swiped his key card. They both hustled inside. Lily dropped her saved shoe to the floor, rose to her tiptoes and wrapped her arms around Noah's neck. He kissed her with such force, she was glad she was holding on to him.

It was like he was sending a message. *I want you.* She not only received it loud and clear, she returned it with the same raw enthusiasm with which Noah had delivered it. Their tongues were a mad frenzy. Noah's hands were everywhere—her waist, her hips, her butt. He scrambled to pull up the voluminous fabric of her skirt, but Lily had no patience for that. He could be searching for her legs for days.

She turned her back to him and pulled her hair to the side. He cupped one of her bare shoulders and pressed his hips against her bottom. She felt his gentle breath at her nape as he skimmed his lips over her skin. She dropped her head to the side as he trailed openmouthed kisses along the slope of her neck. Luckily, he was also drawing down the zipper at the same time. The cool air on her skin was such a delicious contrast to Noah's velvety, red-hot kisses.

He slipped the straps from her shoulders and they both let the dress flounce to the floor. Lily fought the urge to cover herself, standing in nothing more than a bra and panties in front of the man she'd fantasized about countless times. Noah was accustomed to such flawless beauty it was hard not to worry about every little imperfection.

He cupped her shoulders with his hands, drew his fingers down her arms, twining his hands with her own. He pulled her closer, her back against his chest.

"I want to make sure you're okay with this," he muttered into her hair. "This was never part of our arrangement and I respect that, no matter my frustration. Just say no and I'll jump in the pool."

She giggled. "Does that really work?"

"It did yesterday when I first saw you in your bikini."

"You're joking."

"Nope. Boner city."

She closed her eyes, realizing that things might not have been the way she'd thought they were over the last few days. She wasn't the only woman he didn't want. He'd been resisting. She turned in his arms and raised her hands to his handsome face, forcing him to look right at her. She wanted her words understood. She wanted them to make an impression. Then she wanted to forget about them and take off his clothes. "I am more than okay with this. I want you. And I'm more than a little excited by the fact that you want me."

A smile crept across his face and he took his jacket off so fast that she was surprised he didn't tear the sleeves off.

"Careful," she said. "I'm sure that suit cost a fortune."

He unbuttoned his shirt and she helped. "Like the shoes, that's the exact last thing on my mind right now."

As soon as his chest and torso were naked, she took a moment to admire the carved contours of his body, but she also didn't waste any time unhooking his belt and unzipping his pants. Noah shucked them nearly as fast as he'd dispatched the jacket.

Finally, they were on a more even footing, Noah in dark gray boxers, Lily in something that seemed to be making an impression—thank goodness for the power of lace and satin. He grasped her rib cage and squeezed, making her breasts plump inside her strapless bra. She never imagined Noah would see her lovely underpinnings, except perhaps by accident, and she was so glad she'd been judicious with her selection.

His hands slid to her back and he unhooked the bra. Lily flung it across the room and it connected with the flat-screen TV. Noah slid his palms to her breasts, molding his hands around them, then rubbing her nipples in small circles with his thumbs. Lily gasped at the pleasure. Noah was a master.

He dropped his head and drew one tight bud into his mouth, drawing circles with his tongue and sending Lily into near oblivion when she dared to watch him. His lips against her skin, his thick hair slumping to the side—each inviting detail was almost too much to take. This was happening. With Noah. She wanted him with every ounce of desire she had built up inside. Everything between her legs yearned for his touch, longed to have him make love to her.

She reached down and took his hand, rushing into the bedroom. She kissed him, hard, cupping her fingers around his stiff erection. She pressed into him with the heel of her hand, which brought a sexy rumble from his throat. Then she wiggled his boxers past his hips and took his length in her hand, stroking intently, watching his face as his eyes shut and his tempting mouth went slack. Having Noah Locke at her command was an awfully emboldening experience. She had to wonder if once would ever be enough. She worried that it wouldn't.

"Do you have a condom?" she asked, trying to hide the desperation in her voice. If the answer was no, she might explode.

"I do. In my shaving kit. One second." He ran off to the bathroom. Lily loved watching the defined muscles of his frame in motion, especially his butt. Noah had an especially amazing butt, complete with heartbreaking dimples right above it.

Lily sat on the bed, swishing her hands against the silky linens as the seconds ticked by and anticipation bubbled up inside her. Noah appeared in the doorway, tall and muscled and ready for her. She thought she might faint. The only thing that kept her from doing exactly that was the fight inside her. She'd waited for a long time to have sex with Noah Locke. She wasn't going to let anything ruin it.

That first glimpse of Lily perched on the bed, wearing nothing more than maddening black panties and a smile, stole Noah's breath right from his lungs. She was so much more beautiful than he'd ever imagined, just as she'd been more heavenly to kiss than he'd ever fantasized. He wanted her with every inch of his body, but some parts of him were more insistent and begging for attention. He was glad he'd opted to put on the condom in the bathroom. He was sure he'd never been so hard, was sure he'd never ached for a woman the way he did for Lily. He couldn't wait much longer.

He dropped his knee on the bed and stretched out on his side, smoothing his hand over Lily's bare stomach and urging her to her back. He caressed her breasts, cupped her cheek and brought her lips to his. They fell into a kiss that had no logical end. He could've kissed her forever then, their tongues winding in a perpetual loop. He could've dug his hands into her silky hair forever, rubbed her soft skin with his fingers. He breathed in her sweet scent, which seemed even headier in the sticky tropical air.

His fingers slowly trailed along her spine, building the anticipation when he honestly didn't want to wait another minute. Lily arched her back, and a smile interrupted their kiss. They exchanged a breathless laugh, their lips softly brushing together, then things got serious again when his hand slipped into the back of her panties. He cupped her bottom and pushed them past her hips, removing that final barrier between them. Lily hitched her leg up over his hip, grinding her center against him. She needed him and he loved her urgency, the way she told him everything he wanted to hear with an insistent rotation of her hips. He slipped his hand between their bodies and found her apex. Lily groaned so fiercely that he wasn't sure at first that the sound had actually come from her. She nipped at his lower lip. He moved his fingers in rhythmic circles, listening for the changes in her breath as they were drawn back into another perfect kiss.

Lily nudged him gently to his back and she straddled his

hips. In a move he never expected, she sat back for a moment, lazily drawing a single finger back and forth across his chest, then trailing it down his midline. Noah watched in utter fascination. She was so beautiful it boggled the mind, but he was drawn to some features in particular—her deep rose lips, the swell of her hips, those beguiling blue eyes.

She shifted and raised one leg, taking him in her hand and guiding his erection between her legs. As she sank down onto him, a torrent of heat and pleasure rushed through him. She molded around him. Warm. Hot. Soft and hard all at the same time. Being inside Lily was so much more than he'd hoped for. They moved together, Lily lowering her chest to his, but not resting her body weight on his. Instead, she rubbed her nipples gently against his bare chest. That vision alone was enough to send him over the edge.

Her breaths were already rough and short. Her eyes drifted shut, then opened, and closed again. She rolled her head to the side, shoulders rising up around her ears over and over again. He loved the way she surrendered to the pleasure. It was such a turn-on.

Finally, she pressed her chest against his and he was able to kiss her deeply, the way he wanted to. Things were different now—frenzied and fitful, like neither of them could settle down. Noah thrust more forcefully, lifting Lily from the bed. The need coiled in his hips. It was like a cat about to pounce. He pulled her flat against him and flipped her to her back. He might have been a bit too forceful, judging by the way it sent her hair up in a flurry, but she seemed to like that, a lot.

"I'm so close," she mumbled, digging her fingers into his shoulders, her heels into the backs of his thighs, and bucked against him with her hips. He was soaking up her raw beauty, the way the color had rushed to her cheeks, when her chin rose, her mouth fell open, and the orgasm hit her, causing her to gather tight around him.

His own pleasure felt like it was torn from the depths of his belly, relentless waves of tension letting go. Lily gasped and pulled him close, kissing his cheek and neck over and over again. He rolled to his side and they were in each others' arms, breathless with contentment. He could hardly believe he'd finally had a taste of this woman he'd desired for so long.

She turned to him and nuzzled his chest with her nose. When she lifted her head to look at him, the vivid blue of her eyes kept him in the moment like a jolt of caffeine from a potent cup of coffee. They'd given in. This had really happened.

"That was wonderful," she murmured, kissing him softly.

"I couldn't agree more." He wanted to tell her how long he'd waited for this, for her, and that he'd spent so much time thinking that it would never happen. But that would ruin everything when they had to return to work. Better she think that this was just another Noah tryst. Hopefully she already knew that she meant a lot to him on other levels, most important was friendship.

"I'm wiped, though. I hardly slept last night. It was tough being in the same bed with you, knowing I was supposed to keep my hands to myself."

"Really?" He was surprised by her admission. He'd assumed that his frustration with physically staying away from each other had been one-sided.

"Yes, Noah. Really. Have you looked at you? I'd be a fool to not want to try something."

He smiled and pulled her closer. "And why didn't you?"

"I was waiting for you to give me a sign."

A sign. Had it been as simple as that all along? If he

had met Lily in a bar or at a party, yes. But they'd met at work, she'd become indispensable before he could figure out a way around it and the rest was already determined. Tomorrow, they'd go home, the charade of their fake engagement would be far less necessary, and it would end as soon as the Hannafort deal was signed.

Lily's breaths were already soft and even. She was falling asleep in his arms and it was a surprisingly pleasant feeling. He kissed her temple, wondering if he should let her sleep for long. Now that he'd done the thing he'd sworn he wouldn't, he refused to live with regrets. He wanted more of her. If he was going to get her out of his system, and he really wanted to, tonight was his only chance.

Eight

Lily woke up to two things—the amazing landscape of Noah's naked back and a knock at their cabana door.

"Did you order room service?" She was half-awake and more than half-tempted to tell whomever it was to go away. Forget food. She wanted to press up against Noah and get him to go for one last round before they had to leave for New York.

"No. I hope it's not more champagne. We still have another bottle to drink before we leave." He rolled toward her, now flat on his back. He absentmindedly scratched his stomach, eyes still sleepy. The sheet was barely covering him. He was so hot she was surprised the bed wasn't on fire.

Another knock came at the door, this one more insistent. "Do you want me to get it?" he asked.

"I'll get it. Maybe they have the wrong room. Or it's housekeeping." Lily scrambled for some clothes, but all she could find was Noah's shirt from last night. She threaded her arms into the sleeves and buttoned up lightning fast, then bolted for the door.

Lily was greeted by Charlotte, wagging her fingers.

Oh crap.

"Morning. I think you lost something." Charlotte held up Lily's sparkly shoe.

Lily felt the blood drain from her face. So much for keeping this quiet. In the flurry of rushing to bed with Noah, she'd completely forgotten about sending him out again to retrieve her beloved shoe. "Thanks. I was wondering where that went."

Charlotte bounced her all-knowing eyebrows at Lily. "There are only three things that make a woman leave behind a brand-new designer shoe. A flood, a fire, or a man. So which is it?"

Lily wedged herself into the door opening. "Unless I missed something, I don't think there were any natural disasters last night." *Woman-made disasters, yes.*

"Nice shirt, by the way. It looks better on you than Noah."

That was impossible, but there was no use arguing the point. Plus, if there had been any doubt that Charlotte knew exactly what had happened last night, it was gone now. "Somebody was pounding on the door. I had to answer it wearing something."

"Where is my brother, anyway?"

Lily cleared her throat. "In bed."

Charlotte handed over the shoe. "Look. I'm all for a woman taking whatever she wants. I just want to be sure that you're watching out for Lily. I love my brother to pieces, but I guarantee you that he isn't worrying about your career or your feelings. It's not on his radar at all. Honestly, I don't know that he's capable."

Lily didn't want to believe that either. Noah had been

the most attentive man she'd ever gone to bed with, by a long shot. Simply thinking about it was enough to send Lily grabbing the wall to steady herself. But Charlotte was probably right. Noah had a horrible track record, one he did not try to hide. Plus, he was her boss and this was technically the last day of their fake engagement. Tomorrow, they would be back in the office working together. No more kisses. No more holding hands. Certainly no sex. *Bummer.* "Okay. I'll take that under advisement. Thanks."

"See you out at the dock in an hour? The boat will be there to take us to the car." Charlotte turned away for a second. "Oh, Lily. Can you let Noah know that Sawyer and Kendall ended up leaving late last night? She still wasn't feeling well and the doctor thought it best she get home and see her own physician. Everything's fine, though. I got a text from him thirty minutes ago."

"Oh, sure. I'm glad everything is okay." Noah was going to be so mad he didn't get that call. "We'll see you at the dock." Lily closed the door and padded back into the bedroom.

Noah was on his side, head propped up on his hand, the silky white sheets covering very little of his sun-kissed skin—just everything between his waist and knees. No question about it—Noah was a slice of heaven. That long torso, narrow waist and the alluring trail of hair under his belly button was enough to make her choke on the words she had to say. His come-hither smile and the flicker in his eyes made it so much worse.

"Coming back to bed?" he asked.

Yes. I am. Forever and ever and ever. "No. Sorry. That was your sister. She knows what happened last night." Lily held up the shoe as proof.

Noah shrugged and patted the mattress. "Charlotte likes you. She won't say anything to anyone. I promise."

Lily plucked her dress from the floor, turned it right side out and draped it over her arm. "I'm not worried about discretion, although I definitely do not want Sawyer to know about this."

"Why not?"

"Because I have to work with your brother and it's going to be bad enough going into work every day and seeing you, knowing that you know what I look like naked. It's not professional, Noah, and that's really important to me." Every word out of her mouth was a potent reminder of what she was really supposed to be doing at this wedding—securing her professional future, not sleeping with the boss. There was only one future for Lily and it was wrapped up in her 1 percent of Locke and Locke, not with Noah the serial dater. "Last night was fun, but I think we both know that we're better off if we pretend like it didn't happen and just move forward."

He pursed his lips and looked back over his shoulder, out at the gorgeous ocean vista. "You're right. It wasn't a good idea. I was serious when I asked if you really wanted to cross that line last night."

Why did he have to swing so far in the opposite direction? "No. It was my choice and I refuse to regret it. We're both consenting adults. But I think..." Her voice tapered off as she searched for the right words to say. It was as if the devil was on her shoulder, urging her to ask Noah for one more roll in the proverbial hay. She wanted his hands all over her, his kiss on her lips, his body weighing her down. She wanted him to make her fall apart at the seams again and again.

Noah turned back to her. "Let me guess. What happens in the Florida Keys, stays in the Florida Keys?"

Lily didn't even bother holding back her sigh. "Trite, but yes. That's the perfect way to put it."

He knocked his head to the side and threw back the covers with zero regard for the fact that she now had a full view of everything she wanted so desperately. "Okay, then. I'm taking a shower." He hopped up from the bed and traipsed into the bathroom. Lily stole her final chance to watch Noah's perfect butt in motion. She was going to miss that view. She'd rather look at him than the ocean.

"Just start packing," she told herself. "You had your fun, now it's time to go back to work." Lily did exactly that, wondering if she'd ever again wear some of these beautiful designer clothes she now owned. There was no telling when she'd be invited to another event as fancy as this wedding, but now was not the time for pessimism. Knowing she'd never sleep with Noah again was depressing enough.

An hour later, she and Noah made their trek out to the dock, ready to go. Charlotte and Michael were chatting with Lyle and Marcy. Lily could only hope that Noah's claim that his sister was discreet ended up holding water. Loose lips sink ships, as her mother used to say.

"Where are Kendall and Sawyer?"

"Oh, shoot. I forgot to tell you they headed back early because Kendall still wasn't feeling well."

"You'd think my brother would want to share these things with me, but apparently not."

"I'm sure he was just worried about Kendall and figured Charlotte would tell you."

"Yeah. I guess you're right."

Marcy Hannafort turned and caught sight of Lily and Noah. She beelined over to them, looking like a woman on top of the world. "Honestly. What a handsome couple you are," she said.

"Thank you. That's sweet of you to say." Lily shifted

her weight uncomfortably. They *were* a handsome couple. What a waste of two perfectly good people.

"We're very happy." Noah pressed a dutiful kiss to Lily's cheek that nearly knocked her off her feet. "Thank you so much for including us this weekend."

"I know it was my daughter getting married, but I just love weddings so much." Marcy Hannafort smiled and stared off wistfully, as if she were reliving the last forty-eight hours.

"It was a lovely event. You and Lyle must be relieved it went so well." Lily shifted her weight again, glancing at Noah, wishing he knew to change the subject to anything other than weddings. Unfortunately, memories of last night, the ones seared into her memory, were dug up every time she looked at him. She was starting to realize exactly how difficult it was going to be to work with him. She would never be able to forget what his touch was like. She'd probably spend at least the next month avoiding eye contact completely. She never should've crossed that line, but she couldn't have helped herself last night if she'd wanted to. Noah was too irresistible and the wait had been too long.

"Honestly, weddings are like a drug for me, so I'd gladly redo the whole thing over again," Marcy continued.

Lily merely nodded. Considering her history with weddings, she was proud of herself for having lived through this one. As for drugs, she might prefer a horse tranquilizer to witnessing more marriage vows anytime soon.

"You know, I was a wedding planner for years and years. Before the hotel business really took off and Lyle needed my help."

"Oh, I didn't realize that." Noah acted as though he were genuinely interested.

"I helped Annie quite a bit with planning this weekend,

although she's such a Daddy's girl. She wanted Lyle's help much more than mine. Even when it came to things like picking out the flowers and tasting cake. You know, normal mother-of-the-bride things."

"That's sweet, though. She loves her daddy very much." Lily desperately wanted to get out of this conversation. Simply thinking about picking out flowers and cake made it feel like someone was jabbing a knife in her side. The mere mention of it made her feel ill. But she couldn't be even the slightest bit rude to Marcy Hannafort. The big deal wasn't even close to being signed.

"To be fair, Lyle didn't have to do much. Once he came up with the idea of using Key Marly, and she agreed to it, the staff took over most of the planning."

"That's wonderful." Lily tried to send psychic messages to Noah to get his gorgeous mouth working harder so he could charm Marcy into a different topic of discussion. "And now you don't have to worry about it at all."

"I know. It makes me so sad." Marcy flashed her eyes at Lily and rubbed her hands together like she was scheming. "So, tell me what you two have planned for your big day. I understand that yours is the next big wedding on the horizon since Michael and Charlotte opted to get married at City Hall."

"Oh, I guess you're right. Well, we haven't really had a chance to get to the meat of it yet." Lily laughed nervously. Where was she going with this? Lily and Noah were fake engaged, not fake getting married.

"Noah, you mentioned that you and Lily have been discussing how big of a wedding to have. What's the date?"

Lily was struck with panic unlike anything she'd ever experienced. She was the prepared one. She was the person who was always on top of things, but she was out of her depth and Noah had apparently thrown them both under the bus by delivering factoids about their non-wedding. Lily had to be very careful here, or everything could go up in smoke. "Oh. Uh. June. I know it's a cliché, but we liked the idea of it." She shrugged it off.

Mrs. Hannafort gripped her elbow, her face showing deep concern. "But what's the actual date? Where are you having it? Have you sent out the save-the-date cards? Have you put together the guest list?"

Lily found herself glaring at Noah like she was drowning and he was the life preserver. She didn't even know when the Saturdays in June were. "Oh, I forget. So many dates swirling around in my head right now."

"It's whatever that last Saturday in June is." Right then and there, Noah upped the ante. Lily bugged her eyes at him, but the look on his face said he was winging it as much as she was.

"Neither of you knows the actual date?" Enough confusion crossed Marcy's face to cause Lily more than a little worry. Surely she and Noah were sending mixed signals right now.

Lily grabbed Noah's arm and cozied up to him, digging her fingernails into his biceps for good measure. If she was going to suffer, he could, too. "You mean June 28. Remember?"

"We haven't settled on a location yet because we haven't decided how big the guest list should be. We're still making up our minds. Lily has been so busy at work," Noah said.

This is my fault? "Noah won't admit it, but he's the real reason we haven't made any decisions. He's very hard to pin down." *Although he had no problem pinning me down last night.*

Marcy's face appeared positively horrified. "No. No. No. Lily, darling. This will not do. You hardly know the date of your own wedding? And you haven't picked a venue yet? We need to straighten this out right away." She turned to Noah and stuck her finger in his face. "And you need to stop being so indecisive. No bride wants to deal with that. If she wants your two cents, you give it to her."

"Right. Of course." Noah looked as though he'd never been scolded so harshly in all his life.

Marcy shook her head. "I swear you two are exactly like Annie and Brad. You need to take this more seriously. Chop-chop." She popped up onto her tiptoes and waved down her husband, who headed right over. "Luckily, I have an idea."

Lyle set his hand on Marcy's shoulder when he reached them. "Looks like we're having a real confab over here."

"I was talking to Lily and Noah about their wedding. It's June 28 and they don't have a venue yet. What if they did it at the Grand Legacy? And we could use the wedding as part of a publicity plan in conjunction with announcing the joint venture between Hannafort and Locke? Sort of like we used this weekend to have our soft opening of Key Marly."

Lily could see the gears turning in Lyle Hannafort's head and that scared her right down to her bones. "My darling, you are a genius. I love it. We're going to have to light a fire under the lawyers if we're going to get the deal done that quickly, but you know me. I don't like to sit around and wait. Plus, I can just see it. A big, fancy Locke family wedding at the newest beauty in the Hannafort Hotels stable. I think it's a fabulous idea. Lily? Noah? Would you be up for that? It'll get the deal going on a quicker timetable."

"Yes," Noah blurted. "Absolutely. It's a wonderful idea."

"Maybe we should talk about it first?" Lily asked, giving Noah's arm an extra hard squeeze.

Marcy shook her head at Lily while a sweet but condescending smile spread across her face. "I know you're nervous, darling, but trust me. You need to make these decisions now or you won't have your dream wedding. You only get one shot at this."

Or two, if you're me. Lily did not like this scenario at all. Pretending for a weekend was one thing. This was an entirely new level of deception and lying, all tied up in a bow called mental anguish. Could she do this? Noah shot her a look that said he was sorry, but she'd better fall in line. She hated it when he looked at her like that. She had no good answer for it. She scanned Marcy's and Lyle's faces and forced herself to see her nest egg. Her secure future. Everything she'd worked so hard for over the last two years. If this meant the deal happened faster, she and Noah could break things off before the actual wedding happened, and hopefully it wouldn't have to be that big of a deal since everything would be easily canceled with the Grand Legacy.

"I'm sure Sawyer will be pleased." Lyle reached over and patted Noah on the shoulder. "And to think I almost pulled out of it after seeing that silly video. Now I know what a good guy you are."

"Then it's settled," Marcy said. "And I want to donate my services as wedding planner. Lyle and I will be back in New York in a few days and we can start working on it then."

Lily's heart sprang into a full-on panic. "Oh, no, Mrs. Hannafort. That's totally not necessary. I'm sure that Noah and I can handle it on our own."

"But you don't have my experience. And Noah just told me how busy you are at work. This will save you more time than you can possibly imagine. And you won't have to worry about making any big mistakes. I'll make sure that doesn't happen."

Lily looked at Noah's handsome face, colored by an expression she could describe only as surrender. He was on board. Lyle and Marcy were on board. Lily needed to concede and figure out the rest later. "Okay. That sounds great."

Except Lily was sure of one thing—the only thing about this that would be great would be her regret.

Nine

Lily was the first to arrive in the office Monday morning. After being away on Friday, she'd have a ton of email to catch up on, as well as faxes, mail and voice mail messages. She wanted Sawyer and Noah to come in to their usual well-oiled machine. She also wanted to be capable, on-top-of-it Lily when Noah arrived. She wanted to avoid the sense that he was imagining her flat on her back and at his mercy.

One thing she could not avoid today. Sawyer was about to learn that Lily and Noah were now planning a fake wedding. Hopefully, he'd appreciate the business side of what had happened—Marcy Hannafort had backed them into a corner, and they'd done the only thing they could to keep moving forward with the deal. Lily also hoped Sawyer wouldn't give Noah a hard time about it. Until Lily had been folded more fully into the inner workings of Locke and Locke, she hadn't been quite so aware of the friction between Sawyer and Noah. Noah clearly looked up to his brother very much, and felt dismissed or ignored at least some of the time.

Sawyer arrived fifteen minutes after Lily. "Sorry we missed you and Noah yesterday. I trust Charlotte told you we had to leave early?"

"She did. Is everything okay with Kendall?" Lily got up from her desk.

"Yes, thankfully," he answered. "The doctor thinks it was a mild case of food poisoning. A bad shrimp or something. Don't say anything to the Hannaforts. I'm sure they'd be horrified."

"Yikes. I didn't hear anything about the other guests getting sick, so hopefully it was a blip on the map." The mention of the Hannaforts made Lily jittery.

"Any sign of Noah yet?"

Lily was able to assuage her paranoia over whether or not Sawyer might know about recent developments. It was apparent he didn't. "No. But I'm guessing he'll be here soon."

"Did I miss anything important yesterday?"

"Noah can fill you in on everything." Lily was torn over her answer, but if she told Sawyer now and Noah walked in on them discussing it, he would once again feel out of the loop.

"Were you happy with the way everything went with you and Noah this weekend?" Sawyer took a seat in reception. "I hope it wasn't too awkward."

Lily fumbled for her mug and took a swig of lukewarm coffee. She needed a second to think. A million different answers sat on her lips, none of which she'd ever share with Sawyer. "It was fine. I had a nice time."

The office door opened and in walked Noah. He stopped

dead in his tracks, sights sweeping between Sawyer and Lily. "What's up?"

"Just chatting about the weekend."

"Did Lily tell you what happened right before we left?"

She shook her head. "I thought it was better if we were both here for it."

"Good. I agree."

"Whoa. That does not sound good. Do you want to tell me what's going on?" The tone of Sawyer's voice was unmistakable. The Hannafort deal meant too much for there to be any new problems.

Noah took off his coat and Lily had to ignore the memories that flooded her mind. That moment when she first saw him take off his shirt and she was able to have her hands all over him. "Well, the easiest answer is we have news. Mr. and Mrs. Hannafort want to have the wedding at the Grand Legacy. They want to use it for publicity as part of the official deal announcement."

Sawyer's eyes narrowed. "What wedding? Is one of their other daughters engaged?"

"Our wedding. Mine and Lily's."

The words *our wedding* made Lily flinch. Any hope that the state of affairs might appear better in the light of a new day was gone. It only looked worse.

"A wedding? You're actually getting married? How in the hell did this happen? And why didn't one of you call me last night?"

"It's my fault," Lily blurted. She was prepared to do anything to get Sawyer to stop using words like *wedding* and *married*.

"No. Lily. That's not fair." Noah was quick to step in. "Marcy had you in a corner. Who knew the woman was so obsessed with weddings?" He turned to his brother. "She asked Lily about the date and kept asking until she finally had to give her an answer. I figured that we had to do everything we could to keep the deal together. We didn't really have a choice."

Sawyer raked his hands through his hair. "I'm so sorry, Lily. If I would've known it was going to get this out of control, I never would've allowed this in the first place."

"Hold on a minute." The anger in Noah's voice was so unfamiliar Lily wouldn't have believed it had come from his mouth if she hadn't seen him utter the words. "You *allowed* this? I seem to remember that this was ultimately my call, along with Lily. We knew what we were getting into. No, it's not what either of us would've planned, and it's certainly less than ideal, but we have it under control."

Seeing and hearing Noah be firm with Sawyer created a pleasant flutter in her chest. She loved the idea of them as a unified front. He'd been so right two days ago on the dock. They were in this together. "Sawyer, it's fine. We did what we had to do to make the deal work. We're a team."

Sawyer shook his head in dismay. "I hope you two know what you're doing."

"We do."

The fax machine on Lily's desk sprang to life. She only needed to see a few inches of the letterhead to know who it was from. "We're getting something from Lyle."

Noah and Sawyer stepped closer. They all watched the machine chug out the first page. Lily swiped it from the paper tray. *Subject: Deal Memo.*

"This is it." Noah leaned into Lily, subtly enough that Sawyer would never notice, but close enough for his body heat to make her tingly from head to toe. Between Noah and the anticipation of the official offer, this was almost too much to take. "We don't look until every page comes out."

"Fine," Sawyer said. "I'll be in my office. Let me know when it's all here."

Lily and Noah stood sentry over the fax machine until all twelve pages arrived. She collected them in her hands and handed them over to Noah. This was his deal now as far as she was concerned. He'd been in it from the beginning, he'd yanked it back from the precipice every time it was in danger of falling apart.

Noah took a step away from her desk and turned back to her. "Coming?" That flash of his eyes turned her knees to rubber.

Lily was so excited and scared she didn't know what to think. She swiped her notepad from her desk. "Yep. Coming."

A short ten minutes later, they were all still in shock. Sawyer looked out the window. Noah sat back in his chair, staring up at the ceiling. Lily was unsure of the appropriate reaction from her, so she sat perfectly still. This was her first time in on a big deal. She had to tamp down her desire to leap out of her seat and dance around the room. Her nest egg was about to be a lot bigger than first thought.

"We still need to have the lawyers look everything over," Noah said. "And run everything by Charlotte. She should be able to come by the office this afternoon."

"Yes. Of course." Sawyer pinched the bridge of his nose. "I just… I knew Lyle was excited about this deal. But I'll be honest, I never thought the offer would end up being two times the number we started at."

"It's amazing," Lily offered, still feeling out of her element.

"It really is."

"We should go out and celebrate, don't you think?" Noah asked.

Sawyer dropped down into his seat. "Sure. A drink after work? Kendall is still feeling a bit under the weather, so I'm probably not good for much else."

"Six o'clock?" Noah asked.

"Perfect." Sawyer picked up his phone.

Noah and Lily took that as their cue to leave. As they reached her desk, Noah put his hand on her shoulder. "This wouldn't have been possible without you. I want you to know that. And it's more than the stuff that's happened over the last week. It's everything you've done for us over two years. We're both happy to have you here, but I'm especially happy about it."

Lily didn't want his words to make her feel the way she was feeling right now—soft and mushy on the inside. It contradicted the strength she needed to convey in business situations. Still, she so appreciated the kind words. "Thank you very much."

"No problem." He patted her on the shoulder, almost as confirmation that their relationship had returned to being only about business, exactly what she'd wanted. "Now let's get to work."

Lily sat at her desk, a ridiculous smile on her face, and got busy on the hundreds of things that had been pushed aside on Friday. They ordered lunch in and Lily devoured a Cobb salad while poring over spreadsheets and construction schedules. She had calls with two contractors, scheduled meetings for Noah and Sawyer. Six o'clock arrived in no time.

Noah had reserved a corner booth and had champagne waiting at a bar a few blocks from the office. It was a hot spot on weeknights for the after-work crowd, and the place was bustling with people. Lily, Noah and Sawyer were getting settled just as Charlotte joined them.

"I'm only here for a minute." She plopped down her enormous handbag and took the seat next to Lily, who was left shoulder-to-shoulder with Noah. "It's too depressing for me to be around people drinking right now. I would kill for a glass of wine."

Lily laughed. "I bet. Only a few more months to go, though, right?" Pregnancy was a life event that seemed so far off for Lily that it might as well be her retirement.

Charlotte smoothed her hands over her belly. "Yes. And it's all worth it. Doesn't mean I don't enjoy making others pity me."

"Not gonna happen tonight, Charlotte. There's too much to be happy about. We ordered you a glass of ginger ale. Hopefully the thought of all that money will make it tolerable," Noah said.

Right on time, the waiter delivered Charlotte's drink. She raised the champagne flute. "To Locke and Locke. And Lily. And Lyle Hannafort. That's entirely too many *L* names for one toast, but I couldn't care less." She grinned as glasses clinked and they took their celebratory sips.

"Well, that's it for me." Charlotte pushed her drink to the center of the table.

"I thought you were kidding," Noah replied.

"I have a super-hot husband waiting for me at home and he's ordering a pizza. No offense to you guys, but that's way more tempting." Charlotte popped up from her seat and hooked her handbag on her arm.

Sawyer finished his drink. "Hold on. I'll see you out. I need to go meet Kendall."

"Bye," Noah said, seeming annoyed.

Charlotte leaned over the table, looking both Noah and Lily directly in the eye. "If you're staying, be sure to put on the Lily-and-Noah show. You're out in public, and it's only a matter of time before news of the big wedding gets out. If anyone has loose lips, it's Marcy Hannafort."

"Yep. Of course." Lily watched as Noah slipped his hand on top of hers. Lord help her, she would never get accustomed to his touch. His skin against hers would always awaken every nerve ending in her body.

"We're big kids, Charlotte. We've got it under control. You can go now." Noah took another sip of his drink.

Charlotte rolled her eyes. "Bye."

"Do you ever get tired of taking orders?" Noah asked. "Because I do."

"Your sister has a very defined idea of the way things should be done. I get that. I'm the same way."

"It's not just Charlotte. Sawyer does it to me all the time."

"So tell them to stop."

Noah shrugged. "The thing is, most of the time they aren't wrong. And if I had told them to stop when they suggested our engagement..." He cleared his throat. "I wouldn't have had nearly as much fun at the wedding."

Fun. Was that what Lily was to him? It was hard to imagine she was anything more. Not that she had any right to be disappointed about it. She'd eagerly grabbed her chance to be with Noah, to have that heavenly taste of him, no strings attached. "It was fun, wasn't it?" She drew her finger around the rim of her glass. She knew her voice shouldn't be so flirtatious, but now that she'd finished her first glass of champagne, she had no need for defenses. Not with Noah. They'd had major good news today. He was in a great mood. She had her nest egg secured.

"My favorite kind of fun." He put his hand on hers again. His fingers slipped between hers, gently spreading them apart. Down and back he rubbed, going deeper with his touch on every pass. Lily stared at their hands and nearly gasped from ecstasy. "I know we said Florida was the end of it, but maybe we should try to get everything we can out of our arrangement." He turned toward her, dropped his chin and nuzzled the spot behind her ear with his nose. His warm breath skimmed the length of her neck. The scruff on his cheek scratched at her skin.

"What did you have in mind?" she asked.

He laughed quietly in response, but she didn't think it was that funny. She wanted to hear him say the words. "This." He kissed the delicate skin beneath her ear. It took every ounce of self-control not to push him back against the booth, straddle his lap and pop the buttons off his shirt. He kissed her cheek, then moved to the corner of her mouth. The anticipation was killing her. "And this."

His lips brushed hers and she went in for one of Noah's mind-bending kisses—where constructs like time and place mean nothing. They pressed against each other, her hand dug into his hair. She was only vaguely aware of what was going on around them. People milled about, but she didn't care. They were engaged, dammit, and if people couldn't handle a public display of affection, that was too bad.

Noah pulled back, his mouth sexily slack. "We need to slow down or I won't be able to walk out of here without embarrassing myself."

She loved having that effect on him. It was not only a total turn-on, it made her want to give him the night of his life. "Why don't you get your driver to bring your car around? So we can go to your place."

Noah had never heard sweeter words. He'd been certain she was determined to keep things as they'd been before Florida, but apparently not. Unfortunately, he saw trouble out of the corner of his eye—tall and gorgeous and for the life of him, he couldn't remember her name. Whatever it was, she was definitely a woman he'd dated and she was zeroing in on him like a heat-seeking missile.

"Noah Locke, you are a royal jerk." The woman swished her long brown hair over her shoulder.

"I'm sorry?" It was the only thing he could think to say. The look of horror on Lily's face was making it hard to think straight.

"Was I not clear? You're a jerk. I saw the pictures in the tabloids. We went out two weeks ago and now you're engaged to be married? So what was I? A little something on the side?" The woman directed her sights at Lily. "I hope that ring is worth it, because I'm not sure he is. Unless you want to be treated as if you're disposable."

Lily sat a little straighter, but didn't say a thing. She merely cocked an eyebrow at Noah.

Noah scooted out of the booth and stood. "I'm sorry, but I'm going to have to ask you to leave. My fiancée and I are trying to enjoy ourselves."

"I'm sure you're not used to women calling you out on your crap, but somebody needs to do it. I hope the marriage works out, because I think you've run out of single women in Manhattan anyway." With that, she stormed off.

Noah plopped down, unsure of what had just happened, but certain that was his pride she'd ground into the floor. "I'm so sorry. That has never happened. Well, almost never."

"You certainly increase your odds when you go out with enough women to warrant a tabloid video."

"You know that's not me."

"I do know that. It still doesn't make what just happened any better."

"She was terrible, wasn't she?"

Lily squinted at him. "What? No. That's not what I was saying. She felt used, Noah. No woman should feel like that. Do you have any idea how many times I've been that woman?"

"Approaching a former boyfriend in a bar and making a scene?"

"No. The spurned lover. The woman who gets dumped by the handsome guy who can have whatever and whomever he wants. I've been in her shoes and it's not fun. I nearly made room for her to sit and offered to buy her a drink. Or at least tell her that our engagement isn't what it appears to be."

"It's not my fault if other guys treated you badly."

"This is not about me. But for the record, I have several of those. It's not fun to be yanked around."

"Hey. I didn't yank her around. I don't do that. I'm always up-front. I'm always clear it's not serious. Sawyer practically drilled that into my head."

A breathy laugh left Lily's lips. "And you're going to keep walking in Sawyer's footsteps? He managed to figure out that wasn't the way to live his life."

Noah felt as though Lily had plunged a dagger into his heart. Yes, he looked up to Sawyer. How could he not? Sawyer was the one positive male role model in his life. So, yes, they'd shared the same attitude toward women— don't get involved, don't buy into that moment when everything is new and it's easy to get swept away. Their dad had made an embarrassing habit of that, leaving a trail of broken hearts in his wake.

"I don't need you to psychoanalyze me, especially not on this topic. There's plenty you don't know."

"Seriously? I've had to spend the last two years hearing you sweet-talk women over the phone or even worse, bring them by the office. I know exactly what your modus operandi is." She grabbed her purse and coat and scooted out of the booth. "I'm just going to take a cab home. Good night, Noah."

He was still catching up with what she'd said. Had he

hurt her by letting her witness glimpses of his love life? "Lily, wait. My driver can drop you off at your place. We can talk about this."

She took off and Noah had no choice but to wind his way through the throng of people in the bustling bar. He followed her out onto the busy sidewalk. Dozens of people walked past, some filing in and out of the bar. The sun had set and the air held a chill.

"You and I both know what happens the minute we get in the back of that car, Noah," Lily muttered while tugging on her coat. "We can't keep our hands off each other. But we have to. That's the only way I get out of this ridiculous situation with my pride and job intact. Those are both supremely important to me."

"So you've said."

Anger blazed in her blue eyes. "Don't you dare fault me for putting my career first. A man does that and nobody bats an eye. I'm going now. See you tomorrow. At *work*."

Noah looked around. There were people everywhere and Charlotte had been clear that they had to remember the show they were putting on. They were so close with the Hannafort deal. "No kiss goodbye? We're supposed to be getting married."

Lily sidestepped to the curb and thrust her hand up in the air. A cab zipped right over. "Nobody's watching. We're fine." She opened the door and climbed inside without another word.

Noah stood there feeling like an idiot. He'd been so stupid to think that a little role-play with Lily would be harmless. He felt as if his entire sense of self was dissolving, and he knew he'd played a huge role in that. Why did it have to be that the allure of Lily was so great, and she was the one person who could send this all tumbling down?

Ten

At the office the next morning, a number came up on Noah's caller ID that made his stomach lurch—his dad. He picked up, slumping back in his office chair and pre-emptively kneading his forehead. "Dad. Hi."

"You don't have to sound so excited to talk to me."

Last night at the bar had nearly killed Noah, kissing Lily's neck and having it all blow up in his face. Now this. It was going to be a brutal day. "Trust me. I'm thrilled."

"I was hoping this would be a happy phone call, but after seeing the papers this morning, it looks as though this engagement of yours isn't going to stick. I'm sorry to see that."

Papers? Noah had no idea what his dad was talking about. He cradled the phone between his shoulder and cheek, typing his own name into the search bar on his computer. It only took a fraction of a second for the story to come up. Trouble in Locke Paradise. Beneath the headline was the photographic evidence of his argument with

Lily in front of the bar. This would've been a very different article if she had just listened to him.

"It's the tabloids. This is what they do. It's nothing." His words might have sounded cool and collected, but Noah was feeling anything but that on the inside.

"Pictures don't lie. I really was hoping you'd finally get your act together. You can't always let Sawyer be the perfect son."

The perfect son. This was a classic example of their father's cruel ways. He'd never seen Sawyer as the perfect son. If anything, their dad put more effort and attention into sabotaging Sawyer than he did Noah. But he liked to tell Noah that his older brother was the perfect son merely to get under his skin.

"My engagement to Lily is great. Thanks for calling to congratulate us, by the way."

"Thank you for calling to tell me about it."

Touché. "I would've gotten around to it eventually. Work has been incredibly busy." The instant the words were out of his mouth, he regretted them. Giving his dad any inkling of what was going on with their business was always a bad idea.

"So I gather. I understand that you attended Lyle Hannafort's daughter's wedding. There isn't something brewing between your little company and Hannafort, is there? That would be a real slap in the face to everything I've worked so hard for. You know I despise Lyle. The man is a self-righteous blowhard and a terrible businessman."

Noah's pulse thundered in his ears. He and Sawyer had long suspected that somebody was feeding their dad information on the Locke and Locke business dealings. Noah couldn't take the chance that his dad would get wind of the Hannafort deal. He and Sawyer had taken great pains to keep everything under wraps. "For a terrible business-man, he's got quite the empire."

"And looking to add to it, from what I understand."

That one hit a little too close to home. Noah had to end this, now. "We went to a wedding. Charlotte used to work on weddings with Lyle's wife. Stop reading so much into it."

"You and your brother can be as coy as you like. I just want you to know that I'm watching."

Noah sat up in his chair and plopped his elbow down onto the desk. "Is there something else you wanted? I have some work I need to get to."

"No. Merely calling to make sure everything is okay. I worry about you and your siblings."

No, you don't. "Everything's great."

"Okay, then. I'd like to meet my future daughter-in-law at some point if that's possible. That's a courtesy your brother wasn't willing to extend to me. I had to meet Kendall on my own."

Another lie. Dad had met Kendall weeks before she and Sawyer were engaged, and only because he'd tried to buy off Kendall to spy on Sawyer or at the very least sabotage the reopening of the Grand Legacy. "We'll see. I'll let you know."

"Have a good day, son."

A low grumble fought to leave Noah's lips. "You, too." As soon as he hung up, he tossed his phone aside onto a stack of paperwork. He didn't want to look at it again anytime soon.

Just then, Lily marched into Noah's office and tossed a copy of one of the most infamous New York tabloids on his desk. "Page five." She jabbed her finger into the headline then dropped down into the chair and crossed her legs. Even when she was obviously mad, she was ridiculously hot. Last night had been torture. He'd been so close to taking her home.

"I've already seen it. I told you we should've kissed each other goodbye."

Lily dropped her chin and shot him a pointed glance. "Don't make this my fault. We wouldn't have had that argument in the first place if it hadn't been for your former lady friend stopping by for a visit."

Noah took one more look at the paper. He and Lily were both attractive people, but it was amazing the unflattering angles the paparazzi were able to capture. He hated the tabloids. That much was official. It didn't even matter anymore that they were what had brought Lily closer to him. Now they were driving her further away.

"I hate this, Noah." Lily sat back in her chair, staring out the window, her head wagging slowly back and forth. "It's too much. This is way more than we ever talked about."

"What do you want me to say? It's not like I can control this."

"My neighbor saw this. The little old lady who lives down the hall from me. She was so upset and I had to convince her that we were still together, when the reality is that it's all fake."

Don't remind me. This was getting to Noah, too. Being around Lily while she tried so hard to keep him at arm's length was much worse than the misery he'd been experiencing before.

Sawyer poked his head into Noah's office. "Did you guys see the story in the paper? Kendall showed it to me. Not good." He stepped inside and leaned against the doorframe.

Noah didn't get headaches often, but today was already an exception. "It gets worse. Dad saw it. And he knows we went to the wedding. He suspects something is going on with Hannafort. It's only a matter of time until he finds out. My worry is that it's going to happen before everything is signed and he finds some way to interfere. For all we know, Dad was behind the tabloid video in the first place."

Sawyer sucked in a deep breath, adopting his trademark look of concern. "It could happen, especially considering everything he did to mess with the Grand Legacy."

"I also think Dad suspects there's something off about my engagement to Lily. He could out us, easily."

Lily's gaze flew back and forth between Noah and Sawyer. "Do you think he could put the deal in true jeopardy? I haven't done all of this extra work for that to all go south."

Noah couldn't for the life of him figure out what Lily wanted from him anymore, but he was starting to get a better idea. Between sticking up for the woman in the bar and now treating their fake engagement as nothing but work, it was clear that everything that had happened between them in Florida had meant very little to her. Noah was getting a taste of his own medicine and he didn't like it at all.

"We have to do something," Sawyer said. "Any suggestions?"

"I have one," Noah said. "How about we not give the tabloids any more free material?"

Lily shot him a look so fast it could've sliced his head off. "That's not fair. We can't exactly control that."

"Or can we? I mean, at least circle the wagons and keep you two away from negative publicity." Sawyer nodded, clearly calculating. "I think we need to double-down on the engagement. Lily, I think you need to move in with Noah."

Lily's eyes grew as big as saucers. "Move in with him. As in pack up all of my stuff and move into his condo in the Grand Legacy. You do realize this is far more than I was originally asked to do. Way more." Her voice was reaching a pitch that would soon only be audible to dogs.

"Don't forget, I have to go meet Marcy Hannafort in a few days and plan a fake wedding."

There was no mistaking what Lily was saying. She wanted more money. Noah knew it. "Fine. Then we up your percentage." If ever there was a message that everything was back to being business, that was it. Part of Noah hated that it had come to this, but it was unavoidable. It was a tangled mess and Lily was not wrong. They were asking her to go well beyond the call of duty.

"Three percent?" Sawyer asked. "That seems fair to me."

Lily took in a deep breath through her nose and nodded. "Yes. That sounds fair."

"Great. Done." Noah shuffled some papers on his desk, wondering what in the hell he'd just proposed and agreed to. He and his brother were buying off the woman Noah couldn't get out of his head, all so she could move in with him. This was all kinds of wrong.

"In the meantime, we need to double our efforts into figuring out where Dad is getting his information. I read an article about a security company specializing in corporate espionage. I don't like that word when we're talking about our own dad, but it's pretty much come to this." Sawyer rapped on the door casing two times and walked away.

Painful silence hung in the air with Sawyer's departure. Lily sat in the chair, arms crossed, her foot bobbing. Noah vacillated between staring at papers he couldn't care less about and trying not to look at Lily's legs. He really needed to get his act together.

"So. When do you want me to move in?" Her tone said she was resigned to this new reality. That extra 2 percent apparently made the idea tolerable.

"Whenever. Tomorrow?"

"Okay. Sounds good. I'm going to get back to work. I

have a ton of emails to answer." She rose from her chair and headed for the door.

Noah wanted to let the events of the last half hour go, but he couldn't. "Extra work, Lily? Is that what this has been to you?"

"Excuse me?"

"I realize we've had some uncomfortable moments, but it's not like you weren't taken care of. We went to an amazing destination wedding together. And I guess more than anything, I thought we had fun in Florida."

"We did have fun, Noah. We talked about that last night. But that still doesn't mean that I wanted all of this other stuff to happen."

He didn't believe for a minute that she was so naive. "What do you want from me? You had to know what you were getting yourself into when you agreed to this in the first place."

"Like I had a choice, sitting there in Sawyer's office while everyone basically laid the entire future of Locke and Locke on my shoulders. Plus, I agreed to a weekend. That was it. Now we're moving in together. This was the last thing I planned on."

"Yeah. You and me both."

In case the tabloids were watching, Lily moved into Noah's brand new condo on the seventeenth floor of the Grand Legacy in broad daylight, around noon the next day. They made a show of the movers hauling her things into the building, but more than half of the boxes were empty. This was a temporary measure and Lily was, quite honestly, tired of the act.

"Is that the final load?" Noah came out of his home office as the movers marched by with more boxes.

"I think so." Lily was doing her best to remain upbeat,

but this was yet another life event she hated faking. She'd never moved in with Peter, which ultimately ended up being a blessing, but that made this a first for her, unlike getting engaged. And it put her in whisper-thin proximity to Noah, when every warning sign imaginable was going off in her head.

One of the movers had Noah sign some paperwork while the rest of them filed out of the apartment. Once he was gone, Lily was alone with the man she couldn't resist, who held her professional future in his hands.

"I guess I should get myself set up in the guest room."

"Sounds like a plan. I have some more work to do." Noah went down the hall to his home office and Lily decided that distance was the best. Things were still chilly between them after the argument yesterday.

Lily unpacked her clothes. She hung dresses, skirts and blouses in the closet and put everything else away into the bureau. Noah's apartment was straight out of *Bachelor Pad Monthly*, lots of expensive modern furniture and not a single soft touch anywhere. Her bed was a platform style in dark wood with built-in floating bedside tables. The bedding was dark gray. She would've called it austere if it wasn't such a high thread count. Lily had no idea how long she'd be living here, but if it ended up being more than a few weeks, she might need to go shopping for cute throw pillows or a scented candle. A few weeks? Her nerves would be rubbed raw by then. It was that difficult to be around Noah and pretend like everything was fine and that nothing had happened.

Still, he had not only agreed to the 3 percent, he'd suggested the increase. And there was an argument to be made that their predicament was exactly that—theirs. They were in the same boat, for better or worse, and perhaps Lily needed to stop being so hard on Noah.

She headed down the hall to his office. "I was thinking that I'd make dinner. If you're up for that."

Noah looked up and his green eyes worked their way into her soul. The part of her that had been mad at him was a distant memory now. "You don't have to do that. I order in most nights."

"May I?" She gestured for the brown leather chair opposite his desk. Noah's office was by far the most comfortable room in the house. Beautiful antique desk, soft lighting and an array of cool art on the wall—black-and-white photographs and some old playbills from jazz shows at the Village Vanguard.

"Yes. Please." He got up from his seat and walked over to a turntable in the corner and flipped the record. When he moved the stylus over to the spinning vinyl, some familiar jazz began to play.

"Oh, wow. I haven't heard this since I was a kid. Art Tatum?"

Noah nodded. "The one and only."

Lily looked behind her. There was an entire wall of records at the far side of the room. She got up to peruse the spines. "My grandfather used to play this all the time."

"Are you calling me an old man?"

"No, but you are the man with a record player. I don't think I know anyone else who has one."

"Vinyl's making a big resurgence. It sounds so much better than anything else, especially if you're into music recorded in the '50s and '60s. That music was engineered for this medium. It's not really meant to be listened to any other way."

He might not be wrong about that. The record sounded amazing. "I also don't know anyone who has this many records. You must've been collecting forever."

"Not forever, but I did go through a big audiophile stage

when I was a teenager. I took my dad's record collection since he never listened to it and I built on that. I would take the train into the city on the weekends and spend hours in record stores."

"Interesting. Were you just bored?"

"I don't know. Aren't all teenagers bored? I know that for me, Sawyer had moved out and Charlotte was off doing her own thing. Partying, mostly. I was a nerd. I was not out partying."

Lily could hardly believe the words out of Noah's mouth, but he had hinted at this the day they went out to lunch after he bought her the engagement ring. "I really have a hard time believing that."

He held his hands up in surrender. "True story. I didn't have my first girlfriend until I was a senior in high school. I went through a very unfortunate pudgy stage."

"Okay. Now I really know you're lying. You're so trim." Remarking on Noah's physique was bringing back the memories of their tryst at the Hannafort wedding. Noah wasn't just slim, he was all lean muscle. Yes, a bit lanky, but she had a big weakness for that.

He held up a finger. "Hold on one minute. Allow me to dig up some very embarrassing photographic evidence." He crouched down and slid open a panel in a midcentury oak credenza. He rummaged around and eventually pulled out a photo album. He flipped through several pages, finally showing it to her. "There."

Lily sat on the Persian rug, hardly believing what she was seeing. Sure enough, there was Noah's hair, and definitely his straight nose, and what appeared to be his beautiful green eyes, but they were in a decidedly rounder and much shorter package. "You were still cute." Her voice broke a bit and she wasn't quite sure why. Maybe because she so often saw Noah as superhuman. The golden boy with the world at his feet. This made him seem more real, which was a ridiculous concept. She worked with him every day. She'd seen him get angry and upset. She knew that he was human. But still, this was not something she'd ever expected to see.

"I really wasn't cute, but thank you for saying that."

"How old are you in this picture?"

"Fifteen. I grew about a foot and a half the next year."

"And Sawyer was out of the house at that point?"

"Yeah. He left as soon as he could. Went into the military, which really pissed off my dad. He'd wanted him to go to business school and work for him, but it didn't happen that way. Plus, I think my dad felt like Sawyer was always making him look bad. Dad went to a military school as a boy, but didn't have the nerve to do what Sawyer did."

Lily lifted the page to look at more. "May I?"

"Yeah. Of course."

She flipped to the next set of photographs, some more formal-looking portraits around a Christmas tree. "Who's in this one?"

Noah went straight down the line. "That's my dad, my dad's second wife, Charlotte, me, Sawyer and then my stepsiblings, Todd and Beth."

"Did you like them?"

"I did. A lot. We were actually quite close. But then my dad divorced their mom, they moved out and I had another set of siblings to get used to."

"Not exactly your normal upbringing."

"No. Not really." Noah took the photo album from her hands. "What about you?"

"Hey. I wanted to look some more." She let her voice express her true disappointment. She loved looking at old photos, especially of Noah.

"I promise it's more of the same."

"No baby pictures?"

He laughed. "Hold on one second." He put the photo album back and pulled out a small leather box. Inside it was a tidy stack of old photos. "Here you go. No laughing. This was the origin of chubby Noah."

Lily couldn't help but smile as she looked at the photograph. There was a very happy baby in the arms of a beautiful woman. "All babies are chubby. And you were adorable with your big bald head and thigh rolls."

"Exactly what every guy wants to hear."

"Is that your mom? She's beautiful."

"Yep. She really was beautiful. I miss her a lot. You know how they say some people are the glue that holds a family together? Well, my mom was the glue. Things were never the same after she died."

"I'm so sorry, Noah. I'm sure that was hard for you." Lily noticed that there was a blue Tiffany box inside the leather box. "Made more than one trip to Tiffany?"

He shook his head. "Actually, no. This is my mom's ring. Remember I told you about it the day we went to get yours?"

"Right. Of course." Lily didn't ask to see it. It was just a reminder of their arrangement.

"You didn't answer my question. What about you and your family? For as much as we've worked together, I don't know much."

"I'm boring. My parents are happily married. I have one brother. He's two years younger than me. Grew up outside Philadelphia. My mom and dad managed a small hotel. That's how I ended up in hospitality."

"That doesn't sound boring at all. That sounds really nice."

"It definitely wasn't bad."

"And then what brought you to New York?"

"Honestly, I just needed to get out of Philadelphia. I figured all of the best hotels were in the city, so I moved here to get a job. I switched around a few times, trying to get a position as a general manager, but I wasn't getting anywhere. But then I read in a hospitality magazine that you and Sawyer were going to renovate the Grand Legacy and I wanted to be a part of it." She picked at a spot on her jeans. At the root of that story was Peter and the failed engagement.

"Hold on. Back up. Why did you feel like you needed to get out of Philadelphia?"

Lily could've easily talked her way out of this, but Noah had shown her some pretty embarrassing things about himself. Maybe it was time to let him know at least a little bit about her past. "Yeah, that. A bad ex."

He turned to her, his eyes saying he was eager for more. "One of the guys who yanked you around?"

"Yeah. You could say that." The words were like a rock lodged in her throat. "He broke off our engagement."

Noah's shoulders visibly dropped. "Lil. Why didn't you tell me about this?"

"It's not exactly something that comes up during a job interview or in normal office chitchat."

"Well, yeah, but I took you to Tiffany and bought you an engagement ring. Now I feel like an ass. I mean, even more of an ass than I felt like before. I'm so sorry."

She hated hearing the pity in his voice. "Don't be. It's not your fault. And I dodged the proverbial bullet. He got married and divorced since then."

"Yeah, but that day at the jewelry store had to have been uncomfortable for you. I never would've even known it."

She shrugged. "I guess I'm really good at hiding things."

"I don't want you to feel like you have to hide things from me. You know, no matter what happens, our friendship has become really important to me. It's funny, I always used to think of Sawyer as my best friend, but it might actually be you."

Lily felt like she needed to hold her breath, if only to hold on to this moment. Tears misted her eyes. "Now you're going to make me cry."

"Don't do that. Come here."

Noah pulled her into a hug and she sank into his embrace. Right or wrong, Noah's arms were the only place she wanted to be. She felt safe, like nothing could ever hurt her. That was saying a lot considering the chaos in which they were currently living. He caressed her back and rocked her back and forth. It felt so good. Impossibly good.

"It's okay to cry if you need to. You've been under a lot of stress. I'm sorry for that. I know my brother and I have been the source of a lot of it."

She clung to him, not wanting to let go. If only he knew that this hug was about so much more than her painful past or a bad boyfriend—it was about having what you want within your reach and not being able to take it. She wanted him even more now than she had at the wedding. She wanted things to be uncomplicated. She wanted a chance at Lily and Noah. But everything seemed to be standing in their way—the business, her career, his reluctant heart.

It was difficult, but she extracted herself from the hug. Giving herself false hope was a one-way ticket to misery. "So? Dinner?" She discreetly wiped a tear away from her cheek.

"I have no clue what it's in my fridge, but there's definitely wine."

"Good. I'm going to need that. Maybe a permanent IV drip."

"Moving got you that stressed out?" He got up from the floor and extended his hand to help her.

"Among other things." Now that she was standing, it took everything she had not to hug him again, but she didn't need to tell him that he was most of the reason she needed wine. "I get to meet Marcy in the grand ballroom downstairs tomorrow afternoon to start planning our wedding."

"Can we have a chocolate cake? I hate those plain vanilla ones."

"You can have whatever you want." She laughed, but her heart ached at the thought of what her words really meant. This wasn't a joke. They were spinning a fictional web and it was messing with her head and her heart. She didn't want to be pretending anymore. It hurt too much. "We both know the wedding's not going to happen."

Eleven

Lily liked spending time with Marcy Hannafort just fine, but she had been dreading their wedding planning meeting. She hated everything about this—pretending to have a life that she'd never have, with a man she could easily end up wanting forever, and now they were planning the one thing Lily couldn't stomach the idea of—a wedding.

She did like spending time in the other parts of the Grand Legacy, though, so she tried to focus on the positives of that. She and Marcy walked around the grand ballroom, Marcy discussing seating and flow while Lily admired the glorious art deco glass ceiling and other historic details Noah and Sawyer had so painstakingly restored.

"Lily, darling. I feel like you aren't really here with me. Is everything okay?"

Apparently, Lily wasn't as good at faking some things as she'd thought she was. "There's so much to think about. It's overwhelming." The truth was that it wasn't overwhelming at all. If this were her real wedding, Lily would be organizing the heck out of it, exactly as she had the first time. No detail would be overlooked. The groom would have whatever flavor of cake he wanted. The guest list would've been set weeks ago. Lily would have her perfect dress, just like before. It would be a different gown the second time, though. The first had landed at a thrift store. Hopefully a bride-in-need had found it *and* her happy-ever-after.

"I don't know, Marcy. This is stressing me out. I have a million things I need to do back at the office and we're trying to make all of these decisions. This isn't really my sort of thing."

"Do you want me to take over? Because I can. I can promise you a beautiful wedding. It'll be your dream day. Just like you've probably imagined since you were a little girl."

Lily was instead stuck with the indelible vision of her nightmare day, of standing in the back of the church and never getting to walk up the aisle. Brides don't get left at the altar. There's no reason to even go into the chapel if the groom-to-be isn't standing there, waiting. Brides get left in the lobby.

As Lily learned, canceling a wedding at the last minute was a horrific task. She'd had to break the news to her guests, standing at the front of the church about to fall apart and saying that she was so sorry they'd come for nothing. Lily had to suggest that everyone take their wedding gifts with them when they left. All the while, she was crumbling on the inside because the man she'd thought she would spend her life with had decided that wasn't going to happen.

Never mind that Lily had never been convinced that Peter loved her. That was a realization that had taken a long time to reach. She was a solid choice, and he was, too. But there was no fire between them. Zero spark. Just safety and security. In many ways, their wedding had been a game of chicken. And Peter had the guts to end it first. Lily could be thankful for that now, since she couldn't imagine a life with him, but it didn't mean that it still didn't hurt. She'd spent a lifetime as the girl who made a habit of seeking unattainable guys and it never working out. Just when she'd resigned herself to something more realistic, a man who wasn't quite a romance novel hero, she'd managed to fail at keeping him, too.

"Maybe we should postpone the wedding," Lily blurted. She was ready to try anything at this point. "You said it yourself. We have so little time."

"Lyle seems awfully set on the publicity we can get out of the event. I'd hate to disappoint him."

"Yeah. Me, too." Never mind that Marcy's reason was no reason at all to have a wedding.

Marcy shook her head and took Lily's hand. "Do you have cold feet? Are you questioning your love for Noah?"

Lily almost laughed. She didn't question her attraction to Noah, at all. She didn't question her affection for him either. But love? She wasn't there. Her heart and her head kept telling her those were treacherous waters. She would not fall in love with Noah, however much she had zero problem imagining it. Her pride and her future depended on staying wedged in practicality.

"No," Lily answered. "I just don't want to make a mistake." That much was not a ruse.

"Do you mean the wrong man? Was that video about Noah really the truth?" Marcy shook her head. "I had a feeling there was something off about this. I told Lyle I had misgivings, but he didn't want to hear it."

Lily had to squash Marcy's misgivings. "No. No. That

video was not the real Noah. That much I can promise you. He's a very sweet and caring person. He's taken good care of me." Financially, that was true, as well. "Maybe I need a night to sleep on it. Think over everything we talked about today."

Marcy nodded. "Sure, hon. That makes sense. Let me give you this list of the things we need to decide on. The guest list, the cake, the menu, the place settings and tableware, the chairs, the color scheme. Good God, yes. We haven't even chosen a color scheme."

Lily felt like Marcy was trying to drown her in details. "I have the list. I promise I will go through it and make some decisions."

"Don't take too long. We've got to get this show on the road."

Noah had left work early. He couldn't concentrate without Lily in the office, knowing that she was at her meeting with Marcy. Normally, it was Lily's presence that was distracting. Today, it was her absence.

He tracked down Marcy and Lily just as they were leaving the grand ballroom. "There you are. How'd everything go? Did I get my chocolate cake?" The minute he started asking questions, he could tell from Lily's face that things had not gone well.

"Chocolate has been decided. Everything else is up in the air, I'm afraid," Marcy said.

"I wasn't much help today. Maybe you and I can talk about it upstairs," Lily said.

Noah took her hand and kissed her cheek. "Don't worry. We'll get it all done."

The three of them wound their way through the back hall to the elevator. The lobby was straight ahead. "You know where you're going, right?" Noah asked Marcy.

"I do, thank you. Lily, we'll talk tomorrow? Maybe a good night's sleep will help." Marcy smiled at Noah. "Or no sleep might help, too."

Noah laughed, wishing that was an option available to him. "Thank you for your help, Marcy. Lily and I both appreciate it." As Marcy walked away, he punched the button for the elevator, which opened right away. He and Lily stepped on board. "Do you want to talk about it?"

She stared up at the numbers above the door and shook her head. "Not right now. Upstairs."

Noah took her hand and her cue, staying quiet. He sensed she needed him right now, and he'd be lying if he said it didn't feel good. Having her move in yesterday had been the best and the worst thing that had happened to him in a long time. Last night had been amazing, the two of them staying up late and talking. He'd never done that with a woman. He'd never felt comfortable enough to open up. Lily was his safe place. Those two years of frustration over working together and not being able to touch her or kiss her or tell her everything going through his head had not been for nothing. It had built a solid friendship. It had established trust, and Noah understood just how important that was.

The elevator stopped on his floor, seventeen, and he and Lily ambled down to his end of the hall. As soon as he opened the door and they stepped into his foyer, she let loose. "That was a disaster."

"That bad?"

"It's a nightmare." She marched right down the hall, past the kitchen and into the living room, and he had no choice but to follow. "There's the cake that will never be baked and the dress I'll never buy and the guests we'll never invite." She turned back to him, her face strained in a way he'd never seen before. "I can't do it, Noah. I can't.

The lies, the standing there and chatting about place settings and DJs. It's impossible. We have to say or do something to put her off."

He went to her and held her hands, rubbing his thumbs over her fingers to reassure her that everything would be okay. She looked so stunning today in a simple black dress she'd worn to the office at least one hundred times. Her eyes were stormy and sad right now. He hated seeing her so upset. "Okay. We'll come up with an excuse of some sort. I don't know what. Come on and sit down with me and we'll have a drink and we can brainstorm some reasons why people cancel weddings."

Noah went to lead her to the couch, but Lily was frozen. "Lil. What's wrong?"

"I…" A single tear rolled down her cheek. "I can't."

"Just tell me." He wasn't sure what the awful sensation in his chest was, but it felt like his heart was being torn in two.

"I'll tell you why people cancel weddings. They do it when they decide they don't love the bride. When they decide that she isn't special enough or smart enough or kind enough or pretty enough to spend an entire lifetime with. That's why people cancel weddings."

Noah swallowed hard. *The broken engagement.* "Hold on a second. Are you talking about…"

Lily nodded frantically, her lips pressed tightly together, her eyes welling with tears. "He dumped me in the church, Noah. He didn't want to marry me and it was the worst day of my life. And now I feel like I'm reliving every stupid minute I spent planning it. Only this time, the groom is you, which might be amazing if it were real, but it's not. This wedding isn't going to happen either."

Noah struggled for breath as her words tumbled around in his head. Did Lily have feelings for him? It sounded like she did. If ever there was a time to come out with his own feelings for her, this was it.

"I have something I need to tell you."

"I can't take any more bad news."

Just say it. "I've wanted you for a long time. A really long time, Lily. Probably since the moment you walked into our office that first day." It was such a relief to finally come out with it. How foolish he'd been to keep it bottled up all this time. "So when I admitted at the wedding that I was frustrated, it was about far more than seeing you in a bathing suit or because we'd been holding hands and kissing. It was because I finally had a taste of what I'd wanted for so long, but I couldn't have you for real. All because you were too good at your job to let me screw it up. I couldn't let my brother down like that, but it's been killing me. Slowly. Every day."

She looked up at him, her eyes wide, traveling back and forth and searching his face. Her lower lip dropped. A puff of breath left her lips, but no words came out. It was torture to come out with his truth and have it met this way. Was she about to tell him once again that her job was too important?

"Talk to me, Lily. If you're going to hurt me, it's okay. I can take it. Nothing could be worse than the last two years. And if you need to forget that we ever had this conversation, we can do that, too. We can pretend like it never happened. By now, I think we both know we have a talent for putting on a show."

"Will you just shut up and kiss me? For real. No more pretending."

The words echoed in his head. "Are you saying that this is a good thing?"

The sweetest, sexiest smile broke across her face. "You aren't very good at following directions, are you? I told you I wanted you to kiss me. For real, Noah. Kiss me like you want me."

"But I do want you."

"So show me."

Everything in his body went tight as he pulled her close, lifting her to her tiptoes. Her lips met his, soft and giving. It felt like a second try at their first kiss. It was all new between them now that he was no longer burdened with the secret he'd been carrying around so long. He had so much to say to her now, every word crammed into a kiss. *I think about this every day. I wonder about you. Do you want me? Could you want me?* Her lips parted and he hoped like hell that was the answer. She bowed into him. Their tongues met and tangled, a return to that moment of bliss at the wedding when she'd wanted him the way he wanted her.

But it meant more to him now, and he had to know that she felt the same way. He could've kept going, he could've made his move and unzipped her dress, but he wasn't sure he deserved to have her if she didn't feel the same way. As much as he didn't want their kiss to end, he broke it and settled his forehead against hers. "See? Do you get it now?"

She nodded slightly, her eyes only part open. "I have my own confession to make."

"Tell me."

"I've wanted you from that first day, too. I have fantasized a million times about you backing me up against the filing cabinet and kissing me. When I'm standing there rubbing the back of my leg with my foot? I'm thinking about you."

Noah's heart was about to punch a hole through the center of his chest. "Tell me more." Every muscle in his body flooded with white-hot need.

"When you sit on the edge of your desk? I want to walk

up to you and stand between your knees and unbutton your shirt." She popped one of his buttons. "Like this."

Noah had never been more turned on. "That afternoon in the car, the day we went to buy your ring? I thought I was going to explode I wanted you so bad."

"You can have me, Noah. Right now. For real. No more pretending."

"There's no going back if we say it's for real."

"I know." She untucked his shirt and went to work on the rest of the buttons. He watched as she rolled the garment from his shoulders, spread her hands across his chest. "Your skin. It's so warm."

"It's you, Lily. You make it like this."

Lily had never had such a reversal of fortune in all her life. An hour ago, she'd been miserable. Now she was on cloud nine. Her fingers scrambled through the buttons on Noah's shirt. She made quick work of his pants, too. He unzipped her dress and they let it drop to the floor right there in the living room. Of course, today, she was wearing stockings—black ones from France, with a seam up the back and a wide band of lace at the top. Noah groaned when he saw them, his eyes now half-closed with desire.

"Is it possible to keep those on?" He reached around with both hands and grabbed her bottom.

Lily laughed as her lips trailed over his cheek. "Anything is possible if you believe in yourself."

"Good."

He took her hand and tugged her over to the couch. He sat down, his legs spread, his glorious chest and shoulders on full display. She could also see exactly how ready he was for her and it made her absolutely ache for him. It had been only a few days since they'd made love, but even that had been far too long. There were also quite a few things they'd never gotten around to in Florida, and she was keenly focused on pleasing him right now. He'd been so sweet to her the last few days. Lily dropped to her knees and caressed his erection through his black boxer briefs. She smiled up at him and he returned the expression, but it was clearly hard for him to keep it together. His head was bobbing. He was floating between pleasure and paying attention.

"Touch me, Lily. Please."

Noah raised his hips off the couch as she teased his boxers past his hips and down his legs. She wasted no time taking him in her hand and stroking firmly, then wrapping her lips around him gently, sucking and grazing his taut skin with her tongue. Noah dug both hands into her hair, softly massaging her head, gathering the strands in a handful at the nape of her neck. He piled her hair on top of her head, holding it in place as he moaned with every pass. She felt so damn sexy and wanted right now, she wasn't sure which way was up.

"Come here, Lil. I need to kiss you."

She released the grip of her lips and stood before him. He sat forward and wrapped his hands around her waist, kissing her belly, then slipping his fingers into the waistband of her panties and shimmying them past her hips.

She gazed down into Noah's gorgeous green eyes and knew she was with exactly the right guy. "Make love to me, Noah. I want you. I need you."

He stood and took her hand. "Not here. The bedroom." They rushed down the hall and Noah ducked into the bathroom, returning quickly with a condom.

"Come here. I'll put it on." Lily was standing next to the bed, waiting for him.

He walked up to her and they fell into another deep kiss as she took his length in her hands and took care of him.

He reached behind her and finally unhooked her bra, taking her breasts into both hands and nearly sending her into oblivion with flicks of his tongue against her nipples. Heat rushed to the surface of her skin. Her center ached for him. She stretched out on the bed, wearing only her stockings.

"I'd say that the ensemble is super sexy, but in reality, it's you." He took her foot and planted it in the center of his chest, trailing his fingers from her ankle to her knee. He bent her leg and kept going with his hand, down the inside of her thigh, making her need for him that much more pronounced. When he reached her center, she thought she might burst into flames. He remained standing, towering over her, caressing her apex with teasing, delicate circles. With every pass, she was closer to her climax, but that restless need for him wouldn't go away.

"Don't make me wait any longer, Noah. It's not nice."

He smiled and put his knee on the bed, spreading her legs wider with his hands. He positioned himself at her entrance and drove inside so slowly she thought she might pass out. Lily's mind swirled with the pleasure, especially when she heard the primal moan that came from Noah's sexy lips. He felt so perfect inside her, she didn't want it to end. But the peak was already bearing down on her, just like Noah's body weight against the ideal spot to send her over the edge. Every thrust he made was purposeful and strong. His breaths were hard and fast now, and his actions matched them.

Her peak was coming at her so quick, she could almost see it in her mind. The pressure coiled inside her, it fought to wind in on itself further. She thought she couldn't take it anymore right when the pleasure slammed into her and Noah followed almost immediately. He let his full weight rest on her as they kissed, their bodies damp with perspiration. She wrapped her arms and legs around him, pulling him closer when there was nowhere else for him to go, all while his body gave her relentless pulses of beautiful bliss.

They collapsed on the bed together in a lovely, breathless tangle. The beauty of that moment didn't fade, it only created an imagined glow around them. "That was amazing," Lily muttered into Noah's chest.

"Amazing, yes, but I can do better. Give me ten minutes and a drink of water and I'm ready for more."

"Better?" Lily could hardly speak, let alone open her eyes. She instead breathed in Noah's masculine scent and reveled in having made her way into his actual bed. Next, she'd have to focus on working her way into his heart. "I don't know how you can possibly top that."

"You have no idea, darling." He skimmed his fingers from her knee to her thigh, past her hip and up to her breast. He cupped it with his hand and pressed a hot, wet kiss against it.

Lily arched her back. Everything Noah did when he touched her was exquisite. "I think you're trying to unduly influence me."

"Absolutely. I intend to do nothing else all night."

Twelve

Noah wasn't sure he'd ever been so happy to wake up with a woman in his bed. He never wanted Lily to leave it, ever. He never wanted either of them to bother with clothes again, or work for that matter. He wondered if Sawyer would be okay with it if they both called in sick for the next month or two.

Lily rolled over and opened one eye. "What time is it?"

Noah stroked her arm gently. "A little after six. We have time to sleep if you want." Touching her bare skin was bringing every nerve ending in his body to life. "Or we could do something else to spend the time."

A smile rolled across her lips. She'd closed her one open eye. "You're a terrible influence on me. You realize that if we start, we're going to have an awfully difficult time stopping, which will only end up making us late to work. As my boss, I would think that would be the last thing you would want."

He scooted closer until his naked skin was touching hers. The blood began to rush through his body, spreading heat, narrowing his ability to think about anything more than sex. "As the boss, I think I can approve any activity I deem appropriate, regardless of whether or not it makes us late to work."

"What if we can have the best of both worlds?" Her voice was still sleepy and sexy.

"I'm not sure I know what you mean."

"Well, we both need to take a shower, right?"

Bingo. Noah was ready to launch himself out of bed. "I'll start the water."

Lily laughed and threw his pillow across the room.

Even after a long stay in the shower and a quick breakfast, Lily and Noah were only five minutes late for work. It felt a bit like they were conspiring when they stepped off the elevator, especially when they ran square into Sawyer.

"Good morning," he said, but there was nothing good-sounding about it.

"What's wrong?" Noah asked. Whatever it was, it couldn't bring him down. His brother could hurl one hundred problems at him today and it wouldn't matter. Noah reached for the door to their office.

"No. Noah. Out here. We can't talk in there."

"What the hell? Why not?"

Sawyer ushered Noah and Lily to the far corner of the hall, next to an empty office. "Dad called me about an hour ago. He knows about the Hannafort deal. He knows the details of the term sheet and everything. He knows that we lied to Lyle about your engagement and he's threatening to out us unless we meet his demands."

"Demands? What demands? He can't do this. It's blackmail."

"He wants the Grand Legacy back. I think this is what

all of this BS has been about. He just couldn't get over the fact that I inherited the hotel and not him."

"He can't do this. It's blackmail. We should call the police."

"And tell them what, exactly? He made the threat over a phone call. It's not like I had a tape recorder going. And I dislike him as much as you do, but he's our father. I don't want him in jail."

I do. Noah forced himself to take deep breaths. There was a war being waged inside of him right now. He was furious with his father, but not just for what he was doing and what he was after. He was mad because he'd gone to Sawyer first. Everything always boiled down to Sawyer. "Why didn't you call me the minute this happened?"

"Have you even looked at your phone, Noah? I left you a voice mail."

Noah dug it out of his pocket. Sure enough, there was a notification for a missed call from his brother. "We have to call that security company. The one that specializes in corporate espionage."

"Already done. They'll be here any minute."

Of course. Sawyer had everything under control, as he always did. "What can we do in the meantime?"

"Nothing. They told us to touch nothing. They don't even want us going into the office."

The elevator dinged and the doors slid open. A handful of men and women wearing black pants and matching black shirts, all carrying armfuls of equipment stepped into the hall. Sawyer rushed over and introduced himself to one of the women, then waved over Noah.

"We'll do a full sweep of the office for listening devices and cameras," the woman said. "We'll also run diagnostics on every computer, looking for spyware." She glanced down at Noah's hand. "Is that a work laptop?"

"Yes."

She reached down and took it from him. "I'll need that, too."

"How long will this take?" Sawyer asked. At least he had enough sense to ask the question. Noah was still reeling. Lily was standing over in the corner, seeming equally confused.

"Not long for an office of your size. A few hours. I'd go get a cup of coffee or something."

The woman opened the door to their office and her team followed her inside.

"As if today couldn't get any crazier, I'm supposed to meet Kendall at the obstetrician's office in a half hour. You two should find some way to keep yourselves busy."

Now you tell me. Noah would've much preferred to be at home with Lily, back in the shower. "Okay."

"Call me if you find out anything. I hope to be back before they're done." Sawyer jabbed the button for the elevator. "Then we start strategizing on what to do about Dad." He stepped on board and the doors closed behind him.

Noah ran his hands through his hair as Lily approached him. "This is so weird."

She took his hand. "I'm sure it'll all be fine. You and Sawyer have faced bigger challenges."

"Aren't you the least bit worried about this? Your nest egg is on the line if the Hannafort deal falls through."

She nodded. "I know. I just don't want to get all stressed out about something that might end up being nothing." She popped up onto her toes and kissed his cheek. "Now come on. Let's go get that cup of coffee."

They took the stairs and strolled a block down to a corner coffee shop that had killer pastries. After ordering two lattes, a lemon poppy seed muffin and an almond scone, they grabbed one of the café tables in front of the window. "Are you worried?" Lily asked. "I don't want you to be worried. You're too handsome to worry."

Noah laughed, but it was born of exasperation. When would everything go right at once? He and Lily had made a big breakthrough last night, one that he'd never thought he would ever make. He'd never professed his feelings to any other woman. He'd not only never wanted to, he'd never had the feelings he had for Lily.

"How are you so together right now?"

She looked down at her coffee and gave it a stir. "You need me right now. I don't know how else to be. I guess that's what makes me a good employee."

He reached across the table and took her hand. "It's also what makes you an amazing friend." *And what makes me love you.* The words were right there in his head, but they were as foreign as a language he could neither read nor speak. He wanted to say them to her, but he was as unsure right now as he'd ever been. He knew he couldn't take them back if he'd said them only out of weakness and ultimately couldn't live up to them. Lily deserved better.

She rubbed her thumb back and forth across the back of his hand. "You're an amazing friend, too. And my favorite person to take a shower with."

He smiled and raised her hand. Her engagement ring hit his lips when he kissed her fingers. Could that ring ultimately end up meaning something? "I feel the same way."

Several moments of silence played out between them as they sipped coffee, ate and watched the other patrons in the café. Still, neither let go of the other's hand. Once again, they were in this together. In so many ways, Lily was more important to their surviving this ordeal. Just like his mom had been the glue that kept the family together,

Lily was the glue of the business. It all started and ended with her. And Noah was starting to think the same thing about his life. He couldn't fathom the idea of not having Lily around.

"We should probably head back, don't you think?" he asked.

"Feeling antsy?" Lily got up and put on her coat.

"I want this resolved. That's all. I'm tired of the turmoil."

"You and me both."

The office looked like a war zone when Lily and Noah returned. The security team had taken everything apart, even going so far as to cut holes in walls, looking for listening devices. It was like something out of a spy movie. Sawyer was already back, and called Noah into his office.

A burly, bearded man from the security team cornered Lily. "I'm going to need you to stay right here." He pointed to one of the chairs in the reception area.

"But I have work to do."

"I understand, but we're still sorting things out. I can't allow you to touch your computer or answer the phones, either."

Lily plopped down into the seat. What in the world was going on? She racked her brain, wondering if she somehow knew the source of the leak. A member of the cleaning crew? The guy who came in to fix the copier? At least she knew it wasn't her, even if she had a very stern man fifteen feet away from her, staring her down, that made her feel as though she might have been responsible.

The entire premise of Sawyer and Noah's father having an inside source was so ridiculous to begin with. How could a parent go around purposely sabotaging his own children? Because of professional jealousy? Because they demanded their independence? It was terrible.

Sawyer's office door opened. "Lily. We need you to come in now."

She stood, but with every step, her heart beat a little more fiercely. It was hard not to feel like this was a walk to the gallows.

"Please, Lily. Sit down," Sawyer said when she'd stepped inside.

She did as instructed, which meant she was sitting right next to Noah. He turned and looked at her, his expression inexplicable. "Please tell me you didn't do it."

"Noah. Stop." Sawyer's tone made Lily jump.

"No, Sawyer. I can't. I can't even stomach what you're about to say to her."

"We have our evidence. We have to move forward."

"Does somebody want to tell me what's going on?" Lily asked, wishing it was appropriate for her to hold hands with Noah. She needed him right now.

Sawyer looked right at her. "We need you to be completely honest with everything we're about to ask you. If you can't be forthcoming with the facts, we'll have no choice but to press charges and talk to the police."

"The police?" It felt as if the ground beneath her had cracked open and she was plummeting through space. "Whatever it is that you're about to ask me, I will of course tell you everything I know. I would never hide anything from either of you."

"I told you, Sawyer. Lily would never do what you're about to accuse her of." The desperation in Noah's voice only made Lily feel worse.

"Will you let me get through this?" Sawyer asked. "Lily, we need you to tell us everything about your involvement with our father."

"I don't understand. I don't even know him."

A dismissive breath left Noah's lips. "Sawyer. This is absurd." Noah turned to her and the look in his eyes was full of remorse. Lily had never seen that expression. He was too laid-back to get worked up about much, which was part of why the entire morning had been so hard to deal with. "Your computer is the source of the leak."

"What? No. How is that possible?"

"Every night, the contents of your email folders are uploaded to a server owned by one of our dad's businesses. That's how he's been one step ahead of us this whole time, going all the way back to the renovation of the Grand Legacy."

Lily didn't know what to say. She was in shock. "I honestly have no idea what you're talking about. I would never do that. You have to believe me."

Sawyer crossed his arms over his chest and sat back in his chair. "Well, I don't know what to say. Until we straighten this out, you're on leave. I can't even allow you to look at your computer or touch anything before you leave the office. Noah will walk you out."

Lily stood and did as she was told, but she was on autopilot. As soon as they were out of Sawyer's office, she grabbed Noah's arm. "Please. You have to believe me. Do you honestly think I could do such a thing?"

"I do believe you, but this is an impossible situation right now. All evidence points to you. Sawyer seems convinced."

All she could think about was everything that had happened in the office for the last two years. She'd feared that things would end badly if she got involved with Noah, and that had come to fruition, but not in the way she'd thought it would. "Doesn't everything I've done for Locke and Locke count for anything?"

"Of course it does. But it also incriminates you. The transmissions started the week you began working here. And you made yourself indispensable, which put you right in the thick of some very high-level meetings."

Lily's brain was working double time to find some bit of information that could exonerate her. "If I was working for your dad, why would I have agreed to move in with you to save the deal? I could've let the Hannafort deal fall apart right then and there."

"But that's not his true motive. He doesn't want the story to come out. He wants the Grand Legacy. He always has. He tried to make our lives miserable through that project in the hopes that we would abandon it."

Lily looked up at the ceiling, in utter despair. She loved her job more than anything. Except Noah. She loved him. She knew it. And she definitely loved him more than her job. But what if she ended up losing both of the things she loved? And her nest egg? She couldn't bear the thought. The tears started to come and they weren't about to stop anytime soon.

"Mr. Locke." The security guy with the beard was standing right next to Noah. "Ms. Foster should not be in the office right now. We need to ask her to collect her things and leave."

Of the many things Lily had worried about, leaving this office she loved so much in utter disgrace was not one of them. "Okay. I'll go."

"I'll help you. And I'll call my driver and get him to bring the car around to take you back to the Grand Legacy."

Lily watched as Noah retrieved her bag and coat. She wasn't even allowed to touch her desk. Sawyer didn't even say goodbye. He was still holed up in his office. Noah walked her down to the street. It was starting to rain and she had no idea where her umbrella was. Somewhere in a box, back at Noah's.

He pulled her into a hug while the driver stood, waiting, the car idling. "We'll figure this out. There has to be some other explanation. I'll convince Sawyer somehow that he's wrong."

"Okay." She looked up into Noah's face, making a point of remembering every perfect angle, his amazing lips, his unforgettable eyes. She'd suspected all along that he wasn't meant for her and right now, it felt like every circumstance in the world was pointing to that very fact. If she wasn't proven innocent, Sawyer would fire her. He would bring criminal charges. If anything was going to make Christmas morning awkward, it would be spending time with your former boss and boyfriend's brother, the guy who'd tried to send you to jail.

The words she wanted to say were on her lips, but they would do no one any good now. They would only complicate things, make them worse when they were already impossibly bad. *I love you* was not going to fix anything today.

"Will I see you at home?" Noah's question dripped with the same doubt Lily was carrying around in her heart.

"Maybe. We'll see."

"Thinking about going to the bookstore? What's it called?"

"Petticoats and Proposals."

"Right. How could I forget?" He laughed quietly.

"And it's only Thursday. I go there on Fridays." Even the promise of a romance novel couldn't lift her spirits right now.

Noah pressed another kiss to her forehead. "I'll see you soon. It'll be okay. Somehow."

She nodded, even though she wasn't sure what she was

agreeing to. "Okay." She climbed into the car and the tears rolled down her cheeks.

"Are we headed to the Grand Legacy, ma'am?"

"For now, yes."

Thirteen

Noah got home early that night. He couldn't stand being around Sawyer or the office anymore. "Lily?" he asked. "You home?" He dropped his keys on the foyer table, but the sound echoed through his apartment in a way it never had before. He felt her absence in his bones. Coming home to an apartment that had no Lily was a whole new level of empty. Warmth and happiness were gone, and in their place was the clatter of metal keys on hollow wood. "Lily?" he called one more time, but there was no response. Noah had never felt more alone.

He still refused to believe that Lily had betrayed Sawyer and him. It didn't seem plausible, but the evidence was damning. After she'd left, he and Sawyer had talked over the timeline and it all made her look that much more guilty. Had she pulled the wool over their eyes? Was there a cold and calculating woman under that guise of perfect employee? She was no ordinary employee, either. She had the paperwork to claim her 3 percent of Locke and Locke forever, which was awfully convenient. The thought of Lily conspiring with their dad, undermining them, sabotaging their hard work was unthinkable, but the evidence was there and Sawyer was pushing him hard to believe every shred of it. *Use your brain, Noah. It's right here in black-and-white. She screwed us over.*

This was the price he'd avoided paying for so long. If you don't get close to people, they can't hurt you. Noah had never had to worry about money. He'd never had to worry about his career or the roof over his head or whether or not his future was secure. The only thing he'd ever had to worry about was whether anyone would not only love him, but whether they would actually stick around. He was the unlovable one—the guy who only skimmed the surface and was, thus, easy to walk away from. He'd feared that for half of his life and been sure of it for the other. And Lily had only proven his theory. She'd walked away from him today.

He wandered into the kitchen. She'd cleaned up. So much so that it was as if she'd never been there. Her tin of tea bags was gone. The flowers she'd put on the center island were, as well. He opened the refrigerator and everything was neat and tidy, and exactly the way it had been before she moved in. No nonfat yogurt. No bowl of strawberries. Just milk for cereal, orange juice and beer. Bachelor staples. And that was about to be his life again.

He closed the refrigerator door. He couldn't fathom deriving pleasure from food ever again. Instead, he headed for the home bar, loosened his tie, poured himself a double tequila and downed it. He stared straight up at the ceiling and focused on the burn. It hurt all right. Everything hurt right now and he'd better get used to it. There would be no more covering up pain with meaningless hookups or laughing it off with a joke he'd made one hundred times. He couldn't live like that anymore. He needed to embrace the pain of his existence, wrap his head around the reality and find a way to get up tomorrow morning, go back to work and hope that he and Sawyer could hold on to the Grand Legacy and keep the Hannafort deal together.

But first, one more drink. The second one burned as badly as the first. So much for numbing himself to anything at all right now. He replaced the stopper on the bottle and shuffled down the hall and straight back to his bedroom. He took one look at the bed and was smacked in the face with a memory he'd been so eager to cling to. Twenty-four measly hours ago, he'd been as happy as he'd ever been. He'd climbed out from under the secret he'd kept for two years, confessed that Lily had always had his number and her reaction had been everything he'd been so terrified to hope for.

Last night put their night at the wedding to shame. It was no longer lust and forbidden fruit—delectable and worth having, but not on a par with what had happened when he'd dared to bare his soul. The things they'd done to each other in that bed, the pleasure they'd given and taken, was unrivaled. He'd planned to hold on to it forever. Now he couldn't wait to be rid of it, although he couldn't imagine how he was ever supposed to go about doing that. Lily was seared in his memory. No woman would ever make him feel like that again.

He dropped down to a crouch, buried his head in his hands, then screamed right into his palms. The air tore from his lungs, but he felt no better after he'd done it. If anything, he only craved the release that much more. There was no way he was going to be able to sleep in that bed tonight. He couldn't sleep in the guest room either. It undoubtedly smelled exactly like Lily. Maybe he should move out of the Grand Legacy. Hell, he'd have no choice if his dad got his hands on the hotel. Maybe he should change his entire existence. Grow a beard and buy a cabin in Maine and spend his days chopping wood for the winter and learning to fish. He would look terrible with a beard. Good. It would keep women away.

Noah straightened and opened his eyes. That was when things got even worse. There on the nightstand was Lily's engagement ring, resting on top of a note. It felt as if his heart was being ripped from his chest for the third or fourth time since that morning. There'd be nothing left of him when this was over. Forget the beard and the cabin. He'd disappear.

He perched on the edge of the bed, picked up the ring and held it in the palm of his hand. He'd known that day at Tiffany that what they were doing was wrong, but he'd wanted to do it anyway. Even when he feared it would mess with her head and his. He would've done anything to be close to her. What a sap he'd been.

He flipped open the paper and Lily's sweet voice filled his ears.

Dear Noah,

Despite the deal we made, I can't keep the ring. It's too painful to keep. Without you, it means nothing.

For that same reason, I can't keep my 3 percent of the company. Even though I worked my ass off for that share, I don't want it if Sawyer doesn't trust me. I don't need it if there's even a chance that you doubt me. It will just be a reminder of everything we had and the way it all went away.

For the record, what we had never felt fake to me.

Even when I was keeping my distance. I was only protecting my heart. You were the guy in the ivory tower and I was the girl standing on the ground, peering up at you, desperately hoping you'd take a minute to look at me. And notice. That part had always been important to me. I always wanted you to notice. Even if it was only for a few minutes or days. I guess I got my wish. It's just that nobody tells you that when you get your wish, you might not get to keep it. That's a life lesson I'm still not comfortable with. I wish it wasn't true.

I hope you know with every bone in your body that I would never, ever betray you. After today, it's pretty clear to me that Sawyer doesn't know that. I guess I'd allowed myself to believe that I was part of the inner circle, but I never truly was. That's okay. I understand how strong your bond is with your brother. He's your rock. I had hoped to be that person in your life, but some things just aren't meant to be.

Lastly, I want you to know that I harbor no ill will. It's just not part of who I am. I will never understand vengeance or an anger that never dies. I can only understand loyalty, friendship, love and good intentions. Those are the only things that make any sense to me. I hope you saw that in me, for however long it lasted.

Love,
Lily.

Noah ran his fingers over her name, while visions of her wouldn't stop playing in his head. How was it that the one time he actually had his act together with a woman, it all had to blow up in his face? It didn't seem fair, but it did seem like confirmation from the universe that Noah and love were not meant to be. Yes, he'd fallen in love with Lily, but she and her apparent actions were now standing between him and the only other thing he could count on in life—Sawyer.

Sleep had not come easily that night, especially since Noah had opted for the couch. He tossed and turned, mulling over everything that had happened in the office yesterday. None of it added up. The supposed evidence was too obvious, too easy. Almost like it was being spoon-fed to them by a person with ulterior motives—their father.

But who else had access to Lily's computer? Nobody other than Noah and Sawyer.

He turned off his alarm before it sounded, got in the shower and then headed to the office. The sun was still coming up when he arrived. He went straight to his old planners, stored in the bottom drawer of a filing cabinet. The one from two years ago prompted a strange feeling when he saw it. The cover was burgundy leather, not his normal black. That year, his favorite color had sold out early and he'd been stuck with one he wasn't crazy about. But that wasn't the thing that struck him about it. It was that he had such vivid memories of closing it at the end of every work day that year—the year he started to fall for Lily.

He flipped through the calendar until he got to March. Lily had started on March 12. He would always remember the date. It was the first time he'd laid eyes on her. Sawyer had conducted her only in-person interview. Noah had only spoken to her on the phone. Noah then went back one week to find the name he was looking for—Robert Anderson. His phone number was right beneath it. Robert had been the guy who came in the week before Lily started work to deliver and set up her new computer. Noah and Sawyer had decided that they would use the one week of downtime between administrative assistants to get a few things in line—they bought a new desk, had the reception area painted and even put in all new furniture. But it was the computer that Noah was fixated on.

Noah glanced at the clock. It was only 8:00 a.m. But he decided to try the number anyway. He got voice mail for a nail salon in Queens. He double-checked the number and called again. Same message. Something was definitely up. The realization made the hair on the back of Noah's neck stand up. Robert Anderson was a mole. Noah knew it with every fiber of his being. He pulled up the website for his dad's development company and began doing image searches for every one of his father's employees he could find.

After about an hour, Sawyer came in. "You look like I feel."

Noah ran his hand through his hair, beyond exhausted. "I feel like hell. I didn't sleep. At all."

"The Lily thing really got to you, didn't it?"

Noah shook his head and got up from his desk. He loved his brother, but damn, he was being dense. "Yes, Sawyer, it did. It bothered me a lot. Do you want to know why? Because I let you mow me down yesterday."

"I was acting on the facts we had. What else was I supposed to do? Our business is the most important thing we have."

"No, Sawyer. Kendall and the baby are the most important thing you have. The business is what you *do* all day. I know it's your passion, but you have more in your life and I'm tired of believing that only you and Charlotte get to have that. I want it, too."

Sawyer set his laptop bag down in a chair. "I never said that I didn't want you to have that. Your track record never suggested anything else."

Noah was ready to scream again, but that wasn't going to accomplish anything. "Look. Stop digging up the past. I'm tired of it. The only thing that matters right now is that I don't believe Lily is capable of the things we have accused her of. She's our partner, she's an amazing employee and, most important, she's the woman I love."

"Hold on a minute. You love her? Did you two sleep together?"

"It's more than that. A lot more."

"You can't let your libido get between your own brother and the truth."

"I'm not. I'm going to find the real truth. I have to find a way to fix this."

The look of pity on Sawyer's face made Noah want to knock it right off, and Noah had never hit his brother. Not even when they were kids. "You're wasting your time."

"Think about it, Sawyer. If Lily was working for Dad, why be such a flawless employee?"

"That put her further into the inner circle."

Noah hated that his brother had an answer for everything. "I don't buy it. I also don't think Dad would've kept her on after the Grand Legacy was finally open. He would've had her disappear. The hotel is Dad's real obsession."

"Okay, then. Prove to me that Lily is innocent."

"I will. And then I will say I told you so when I'm done."

Sawyer left and Noah got back to work. After what seemed like hundreds of searches, he finally stumbled across what he was looking for, but Robert Anderson went by an entirely different name—Dan Lewis. The man worked for their father's IT department out of his main office in New Jersey. Aside from the name change, he was practically hiding in plain sight. Noah printed the page from the website and walked into Sawyer's office.

"I found the guy who sabotaged Lily's computer."

"What? Is that what you think happened?"

Noah explained his theory. Now that he was going through everything a second time, it made perfect sense. "And now I'm going out to Long Island to make things right."

"If you're going to talk to Dad, I'll go with you."

Sawyer wasn't going to lead the charge on this one. This was much more about saving Lily than rescuing the business. Only Noah could do that. "I need to do this on my own. I need to end this."

Sawyer nodded. "Okay. You do what you gotta do."

Noah grabbed the printout from the website and reached for the door. He turned back to his brother one more time. "Oh, and Sawyer. I told you so."

In the car on the way out to the Locke estate on Long Island, Noah did the unthinkable. He called Lyle Hannafort and told him everything. It was not a pleasant phone call, but Noah smoothed the ruffled feathers by the end. A man like Lyle Hannafort doesn't make a deal solely based on a man's reputation. Plus, Lyle seemed to appreciate that Noah would do anything for his business. In the end, it came down to zeroes and dollar signs. And the promise of an in-person apology to Marcy. That much Noah could do.

When he arrived at the stone-and-iron gate, he got the usual runaround from Tom, the guard stationed at the estate entrance.

"I'm not supposed to let any of you kids onto the property. You know that."

"Tom, I'm thirty and you've known me since I was ten. Maybe longer."

Tom grudgingly pressed the button opening the gate. "If I lose my job, I'm coming to work for you and your brother."

"Do it anyway. I promise you'll be much happier."

The car started down the crushed stone driveway, along the manicured hedges. The sprawling and stately white house with the black slate roof rose from the stand of trees starting to leaf out. What was it like for other people to return to their childhood home? For Noah and his siblings, the mixed feelings were too numerous to count. There had been more unhappy moments than happy in the house, but this was the only place they had known their mom. As far as Noah was concerned, this house was where love had once had a chance, but was squashed under the weight of their father's ego. Everyone around him—children, spouse and employees—existed only to serve him. To laud him. To shower him with affection he never deserved.

A member of his dad's security detail was standing outside when Noah arrived at the front door. Noah had to once again talk his way in. Since the kids had left home, their dad had practically turned the house into a fortress. As the guard radioed for approval, Noah stood with his hands stuffed into his pockets, noticing how the grounds and house were starting to look dilapidated. There were browned-out sections in the hedges and green algae bloomed near the foundation. Maybe his dad was losing touch with reality. Or maybe this deluded attempt to grab the Grand Legacy was about money and a man desperate to maintain a level of success beyond that of his own children.

"You can go in now. Mr. Locke is waiting for you in his study."

"Thanks." Noah saw no point in being rude to the guard. He was doing his job.

Noah strode through the familiar marble-floored foyer, under the antique crystal chandelier and to the left, down the long hall that led to the private quarters. Even this space, which could have easily been more humbly decorated, had a fine Persian runner and museum-quality paintings in gilt gold frames. The house was deadly quiet. A library had more life.

His father's study door was open and Noah didn't wait to go in. This would not be a long visit.

"Noah." Like a king who has no time for commoners, his dad didn't bother rising from his seat behind the tank of a desk to greet his youngest son. "I was hoping you'd bring your lovely fiancée. Or is there trouble in paradise? Perhaps you should've stayed in Florida with your friends, the Hannaforts."

Noah stood dead center in front of his dad's desk. "Honestly, things could be better. That's for sure."

His dad was smugly fighting a smile, but Noah noticed how much he'd aged. His salt-and-pepper hair was thinning more, his wrinkles were more pronounced. "Sit. Let's catch up."

"I'm good. I'm not staying."

"If things could be better, I take it your brother is having a hard time after we had our conversation?"

"It's not just Sawyer. I'm having a hard time with it, too. You can't have the hotel, Dad. It rightfully belongs to us."

"You mean it belongs to your brother."

Noah shook his head. "No. It belongs to all three of us now. Sawyer cut both Charlotte and me in on it."

"He'll bring you two on board, but he won't give his own father what is rightfully his?"

His father's sense of entitlement had always bothered

Noah. "I like how you care about fatherhood when there's something in it for you. Sawyer brought us in to protect the hotel from you. The Hannafort deal is part of that."

"So you admit that you're cutting a deal with one of my oldest business rivals, on a property that should belong to me? Do you have any idea how insulting this is?" The anger in his dad's voice was clear, but Noah preferred it that way. No hiding his true feelings.

"You treat everyone like they only exist to do your bidding and this is what you get."

His father's nostrils flared. "This is not what I get. I want the damn hotel." He pounded both fists on the desk. The sound reverberated through the room, but Noah stood firm. He didn't let it faze him.

Noah planted both hands on his father's desk and looked him square in the eye. His pulse pounded in his ears. Rage coursed through his veins. "You don't get the damn hotel. Great-Grandfather saw you for what you are. You never cared about it. You cared about appearances. Your own flesh and blood cut you out of the will and you can't stand the way it made you look." Now that he was on a roll, he couldn't stop. Noah reached into his pants pocket. He fished out the printed page he'd brought from the office, placing it on his father's desk. "We know about Dan Lewis and what he did to Lily's computer."

His dad hardly glanced at the picture. "I'm impressed. Dan's one of the best in the business."

"I don't really care what he is. The reality is that you tried to sabotage our company and we have the evidence. We'll bring charges of corporate espionage against you, but I'm hoping it won't get that far. I'm hoping you can finally learn to let your children live their lives." It felt so good to get that off his chest. Avoiding a brass-tacks talk with his dad had left a huge weight on his shoulders.

"Fine. I'll just give Lyle Hannafort a call after you leave. We have a lot of catching up to do."

"Tell Lyle whatever you want. I called him from the car a half hour ago and explained everything."

As that bit of news settled in the room, his dad's eyes reflected the defeat Noah had come for, but didn't relish. He didn't want things to be like this. But his dad had insisted on stirring the pot. Hopefully this could be the end. "So you told him the engagement was fake?"

"Was, as in past tense. Today, I ask Lily to marry me for real."

Fourteen

Even from across the street, Noah could see that Lily's favorite bookstore, Petticoats and Proposals, was packed. A steady stream of people was filing inside. More were out chatting on the sidewalk in front of it. This was not what he'd expected. Lily had always said she liked Fridays because the store was especially quiet and she could sit in the back corner and read in peace. Would she even be there? There was only one way to find out. Even when turning up at a busy romance bookstore with a bouquet of roses and a ring in your pocket was a sure way to look like you were trying too hard.

The signal turned green and Noah marched across the street, his heart pulsing at a rate he wasn't sure he'd ever reached when running. He spotted the sign on the door as soon as he got closer. An author was doing a reading and signing tonight. Judging by the crowd inside and out, this author was extremely popular. Noah really hoped Lily was a fan.

Noah pulled the door open. A bell jingled against the glass. A gray-muzzled beagle sauntered past him, winding between the people gathered, not noticing Noah at all, exactly as Lily had once described him. The bookstore had that familiar aroma of paper and coffee and ink. Lily loved it here. She'd talked about it many times. The stories contained on these pages represented the part of her that refused to believe anything other than love conquers all. Even when real life had shown her that loving someone only hurts, she still clung to the notion that it simply wasn't the right love. She'd taught him that. And now it was time to show her that their love was the right one, the one they'd both been waiting for.

He walked past the front counter, where the clerk was busy ringing out a customer. Noah walked down the center aisle between the bookshelves. This was the moment when everything would either come together or fall apart. He had spent a lifetime avoiding scenarios like this, never pushing things to their limit to test how strong they were. Whether he'd realized he was doing that or not didn't matter. He couldn't allow it to happen anymore.

He reached the back of the store and looked left, seeing only more books and customers. He turned right, and down at the end of the aisle was exactly the picture Lily had painted for him—a comfortable red chair and a reading lamp next to it. Noah's heart sank. The chair was empty.

A young woman approached him. "Can I help you find a book? Or did you get lost on the way to a photo shoot for a romance novel cover?" She nodded at the bouquet in his hands.

Noah felt foolish, but he was determined. "I'm hoping you can help me find one of your customers. Her name is Lily and she comes here almost every Friday night. She reads in this chair. She told me all about it."

A look of recognition crossed her face. "Pretty blonde?"

Noah nodded eagerly. "Yes. The most beautiful blue eyes you've ever seen."

"I know exactly who you're talking about. Come on." She waved Noah to the center of the store, near the back room where the reading was taking place. When they arrived at the door, she pointed to the front of the jam-packed room. "She's right there," she whispered.

Noah scanned the rows and rows of people, and the instant his eyes landed on Lily, his heart flip-flopped in his chest. There she was, as gorgeous as ever, listening intently to the author's reading. "How do I get in there?"

Several people standing in the doorway turned around and shushed him.

The clerk pulled him aside. "You can wait until she's done with the reading. It should only take another twenty minutes or so."

He considered this option, but it didn't feel right. "I don't want to wait. I feel like I've been waiting my whole life for her."

A look of charity and pity crossed the woman's face. "Maybe text her?"

Noah hated his phone, but it might work. Otherwise, he'd be forced to walk into that room. Talk about scrutiny—getting down on bended knee and popping the question was likely to get healthy critiques from romance readers. He fished his phone from his pocket. Turn around. I'm here.

He watched as she scrambled for her purse. He'd never studied a person's facial expressions more than at that very moment. When a smile crossed her face, the relief he felt was immense. She turned and their gazes connected. The room of hundreds of people seemed to fade away.

"Come here," he mouthed.

She got up, but it was no easy task to make her way through this room. Noah watched as Lily had to sneak her way out, crouching down and tiptoeing past row after row of people. By the time she reached him, she practically stumbled out of the room. "What are you doing here?"

The women who'd shushed him turned around again. He knew he had to redeem himself. "I'm here to hopefully make everything better." He held up the bouquet as evidence.

A wide smile crossed Lily's face and she took the roses from him and smelled them. "Thank you. They're lovely."

"You're welcome. Can we talk?"

Lily looked around. "Outside? There's no privacy in here."

Noah was so relieved. "Yes."

Out they went onto the street. Lily tugged on her coat and Noah helped her, but every second he had to put this off was grating on him. "Did something happen with the computer and Sawyer and your dad?" Lily asked. "It doesn't seem like you'd bring roses if there was more bad news."

Noah told her the whole story, complete with the admission that even Sawyer didn't know about yet, that he'd called Lyle Hannafort and told him everything.

Lily clasped her hand over her mouth. "I can't believe you spilled the beans."

"I had no choice. I didn't want us to live under the shadow of that anymore. It wasn't right."

"And it didn't jeopardize the deal?"

Noah shook his head. "In the end, the almighty dollar was stronger than a silly story in a tabloid or a fake engagement."

A contented smile crossed Lily's face. "If flowers are your way of inviting me back to work, I would've come back anyway. I love working for you and Sawyer. I'm so relieved it all got worked out."

He took Lily's hand and knew this was his moment. This was his chance to go for everything he thought he'd never have, his one shot to get the girl. Right there on the sidewalk, he dropped to one knee. Lily's eyes were bigger and more beautiful than he'd ever seen. Her smile grew, too. "Lily, I love you. I love you more than anything in the whole world and I can't even conceive of a life where you aren't at the center of everything." He reached into his pocket and pulled out the blue Tiffany bundle, hoping this was the right thing to do. "Will you be my wife?"

When he popped open the box, Lily gasped. She reached for the ring, her hand trembling. She didn't even take it. She only looked at it in awe. "Noah. The sapphire. Your mom's ring."

"The right ring. The only ring. The one you were meant to wear."

She gazed down at him, her eyes watery, but it was unlike the other times he'd seen her cry. He saw happiness and joy. He saw everything he'd ever wanted. "Yes, I will marry you, Noah. Yes, I will be your wife."

Noah rose to his feet and pulled the ring from the box, slipping it onto Lily's finger. "That other ring looked pretty good on your hand, but this one is perfect." He took another look at her and didn't wait, pulling her into his arms and planting a suitably hot kiss on her lips. He couldn't wait to get her stuff back from her apartment and move her in, again. This time, for real.

Lily ended the kiss and grinned. "I'm so happy, it's ridiculous." From inside the store, the muffled sound of applause came. A customer opened the door and hoots and hollers erupted from the store entrance. The window was lined with customers who must have seen the proposal. Lily laughed. "It appears we've attracted a crowd."

Noah wanted one more kiss. "This is one time I don't mind anyone watching."

Lily's second visit to the New York City Clerk's Office for a wedding was much more romantic than the first. She gazed at Noah, knowing now that he was hers. The years of longing for him were nothing more than part of their journey, the story they could tell their children someday. She'd done her time with unrequited love. Now she had it—Noah's affection, his devotion and his glorious self. She couldn't have been any happier if one of her favorite authors had written this happy ending. It was the one she never saw coming.

"By the power vested in me by the state of New York, I now pronounce you husband and wife."

Noah grinned like a goof, but there was that sexy edge to it, the one that said he couldn't wait to get her home and take off her clothes. Of course, there would be no tearing off the wedding dress. There would be careful and judicious removal of said garment, followed by hours of hot sex. She was going to get everything that Lily Locke was entitled to. Or Lily Foster-Locke. She still wasn't sure which was better.

"Do I get to kiss her?" he asked the clerk, suddenly seeming unsure of himself.

"Come here." Lily popped up onto her tiptoes and wrapped her arms around his waist, pulling him closer. The kiss was steamier than was probably warranted for a government building on a Tuesday, but Lily didn't really care.

They both lingered for a moment, lips still a whisper away from each other. Their breaths were in perfect sync.

The spark between them, the magnetic pull that made it impossible to stay away from Noah, was making its presence known. It took everything Lily had not to kiss him again. Lily heard a woman in the office speak. *I want a man to kiss me like that.*

Lily sighed, contented, and landed back on her heels, still grasping Noah's arms. She not only had a man to kiss her like that, she got to keep him. This was so much better than the first time she tried to get married, aside from the obvious upside of the desired outcome. Today felt like a happy dream, the kind you never want to wake up from, rather than an unthinkable nightmare. But even better, the pain she had gone through the first time was now a good thing. If she hadn't been dumped, she never would've moved to New York. If she hadn't moved to New York, she never would've found Noah.

She slipped back into her lovely new reality when Noah spoke. "Can we get out of here? I'm starving."

Charlotte was the first to congratulate them. Sort of. "Don't you dare screw this up, Noah. Or I will hunt you down and slap you silly."

Lily laughed, but Noah's forehead crinkled with annoyance. "Don't worry. I'm not about to let Lily out of my sight." He took her hand and squeezed it three times.

Sawyer appeared and held his arms wide for Lily. "I need to give my new sister-in-law a hug." When they were cheek to cheek, he said one more thing. "I hope you know how sorry I am that I ever doubted you."

Lily waved it off. "Water under the bridge. I don't believe in grudges."

"So I've been told," Sawyer said.

Kendall was right behind him. "Welcome to the family, Lily. I hope we can become good friends."

"Absolutely," Lily replied.

"Now let's eat." Noah kissed Lily's temple. "On to the Grand Legacy."

With a wave of his hand, Sawyer made way for Lily and Noah to lead the procession out of the building. A stretch SUV was waiting to take them to lunch at the hotel. Noah and Lily sat in the back, holding hands.

"I can't even believe today, Noah. It all feels like a dream. Pinch me."

"That sounds like something for later tonight." He nuzzled her neck and kissed that delicate spot beneath her ear, making her go weak in the knees, even though she was sitting.

"I can't wait."

The car pulled up in front of the hotel and they all climbed out. Sawyer, Kendall, Michael and Charlotte filed straight into the revolving door, but Noah held Lily's hand and kept her back.

"Is everything okay?" she asked.

"Everything is perfect. I just want to make sure you're okay with not having the wedding here at the Grand Legacy. Of not going through with the things you started planning with Marcy. I hope you know that I only made this suggestion because I didn't want to wait, but if you want to have a more formal ceremony, we can still do that. I don't want you to feel cheated out of your perfect wedding."

Lily raised her hand and dug her fingers into Noah's hair, admiring his fine face that she now got to kiss as much as she wanted. It was so sweet that he was concerned about this, but it was time and effort wasted. "I don't need the perfect wedding, Noah. I got the perfect guy."

* * * * *

MILLS & BOON MODERN IS
HAVING A MAKEOVER!

The same great stories you love,
a stylish new look!

Look out for our brand new look
COMING JUNE 2024

MILLS & BOON

afterglow BOOKS

Afterglow Books are trend-led, trope-filled books with diverse, authentic and relatable characters and a wide array of voices and representations.

Experience real world trials and tribulations, all the tropes you could possibly want (think small-town settings, fake relationships, grumpy vs sunshine, enemies to lovers).

All with a generous dose of spice in every story!

OUT NOW

Two stories published every month.

To discover more visit:

Afterglowbooks.co.uk

LET'S TALK

Romance

For exclusive extracts, competitions and special offers, find us online:

MILLS & BOON

MODERN

Power and Passion

Prepare to be swept off your feet by sophisticated, sexy and seductive heroes, in some of the world's most glamorous and romantic locations, where power and passion collide.

MILLS & BOON

MEDICAL

Pulse-Racing Passion

Set your pulse racing with dedicated, delectable doctors in the high-pressure world of medicine, where emotions run high and passion, comfort and love are the best medicine.